When he gets up to leave, we move to the door, and I realize: it's That Awful Moment. Will he kiss me? On the cheek? The lips? If he does, does he bend to me or do I stand on tiptoes to meet him halfway? This is so complicated—how do people date and survive? It's a non-issue when he gives me a hug, thanks me for dinner one last time, and is out the door.

What, no kiss? He's not attracted to me? Not that I imagined him shoving his tongue down to my tonsils, but a kiss…a little, polite kiss.

Is it me? Give it time. It's our first…quasi-date. We've been neighbors for a year and a half and it took him this long to ask me out for a drink. And only when he saw me straight from the beauty factory. I must've looked like a rag every other time he'd seen me. Mom was right.

Maybe it's not me. Maybe he's gay. After all, he's an architect, and that's almost like being in the arts...

Maybe he thinks *I'm* gay?

Omigod, girl, get a grip. Next thing, I'll be waiting up for him to call. But he didn't kiss me, and that could mean so many things. He's shy; no. He's old fashioned; possibly. Maybe he thinks I'm not attracted to him; what, I should have flung myself at him? Jesus, Mary and Joseph, I haven't dated in a hundred years.

No wonder people throw up their hands at the idea of dating. It's so complicated. Who pays for what? What are appropriate first dates? Who provides the condoms, if it ever gets to that? For people over 50, it's a minefield whose rules have been re-written since our own mating rituals. Do people today just meet and jump into bed, then tell each other their favorite foods and movies?

OK, Callie Cat, here's the leftover salmon. Enjoy it, girl. It may be the last "special dinner" I ever fix for a gentleman caller. Who didn't kiss me. You, girl, you've been spayed, so you're out of the uproar, the chaos, the insanity. Of course, cats don't really date. You gals just yowl, the guys come over, and no one even buys you dinner first. All things considered, you're best out of it.

# *Mommy Machine*

Kathleen M. McElligott

7/8/08

To Judith —
  Forget all preconceived notions,
embrace your inner
        Mommy Machine
    Enjoy,
      Kathy McElligott
          Kmcelligott@AOL.com

Heliotrope Press
Orland Park, Illinois

© 2008, Heliotrope Press
ISBN 0-9788347-0-4

Printed in the United States
10 9 8 7 6 5 4 3 2 1

# Dedication

*Mommy Machine* is dedicated to all who follow their dream. On your journey, be healthy in mind, body and spirit.

# Acknowledgments

Writing Mommy Machine has been a journey of discovery. It's taught me many things, not the least of which is patience. A friend commented, "You've been writing this book since I've known you." Thanks to my family for supporting my writing and coming to my readings at The Red Lion and the Book Cellar in Chicago. To my partner, Ed, who literally became a 'writer's widow' while I wrote, rewrote and met with my editor for countless hours—my heartfelt appreciation. To my excellent editor, Whitney Scott, who claims I received the equivalent of a master's level education in writing during the course of our work together. The relationship between an editor and writer is unique...when we began finishing each other's thoughts and sentences, it was uncanny. Thanks to Lee Cunningham, who proofread the manuscript and said it read 'like a movie' playing in her mind—very encouraging.

Appreciation for Fran Beukelman, School Psychologist, who advised me about Colin's behavior, Bret Angelos, attorney for DCFS for his advice on custody and guardianship; Mark Ruttkay, Foster Care and Adoption Manager, CYFD, Protective Services, Santa Fe, New Mexico; Susie Benavides, from the Santa Fe School District, Trish from the Santa Fe Chamber of Commerce, and Carol Mcbride, Realtor with Santa Fe Properties.

# Part I

# *Elaine*

ursts of green leaves and early spring grass intensify in color as the sunlight fades. My frayed navy tote bag bulges with pounds of student files, team meeting notes, a school calendar, health histories in progress, and the latest book on ADHD management in schools. Checking its torn corners, I wonder if the bag will last through the end of the school year.

The garage almosts bursts with plumbing supplies, old paint and ladders, the lawn mower, flower pots, rakes—the whole suburban scene. No room, as usual, for my worn but dependable, seven-year-old Corolla. It has held up well, even though it's had little more than regular oil changes since the day I drove it home in 1988, my pride and joy, my first new car.

Today I could use an oil change myself, and maybe a little pure oxygen. Too many sick, injured and simply malingering students in the health office plus two hours of team meetings have drained my energy and caused this persistent throbbing behind my eyes. So it's a matter of carefully steering myself up the creaky back steps, hoping this headache won't turn into a full-blown migraine. I've learned over the years, however, that it's better to act earlier than to wait and see.

Once inside the house, I lean against the kitchen counter and reach for my economy size bottle of ibuprofen in the cabinet over the sink–the sink that is empty! Empty because I forgot to defrost anything for dinner. My shoulders tighten, rise and slump with the big sigh I allow myself. There will be no dinner tonight, I decide, at least none I cook. Frank and Roxy can order a pizza. It seems they like that better than my cooking anyway.

My office upstairs still has dried prom flowers on a bookshelf and stacks of U2 cassettes, remnants of Stephanie. Maybe I'll find an email from her this afternoon, less personal but cheaper than a trans-Atlantic phone call from Dublin.

Her last call informed me that she and her boyfriend, Liam, want to spend his summer holiday traveling around Europe. The corporate position she'd wanted hasn't materialized, so it's no problem taking the summer off from the most recent in a series of menial jobs. Lack of cash is a problem, however, and she asked for some money—to be repaid when that dream job comes along. Yeah, Stephanie, dream on. Throb on, my head answers. A year ago she'd waved good-bye at O'Hare, a pretty green-eyed redhead with a jaunty pink beret as I walked away alone, head down so she wouldn't see my tears.

Now, after my repeated cash infusions for her rent and bus fare, I have to set limits. Stephanie may think she's the only one with plans, but I need some R&R for myself this summer. At 50 my batteries need a recharge, and a trip to Hawaii with Frank is my dream. If I lend her more money, I'll be the one staying home. Besides, I want to go to Hawaii while I can still wear a bikini, something I'm quite proud of.

The ring of a phone interrupts my visions of sandy beaches, palm trees and pina coladas. People say my voice sounds very young over the phone. So much so that when I answer the phone, which is rarely because it's almost never for me, I am usually mistaken for Roxy, my 16-year-old daughter. Sometimes the voice on the other end of the line starts with, "Hey, Roxy, wanna go down to the forest preserve–get blazed?" At those times I imagine doing a high-class, uppity accent, "Oh, please–my Roxie is a lah-dy," but to avoid embarrassment, I jump in as quickly as possible. "Whoa, this isn't who you think it is. Hold on." Then I call for Roxy. If I were devious, I could make life pretty miserable for her, but the truth is that there are some things about her life I just don't want to know. As a single mom, my fingers are crossed, and toes, too.

It's Dave of the hoarse baritone calling for Roxy, but there's no answer when I yell her name. "I'll call back," he says eagerly. *Yeah, I know.*

Finally, I'm able to sit down and double-click email on my five-years-ancient computer. The darn thing takes so long! Finally, the familiar robotic male voice announces, "You've got mail." Hesitating, I click on Stephanie's message; her acerbic response to my limit-setting: "Don't worry, Mom. Isn't that just like you? Why did I think you would help us make this work? I love Liam. Don't you get that?" So much for improving European-American relations. Stephanie thinks guilt will get her whatever she wants and, I admit, it used to work when she portrayed herself as the tragic product of a broken home. But enough is enough.

Real tragedy in my work is all too familiar. It's a relief when I don't have to call the child welfare authorities again, a contact that's fast becoming a routine part of my job as a school nurse, and one I can stomach less and less. In the past week, there were two abuse cases. Both victims were eight-year-old black boys. One little guy was beaten with closed fists and kicked in the ribs by his stepfather because the boy *almost* knocked over the fish tank. This skinny little child came to school on Monday with bruises on his face, arms, and back that he said happened Friday night and kept him in bed over the weekend. His teacher saw his bruises and a definite limp, and sent him to me. I immediately sat him in my inner office for privacy. I always sit down to be at the kids' level so they can see my eyes and know I mean it when I tell them I'm concerned for their safety. So many barely make eye contact with the adults they've learned not to trust.

The drill goes as follows: once I've tended to his injuries as much as possible and temporarily returned him to class, I call the abuse hot line and write the mandatory report. A worker from the agency comes to the school and questions the child, usually just before the school day ends. In the vast majority of cases, I get an official form letter a few weeks later saying that my report was "unfounded," which means nothing will be done, and I interpret as, "You're wasting your time." However, if I failed to report these cases, I could lose my nursing license, but fear of that isn't what keeps me making the calls and writing the reports; it's the kids. They deserve better.

If I can stick it out another five years, I'll accept the school district's early retirement option, then take art classes and write a novel. I toyed with writing when the girls were little, and did feature articles from home for the local newspaper until someone complained to the editor about the girls' interruptions during a phone interview. It didn't pay very well, anyway.

My fantasy of the writer's life has always appealed to me: enjoying solitude, wearing offbeat clothes, flipping society the bird. Don't get me wrong; I'm not anti-social. I enjoy what I call my "quiet time." I love to read and I've never been a "dress-for-success" nurse–like I could be, in my job, *not*–since the occupational hazards include contact with all kinds of bodily fluids. I have always dressed as I please, with comfort my priority. Frank once accused me of dressing "too young," whatever that means. But I figure if I can do 'still in good shape at 50,' why not?

I'm supposed to meet Christa for dinner tonight. We used to work in the same school, and now we meet occasionally for lunch or an early dinner. Tonight could be awkward, however, since I heard through a mutual friend that Christa was seriously involved with a man indicted for investment fraud. Then it came out that he wasn't divorced as Christa thought, but had a wife and kids on the East Coast.

We're meeting at a local Italian restaurant, not my favorite, but I didn't make the arrangements, and sometimes it's easier to just go along. Besides it's close to home for me. Even so, I'll need to figure in an extra 20 minutes to take Roxy for fast food and drive her to her friend's house before dinner.

I'm in the parking lot of Emilio's listening to my *Abbey Road* CD. In my mind, no one will ever surpass The Beatles. It's amazing how timeless they sound after more than 30 years. Even Roxy likes the Beatles. She and Stephanie grew up listening to rock music and know most of the words to the songs on the oldies station.

At 7:00 I decide to see if Christa has arrived. How will she be dealing with the breakup?

No Christa in the waiting area. No messages on my cell phone. Christa's recording is a man's voice..."not home, leave a message," etc. Is this the famous felon? Weird. I disconnect without leaving a message.

At 7:15, she arrives. "Christa, how are you?" We hug.

"Elaine, Laney. Sorry to be late. Traffic was a bear." She seems distracted, barely meeting my gaze. In fact, her eyes seem to wander the room in search of someone. Throughout dinner, I wonder if Christa will discuss her failed relationship, but no, and the closest I get to a personal question is a generic inquiry about her private practice–she's a therapist–which is thriving. Eventually, when she's ready, she'll tell me.

After pasta primavera and pumpkin ravioli, we savor our coffee as I do 'plucky mom dealing with rebellious daughter' and tell her about Steph's plan to go on a holiday with her boyfriend.

As we leave the restaurant, I invite her over for a glass of wine. "I have clients I need to call," says Christa, glancing at her watch. "Maybe next time."

Frank and Christa—oil and water, I'm afraid. She's a polished professional woman, and he gets defensive around her.

Too late to go shopping for spring clothes. The Midwestern winter's taken its toll and I've been wanting to brighten my spirits and wardrobe with soft pastels. Generally, I avoid the mall unless absolutely necessary. Usually it's Roxy that wants new clothes, but we don't agree on fashion. The other day she went to school done up in black fishnet stockings, a white tutu she got from God-knows-what thrift shop, topped with a screaming magenta tank top and tiara, finished off with half-laced black combat boots. I try, I really do; but sometimes it's hard to hold my head up high and acknowledge this not-quite-stunning creature as my daughter. I wonder if the lady across the street looks at her, thinking, "There goes the neighborhood."

That image turns me away from the shops and instead I head for my usual Friday night haunt, the bookstore. Not only do I love reading, I love browsing through books, and being around booklovers.

Armed with a decaf latte (made with skim milk, of course), my mission is to find a comfortable chair, investigate the latest hot sellers, and consult my "to read" list as I work my way through books ranging from contemporary classics by Hemingway and Fitzgerald to today's voices–people like Alex Kotlowitz, Elizabeth Berg, and Sue Monk Kidd. Surreptitiously, I enjoy watching the other patrons of the bookstore and even fantasize about a man down the aisle, browsing through travel books. Is he planning a romantic get-away?

On the way home, bookless but content from browsing, I call Frank on my cell. "Hey, what's going on?"

"Not much; getting ready to go upstairs. How about you?"

"I'm on my way and should be home in a few minutes."

"Good. I'm going to take a shower. Want to join me?" Frank asks. This is code for *do you want to have sex?*

"I'll see you soon."

And I do–admiring his thick silver hair and tightly muscled frame toned from workouts in the gym that keep him looking younger than his age, which is 55. He routinely gets second looks from gray-haired matrons–and their daughters.

After five years together, I still tease him about it, especially when he's reliving his high school jock days during Monday Night Football. Then I assure him he could still get any cheerleader on the field. He pretends to wave it all away, doing 'Bruce Springsteen's *Glory Days*,' but eats it up just the same.

Over the years our lovemaking has evolved. Through experimentation, we've learned how to please each other. My orgasms and Frank's erections might not be as intense as when we were younger, but neither of us is complaining. I like nothing better than to snuggle next to him after making love and drift into a contented sleep.

So I still feel attractive when he chases me into the bathroom and smothers me with silly kisses.

"Let's take that shower now," suggests Frank, eager for love, pressing urgently against me.

❖

Frank is usually the first one up on Saturday morning, and today is no exception. I lie languorously in bed smelling fresh-brewed coffee, watching the sun seep through the mini-blinds. "Phone's for you; it's Stephanie," Frank calls up from the kitchen.

*Oh God, what now?* I pick up the phone, aiming to sound upbeat. "Stephanie? Hi! How are you?"

"Mom. I'm glad I caught you."

"Well, it's 8:00 on Saturday morning."

"I know, but you're usually not home when I call."

"Well, you could've left a message…"

"I have something…something…to tell you…it's hard…" She fumbles to finish. "It's hard for me to say."

I hold my breath, doing my best 'Understanding Mom' and wait for a few moments of silence, but blurt out, "Just tell me."

"Mom, I'm pregnant." Dead air. "I know you must be disappointed." Now it's my turn for silence. "Mom, are you there?"

"Yes, I'm here. What are you going to do? Have you talked to Liam about it?" How can this happen to a grown woman who's been to college, unless she wants it to?

"I don't know. We haven't talked about it much. I mean… it's that we're barely a couple. And having children together, well, it's a whole new idea."

"How are you about it?"

"Oh, Mom, this wasn't in my plans." I imagine her tugging at her long, red hair in frustration, a habit held over from childhood.

Looking back over those years, I think I overindulged Stephanie, especially when I was going through the divorce from her father. Now she is going to be a mother, despite her plans. In my own life, there's never been a plan, just a series of events. One of them, a major one, as it now turns out, was her move to Ireland to "ride the Celtic Tiger"—the mid-'90s tech boom there fueled by IT—information technology. Armed with a scant two years of college computer and IT management courses, off she went to seek her fortune. No dream job ever happened for her, although she did find steady work–and, apparently, a steady boyfriend.

Downstairs, Frank waits with a cup of coffee, saying nothing, but questioning me with his look.

"Stephanie's pregnant."

His heavy eyebrows shoot up. "What's she going to do?"

"Well, she isn't sure. She doesn't seem ready to think about it." And I'm not either–not now. "I'm going to the health club. We can talk about it later."

## Roxy

Ever since we moved in with Frank, into his house, I feel like I'm being watched, like I'm in prison. When I come out of the bathroom after taking a shower, he just happens to be walking down the hallway. At first I didn't get it when he'd look at his watch and then give me a dirty look, until I heard him mumbling, "Water costs money…hot water even more." What is he, the Water Nazi, plus the Gas and Electric Nazi, all rolled into one? As if…

That's no freakin' way to live. A chick should be able to take a shower for as long and as hot as she needs to. I don't know what my mom sees in him…I think he's lame; no, worse than that…he's one wacked dude. At first I tried to avoid him, like my mom used to say, "Out of sight, out of mind." But now I'm all up in his face. I'll even make a point of announcing, "I'm going up to take a shower," and I'll stay in there until the bathroom is so steamy, I can't even see. Eat my shorts, Frank. Two can play this game. Before we moved in here, my mom never bitched about water and gas bills. Back in the day…things were dope, no worries, you know what I mean? All I can say is, "Deal, Frank."

## Elaine

The week drags by, made heavy with my worry for Stephanie, my first born, and always the problem child, strong-willed even as a toddler and rebellious in adolescence. Roxy, who has no clue about her sister's pregnancy, attributes my edginess to a disagreement with Frank.

"Yo, Mom—you goin' postal on us?"

"It's all good, all good—just work."

Frank can be pig-headed, and with Stephanie an issue—a pregnant Stephanie…Finally, after several days of living beneath this cloud, I'm backed into a corner when Frank forces the issue. "Elaine, what are you going to do about Stephanie?"

"What do you mean, 'What am I going to do?' I'm not the one who's pregnant."

"Right, but we both know how you are. You'll want her to come and stay here with the baby, and you know how I feel about babies in my house. Roxy's enough of a baby as it is."

Though we've lived here under his roof for a year, it is his house, after all, but Stephanie is my daughter. "Don't make me choose between you and my children, because I'll always choose my family. I shouldn't have to decide between people I love. Let's wait to see what she'll do. We don't even know yet."

"But I know what you'll want to do–bring her here with the baby and dirty diapers and bottles and no sleep for any of us." Roxy would have to be down the street to miss Frank's booming voice, and sure enough, she bounces into the kitchen.

"E-eew…baby? Who's pregnant? Not you?" She fixes a withering look at me, then Frank. "That's ghetto!" I believe that is definitely not a good thing. Considering her jeans are more holes than denim, revealing half her butt and a good portion of her crotch, I have to wonder about people in glass houses.

"It's not your mother," Frank starts, then wisely thinks better of it, and falls silent.

"I just want to know what's going on. Who's knocked up, and why are you arguing about some baby?" Her blue-gray eyes darken, holding me with a stare I can't avoid.

"It's your sister. She called and told me last week."

"Oh, awesome. I'll be an aunt."

Frank cuts her off with a furious wave of his hand. "Not awesome at all, especially if your mother thinks Stephanie's coming here to live with some baby."

❖

There was a time when I would have described my relationship with Frank as "solid." We had some rocky adjustments at the beginning, and I had to learn to be unfazed by his bluster. In fact, there were times when I thought I had made a mistake. But in the last couple of years, we both seem to have mellowed. To the casual observer and even to some friends and acquaintances, we seem like a happily married middle-aged couple minus the married part.

But now I may have to choose between two people I love, both difficult in their own ways, yet dear to me.

So if the going gets tough, the tough go shopping...and not just for everyday stuff like clothes. I feel the need for a creative outlet, and my target is the master bedroom, establishing a softer, more feminine look for the room with a new comforter and linens. Last summer I painted a watercolor series of a local pond with purple wildflowers called lupines, and they would surely be ready at the frame shop by now. Some of those paintings would look great hanging in that room and in the hallway leading up to it.

When I leave the house, the glass rattles in the frame as I slam the back door, eager to be on the move and excited at the prospect of a new look for the bedroom. Within the refuge of the car, I safely blast "Friday I'm in Love" by the Cure from their greatest hits, the one I bought myself for an early birthday present.

A quick stop for a loaf of bread and a dozen eggs...add to the shopping an unplanned pint of Ben & Jerry's Chunky Monkey, which I'll hide in the back of the freezer. Frank and Roxy will never find it. It will be a Chunky Monkey pig-out while I soak in the tub later on, cheaper than drugs and better than sex.

Even the thought's delicious as the frame shop's old brick storefront comes into view. A tinkling bell on a spring announces my arrival against the delicate sounds of Debussy's *Afternoon of a Faun*. The music relaxes my shoulders that I had no idea were knotted and tense from the stress of uncertainty. What a pleasure to be here, with the fragrance of wood shavings and varnish mixed with a slight tinge of mustiness in this old-fashioned building. It's a place where I've had many enjoyable conversations over the years with the owner, a balding Greek gentleman who often speaks wistfully about his birthplace, Athens, where he hopes some day to return.

The thirty-something man coming from the back of the shop is definitely not my old friend Nick. This fellow's tall and thin, with a luxurious head of dark, wavy hair and tight blue jeans that I try not to look at.

"Can I help you?" he asks, flashing a dazzling smile. His dark complexion and appealing five o'clock shadow set off his intensely green eyes. He moves fluidly and with the ease and confidence of a model on a runway. Could he be a European fashion model...or a Greek god? I can't help smiling in return. Speechless, I'm undone by his presence and the immediate attraction I feel for him. The violins playing in the background gently crescendo, like a scene from an afternoon soap opera, only this guy is definitely real. Suddenly the uncertainty in my life fades into another world, one I would gratefully leave behind. He frowns slightly, repeating, "May I help you?"

"I hope so," I murmur, willing away the color that threatens to rise in my cheeks. "Are my paintings ready? I'm Elaine McElroy."

As he turns to retrieve my watercolors from the back of the shop, I stare at his firm butt, and I'm transported by luscious thoughts of Chunky Monkey ice cream, a steaming tub for two and this tall, dark stranger.

Who is this Elaine, this horny woman who is old enough to know better? Or am I? Both? Old enough or should I know better? What's come over me, wanting to get all jiggy with this hottie? And since when did I start using these words, let alone think about doing them?

"These paintings are first rate," he comments as he begins wrapping them in brown paper. "Who's the artist?"

This time there's no escaping the warmth and color creeping up my cheeks. Grinning inanely, I ask in an unnaturally high voice, "Do you really think they're good?" Am I a schoolgirl seeking teacher's praise?

"The washes are so delicate, and the mood you've created is hypnotic—it draws me into the landscape." With one wrapped painting on the counter, he pauses, leaning toward me, his eyes sea green in appreciation. "Do you have more? I'd like to see them."

I lean into his approval like melting butter. "I've been painting on and off for years, but wasn't sure..." I say, "...I didn't think..."

"You know, I'm involved with a group that's putting together a show of regional women artists." He leans a millimeter closer. "These would fit right in. Why don't you plan to bring a few more to the gallery, and we'll discuss it."

I gasp, as much from his proximity as from his professional assessment–and the realization that the ice cream in my car is surely mush by now.

I brave leaning forward further, doing 'bold-but-winsome woman of the '90s,' chin in hand. "Do you like Chunky Monkey ice cream?"

"It's one of my favorites," he says, moving the painting off to the side as though making room for a feast.

"Wait right here."

Fingers sticky from the melt-down in the bag, I set the small package on the counter less than a minute later, grateful the bagger separated it from the eggs and bread, and longing to place my sweetened fingers in his mouth.

No spoons. We take turns slurping it from the container, scooping chocolate chunks into our mouths with our fingers. How bold-but-winsome is that!

## Jeff

This Elaine chick picked up her watercolors at the frame shop yesterday, and we pigged out on Chunky Monkey ice cream. I mean we really pigged out. Like fingers in the carton, and slurping it into our mouths. That was kind of cool, like she's edgy, but not really. What is it about her?…shit…I know what it is…she reminds me of my mom; she has that Earth Mother feeling about her. Still, I'd screw her in a minute if she were willing. I'm burned out on so much right now…spoiled blondes and work and too much of the wrong kind of work and not enough of my own…and one thing Elaine is not, is blonde and living off Mommy and Daddy's suburban bucks.

When I said I'd like to show her pieces in the women's show we're planning at the gallery, that wasn't just hype…her stuff was good…better than I've seen in a while. She just seems so…unaffected…like she didn't really think her stuff was any good. I like that.

## Elaine

Faded blue jeans, pale yellow T-shirt with matching cotton socks–that's what I finally decide on after trying several outfits and throwing them on the bed. Somehow what I wear for my meeting with Jeff seems terribly important. The four paintings I choose to bring are desert and mountain scenes from New Mexico. I carefully place them in the oversized portfolio.

I wait until Frank leaves for his Friday night bowling league to spritz on just a hint of perfume. As I put the paintings in the back seat of the car, I hear the phone ring. Something tells me not to answer it, but it could be Roxy calling to arrange a ride home.

"Mom, you sound out of breath."

"Stephanie, how are you? I was just going out the door."

"I'm glad I caught you, then. It's early in the morning here. I couldn't sleep. I've been thinking a lot since we talked. I'm not sure exactly what I'm going to do, but I know one thing," Stephanie says.

I hold my breath.

"I know I'm going to keep this baby. No matter how things turn out with Liam."

Whatever's going on with Steph and her baby's father–or not–I have no control. That it affects a baby–my grandchild–makes it impossible to stay out of it. She's my daughter, and I'm in it up to my eyeballs.

"Steph, I have to run. We'll talk later."

❖

The Bucktown gallery is a somewhat rundown, two-story building made of limestone, probably a wealthy merchant's home at the end of the 19th century. The metal sign on the black wrought iron fence surrounding a mature spruce and some evergreen shrubs says *Prairie Place Gallery* in calligraphic script. The front entrance has a stone lion on each side of the doorway, the match to the brass lion's head knocker on the dark oak door. Hesitating, I feel the weight of the tarnished door-knocker in my hand, then hear its echo inside. No view of the interior is visible through the etched, oval pane of glass, just a dark blur of motion approaching.

Jeff answers the door wearing jeans and a teal turtleneck, looking handsome with his dark curly hair wet, perhaps from a recent shower. It's his eyes, however, that catch my attention, green with just a hint of mischief. "Come on in." He holds the door open. "Good to see you. Let's go to the office. You can set up your paintings."

I'm almost giddy with happiness at the sight of him, and wonder for a moment if I can make my way down the carpeted hallway without tripping. What an entrance that would be! Is it as obvious to him as it is to me that I've got a giant crush on him?

Wing chairs and several empty easels stand by an oak desk on polished hardwood floors. The old stained glass window illuminated by the streetlight outside casts a pale rainbow. The only other light seems to be from an antique brass desk lamp. I arrange the paintings on the easels and take a step back. "So, what do you think?"

He turns on the overhead track lights, a shock to my eyes. His gaze goes from one scene of the desert and mountains to the next, then back, considering before moving on. He pauses before the matted watercolor of the Sangre de Christo Mountain Range at twilight done in rusts, purples and ochers, and lifts it to the light. I step forward, and he accidentally brushes against my arm; a warm feeling radiates through me like a touch of setting sun against amethyst mountain peaks.

"Lovely suggestion of depth in that slanting light." He shifts his attention from the paintings, focusing his intense, now olive-green eyes on me. "Do you have any more? I'd like to see what else you have." It's the second time he's asked for more, and I want to hug him, but restrain myself.

"A few. And some that I can collect from friends and relatives. Over the years I kept on painting just because it was a release for me, like therapy. I'd give them away, and it didn't seem to matter if they were any good."

"They're good, take my word for it. I'm thinking of them for an all-woman show that's still in the planning stages." He sits in a leather chair behind the desk, stretching his long legs and torso, locking his hands behind his neck, doing 'rising young gallery owner.' Just as his trained eye evaluated my paintings, now he evaluates me, seemingly for the first time.

"That's great, and so...unexpected. It would be an honor to be included in your show." We're both beaming.

I'd love to stay there another hour—or three—but the next thing I know he's on his feet and I'm collecting the landscapes. "Are you from Chicago," he asks, probably to be polite.

"Born and raised on the South Side. How about you?"

"I'm from the East, New Jersey. I came to study at the School of the Art Institute," Jeff says. I fell in love with Chicago and I've been here ever since."

"That's easy to do...fall in love with Chicago, I mean. People tell me Chicago always measures up. The Lakefront and Michigan Avenue and museums..."

"Do you have a business card so I can reach you?"

"Oh, I forgot them," I lie. I meant to print up business cards on the computer, but never got around to it.

He reaches around to a cardholder on his desk. "Here, write your number on the back of mine. I'll call you."

❖

On the way home I indulge my fantasies about Jeff, about our broad smiles of parting that promised...what? Being in a gallery show? More? Has he a lover, male or female? Both? Is this a misguided, middle-aged illusion on my part? Maybe. Who is this Elaine who's thinking about more? More what? Like I've got way too much time on my hands, between my job and Frank and Roxy and who-knows-what with Stephanie? And her baby. But the thought of falling into the arms of that gorgeous, artistic stud... it's too delicious, with or without Chunky Monkey. Anyway, there's no harm in dreaming...

With time to stop at the bookstore, I browse through the new fiction section and spot Christa who's engrossed in a paperback. "Christa, how are you? That must be a great book. It's really got your attention," I observe.

"Oh, this," she lies, blushing. I can see the title: *What Your Mother Never Told You About Relationships.*

"Looking for pointers?" I ask breezily, wondering all too readily how I might grab a copy for myself.

"Actually, no, well maybe yes... did you hear what happened with Cooper?" She looks like a kid who's caught with her hand in the candy jar.

"No, what?" I can't wait to hear the details.

"Let's go and get some coffee." She hastily puts the book back on the shelf, and walks in the direction of the café.

At a table in the far corner, Christa spares no detail about her relationship with Cooper, the stockbroker. Her clear blue eyes, which usually sparkle, are lackluster, downcast.

"Wow, and there was no clue that he was married?" What about those weekends and holidays when his phone number was off-limits, I think. It amazes me that someone as intelligent as Christa can be so naive about men and relationships, especially someone in her profession. It's ironic that Christa's always asking me for advice, yet I have never sought advice from her. I think she sees me as a mother figure, a feeling I get partly because she's rarely talked about her own mother.

"Enough about me. What's new with you?" Christa asks, changing the subject. I find myself waving my hands in the air, telling her about my watercolors, but don't say anything about Jeff because there isn't anything to tell, yet...and maybe never. Besides, he is still my deeply personal fantasy, and I am not ready to share that with anyone. We part after promising to get together for a glass of wine some evening.

❖

That night I'm tossing and turning with thoughts of Jeff and paintings and gallery shows and Jeff and Christa and Jeff and Stephanie keeping me up. "Will you settle down? What's wrong? Is it another migraine?" Frank asks, irritated.

"No, a lot on my mind, Stephanie being pregnant…and I'm thinking about doing more paintings for an exhibit."

"Did he ask you to do more paintings?"

"No, but you know me, once an overachiever, always an overachiever." And I want to please him, I think.

Frank turns over to sleep after a perfunctory kiss. I drape my arm over his bulky, comforting frame and squeeze into him, nuzzling his back. He responds with a contented grunt. During the night I awake to Frank's caressing my shoulder and saying, "It's all right; go back to sleep." I remember a nightmare, the kind where you try to run away, but you can't.

In the morning Frank tells me I was moaning and shielding my face with my arm.

❖

The emerging purple and white crocuses bordering the slushy driveway prompt me to think ahead about painting some watercolors of local scenery, and perhaps taking a beginning oil painting class at the Art Institute. If I'm halfway decent at it, I might even follow it with another class in the summertime.

Stephanie will visit in early May, the latest her obstetrician will let her fly. She says she's fine now, past some morning sickness early in the pregnancy. But where will she live with her baby? I can't help but wonder. Will Liam help support them? The last time I talked to her on the phone, she snapped at me when I asked about her plans for the baby and I didn't want to push the issue.

Still, these questions nag at me as I drive back and forth to work, stop off at the library, dry cleaners, post office, supermarket, and gas station. All these drains on my energy, but what about my painting? I register for the Intro to Oil Painting class at the Art Institute website without further delay since I'd ended up on the waiting list last year. A tingle of anticipation surges through me when I receive the confirmation email: "Intro to Oil Painting…Thursday…7 to 10:00 pm…Instructor, J. Dvorak."

Okay, first Thursday in April…and the next day I receive J. Dvorak's student supply list for the class.

The end of the school year can sneak up quickly, so I try to do as much as possible ahead of time, so I'm not overwhelmed in June. I send follow-up letters on vision referrals and medication forms for next year and begin working on next year's supply order: ice packs, bandages in eight different sizes, gauze, Bactine, hydrogen peroxide, flashlight batteries, cotton-tipped swabs, Neosporin ointment, exam gloves (latex and powder-free), bee-sting swabs, red hazardous waste bags, and warning labels for blood, teeth, skin and any other of the many biohazards in my life.

After school finds me shopping for an assortment of oil paints plus a few basic brushes and a palette knife that surprisingly set me back well over a hundred dollars, not including the three canvasses on the list. With Stephanie arriving, and then a baby, I have to wonder about the expense for this…but if not now, when?

The first art class coincides with an early dismissal day at school. The kids' buses pull out at 1:40, so I leave the building right after the staff meeting to avoid the rush hour traffic. Parking in the Monroe Street underground garage is the best choice; it comes up to street level right outside the back entrance to the Art Institute on Columbus Drive. With time to kill, my first stop is the museum gift shop and its exquisite, although expensive, blown glass ornaments, note cards, art books and calendars. After an hour of browsing, I head across Michigan Avenue for a light supper. In warmer weather, many of the cafés have outside seating, but the evening's cool breeze off the lake drives diners inside. I order a bowl of vegetable soup and a crusty French baguette. Sitting by the window, I watch the passers-by, many stylishly dressed office workers rushing now to catch their trains to the suburbs.

About 20 minutes before class is scheduled to begin, I walk back across Michigan Avenue, stopping at the center island as cars stream by, then past the massive bronze lions that have stood guard at the Art Institute as long as I can remember. A lot has changed since my summer classes here as a teen, when the school was in the basement of the museum with narrow corridors and low-hanging steam pipes. Since then a new wing has been built, with spacious, light filled classrooms and studios. After checking my schedule to make sure I'm in the right studio, I pause at the doorway and gasp slightly, my hand over my mouth. It's Jeff, *my* Jeff, from the frame shop and gallery, saying in a loud voice, "This is Intro to Oil Painting, and I'm Mr. Dvorak. Anything else, you're in the wrong place. We'll start in a few minutes." He wears a dark gray turtleneck, his curly dark hair tousled like he has just gotten out of bed; with whom, I wonder.

Stools and easels stand haphazardly about the room. The east windows of the classroom look out onto Columbus Drive. Beyond, Lake Michigan's cold blue-gray water blends into the horizon. I choose a stool and easel near the back of the room and sit down next to a girl whose tight, tattered jeans and multiple ear piercings remind me of Roxy. She's immersed in an animated conversation on her cell phone. A man in faded blue jeans, his salt and pepper hair pulled back in a ponytail, scans *The Reader*, waiting for class to begin. Jeff begins to call the roll and when he reaches my name, he looks up slightly to see where "here" is and smiles at me in recognition. He remembers me! Inside I feel like a schoolgirl with a crush on the teacher, but I try to project an air of detachment; calm, confident professionalism.

The first class is devoted to getting the feel of the oils, creating various textures by using instruments such as a knife, brush and stick. I'm just getting into the assignment as Jeff goes from student to student, stopping, eventually, at my easel. "Expanding your horizons?" he says, flashing me that killer smile.

"I've never worked with oils before..." *Come on, calm, confident, professional Elaine—where are you?* "I had no idea you...were the instructor." He places his warm hand over mine, gently helping me guide the knife, making quick, choppy movements in the paint, then slower strokes. *Dear God, don't let my hands be cold and clammy*, I pray silently. *And does it even matter...what if he doesn't feel the same electricity I feel? And what if he does?*

❖

Each week Jeff spends time at my easel, offering suggestions and praising my willingness to take a risk with form or color. Lost in Frank's oversized flannel shirt, I usually just nod silently, glad to the point of giddiness for the encouragement and the attention Jeff gives me.

During the fourth week after stopping to critique my work as usual, he says, "How about coffee after class?"

"Sure," I respond, wanting to shout and jump up and down, but managing to restrain myself.

All the students leave on time except for a girl who's asking about dropping the class because it conflicts with her new work schedule. I take my time cleaning my brushes, putting supplies away and calling home on my cell to say I'll be a while, getting Roxy, who barely gives me five seconds before she switches back to the other line.

The early April air has an edge to it, a reminder of winter past, as we walk the couple of blocks to the coffee house. Jeff removes the worn leather jacket over his turtleneck and places it around my shoulders, still warm from him. *Who says chivalry is dead?* "You never told me what you do; I mean, for a job."

"I'm a nurse," I say, snuggling into his jacket like a baby into her favorite blanket. *It even smells like him, like paint and turps and maleness. Damn, does that big old shirt of Frank's I wear smell of him—his plumber's putty and Old Spice? I hope not.*

"At a hospital?"

"…a school district."

"I think of a school nurse with gray hair pulled back in a bun. You don't fit that image at all." He looks me up and down, taking in my Gap khakis and apricot-colored cashmere hoodie that I hope flatters my petite frame. "You look stylin' to me…"

*There's that great smile again!* "Thanks, and you don't fit my image of a college professor hitting on beautiful young coeds."

"You are brutal." The smile fades to a grin. "Believe me, I did my share of dating students, but it's like Chinese food; you fill up fast and it leaves you wanting more." *Is that a hint of regret? Is he doing 'hip, cool, been-there college prof' or does he mean it?*

"Technically I'm one of your students, Mr. Dvorak. What have you got to say about that?" I tease.

"Technically, but I knew you before you were my student," Jeff shoots back.

He holds the coffee house door open for me, which is sweet, but would he do that for a younger woman? The interior is dark with a lit candle on each small round table, so it takes a minute for my eyes to adjust. Jeff chooses a table away from the other patrons, and I order decaf latte with skim milk, ever health-conscious. Besides, I'll have a hard enough time sleeping tonight.

We talk there for about an hour, easily, like new friends that immediately connect. I make sure I let him know I have no husband, though I do make mention of living with someone. Then, too, there's my teenage daughter (who'd probably be interested in dating him if she saw him, but NO–he's mine, dammit).

He's from a family of teachers (History and French) in the East, with an older sister in California who's a massage therapist. He's the only visual artist in the family, though his mom and sister play the violin, and he grew up listening to the two practicing and playing duets together in the living room.

No wonder he was playing the Debussy when we met...

When it's time to leave, he pays, leaving a tip, and announces he's walking me to my car.

"Will that take you out of your way?"

"I live above the gallery. It used to be gang territory, but now it's getting gentrified and my rent keeps going up." He shakes his head, grins a self-deprecating smile. "Hard to believe I'm still there."

"My Stephanie used to live in Bucktown before she moved to Ireland."

"Who's Stephanie?"

"My oldest daughter." I half-jog to keep up with his long strides.

He slows, facing me, his eyes full of unasked questions. "You're all surprises, aren't you?"

How will he see me with my next revelation? *OK, here goes.* "Which reminds me, *(Oh, yeah!)* I almost forgot to tell you that I might not be at class next week. Stephanie is coming home for a visit before she has her baby."

This stops him in his tracks–literally. *Omigod.*

"Now you're telling me that you're going to be a grandmother!" Doubts flicker in his eyes, at odds with the smile on his face. "What next...you're running away to join the circus? You're really something. I mean that in a good way."

*Oh spare me... or maybe he really does?* "Thanks, I think."

He laughs, breaking the tension and gazing at me intently. "Someone old enough to be a person with a life story. I like that. Something unexpected."

"Well, that's me–unexpected." *How lame was that?*

We retreat to our own thoughts as we walk down the stairs to the parking garage. It's nearly deserted and I'm glad he's with me. We approach my car, and I can't think what to say but "Thanks."

He leans closer (*here it comes, oh God*) and kisses me—on the forehead.

❖

It is past midnight when I get home. The house is quiet as I undress and slip into bed next to Frank. I put my arm around his warm, muscular back and kiss his shoulder, my usual routine. He mumbles something and cuddles closer. I lay in bed next to Frank thinking about Jeff. Am I out of my mind? My Catholic school girl side keeps warning me that nothing good can come of this. But nothing has happened…yet. He's just a friend who shares my interest in art, I rationalize as I drift off.

## Jeff

Let's see where this goes…with Elaine…hell…something different…nothing to lose. She doesn't seem all hung up with bullshit. Is she past that? Whatever, I kind of like it; it's a relief to just chill. Like, there's an age difference, but not really that much, 'cause she's basically into the music (from her daughter, I guess) and we can talk about art and she's not trying to impress me with how she's got it goin' on. She does…in her own way. Shit, does this mean I'm getting old?

A *grandmother*? That's a little freaky, but she doesn't seem to mind, so why should I? She has talent…it needs some polishing, sure, and I can help her, if she wants. Dude, it's like robbing the cradle, but at the other end. I wonder how old she is? She's got a daughter having a baby who had a couple years of college, so unless she had her when she was 15, she's at least in her forties. I wonder what that's like…banging a chick in her *forties*. Dude, chill; go with it.

## Elaine

The next morning when Frank's pouring his coffee, he says, "I looked at the alarm clock when you finally came to bed… it was past midnight, almost 12:30."

"I know. I called, but you were already asleep. I left a message with Roxy."

"Like Roxy's ever going to give me a message from you!" he growls. He takes a long sip from his mug, spilling some down the front of his T-shirt, and swears.

"What do you want, Frank? She's a teenager. They're all surly."

"You always make excuses for her, for Stephanie, too. I know I'm not her father, but she needs to show me some respect!" His bluster is half pout as he ineffectually dabs at the spill with a moist paper towel.

"It's a two-way street, Frank. Why don't you try getting to know her better, try talking to her." *Oh God, how many children do I have…two or three?*

Timing is everything, and it's the worst possible time to remind Frank that I'm picking Stephanie up from O'Hare tonight. Another late night, I realize, feeling the weight of fatigue on my neck and shoulders, exhausted before the day's even started.

He refills his mug with black coffee and takes a long drink. "One more thing." *Uh-oh.* "We never talked about how long Stephanie is staying, or if she's going back to Ireland to have the baby, or what." *Any minute now, he'll fold his arms across his chest and plant his feet on the kitchen floor, battle posture.*

"I know. I don't even know myself. Let's just see how it goes. First things first. I'll be picking her up at O'Hare tonight," I say.

He folds his arms and stands, feet apart, glowering at me. "Tonight. You never told me."

"I did, Frank, but maybe you weren't listening."

"I think I'd remember that," he insists, continuing, "Besides, you know how I feel about babies…crying at all hours, dirty, stinky diapers, and baby stuff all over the place." Frank was married before, but never had children. He is the oldest of seven, though, so he knows what babies involve.

Pressure's building in the space behind my eyes. *Just what I need–a migraine. OK, how do I make my escape?* "Frank, I have to get to work. Can we just let this go for now?" *Three more steps and I'll be by the counter to fill my mug.* "After all, she hasn't even arrived yet…and won't until I meet her plane tonight. At six." *Two more for my keys.* "Let alone, had the baby." *Then a quick dash out the door.* "Really, I've got to run." *Made it!*

The door slams, jolting my budding headache, not at all helped by my bounding down the back stairs to my car.

❖

Work's a vacation after that, and I grin at the sight of Mrs. Rothrock…Lenore, our school secretary, who seems to be part of the building's infrastructure. She's the original Meadowlark Wildcat, as much of a mascot as the snarling cat's face emblazoned on the school stationery, every Phys Ed T-shirt, the gym floor, the principal's door, and the entrance, where its four-foot tall image overlooks the door that is locked each morning at 8:15. After that, you have to be buzzed in by Mrs. Rothrock.

With her sensible shoes and buttoned-up cardigan sweater, she's a no-nonsense bulldog of a gatekeeper who guards the principal's inner sanctum like a mother bear guarding her cubs. Her pulled-back hair reminds me of Jeff's comment last night, and I find myself fluffing my fingers through my shoulder-length bob.

"Good morning, Mrs. Rothrock. It's going to be a quiet day, right?"

"Yes, let's hope so." She barely looks up from her computer monitor.

"Outdoor recess today?"

"Looks like it, unless it rains later on."

Outdoor recess means cuts, scrapes, and bumps. Once past her massive oak desk and into my office, I settle gratefully into my worn chair, hoping to coast through the day, meet Stephanie's plane, get her home and settled, and myself into a hot tub.

Just past the bell signaling the end of the last lunch period, I unhunch my shoulders, daring to hope at 1:00 PM that the rest of the day will be as peaceful as the first half, which has been punctuated only by my "frequent flyers," the ones with headaches and stomach aches needing more in the way of comfort than medical attention. After verifying their normal temps, I send them on their way, reassuring them that they're OK. Some linger with those sad eyes, hoping to stay for even a few more minutes rather than return to class.

"Try to make it through lunch," I say, the classic encouragement, attempting to keep them here for the day. They're not just an annoyance; they're a red flag for deeper issues at home, no doubt. What, I can only guess. It's better to keep them in school until the last bell and on their usual schedule if they're not really sick. At least they're under adult supervision for the better part of the day.

With some parents working in the city, over an hour away by train, I can't send kids home to empty houses, and tracking down the emergency contacts can be tricky. Phone numbers change or are disconnected. But so far, so good today, and the thought of some hot soup for lunch and a little time away from my office perks me up.

Spattered food is baked onto the inside of the microwave oven in the teachers' lounge. A note taped to the door saying *Your mother isn't here to clean up after you!* apparently makes no impression on the harried users intent on warming their lunches and getting off their feet for awhile. Still, if everyone cleaned up their own mess...

I try to ignore what I imagine to be colorful colonies of bacteria multiplying exponentially while my cup of instant chicken noodle soup heats.

Karen Connors, a seasoned second grade teacher, begins quizzing me about the side effects of her blood pressure medication the minute I sit down.

"I got so dizzy I stopped taking it...now I've got this throbbing ache. I can feel the blood surging through my veins." She massages her fleshy neck, just in case I didn't get it: she's got a pain in the neck.

"Stop by my office during your free period and I'll take your blood pressure." *Jeez, am I ever not 'on'? All I want to do is drink my soup in peace.*

"How's your daughter, the one in Ireland?"

"I'm picking her up from the airport after school today." The chicken soup is salty and warm going down. No one at school knows about the baby. I don't want to go there, especially with Karen who can terribilize anything, and would likely broadcast the news to the entire staff.

"What's that noise?" Karen asks, looking around, trying to locate a faint chirping sound.

"What noise? Oh *that!* That's me...it's my pager." Clipped on the waistband of my slacks, under my sweater. *Who's paging me,* I wonder, fumbling under my sweater. Now my cell phone begins ringing, and before I can answer it, the intercom blares. *Mrs. McElroy, report to the office immediately.*

"Gotta go." *There goes my quiet afternoon.* Taking one last gulp of soup, I bolt for the door and speed walk down the hall. Near the office, in the direction of the playground, a spotted trail of bright red leads up to the office door. Through the glass enclosure two boys are visible in front of Mrs. Rothrock's desk; one is crying and holding his cheek while blood seeps between his fingers. The taller boy has his arm around the younger boy's shoulder and is frantically gesturing in the direction of the playground.

"Miz M, Miz M," Javari, the older boy, tugs at my sleeve as Mrs. Rothrock hands me a pair of exam gloves. "A big ole nasty dog came on the playground when we was playing dodgeball. The other team tried to hit Marcus with the ball and got the dog. That dog came right over and bit Marcus on the face." His wailing is a combination of fear and pain.

I gently pry his blood-stained fingers away from his face. Four puncture wounds gush fresh blood as soon as I lift his fingers.

I scoop him up and place him on the cot in my office. He moans and kicks, pressing his dirty hands to the open wounds. Mrs. Rothrock hovers, waiting for instructions. "Call the parent; tell them we're calling an ambulance. Call 911 and the police, and make sure everyone is off the playground. Where's Mrs. Stallings?"

"...An administrator's meeting at the District Office."

"Call her after you call everyone else."

I close the door and Javari is still there at his little brother's side. "Javari, I have to take care of Marcus. You need to wait outside the door." This starts Marcus wailing all the more, his free hand reaching out for Javari. "OK, you can stay, but you have to sit right here and stay out of the way." I motion to a chair next to my desk. The health office is too small for the cot, file cabinet, battered wooden desk, metal storage cabinet, and small computer stand. The bathroom, used by staff and sick kids as well, is a few feet away, behind Mrs. Rothrock's desk. The building is over 40 years old, designed long before anyone heard of universal precautions and bloodborne pathogens.

Prying those small, grimy hands away from Marcus' face proves no easy task, reminding me all over again how strong a six-year-old kid can be when he's scared and hurt. Finally, I'm able to unclamp his fingers. Gauze 4X4s saturated with Betadine serve to clean the wound and soak up the blood, but also take Marcus' cries to higher decibel levels that reverberate throughout the tiny space and out into the main office where Mrs. Rothrock is busy making the necessary calls.

"Hold still, like Big Mama say to do when she's fixing you up," Javari tells his brother, and mercifully, it seems to have some effect. Working quickly, I cover the wound with a clean dressing and apply pressure with an ice pack, all the time murmuring, "It's gonna be all right, Marcus, it's gonna be fine. I'm gonna go with you to the hospital so the doctor can have a look at your cheek."

"The hos-pid-dal—no way a hos-pid-dal!" He gasps for air to support a fresh wail. "Am I gonna get a shot?" He begins crying again at the thought.

"No, Marcus, you had a tetanus shot last year when you started kindergarten." I hug him, careful not to bump his cheek, where he's holding the ice pack in place.

The paramedics arrive, wearing heavy-duty gloves, pushing a gurney that won't fit past the corner of my desk before it bumps into the file cabinet. I lift Marcus onto the gurney and turn to pull his health file from the cabinet. "I'm going with you," and Javari is at my side ready to go along. "Javari, you have to stay here, but I promise I'll call the school and tell you how he's doing."

❖

Radio transmissions crackle their data to the hospital as I hoist myself up and into the back of the ambulance to sit by Marcus and reassure him. Usually, I'd follow the ambulance in my car, but this scared little kid needs me. He gasps for air and clutches my hand as the paramedic monitors his vital signs and checks the dressing. The problem will be getting back to school, but I'll deal with that later. Glancing at the playground, I wonder if there's any sign of that dog. The Animal Control van pulls up just before the ambulance doors slam shut.

The ambulance pulls away, siren blasting, and Marcus howling in fright. There's no comforting him; he's still screaming full force as he's rushed into the ER. A nurse there wheels him back to a cubicle. I hear his cries from the registration area, where I sign him in, giving as much information as I can from the school records.

❖

"Mrs. Rothrock, Marcus is with the doctor right now. Did they get the dog?"

"They're combing the neighborhood for it, and we've had to make out a police report."

"Have we gotten hold of anyone for Marcus?" The clock on the lobby wall inside inches past 3:30 with no relative of his in sight. I pace the sidewalk outside, easing the cell phone to my ear, all too mindful of the lurking migraine I thought I'd dodged earlier.

"I left messages with all his contacts and I'm hoping someone will go straight to the hospital." *Oh no! Who knows when someone will show up? I have to swing by the house for Roxy, then up to O'Hare to meet Stephanie's plane, all in afternoon traffic.*

A blue Ford Taurus pulls up to the ER entrance. An attractive, slender woman, wild-eyed, slams out of the car, clearly a woman on a mission, and my gut tells me it's Marcus' mom. "Hold on. I think the mom is here…"

❖

Roxy and I arrive at the airport just before Stephanie's flight is due. Traffic was worse than I'd anticipated, the result of getting an even later start on the road when I pulled up at home–already running late–and Roxy was only getting out of the shower. Hair and makeup can be done in a car, but basic dressing–no way.

She's still messing with her hair when we arrive at O'Hare. According to the monitor, Stephanie's flight is on schedule, but she'll still have to claim her luggage and go through customs, however long that takes. We approach the waiting area in the international terminal when Roxy stops and looks intently at me. "Yo, like Mom—your name? Listen," she says, a worried look on her face.

"Listen to what?"

"I think your name's on the intercom-thingy. They said to go to Aer Lingus."

"Hmm. Where is their counter?" The pressure behind my eyes increases, and I suspect this headache isn't going away. I fumble in my purse until I find my pill case. Forget a water fountain, I choke down a couple of Advil before the pain gets too intense.

I approach an airport employee who directs us as I unmistakably hear my name over the intercom. "See, Mom, I told you!" Roxy grabs my arm and drags me on.

Concern has tightened my stomach into a knot and turned my palms cold and clammy, not to mention my aching head.

"Maybe Stephanie joined the IRA and got arrested. She needs someone to bail her out," quips Roxy.

"That's not funny." I stop dead in my tracks and turn to lecture her. "What if someone overheard you?"

"Sorry." Roxy sulks, thrusting her hands in her frayed jeans pockets.

I approach the counter. "I'm Elaine McElroy. You paged me?" *How many times can I be paged today? What more in this day from Hell? Now what?*

A young woman with Aer Lingus asks for an ID. "Of course." I wind up rummaging through my purse again for my wallet like the stereotypical flustered woman, even resorting to emptying a pack of Kleenex, several pens, spare keys, a couple of lipsticks, my compact and pill case, cell phone and two power bars on the counter before producing my driver's license. "What's going on?" I ask.

"Do you have a relative aboard Aer Lingus flight 299 from Dublin?"

"Yes, my daughter Stephanie, and she's pregnant. Is something wrong with Stephanie?"

"Over the Atlantic the plane encountered quite a bit of turbulence. Your daughter is reporting labor pains." *Oh no, it's too soon.* "Paramedics are waiting to take her to the hospital as soon as the flight arrives, which is any minute. We have a customs agent to clear her. I'll have security escort you to the tarmac."

I grab Roxy, now very pale. "C'mon." My experience as a nurse taught me to stay calm and react later. Right now my priority is to help Stephanie in any way possible. We arrive at the landing area just as the plane is taxiing into position. Two paramedics, a man and a woman, stand by with a gurney. "I'm the mother of the woman you're supposed to take to the hospital. Do you know how she is?"

"Our dispatcher is in contact with the captain. She seems to be doing OK, but the turbulence and sudden drop in altitude may have caused her to go into labor about two hours ago."

"Can I ride with you to the hospital?" I ask, doing my best to exude the cool, calm demeanor of a woman who'll be no problem.

"Not a problem," replies the woman paramedic, and they're off, right on the heels of a man I assume to be the customs agent.

Before I know it, they've gotten Steph strapped onto the gurney and off the plane. She looks worried, but smiles weakly. "Sorry for all the excitement, Mom." The paramedics load her into the waiting ambulance and I see her baby belly curve beneath her fisherman's knit sweater.

I squeeze her hand, leaning over to kiss her. Roxy just stares.

"Hi, Roxy. How's my baby sister?" says Stephanie, trying to sound upbeat.

"You're having it *here*?" Roxy asks, somewhat breathless. Her eyes, outlined with black liner and mascara, appear huge, astonished.

"I hope not. It's not due for another 12 weeks," responds

Stephanie.

"They'll give you medication to stop the labor. How often are you having contractions? And how long do they last?" *(Here I go into Nurse Fuzzy Wuzzy mode. I can't help it; it's second nature.)*

"About every 20 minutes, but they're not regular." Stephanie replies. The paramedics push the gurney through the automatic doors to the waiting ambulance as people gawk.

As I step up to the back bumper of the ambulance (for the second time that day—is this the universe's way of telling me to consider a career change?), Roxy says, "Mom, what about me?" Her eyes are big, her dark eyebrows raised as she speaks in a thin, shrill tone that does nothing for my nerves, not to mention the headache, which is now threatening to take off the top half of my skull.

A deep breath and exhale. What to do? "You'll need to get Stephanie's bags. Then...do you think you can find your way out of the parking garage and drive home by yourself? You have school tomorrow, and it could be hours and hours waiting at the hospital, honey. If you don't think you can, call Frank on my cell phone." I toss the phone to her, along with the keys and a twenty.

"He'll come and pick you up. Call him anyhow, and let him know what's going on, and he can talk you onto the expressway and home. I love you. Now I've got to help Stephanie." Poor Roxy just stands there dumbly, clutching the cell phone as they slam the ambulance doors shut. Within seconds we're on our way, sirens blaring, only this time it's my Stephanie, my own flesh and blood and a new life as well. *God be with us*, I silently pray.

"You're going to be OK," I say, gently brushing Stephanie's red hair from her green eyes with one hand and squeezing her hand with the other.

"I hope so, Mom. But it's not me I'm worried about," she says. "It's the baby… it's too soon."

"Sweetheart, they'll do everything they can…they can do so much now. It'll be OK…it has to." Her hand clutches mine, nearly crushing it, I fear, and another wave of contractions distorts her delicate features with pain. I send a silent prayer for my daughter and grandchild.

When we arrive at Resurrection Hospital, the paramedics escort Stephanie through the automatic doors labeled, RESTRICTED AREA. AUTHORIZED PERSONNEL ONLY. *It's a good hospital*, I remind myself, staying behind to answer seemingly endless questions about insurance, employment, and social security numbers. I don't know about Stephanie's job, let alone insurance. Even if she is working, it isn't here in The States, so I put down as much as I know, which is precious little. It will be a mess to straighten out later. "Can I see my daughter now?" I ask the admitting clerk, after handing her the paperwork.

"I'll check with the nurse; please have a seat."

The waiting room occupants look as if they had been randomly scooped up by a tornado and deposited unceremoniously onto the institutional furniture. An old woman is rocking and moaning softly, her arms wrapped around her mid-section, a baby cries shrilly, and a man with wild dreadlocks is holding a bloody cloth to his thigh. I close my eyes and try to summon as much strength as possible. *Don't fall apart now, old girl. Stay strong for Stephanie; she needs you now.* Breathe. *God, grant me the serenity to accept the things I cannot change, courage to change the things I can, and wisdom to know the difference…*

"Is there someone here for Stephanie McElroy?" I return to the moment and jump to my feet.

I follow the nurse through the automatic doors, past draped cubicles, gurneys with and without occupants, and harried hospital workers. *Thank goodness they've taken Stephanie right away.* The nurse pushes a drape back just enough for me to enter Stephanie's cubicle. An IV drips fluid slowly into her arm and a monitor at the bedside illuminates a jagged green line working its way to the top of the screen then back down again. "How are you doing, honey?" I grasp Stephanie's hand and kiss her on the forehead.

"The medicine in the IV is supposed to stop the labor, but I'm still having contractions." Her pale, almost translucent skin, like a delicate bone china teacup, is shiny with sweat. She twists my hand, hard. "Here comes another one," she gasps, her face contorted with fatigue and pain. Finally, it subsides, and she lets out a long breath. "The doctor says they will do everything to try and stop the labor, but if they can't, the baby has a good chance…the heart beat is strong."

At 12:07 A.M. Stephanie's son is born by Cesarean section, weighing in at just under five pounds. He looks like a tiny bird that has fallen out of the nest, scrawny with paper-thin skin covered with soft down, and a perfectly formed head. I love him immediately, of course, and feel I must protect him and Stephanie, from what I am not sure. My maternal instincts are honed to a razor's edge.

Stephanie dozes, and I settle into a recliner by the window

in her room to call home and tell Frank the news: He's groggy with sleep when he answers, but I can't help blurting out the news, "I'm a Grandma and Roxy's an aunt! It's a boy! They did an emergency C-section because his heart rate dropped, but mom and baby are doing fine. He's in neonatal intensive care for observation, but he's breathing on his own. They're monitoring him to make sure he's OK." I'm the only one talking.

He grunts. "Lemme tell ya, it was some mess last night, talking that kid home on the expressway. Like some kinda movie. Kept wonderin' if that cell was gonna die out on us. But she made it home." *Do I detect a note of pride in that? A job well done together?*

"Thank God. I want to hear more about it when I see you. You'll come to the hospital after work? See you in the Main Lobby."

Another grunt.

"Let me talk to Roxy." The phone drops with a *thunk*, and he hollers for Roxy.

"Mom?"

"… Oh honey, you're still my baby… I'm sorry you had to drive home alone." I find myself gushing. "Did you find your way? Did you make it home all right?"

"Yeah, it was freakin' to drive on the expressway by myself, you know, but Frank talked me through it, and I made it home, like, OK." She pauses, then laughs. "I rock, dude!" Then, "How's my big sister? Did she, like, have it?"

"She's fine. You're an aunt! It's a boy, 4 lbs 14 oz. He's doing fine. We're all fine. She's sleeping now, which is something I wouldn't mind doing myself. You need to get up for school tomorrow…today, though, and it's late, early, I guess." I'm suddenly overcome with exhaustion. Knowing that my offspring are all safe and accounted for, it's OK to collapse.

"I could come and get you later on today, after school,." she offers hopefully, no doubt wanting another chance to rock.

"No, I think you've had enough solo driving for a while. You've only got your permit, remember? Frank can drop by the hospital on his way home from work. We'll all come home together when Stephanie and the baby are discharged—soon, if everyone is all right. Love you. Get some more sleep. You've had quite a day, and so have I."

"Back at ya. And Stephanie…and my new nephew."

*What a day – two ambulance crises, a new grandson, and Roxy driving 40 miles alone on a major expressway with only a permit and*

*Frank's voice to guide her.*

I welcome sleep, relieved that Stephanie is back in the United States, the baby is cared for, and Roxy made it home safely.

On the edge of consciousness, I perceive shadowy figures floating in and out of Stephanie's room during the night. Morning brings an early visit from my grandchild, all swaddled up in blankets with a little white cap on his lovely, round head. It's amazing to see Stephanie holding her own child, but the happiness is bittersweet. She has an uphill battle as a single mother, I know. Still, my heart aches with happiness when I hold him, wishing I could immediately instill into him and his mom all the lessons I've learned so far, so they can avoid mistakes I've made, but that's impossible, of course. For me to love them unconditionally will have to be enough.

I wash my face and go down to the cafeteria for breakfast. The beginning of a new life holds so much promise. If only the journey had started under more positive circumstances. I'll do everything I can to smooth the way for Stephanie and her baby, but will that be enough?

❖

The day seems a week old before 5 P.M. comes, when Frank will pick me up, meet my grandson, and then we'll go out and celebrate with a glass of wine and a well-earned plate of good pasta after a day of cafeteria food. Stephanie's pain meds help her sleep through the 7 A.M. admission of her roommate, but no such respite for me. Fortunately, the chapel gives me peace, quiet and a place to doze for a while, so I give a prayer of thanks for Stephanie and her boy, as yet unnamed, as well as for the much needed tranquility.

But my serenity does not last long, for my daughter announces before I'm half way in the room, "Mom, I thought about it, and I've decided to name him Colin."

That snaps me out of my grogginess, mother-antennae tingling. "Oh, really," I remark very casually. *Not naming him after his father–does that mean something serious?* "Any particular reason?"

"I just like it...a good Irish name that means 'young cub.'"

❖

When I go down to the lobby, I'm bubbling over with details about Colin; he burped, he yawned, he peed, pooped and cried. How amazing is that? I can't wait to tell Frank all about my perfect grandson, and show him how beautiful this baby is. Frank must be delayed at work or held up in traffic. When he finally pulls up to the entrance and jumps out, leaving the car running, I'm confused. This isn't what we–I– planned.

"You're not parking the car? What's going on?"

He gives me a withering look that I choose to ignore. What's gotten his face all tight and pinched looking? After all, this is a big occasion.

"Well, park and come back, and we'll go see the baby–he has a name, too."

"Not now, Elaine."

"Aren't we going to see the baby together?"

"Just c'mon and get in the car." I'm not prepared for his tone of voice, which is almost unrecognizable to me, it's so deep–almost threatening.

"Wait, a minute, Frank, I thought we were going to go upstairs to the nursery…" I hear my voice rising in a whine.

"Maybe *you* thought I was going to go upstairs to see it, but I never said any such thing." His voice takes on a sharper edge. "So would you just get in the car, for God's sake!"

How can this be–this side of Frank I've never seen before, a side that scares me? His voice cuts the air.

"What do you mean, you're not coming in? This is my grandson we're talking about."

"*Your* grandson, Elaine, yours…"

*Who IS this person?* "Well, if you're not coming in, I'm going back upstairs and say good bye to Stephanie."

"That's a no parking zone, so I'll circle…If you're not down here in five minutes, I'm leaving."

"You're what?"

"You get in this car in five minutes, or call a cab." He is practically whispering now, with an intensity I've never heard before.

It knocks the breath out of me. "You go on ahead." Feelings bubble up inside, reminding me of what I used to feel with Tom when we were married. *How long has it been? Ten years and these memories are still with me? Frank is nothing like Tom, and I know that, after five years together…*

I drop into a chair, grateful for its support. When I pull myself up and head toward the elevator, I barely take two steps before I have to grab at the arm of a passing stranger to steady myself.

"Ma'am, are you OK?" he says as I struggle for balance.

*No, no I am definitely not OK, and I'm not even a "miss" anymore, I've somehow become a "ma'am."* "Fine, really, I'm fine – just a little dizzy after a long day." *The exciting day that turned into the Day from Absolute Hell.*

He steers me toward the reception desk, clearly eager to be rid of me. "Well, if you're sure you're okay…" He steadies me against the counter, turns and bolts.

The receptionist's busy with someone else, giving them a visitor's pass with one hand while she answers the phone with the other, so I inch my way along the counter toward the elevator, determined to make it upstairs. *This is just a minor setback,* I tell myself.

My fingers tremble so hard I can barely push the right elevator button, but soon I find myself in Stephanie's room.

"Mom, you look terrible–what happened? Frank's at the nursery?"

"He can't make it, and I'm feeling a little weak…too much excitement." I collapse into the nearby chair. "I'll call Christa…"

## *Roxy*

Y ou go, girl! That was *sweet*, and a little scary, merging onto the expressway…Frank couldn't help me with that…that was on my own. Dude, I just gunned that Toyota like it's never been. It kind of hesitated right in front of that semi and I thought it was all over, but it came through…*Yessss.* So what if he gave me the air horn and probably the finger…Dude, I *rock.* Now I can drive all the time…yeah…I *earned* it.

Mom taught me, you know, and even though she's this total nerd, she is one wicked good driver. So's my sister. We are one bunch of ass-kickin', gun-that-engine, tear-up-the- road McElroy babes! No duh.

## *Elaine*

T hank God for the sanctuary of Christa's car, filled with books, papers, magazines, tote bags half-filled with more books and papers, empty Dunkin Donuts cups and smelling of amaretto coffee and Estee Lauder's "Pleasures." Wherever she goes, and throughout her home, Christa has a "signature scent," just like Cher, who insists her dressing room be sprayed with the fragrance bearing her name before she'll consider setting foot into it. I lack a signature scent, unless you count Bactine and disinfectant soap, and frankly, right now, I'd settle for some hot food, a cold beer, and the scent of good old, Calgon Bouquet in a steaming bath.

How do I begin–do I even want to discuss it? I'm not sure I even know what happened at the hospital with Frank. Christa fixes me with a look, eyebrows raised in a question, inviting me to spill my guts. "I can't talk about it now. Can we just go get something to eat?"

Over cheeseburgers and fries, it all comes tumbling out: Marcus bitten by a dog, Stephanie in premature labor over the Atlantic, Colin's entrance into the world, Roxy's solo drive home on the expressway sans license, and finally, Frank's transformation into a baby-hating monster. Who knew? Last time I had any semblance of sanity, I was getting ready to go to school for a normal day. Now I don't know what normal is and couldn't identify it if it bit me on the nose.

"Wow–but Stephanie's okay…and the baby?"

"Both doing fine, or I'd still be there. What I really wanted to do was go home and collapse, but Frank's made that impossible." Christa folds her hands on the table and leans toward me, counselor-style, ready for more.

Between bites, I find myself wondering out loud how I can even return to that house, but Roxy's there, with her school and friends…and Stephanie's depending on me to bring her there with the baby, at least for a while.

"You can stay with me if you'd like." Christa's understanding blue eyes, wide and inviting, seem to offer some hope of an alternative.

"But I have to go back there and find out where I stand— where we all stand with Frank." My voice sounds thin and shaky, not at all the resolute tone I'll need.

❖

Christa's reassurances of help linger as I walk past the border of crocuses, daffodils and hyacinths I planted last fall, then make my way up the back stairs. Before I can reach for the knob, Frank's opened the door and stands before me, waiting.

"Elaine, I want to know how all this is going to affect us."

I'm not even in the door. "What?"

"You know… Stephanie and the baby. You know you're going to ask her to move in with us. You don't even have to ask her–it's understood that she'll move in with us, and I wasn't even consulted!" With hands on hips and his face contorted in anger, he stands ready for battle, just when my defenses are down. I don't have the strength to argue, nor do I want to.

"Frank, do we have to have this conversation now? I'm exhausted."

"*Now.* I know you. You just put things off and hope they'll go away. I told you before how I feel about babies. I'm not happy about this!" he thunders.

"You may not be happy about this, but I don't see why you can't just be happy for me. I told you before not to ask me to choose between you and my family." I slam the door shut behind me and stride into the kitchen as Frank, surprised, steps back.

"I'm not asking you to choose."

"That's what it sounds like to me, dammit."

When I dump my purse and jacket on a chair, it seems to signal a fresh attack. He's right in my face when I turn around.

"*Ex-cu-use me!*" Palms up, I give fair warning: *Don't get in my face.* I don't trust myself to say another word, not right now. I imagine shrieks and howls pouring out of me, all pent up from dealing with dog bites and tracking down mothers and ambulances and non-licensed daughters driving expressways, not to mention emergency C-sections and the man I've made my life with turning into a big insensitive, non-supportive, misogynist asshole.

"What did you call me?"

I look blankly at this man who's apparently become a mind reader.

"You called me an asshole!"

"It must have slipped out. But I'm NOT sorry." I feel heat rising in my face and I'm almost choking on the anger that wants to erupt all over his clothes and shoes, all over the floor, all over his damned kitchen that he can take and…"

He crashes the metal chair against the old Formica table, and the sound reverberates off the plaster walls, hollow and cold. "Bitch! You've been living under my roof…"

"You make it sound like I was a bag lady with a shopping cart–I had a perfectly nice apartment that I gave up to come and live in a house that hasn't been remodeled since the Korean War."

"And it's not just you, it's Roxy, too—clothes all over the bathroom floor, loud music, and she's always eating…"

"Wait a goddam minute. I buy all the groceries, remember?"

"Yeah, but I pay the electric bill, and she's forever leaving the lights on. And those 20-minute showers she takes…between the gas, water and electric—they're five times what they used to be, now that you're here with…that…"

"That what? That brat who uses gas and electric and water? Jesus, Frank, you are one cheap-ass son of a bitch!"

"Nice! Nice talk, Elaine."

"You act like this, you better damn well get used to it. Listen, you knew Roxy was part of the package right from the beginning. 'Oh, no problem,' you said. 'She's a sweet kid,' you said—until she starts costing you a little money!"

"She's a slob, a mess, the way she dresses like a hippie out of a horror movie and the way she talks…"

"What do you mean—she talks like a teenager? She *is* a teenager, and that's how they talk. Get with it. You're a stingy old geezer. And don't you ever, ever, attack my child. She is my daughter and that's that. She's a good kid, and you said it yourself."

"Yeah, throw my own words in my face, why don't you, you conniving bitch, finagling your way in here with that kid of yours."

"Finagling my way—huh? Is that what this is about—money? Like you don't eat the food I buy—and cook—or watch the cable-TV I pay for? You love that, you cheap bastard." The look on his face tells me I've hit a nerve. "You never put a nickel into this place, but you sit in your recliner with your feet up watching sports on your big screen TV that's worth more than this whole damned kitchen. Speaking of which, you don't seem to mind having a free live-in cook, not to mention, cleaning lady and landscaper!"

"That is crap, Elaine, that is just plain crap and you know it. There's no way that stuff stacks up against these bills and the roof I put over your heads."

"Well, screw you and your blessed roof!"

"Would you have all this?" he says, gesturing grandly to the chipped metal cabinets and scratched gray Formica countertops as the overhead fluorescent light briefly dims when the 1970s Harvest Gold Frigidaire kicks in.

"I would hope not," I shoot back, trying to keep a straight face as I glance down to the scuffed, faux brick linoleum floor worn to the wood subflooring beneath in spots. "Are you insane? Am I supposed to be grateful? The place I left had up-to-date appliances, floors that weren't as old as me and in a lot worse shape..."

"Don't be so sure about that!"

I freeze, feeling eyes on me. Roxy stands in the arched entranceway, staring, wide-eyed like a stunned deer in plaid drawstring pants and a Red Hot Chili Peppers T-shirt.

"What's going on?"

Frank and I turn to her at the same moment, shouting in unison, "Nothing!"

"It sure sounds like something to me." She makes her way with exaggerated teenaged bravado to the refrigerator and grabs a can of pop. She pivots theatrically, holds the can of Coke up above her head and says, "Carry on," as she flounces from the kitchen.

"Later," Frank says, outnumbered, outflanked and deflated, sinking into a chair. "We can definitely do this later."

Sighing, I fall into one of the metal dinette chairs, careful to avoid its sharply ripped corner. How long had Frank been saying he would mend it? And with what? More duct tape, like the chair across from it?

Frank rises and opens the fridge for a beer.

"Get me one, too." Actually, I am contemplating something between several glasses of Merlot and a shot of Jack Daniels, but a cold beer will do.

"When are Stephanie and the baby coming home from the hospital?" Frank's voice is softer. An unspoken truce is in effect.

"Not for a day or two, at least, for Stephanie, and possibly longer for Baby Colin, depending on how's he's doing." The finality in my voice signals the end of the conversation.

"I'm going to go upstairs and soak in the tub and then go to bed," I say, bringing the beer with me to my bath.

After lighting an aromatic candle, I close my eyes and relax as soothing liquid bubbles around me. An image of Jeff drifts into my consciousness...we're kissing... and my thoughts wander where they will. Retreating to bed with a novel, I doze off, exhausted but relaxed. In a state of twilight sleep, I feel rough masculine hands caressing my inner thighs. I don't open my eyes, but continue with my Jeff fantasy. Thinking of another man brings a heightened sensuality to our lovemaking. I think Frank feels it, too, because afterwards he kisses me sweetly on the lips before turning over and saying, "We haven't made love like that in a long time! Guess we should fight more often. Love ya."

*Yeah, whatever. Is that what you call this? Love?*

## *Frank*

What was it that first attracted me to Elaine? That she had a good body, nice tits, and she was supporting herself and Roxy...self-sufficient. A woman with spunk, with gumption. Sometimes I wish she would look out for her own interests more. I think her girls try to take advantage. She's way too good to those two.

We met at a singles dance at the Legion Hall. Before she came along, it was getting pretty lonely around here after my divorce and all. I'd come home from work, cook some burgers or a frozen dinner, and sit on my recliner and watch TV. Not that there's anything wrong with that. It's just that sometimes a man needs to feel someone soft, someone who smells just right. Elaine and I hit it off. I could see that she was a practical woman, and a year ago she moved in with me...with her daughter Roxy. Don't get me wrong, Roxy's not a bad kid, but she gets on my nerves, sometimes. She's either blasting her music, or she's in the shower forever, or hanging out in front of the fridge. When I was her age, I was bagging groceries at the local Jewel. These kids; everything is handed to them now.

## *Stephanie*

He's so sweet when he's sleeping...a little angel. Look at his perfect little mouth and nose. I remember Roxy when she was a baby...not all sweetness and light. She was cute all right, but it seems like I got stuck watching her when she was a little older...my baby sister. Now I've got one of my own. I can hardly believe it, but he's real, all right, and in a little while he'll wake up and want to be fed.

What do I know about babies? What does anyone know when they first have one? Mom will help me; she won't let anything happen to him–he's her grandchild. Still, those early morning feedings are the pits, and I just had him.

I should call Liam, but there's the time difference, and I'm not sure that I can make an international call from the hospital. I'll have to wait 'til I get to Mom's house. Will he be happy? A son. I met his parents only once, and they seemed ancient to me, like cold fish, but a grandson– how could they help but love him?

## Elaine

I spend the next day shopping for some of the basic things that Stephanie needs for the baby—a car seat, crib and a few baby clothes. It's a relaxing, unhurried day spent savoring my remaining privacy and solitude before Stephanie brings the baby home. The only thing to spoil my quiet day alone is the thought that tonight Frank will want to have the discussion about Stephanie's living arrangements. I review Stephanie's options; go back to Ireland and try to get Liam to support her and the baby until she can get on her feet; ask her father if she can move in with him and his new family; or stay with me and Frank. I will try to convince Frank–I *will* convince Frank to let Stephanie and Colin stay with us until she gets a job and can support herself and her son.

Tonight is my oil painting class so I will pop in on Stephanie and Colin for just a few minutes and let her know I've bought some essentials.

❖

I leisurely prepare myself, bathing and dusting myself with scented powder. Frank gets home, comes upstairs, gives me a look and asks, "What are you all dolled up for? You must have a boyfriend." His tone is joking, but I detect suspicion as well. I know enough not to make an issue of it.

"I do and I'm going to see him tonight and we're going to make mad, passionate love…oh, and did you forget tonight's my art class?"

"Weren't we were going to talk about the Stephanie situation tonight?"

We are, right now," I say, diving headfirst into the unpleasant task and trying not to stab my earlobe with my dangling earring. "Can't we let her stay until she gets on her feet, maximum of a year?" I make it sound like I am asking for Frank's permission, but I have no intention of turning Stephanie away.

"One year max, then she's on her own. Make sure she knows that upfront," Frank says, beefy arms across his broad chest.

"I thought we could both sit down and talk to her when she comes home. I know your attitude will change once you see the baby."

"I doubt it." I detect we're entering dangerous territory with that gravely tone that threatens God-knows-what. "And someone will have to get up with him if he's making a racket at night. I need my sleep," he says indignantly.

"Frank," I say, careful to keep my tone even, "It's not 'he.' The baby's name is Colin. And yes, he will live here."

❖

Stephanie's feeding Colin as I bring her the good news, but she doesn't seem too surprised or even grateful. "I just assumed..." she starts before I cut in.

"Don't assume anything," I snap back. "You have no idea what I had to do to convince Frank...but it'll help you get through the first year."

She returns her gaze to Colin, contentedly sucking from the bottle. "Mom, thanks. I owe you. We both do," she says softly.

Such a Hallmark moment—but for how long?

## *Stephanie*

Where would Colin and I possibly go if not to my mom's? It's not like I can check into the Holiday Inn with a newborn. Frank hasn't changed much, I guess. But I really—make that *we* really don't have a choice. Forget about my dad. He's got his new family now, and it's like he forgets that Roxy and I even exist, except at Christmas and Thanksgiving when we're supposed to show up and act like one big happy family. As if!

As for Liam welcoming us—who knows?

That business office dude came in and asked me about my insurance or lack of it, since that's not an issue in Ireland. He made me sign some papers saying I'd be responsible for the bill, even though I'm not even working in this country.

But as a nurse, maybe Mom knows the system and can help me figure this out, or I'll be paying for this child the rest of my life.

Thank God for Mom, in more ways than one, or I would be calling up old friends that I haven't talked with in over a year. I'm sure some of them don't even know I went to Ireland. So it's Colin and me against the world, or maybe just Frank for now.

## *Elaine*

While driving into the city listening to U2, I savor the idea of my painting class and seeing Jeff. For one night I can step out of my many roles and be Elaine, a still sexy 50-year-old with creative and physical urges. At class Jeff immediately walks over to me and gently touches my arm. "Hello," he whispers. "What's new?"

"So much, like you wouldn't believe has happened in the last couple of days…if you're interested," I say.

"Let's talk after class. I have some great Merlot." Then he's gone, moving on to the next student.

Class time passes quickly as I work to complete last week's assignment. In fact, I'm so focused–*how can I even think about what he's said, that he has good wine–at his place–HIS place*–that I find myself breathing shallowly through my mouth, and when he whispers, "We still on for tonight?" he startles me. How long has he been standing there?

"Oh–yeah."

"Didn't mean to scare you." He smiles disarmingly. "It's just me."

*Does he know the effect that 'just me' has on me?* "Oh…not scared–I just didn't…"

"I wish all my students were as intense…"

*Jeff, you have no idea!*

On our walk to the underground parking garage I'm glad, again, to have him at my side, even though I have walked there by myself on occasion. On the way to Jeff's place, I worry about my car–the magazines and nursing journals strewn about, a half-full Speedway coffee mug in the cup holder, my school tote bag, all the baby things thrown in the back seat. *Will he think I'm a slob? What the hell, this is my life–and I live so much of it right here, in my car.* I tell him about Colin's difficult and unexpected birth. I continue with how I had to stand up to Frank, who, up to now, I'd only referred to as an unnamed live-in, insisting they stay with us until Stephanie is settled. Jeff listens closely, and as I turn toward him, his gaze seems focused, his jaw set, as he listens intensely, without interruption.

"Sounds like you have so much going on…"

"Your art class–that's my escape."

His apartment is as I have imagined it; messy and lived-in, but not disgusting; no piles of dirty dishes in the sink. I smile as he clears a stack of mail from the kitchen counter so I can set down the glass of Merlot he hands me. His paintings dominate the small combination living room/bedroom; on easels, in stacks and leaning against the walls. As I admire a nude of a Rubenesque-type woman, Jeff surprises me, coming up behind me and nuzzling my neck and rubbing my shoulders.

"You like her? That's my best work, I think, and I haven't done anything as good in months, even though I keep at it. Maybe you'll be my good luck charm–like at the casinos."

He gently turns me around, kissing me on the lips, and taking my hand leads me to the sofa. I put the wineglass on a table and savor the newness of the kiss, his lips so soft and moist, his chin prickly with five o'clock shadow. We kiss, talk, sip wine and I completely lose track of time.

"I feel like a teenager who's out past curfew and afraid to go home," I say, breathless from kissing and from the realization that it was past midnight.

"What are you afraid of?" he asks. "You said you're not married to him. Why all the drama?" He sounds irritated.

"That's easy for you to say. People at home are waiting for me. You're not responsible for anyone but yourself."

"That's such a cop-out." Anger clouds his handsome face. "Listen, I'm very attracted to you and I think there's a lot more under the surface than you let on, even to yourself." He attempts to kiss me again, but I pull away.

"I'm very attracted to you…" *attracted, Hell— I want to rip off your clothes and lick your chest…I want you…* "but I have to go now. Stephanie may be leaving the hospital tomorrow."

"It's your choice; we're both adults," he says, anger mixing with disappointment and deepening his voice. *Wait…is he sulking? How sweet. He wants me to stay, and I want to stay, too, but I can't.*

"I'm sorry," I say as I head for the door. Jeff gulps the last of his wine, his eyes all over me as I gently close the door, thinking that I've really blown it with him.

## Jeff

What's up with this? Like I need grief in my life? It's not like I was proposing, for Christ's sake. I just wanted her to stay and have a few laughs. She could use some down time, if you ask me. Just chill and enjoy life instead of worrying about that kid of hers who's a grown woman. Like, what is it with Elaine? Is she some kind of mommy machine? Maybe this was a big mistake, asking her back to my place. What I should be doing is painting, not trying to do someone who's old enough to be...well...older than me.

Haven't even finished a canvas in months...been through this before and it's a downer. So what is this Elaine, an excuse not to paint, or something more? All I know is I was ready to party and she upped and walked out on me. No one's ever done that to me before. Damn, running back to the 'burbs...to what...some guy in a wife beater with a belly to his knees? I don't need this...should do a sketch for a new painting...yeah...

## Elaine

The morning coffee tastes especially good with the sun's rays warming the kitchen and the sounds of birds, probably busy building nests and preparing for their young. The car seat for Colin is ready, resting on the table next to the little blue layette and blanket–his "coming home" outfit. Of course, that's when the phone rings and Steph asks, "Mom...there's someone here to register Colin's birth..."

"Yes, of course."

"Mom..."

I hear a long, plaintive sigh. "I don't know what to put for Colin's last name."

"Well, Liam's the father, right?"

A derisive huff. "Duh, Mom, of course."

"Then his name's Colin Casey. Does he have a middle name?"

"Does he need one?"

"That's up to you, Stephanie."

"Then it's Michael, after the Archangel. And it looks like we'll be coming home later today."

And so it was that Stephanie Marie and Colin Michael came to live with us.

❖

After less than a week with them here, fatigue has become my natural state. I sometimes scare myself as I go through my work days in a blur of yawns. One bright spot is checking Marcus' wound each day now that he's back. I check for infection, apply Neosporin then a fresh dressing, and am relieved the dog was caught—and not rabid.

And at least the school is on one floor. My muscles ache from running up and down the stairs at home with never-ending loads of wash, bags of soiled diapers, snacks for Stephanie and baby bottles...so many baby bottles. School's become a vacation compared to the homefront. But then I drag my weary body home and up the back stairs. Even before I open the door, the sounds of Motley Crue assault me, so loud the doorknob vibrates under my fingers. *Not again*—that familiar pressure rises behind my eyes, and my shoulders tighten. It only intensifies when I see the sink full of dirty dishes, among them empty baby bottles and a half-filled bowl of Chef Boyardee Spaghettios, the empty can sitting on the counter with orange goo dripping down its sides. *Good God, you'd never think three able-bodied adults and one teenager lived here.*

The washing machine's spin cycle sends high-pitched whines from the laundry room as Motley Crue screeches at painful decibels. The 30-year-old dryer protests yet another load of baby clothes with a metallic grinding. Frank says he will take care of it, but obviously he has not. So it's up to the refuge of my room, nearly tripping over a stack of disposable diapers and laundry on the stairs. The baby monitor crackles in the hallway, broadcasting little Colin's plaintive cries from Stephanie's room. *Where the hell are you, Stephanie?* I glance into the bathroom where the door is wide open, and there she is, wearing gray sweats stained with spit-up, using the closed toilet as a chair, painting her fingernails drop-dead red. The baby wails, but, of course, she has tuned everything out but her music. She sways and sings out loud. Her voice more closely resembles the baby's cries than the renegade sounds of Motley Crue, but that is *not* a plus.

I turn away from my preoccupied daughter, shutting the bedroom door with a resounding thunk and collapsing onto the bed. *I've got to get out of here.* Wrapping the pillow around my head doesn't drown out the sound of Colin's cries, amplified by the baby monitor, not to mention the rock serenade.

Try as I may, I simply can't lie here and listen to my grandson wail. Looking into the crib next to Stephanie's bed, I see that his face is red and pinched from the exertion of so many tears, so I lift him up, speaking softly, trying to calm him. His crying turns to sobs as I hold him to me, and walk back and forth several times before I feel his little muscles relaxing. Then the sobs turn into hiccups, and the hiccups into a sucking sound. Our boy is hungry. Stephanie's finishing her nails. Apparently, it takes a major time commitment to get the job done right no matter what, even if the baby's bawling...

"Stephanie." No answer. She doesn't even look up. I step closer to the doorway, gently rocking Colin and not moving too quickly for fear of startling him back into tears. I can't really shout at her because that will probably frighten him, too. Another step takes us across the threshold so that we are practically on top of her.

"Stephanie."

She looks up, annoyance furrowing her forehead. "What?"

I'm doing 'responsible grandma' with an edge to my voice. "You need to feed him. Didn't you *hear* him?"

She displays her bright red nails, waving her hands as she explains (clearly I am too dumb to comprehend the obvious), "Well, my nails. You see, Mom, they're not dry yet."

Words desert me—yes, I am literally speechless for a moment until I hear my voice, shrill and foreign to me, "Excuse me?" I want to shake her, just put little Colin down on the floor right there and shake her. *How do you tell your own daughter how to do the obvious mothering things that little babies need? Why is it even necessary? Like picking them up when they need comfort and feeding them when they're hungry is rocket science, for God's sake!*

I clear my throat, handing Colin to his mother. "He needs you. Now...and lose the music."

Back in the haven of my room, now mercifully quiet, I step out of my flowered skirt, and into my favorite pair of faded blue jeans which are a bit snug, a sure sign that I've been missing my workouts at the gym. A blue cotton sweater over a blouse and matching socks and comfortable brown loafers complete my look: former preppie gone to seed. There are definite streaks of gray, but the hair I see in the mirror is shiny as it's released from a ponytail and shaken free. *Not bad for an old chick.*

I give my daughter (though how she can be mine, I've really no idea) the courtesy of waving good-bye. She glances up briefly, dismissively, and then returns her attention to that beautiful little boy in her arms–still unfed, but held and snuggled.

"*Stephanie.*" It's several decibels louder than I intend. "Do you want me to heat a bottle before I leave for class?"

"You're leaving?"

"It's my art class tonight…I'll go warm his formula."

Relaxed in my car, my home away from home, I think of Jeff, of course. *What is he thinking after last week's episode? Fleeing his place like a scared schoolgirl? But with Stephanie coming home from the hospital and Frank expecting me…still, that's not to say I couldn't have stayed with Jeff…for a little while…*

Once in class, I avoid eye contact with him, concentrating my interest on the painting next to mine, to the right. I've noticed how well this bearded young man's work has progressed, and comment to him. He smiles in pleasure and tells me to lighten the foreground of my painting if I want to bring out the details in the earthenware vase and dried wildflowers of my still life.

As Jeff slowly approaches, making his way to every easel and student, I work on mixing a paler shade of gray to accomplish exactly that, and with a few quick brush strokes, I'm delighted to see immediate improvement.

"Good work, as always, Elaine." He scans the rounded forms of water jug, vase, and pear from top to bottom. Taking my arm, he guides me a few steps away from my easel and others' ears. "I meant what I said last week. The offer still holds. It's all about choices. Wait for me after class if you're still interested."

Am I? Of course!

Our return to the coffee shop is marked by long silences, not always comfortable ones. The last thing I need is a rehash of last week at his place, even though so much of me wants to clarify the situation and replay it, but with a different ending. Fortunately, Jeff's conversation turns to an article he's just read on body painting, where the body itself is painted, then used as a life-sized brush on paper rolled out on the floor. I remember hearing something about that from the '60s, but it was more like painting images directly on naked flesh. Peace signs and crudely drawn marijuana leaves predominated. Jeff's not likely to remember much of that.

"That could be really interesting–arms, legs, the whole body leaving trails of color on the paper." *Jeff applying paint to my naked body–now THAT is interesting. Oh, stop it, Elaine, you're becoming the dirty old lady equivalent of a dirty old man.*

"Are you game, Elaine?" Those green eyes of his sparkle with mischief.

"Count me in." *I've gotta wipe this shit-eating grin off my face. I am certainly NOT going to let this opportunity pass me by.* The tension between us disappears as we share a conspiratorial smile.

The next evening, Friday, Jeff and I are running down the hall to his studio classroom, deserted now after a week of students. His long legs outdistance mine as I struggle to keep up. We're like children escaping the watchful eye of Mother. Or Mother Superior. *She* would never approve of what we are about to do. The image of a young Goldie Hawn, willowy and blonde, with flowers and peace signs painted on her lithe arms and legs and taut stomach pops into my head. I giggle though I'm generally not a giggler. "Remember Goldie Hawn on *Laugh-In*?" I say. He gives me a sideways glance that implies, *what are you talking about?*

"Wasn't she the *Sock it to Me* girl?"

"I'm not sure. Maybe there was more than one." Thank God I wasn't dating myself. He's younger than me, how much I'm not sure, but not *that* young that he doesn't remember *Laugh-In*.

We're out of sequence, colliding with each other as we continue running down the hall, the canvas tote bag full of art supplies thumping against my leg. Somewhat breathless, I begin singing my rendition of the chorus to Aretha Franklin's R-E-S-P-E-C-T: "Sock it to me, sock it…"

"Have you lost your mind?"

"Totally, and not a moment too soon. I've wanted to do this for a long time, and now, thanks to you, I can."

Laughter slows me down as we reach the classroom. He unlocks the door and turns on the lights of the spacious, high-ceilinged studio, revealing wooden easels, metal stools, and work tables loosely arranged around a model's raised wooden platform in the center of the space. The entire east wall is a series of floor-to-ceiling windows overlooking Columbus Drive. My footsteps echo as I run around the room dodging furniture and singing "Sock it to me." As I whirl by, he hooks my arm and pulls me close. His face is inches from mine, his breath hot on my face when he bends over to kiss me and the tote bag drops to the floor as I crane my neck to meet his lips and return the kiss. Excitement registers in his probing tongue. Before we get too hot and heavy, I pull away with a crick in my neck. "You're too tall," I announce, rubbing my neck.

"Ever think you're too short?" he retorts grinning, and massages my shoulders, which immediately relax under the firm but gentle pressure of his slender fingers. Thoughts of Stephanie, Colin, Frank, and Roxy melt away under his masterful touch.

"Where did you learn how to do that? It's fantastic, better than sex."

"Excuse me? That's because you've never done it with *me*." He continues kneading my neck and shoulders, the focus of all my stress. Relaxed and energized at the same time, just thinking about sex with Jeff releases hormones not felt in how long? Months? Years? A gentle tongue on my neck sends me over the edge, that basic instinct almost forgotten in the press of time and day-to-day living focused on getting to the cleaners before they close and trying not to burn the toast. Forget the cleaners. Forget the toast. I'm ready right now.

More kissing, passionate and urgent this time with no thinking, just doing. I begin pulling my sweatshirt over my head and Jeff helps, flinging it across the room where it catches and rests on an easel. Turning to catch sight of this bizarre–and for some reason, bizarrely funny–spectacle, I realize that the man outside walking a large white poodle is looking up at me in my lacy black bra, bought especially for my art classes with Jeff…and his dog is staring at me, panting, with his tongue hanging out. A small group on the corner is all eyes, too. An old woman with a shopping bag is pointing at us–at *me*, because *I'm* the one who's half-undressed–and laughing her head off. She nudges some spindly little guy next to her with such force that he nearly topples over into the street. For an instant I imagine seeing him fall into the stream of oncoming traffic, a screech of tires and horns and then an awful moment of stillness before I race down to minister to him, Nurse Fuzzy Wuzzy to the rescue. I rip off the lace bra to use as a tourniquet before the paramedics arrive, and they praise me for a job well done and cover my nakedness with a blanket just as a reporter for *Channel Seven Eyewitness News* thrusts a microphone at *me*, Chicago's heroine of the 10 o'clock news.

"Jeff, the lights!" He is busy laughing at the woman who is laughing at me. "The lights!" The switch is by the door on the far wall, a good 15 feet away. Meanwhile, a quick glance outside tells me the woman with the shopping bag has succeeded in drawing something of a crowd. They're all standing there gazing at me, some pointing fingers and others shaking their heads in disbelief while an old man in a Sox cap gives me a smile and the thumbs up sign as I cross my arms over my bra, wishing I'd worn a burlap gunny sack and a chastity belt for good measure. At least the people in Edward Hopper's *Nighthawks* have no idea they are being watched–that, plus they're fully clothed.

"Not to worry." Jeff crosses the distance to the light switch in five easy strides, plunging the room into dusk and shadow, and the city glow of street and headlights softly swaddles us. The audience outside looks disappointed.

"Let's get back to what we were doing." Jeff takes my hand, leading me away from the glass toward the middle of the studio, and pulling off his T-shirt along the way. We kick off our sneakers and begin unzipping our jeans and step out of them, but not before I struggle and shimmy to get mine down. What was I thinking, wearing size six jeans I could barely breathe in, or pull down easily, let alone let slip gracefully, seductively, to the floor? Unfazed, Jeff takes a small foil package from his wallet, reaching for my hand and guiding me to the model's platform. "Do I need to use this?"

"Of course."

It's obvious he's ready as well. His hands are all over me. Jesus, I'm a teenager again in the backseat of a car, down to bra and panties, when reality cools my ardor momentarily.

"Here? We're going to do it *here*?" The cold, hard, wooden model's platform is not covered by as much as a drop cloth. This is not what I had in mind for our first time. He continues kissing my neck and shoulders, deftly unhooks my bra, then pulls my panties down past my knees. Before I know it, he's just as naked.

"Could you lock the door…What if someone walks in?"

I watch him walk over to the door, feasting on the image of his firmly defined butt and thighs, his back smooth and muscular.

Jesus, there's moistness where there hasn't been for *ages*. Thank you, God, for this, even if it's just for this one time. I couldn't turn back now even if I wanted to.

His breath, hot; his hands, sure as he guides me to pleasure in places I haven't visited in so long–if ever. I grip him hard, harder, marveling at his energy and stamina, his unbridled joyful enthusiasm. I feel our spirits take flight, soaring together when he says over and over, "Elaine, Elaine, oh, Elaine" *Jeff,* I think, *yes, Jeff, yes.*

The model platform creaks, cold and hard, Jeff is hot and hard and each thrust is a prayer, *thank you, God,* thrust, *for this,* thrust, *Yessssss,* thrust, thrust. *Elaine, you are a slut.*

❖

I take a mental snapshot of us lying on the floor...Jeff napping. I stroke his glorious black hair. After he awakens, I ask him, "Are we going to do it? Are we really going to do body-painting?"

Half asleep, he responds groggily, "For you, Elaine, anything."

# *Jeff*

Who is this person...Elaine...really? So I finally banged her and it was sweet, but it's not like I know her...at all. I only know the bits and pieces that she lets me see: that she's a painter, and quite accomplished for no formal training, and a mother, and she lives with some guy, and, oh yeah, she's a grandmother. But, she's no grandmother in bed. Why should I care, anyway, I was up front, no promises. She's definitely got more going on than the Trixies I've done before. But still, there's something about her and I can't put my finger on it. Maybe it's that she's not all in my face wanting a "relationship" and calling me all the time. That gets old real fast. Still...there are times I'd like to call her and see what's up, just spur of the moment...but I know she lives with what's-his-name. This is seriously twisted.

# *Elaine*

What to wear to the opening? I contemplate my wardrobe in the bedroom closet, heart racing at the thought of my art on exhibit—my first group show. The floral chiffon dress? Too old lady. And too summery—I need something seasonal, something autumnal. Black...artists' classic black. My black suit with a tailored silk shirt, dangly silver earrings and spiky black heels...I'll borrow a pair from

Stephanie…I'm not a spike heel kind of woman, but this is a special occasion.

Heading across the hall, I stick my head into her room, "Aren't you coming with us?" She's laying on the bed, in jeans and a sweatshirt, the crib a few inches away. Colin is lying there gazing at a mobile hanging above him with brightly colored shapes and playing "*Twinkle, Twinkle Little Star*" as it slowly spins around. It was a christening gift from Christa in June, and he has't stopped staring at it since.

"I'm not dressed yet, 'cause the sitter called and said she'd be late. Frank said I could use the truck, so I guess I'll see you there."

Fortunately, I remember what I came for. "Oh, can I borrow your black heels?" She nods and motions toward the closet.

"On the floor, in the back. I can't remember the last time I wore heels…before Colin was born," she says wistfully.

Mirror, mirror on my dresser, tell me please: how to wear my hair…I decide on down, and bend over and run my fingers through my hair to give it what I hope is a kind of wind blown, sexy look. Meanwhile, Frank comes into the bedroom looking like he's about to clean out the neighbor's septic tank.

"Frank, that Sox T-shirt and jeans just won't do. Don't you have a dress shirt? You don't need a tie, but a shirt with a collar and a pair of dress slacks would be nice. And please shower, shave and comb your hair."

"Jeez, I don't see why I have to get all dressed up. Why don't I just wet a wash rag and wipe down, kind of? It's not a wedding or a funeral, for God's sake."

I refuse to address the 'wipe down' suggestion. "Please, Frank."

He sighs, then takes the Sox T off and throws it on the bed.

"Roxy, come on, I don't want to miss my big night." I holler toward the locked bathroom door. "And Frank needs to get in there."

"I'll be right out."

*What, she's putting three more piercings in her ears? Or, God forbid, her nostril?* "I'll be waiting downstairs. After 10 minutes, I'm getting in the car." That used to work when she was younger; fear of being left behind, I guess. I head cautiously down the stairs in Stephanie's heels, and get a glass of water, nervously awaiting my family.

Thoughts of my colliding lives overtake me for the umpteenth time. Jeez. Frank will meet Jeff. Jeff will meet him, plus Christa and my children. What will they think of him? I'll meet the other artists. See their work. Please, God, I hope my paintings are hung in a good place. Not in the back next to the bathroom. Speaking of which, "Roxy! Are you outta the bathroom yet?"

Bet Jeff'll look great. Probably wearing one of his dark turtlenecks. Hopefully with tight blue jeans that show off his butt. I'll be staring at his ass all night, along with every other woman there. And probably some guys as well.

He's never seen me really dressy before, in a suit and heels. Does it make me look old? Maybe I should change. Or undo a couple of buttons. Show a little cleavage.

As I unbutton my shirt, Frank comes into the kitchen buttoning his.

"Is this OK?" He looks down at his white dress shirt and navy blue pants, his arms outstretched, waiting for my approval.

"That's much better. You look fine. Let's get in the car or we'll never get out of here."

What man doesn't look nice in a white shirt and dress slacks, I think, grabbing my purse and heading out the back door toward the car.

Roxy follows a minute later dressed in her Sunday best…frayed denim mini-skirt with thick purple leggings, a tight black off-the-shoulder sweater, and black Doc Martens boots. Three-inch purple hoop earrings, silver bangles, and studded leather wristband complete the ensemble. "How do I look?" she asks breathlessly as she slams the car door.

"Stunning. You look more like an artist than I do."

❖

Frank, Roxy, and I enter the crowded gallery as Jeff walks over and hands me a plastic wineglass filled with white wine. "Here; you'll need this," he says, giving me an air kiss.

"Jeff, this is Roxy, my daughter, and Frank Zowicki." My hottie stud muffin in tight blue jeans steps toward my non-evolved live-in. The guys shake hands, considering one another. Frank has to look up to meet Jeff's gaze, which lingers only briefly before returning to mine.

"This is Elaine's big night," he says, and flashes his killer smile. "There's wine and cheese over in the corner." He motions to a cloth-covered table with bottles of red and white wine and a cheese platter.

People mill around, sipping their wine and chatting.

"But first come see the section I'm sure you're most interested in—Elaine's." He gently takes my arm and leads us toward five of my Southwestern landscapes hanging on the far wall of the gallery. *The best spot—I think? Or maybe not. Or maybe it doesn't really matter, as long as they're here at all. Oh, God, can it really be? I'm in a gallery show as a painter, a bona fide artist.*

"Hmmm," says Frank, in recognition of all my hard work.

Clearly he is not overcome with excitement. Oh well, he's hardly an art critic.

"Yo, Mom, check out the painting over there, with the exploding snakes. How sweet is that?"

So much for my daughter's joy at my success—she isn't even looking at my work.

"Mine are the landscapes."

"Oh, yeah," she says, reluctantly turning away from the reptile viscera and toward my depictions of mountains and desert. "Those are nice, too." After a moment she walks toward the disembodied fangs, entranced.

I will not—NOT—let them spoil this for me, non-cultured boors that they are. Roxy must take after her father's side of the family. And where did I ever find Frank?

"Your work looks exceptionally strong, hung in this sequence," Jeff says. "With the play of light and shadow shifting from dawn to dusk. My personal favorite is this last, with the cactus in twilight and the mountains glowing red."

I want to plant a big, wet one on him, right here in front of everyone, I'm so grateful. Instead, I gently squeeze his arm. Frank makes a beeline for the refreshments.

Jeff introduces me to a couple of people near my largest painting, and after they've said a few obligatory nice things about it, they move away and no one takes their place. *Why aren't they all crowded around my work, for heaven's sake?*

He gives me a quick kiss on the cheek. "Nice work, Elaine," he whispers.

He steers me to the next section before excusing himself. I spend a few minutes with a small gathering clustered around six large black-and-white photos of female nudes defined by subtle gradations of shadow. Their power makes me see my own work as weak and unimportant. There's little opportunity for more than introductions to the photographer, a tall, commanding woman with a braid of silver hair and a set of false eyelashes no one could ignore. Her talent humbles me, and I'm eager to move on. As I'm standing before a painting of a female with the feet of a chicken, one breast, a scar, and no hands, its creator, a short, heavyset woman, discusses 'Fat Politics' with a tall, lanky man. Stephanie comes over with red wine in one hand and a cracker in the other.

"Sorry I'm so late, thanks to the sitter. The good news is, Colin was already asleep when she arrived. Where's the john?"

"Where everyone's lined up, I guess. Over toward the back."

Frank approaches looking bored." Mind if I take off? This artsy-fartsy stuff isn't for me."

"Sure, you did your time." He stands there waiting, and I'm caught off guard as Jeff approaches. Frank just stares at me. I hear myself say somewhat stiffly, "Oh, Jeff, you're back. Stephanie, meet Jeff Dvorak, my painting teacher who helped arrange for this show. Jeff, Stephanie's my other daughter."

He flashes that smile to her and I wish she'd get in line for the bathroom without delay. They've met; OK, move on.

"Hi," he says. "It's good to meet you."

"Hey." She's grinning like a fool and batting her eyes. I want to remind her, as if she were a toddler, *Stephanie, isn't it time to use the bathroom, sweetie? We're wearing Pull-Ups now, like a big girl.*

"Elaine." Frank is still standing here. Why?

"The car keys."

"Oh, yeah." Fumbling around in my purse, I add, "Don't worry about me. I can go home with Stephanie or Christa, if I see her. Has anyone seen Christa?" I ask, scanning the room for her.

"She was talking to someone in the other room," Stephanie says, and then nods to Jeff before leaving to join the line—*at last.*

Christa and a stunning woman with smooth mahogany skin and shiny black hair pulled into a chignon are deeply engaged in conversation. They don't see us approaching until we are almost upon them.

"Elaine," Christa takes my arm and pulls me toward her. "This is Mercedes Martinez. She's been explaining the inspiration for her work." Martinez' section of the exhibit consists of four paintings of large women lying together in erotic poses.

I extend my hand. "This is my first show. It's a pleasure to be among such talent." I turn to Christa. "Please meet Jeff Dvorak, who's responsible for including me in the exhibit."

Christa acknowledges Jeff's smile before returning to Mercedes and their conversation. A knot of professionally dressed women, all very expensively turned out, are off to the side. They whisper among themselves as they jot down notes between glances at the erotic paintings.

Jeff deftly steers me away. "Back in a minute. There's someone I have to see." I'm not alone long when Roxy and Stephanie find me to offer hugs and congratulations before leaving.

"Jeff is some hottie, huh? Any chance you could fix me up?" Stephanie is practically panting.

*Not a snowball's chance in Hell.* "Actually, I think he's taken." *Yes, definitely.*

"I'm driving," Roxy informs me, almost grabbing the keys from her sister. "I get to drive a truck. Yesss."

"Be careful," I call to them as they head to the door.

❖

All the way home in Christa's car, and even at the place where we stop for a sandwich, I'm barraged by her nonstop talk of Mercedes...her fantastic paintings, her flawless skin, her straight black Cher hair. The best thing I hear about is her upcoming–and lengthy–trip to Spain. Seems Mercedes will be leaving soon, and for some reason, that's a relief to me. Christa catches herself as we pull into my driveway, realizing she's been going on and on. "Laney, you know I love your paintings. I've told you time and again."

"Thanks, but I still like to hear it."

"Did you enjoy your special night?" *Thankfully, it's not another litany of praise for Mercedes. So are we done with that?*

"I think so...I didn't *not* enjoy it. It was different, to say the least."

"Well, it's after eleven, so..." Christa's voice trails off as her face takes on a preoccupied, almost dreamy, expression.

❖

The house is dark and quiet when I get in, happy to kick the spike heels off my aching feet. I try not to awaken Frank when I crawl into bed, so am startled when he announces to the darkness, "Don't make me go to any more of those high falutin' art shows, OK? That lezzie art!"

"OK, Frank, go back to sleep."

## *Jeff*

Good show and even a few sales; two of them Martinez' paintings. No real surprise once I saw those women whispering together. It was just a matter of who bought what. None in the "Distressed Reptiles" series sold, but they need a specialized market. I'm frankly surprised nobody bought one of Elaine's landscapes, but the exhibit's up for another couple of months, so we'll see. Really, the importance of the show is to spotlight work by women artists, so at least Elaine's off to a good start.

As for her family…her live-in, whatever his name is, seemed like he didn't even want to be here, and the little girl reminded me of so many students at AIC. She loved the "Reptiles"—of course. But the older daughter, the redhead; now *she* is hot.

## *Elaine*

Colin smashes chocolate frosting from his first birthday cake into his eyes and hair. Stephanie, whose fiery red hair's up in a pony tail and whose droopy T-shirt is stained with mashed carrots (which Colin spit out in a fit of self-assertion), cuts the cake. I pass paper plates to Roxy and Frank. "Great cake," says Frank. His eagerness for seconds is becoming routine. The pot belly that was once just a hint of a bulge beneath his shirt has become more obvious. Actually, in addition to Frank's added heft, a strange thing is happening: Frank has really mellowed when it comes to Colin. It seems that Colin has become the son that Frank never had. He spends time reading to him, playing Playskool trucks with him, teaching him to stack blocks, and trying to get him to catch a ball. The baby doesn't see much of his grandfather since Tom's on the north side of the city with Cheryl and their little girl, so I think Colin is lucky to have a strong male figure in his life on a regular basis; otherwise, all his experiences would be colored by the female perspective.

Frank and I have turned into an old married couple, with the passion long gone, for me at least. We still occasionally make love, but it is nothing like what I feel when I'm with Jeff. There's an intensity with him I crave, and I can honestly say it's clear now it was never there with Frank. I see I settled into a relationship with Frank, and the comfortable routine of it has taken over and gone stale. It's hard to remember a time when I felt I was 'in love' with him, though I believe there was a time we both felt we 'loved' each other in some sort of committed way, but what does 'love' mean in a day-to-day life, after all? Is it based on needing to know someone is there? And what does 'being there' mean? Being held when you need to cry after an exhausting day of dealing with abused children? And feeling that your interventions fall far short of making a difference?

Does 'being there' mean listening, even when you don't expect a solution? Does it mean going to my sister's house on Christmas even though she can't cook, but refuses anyone's offers of food and would never consider spending money on a prepared meal from Jewel or—perish the thought—a catered dinner? Give Frank credit for putting up with her, certainly.

'Being there' is so many small things, or the things we wish would happen when they don't. But how does the 'being there,' the caring, go bad, disappear, or never appear at all?

When we change in ways that leave others not so much behind, but to the side somewhere, we can surprise ourselves, flourishing in unexpected ways, like houseplants on Miracle-Gro.

*It's comfort, Elaine, rather than passion.* I guess the absence of a marriage license doesn't prevent that from happening. Knowing Frank is *there,* will be there—the there-ness of him—that, plus the habitual smell, feel, and taste of the familiar—is that what keeps me with him? Or is it the monster truck he got for Colin's birthday? I didn't realize the man even knew Toys "R" Us existed.

Enough. Colin's gift from his dad, a mini soccer ball, sits ignored on a chair next to the stacking toy from Christa and the large stuffed bear he got yesterday when Stephanie took him to Tom's. Another party there. Birthday Boy's definitely enjoying these parties, and right now is smearing frosting all over his face and sandy hair in a way that cries out for the camera.

Stephanie agrees. "Mom, take a picture. We don't want to miss this!" Her hands are full of ice cream and milk and the old refrigerator door refuses to close unless you grab its handle forcibly—with both hands—and push it shut. Why do I stay with Frank? God knows it's not his kitchen appliances.

## *Roxy*

That little rug rat Colin's a year old now. It's been…interesting having him and my sister at home. The place is jumping, not quiet like a morgue anymore.

Still, I have to keep my door closed because Mini Me is into everything, and there's some stuff I definitely don't want him messing with, like my CD's and my headphones, and backpack and drooling on my clothes. Other than that he's a cute little kid as long as I don't have to baby-sit. I got Steph straight on that pronto. No baby-sitting. I'm not trashing my life just because she had a kid. No way. No kids for me, ever.

I can't even play my music loud anymore because "The Baby's sleeping." So I head over to friends to jam. I'm not home that much. It's not like anyone's missing me there. Before dinner I'll call and check in: "I'm eating at Katelyn's. Her mom asked me and yes, it's all right, and oh, Mom, of course I'll say 'thank you'; I'm not three, you know." That buys me more time until I make it home around 10:00. Frank is zonked out in front of the TV, Mom may be home–or not–and Stephanie is crashed upstairs along with Colin. I could walk in dressed up in a clown suit and not get a rise out of anyone.

## *Elaine*

Christa has become rather militant when it comes to men: not needing them. Her string of failed relationships has left her bitter. I don't ask her about her love life anymore. I figure if she wants to tell me she will. She and I have started doing more things together. We sign up to walk 60 miles over a weekend in June to raise money for breast cancer research, sleeping in a tent together for two nights. It would be fun, we figured, like an adolescent sleepover.

After the first day's walk we stay up late, giggling and drinking contraband wine that I smuggled in empty plastic cosmetic containers. Anyone seeing how many cosmetics containers I have in my duffel bag would think I'm pretty high maintenance for hiking. We lay side by side with our heads at opposite ends and massage each other's tired feet with tea tree oil. "Mmmm, that feels good," murmurs Christa. "Where did you learn how to do that?"

"I've had massages before. The first full body massage I had– the masseuse was a woman, I'm guessing in her thirties, with buff arms and shoulders. I was at a day spa, and I'd never been to one of them before, either."

"What about the woman who massaged you?"

"She worked there–at the spa. Kind of like a staff regular, like the hair stylist or the skincare lady."

"What was she like?"

"Petite, blonde, with hands so strong I thought she could bend steel with them."

"How did they feel on you?" Christa's eyes are large, interested.

"Incredibly relaxing. She started with my neck and shoulders, with her fingers kneading the muscles deep, deep down. Then all up and down my spine. Since I'm left-handed, she took my left arm out from under the sheet first..."

Apparently surprised, Christa says, "You had a sheet over you?"

"Well, yes, and as she finished with one part of my body, she'd re-cover it and move on."

"*Every* part of you?"

"Except for breasts, stomach and butt, yes–even my scalp. When she got to my legs, she became fixated on my upper thighs, rubbing over and over with deep pressure." I pause, feeling uncomfortable. "I was surprised...it was extremely arousing. I wondered if everyone got the same treatment. When it was over, I tipped her twenty dollars! I felt like I was paying for sex and wondered if I was a closet lesbian and didn't even know it."

"Want to find out?" Christa asks, turning on her side and facing me. She brushes her long brown hair off her shoulders.

"Do *you*?" I ask, surprised at her boldness.

"I just know it would feel wonderful to have a relationship with someone who understands what it's like to be a woman," she continues, "someone who's gentle and nurturing."

*I can't believe I'm even thinking about this at my age! Did the temperature in this tent just go up 20 degrees? Is it just me? Another reminder of menopause?* "If I were gay, I think I would have realized it a long time ago." We each start on another plastic bottle of wine. "Christa, I think of you as a friend, not a lover." Her face clouds briefly. I am trying to do 'I know what's best for both of us here.' "It would change everything between us." She looks at me with disappointment darkening her eyes to navy.

"I mean, I'm flattered that you would consider me for a partner, but my pattern has been, sexually...with men," I can't meet her gaze. I don't want to hurt her.

After a long, awkward silence, she says, "Would you mind giving me a back rub before we go to bed? My shoulders feel pretty tense." Her earlier intensity is gone.

"Sure," I respond, taking this as a change in direction–or is it? Christa is sitting Indian style, wearing only a worn pair of guys' boxers and a T-shirt. Cooper's maybe? I scoot over behind her with my legs in a 'V.' She wriggles her rear end close to me, and I squirt the tea-tree oil on my hands and rub them together. Slipping my hands under her shirt, I begin massaging her shoulders.

"Hold on, let me take this off," she says, as she pulls the cotton T-shirt over her head. I continue, massaging her shoulders, back and upper arms. Her body is warm and I can feel her muscles relaxing.

*Why would an attractive, 30-something woman–an accomplished woman–want me...with her? Couldn't she have her pick, of women as well as men? And the hurt, the terrible, awful hurt if we did it and it wasn't...am I willing to risk our friendship...*

"That feels good." She leans forward, holding her head in her hands, relaxing even more.

*Omigod! She's got a tattoo! How did I not know? Well, maybe because it's not in a place I'd normally see it–the small of her back–but this doesn't feel like a 'normal' situation.*

"Christa, what's with the tattoo? Chinese calligraphy?"

"Did it one night with Cooper." A long pause. "You can imagine his wife's reaction when she saw his."

I have to laugh. "Imagine him trying to explain it."

She stiffens under my touch. "It wasn't funny at all."

"Sorry. I didn't mean to…"

"Well, it wasn't," she snaps. "In fact, that's when his wife started to wonder…" She breaks off, and I feel a sob rising through her body, tensing and releasing.

"Oh, honey, I'm so…"

Christa jerks loose, turns and faces me, hugging me close to her, burying her wet face into my shoulder. Rocking her as though she were a child, like I'd rocked Marcus, I have to wonder…

"Anyway," she says, pulling back and wiping her face with her hand, "That's that." Her rounded breasts; they're so firm and her nipples pink… it's obvious she's never nursed an infant. She sees me looking at her breasts, smiles and turns slowly, her naked back to me, ready for more.

"The tattoo means 'Eternal Love'–some joke, huh?"

"Would you have it removed?"

"I've heard it's more painful than getting it done in the first place," she says.

"And it hurt?"

"Like you wouldn't believe."

"So you wouldn't get another?" *Can't really imagine getting a first one.*

"Dunno–depends on the tattoo. Maybe the next one would mean 'Long life and good fortune.'"

*Or 'live and learn'?*

"Do you think this one could mean that–if you say it does? Who would know?"

After a few moments she says, "Do my legs, too, OK?"

Before I know it, she's stretched out on the floor of the tent we've covered with an old quilt, face down, waiting for me. I kneel at her feet and began kneading her muscular calves. I silently minister to Christa, occasionally sipping wine, completely lost in the moment, the feel of her warm, toned legs under my hands and fingers.

"That was fabulous," announces Christa. "Now it's your turn." She pats the floor between her outstretched legs. "Come on, plant your butt right here. You won't be needing this," she says, lifting my T-shirt above my head. She begins kneading my shoulders like a human breadmaking machine.

"Jeez, you've got a knot here like a golf ball."

"Ouch." The brief flare of pain makes me wince. "That's where I carry the weight of the world–on my shoulders."

She softens her touch for a moment, then reconsiders. "Let's try to break up that knot." She concentrates on my shoulders, which hurt like hell in the beginning. After awhile I feel the muscles of my upper body relax. I stretch out face down on my sleeping bag so she can work on my tired legs.

And the next thing I know, daylight filters through the blue nylon tent. My mouth feels like cotton as I glance over at Christa, curled into a fetal position, sleeping peacefully.

## *Christa*

When I found out Cooper was married, that did it for me. I knew I couldn't trust another guy. It seemed so good between us...guess it was too good to be true. He was The One, I thought, but I was wrong. How could I have been so off base? All the signs were there…he said he was working on a "special project" on weekends; the special project was apparently his wife. I didn't even know his home number, only his cell phone. You only see what you want to see. OK, I admit it; I was in complete denial. I wanted our little fantasy to go on forever.

The night that Elaine and I met for dinner at Emilio's, that was my lowest. I even thought about suicide, but I knew that was something I could never do. Christa, the therapist; the irony is not lost on me. When Elaine and I first started working together at Meadowlark School, before I went into private practice, she struck me as being so strong, so in control. After my break-up with Cooper, I wanted some of that strength. How was it that she always bounced back? I knew a little about her marriage to Tom, and from what she told me, it sounded like a horror story: drinking…infidelity. I reached out to her, and I'm not sorry I did.

She was kind, but a refusal is still just that…a kick in the gut. I need time to deal with that before reaching out again.

## *Elaine*

Lately my life seems a lot more complicated. I feel like everyone wants a piece of me and there's nothing left for me. When I'm spending time with Colin, I'm preoccupied thinking about Christa. When I'm with Christa, I'm thinking about Jeff, and when I'm with him, I'm thinking about Frank and Roxy and feeling guilty about not spending more time with them. Am I losing my mind? It's to the point that my only refuge is work, where I can completely lose myself in the needs of the kids. I don't have time to think about the abysmal state of my personal life for at least eight hours at a stretch. And in a week, when school's out, that will be over, too.

I know, however, that I can't continue to function this way. I am on edge and unusually short with people, even the kids, where I usually have patience. As for Mrs. Rothrock–forget it. Yesterday I was swamped with vision referrals and three kids were lined up, waiting for their meds while I tended to the fourth, an injury. In the middle of all this, she yelled into my office, needing me to pull a health record for a transferring student.

When I didn't respond, that old biddy started in on me. "Mrs. McElroy–I am waiting!"

"Not now! Can't you see I'm busy?" *The old bat must be going blind as well as deaf.*

I applied the Neosporin ointment to the child's scraped elbow and went to the cabinet for an elbow bandage.

"Mrs. McElroy…"

The beauty of elbow bandages is their H-shape construction that molds to the elbow, allowing flexibility. I finished by charting the student's name and the time of day, then sent the little girl back to her class. Three boys shuffled in line, with the smallest not so surreptitiously poking and jabbing the others as they waited for their hyperactivity meds–*and not a moment too soon*, I was thinking, as Jimmy Barnes retaliated by shoving his younger brother, Julian, into the edge of my desk. Julian's high-pitched shriek echoed out into the main office as his brother smirked and DeAndre gave him a big toothy grin. That meant getting an ice pack for little Julian, who, by then, was howling like he'd lost an arm.

I heard an authoritative clearing of her throat, as she did 'responsible professional forced to deal with incompetent co-worker,' then, "Mrs. McElroy, THERE IS A PARENT HERE – NOW. And *I* am waiting." Her phone rang for the umpteenth time that day, and she barely got it before her other line rang.

*Talk to the hand, you old fart.*

An ice pack for Julian's upper arm, which, thankfully, he had to hold in place, at least temporarily prevented further mischief on his part. Then the prescription bottle on the top shelf.

Another clearing of the throat, this one louder and longer.

I turned and faced her, hands on hips. "EXCUSE ME. I SAID I WILL GET TO IT WHEN I GET TO IT – AND NOT A MINUTE SOONER!" And wouldn't you know it–the sweat's popping out on my face. Menopause has no mercy.

She looked at me, red-faced, as though she were seeing an alien, and the parent in front of her desk had her eyebrows all the way up to her hairline, she was so scared and embarrassed. "You…you could just mail it…mail it to me," she said, eyeing the door and escape.

Rothrock and I look at her. "No!" we bawled at her, and the kids started to back away in fear.

Great. Now we've got an "incident" in front of the kids–and a parent. Let's hope Mrs. Stallings is at lunch.

No such luck. Her door opened and she stuck her perfectly coiffed head out. "Is there a problem out here?"

"I'll…I'll just leave…now," the parent said, backing out.

Two seconds after the poor woman was past the counter and out the door, Patricia Stallings fixed both of us with a look to melt steel. "I'll see both of you in my office. Five minutes," she added, seeing the kids in my office.

❖

Most of the principals' offices I've seen were not neat. In Stallings' office, stacks of reports vied for desktop space with new textbooks that may or may not be approved for purchase. Family photos, a couple of empty coffee mugs, a withering philodendron, two laptops, but only one turned on, and a large, multi-line speakerphone next to the walkie-talkie she uses to contact lunchroom and playground staff left very little of the polished walnut desktop visible. Her degrees, framed in matching walnut, hung on the wall behind her chair so visitors couldn't miss them.

"Sit," Patricia Stallings indicated with a wave of her hand to the two empty chairs facing her desk. The door was left open, of course, to keep an eye on the unstaffed outer office space. When she remained standing behind her desk, arms crossed, brow furrowed, I knew we'd be looking up at her for the duration of this conversation, and she was not happy.

"What, exactly, was going on out there, ladies?" She was doing her 'stern principal voice,' complete with arms crossed over her chest.

Rothrock and I exchanged glances, each waiting for the other to go first so we could dispute the opening statements.

"Four students were in my office—one injury and three waiting for their meds when Lenore asked for a student record. In my mind, the kids' needs came first."

"But there was a parent…waiting," she cut in.

"I told you that you'd have the file after I finished with the kids…"

Hands on hips, Patricia spoke. "Enough. We have a busy office here and you two need to work together efficiently and courteously. Let's hope this parent doesn't go to the superintendent with this incident." A brief gaze from her to each of us in turn, then: "No matter who said what, make sure this doesn't happen again." Her steps toward the door told us we were excused.

If I hadn't been a time bomb waiting to explode before that little interchange, I certainly was one by the time I left her office.

❖

Inevitably, the Universe intervenes.

When I get home, Frank calls me and says he hasn't been feeling well all day. He's going to stop at the urgent care clinic on his way home. I am concerned. It isn't like Frank to go to the doctor on short notice, especially on a Tuesday night when he likes to bring home a pizza. My antennae are up.

Another call a half-hour later, from the clinic doctor, comes to the point: "Elaine McElroy? I'm Doctor Marino from Urgent Care. Frank Zowicki asked me to call you. He's being transported to Forest Community Hospital. He wants you to meet him at the emergency department."

"Is it his heart?" I ask, recalling his high cholesterol and strong family history of heart disease, plus his recent weight gain.

"That's what we suspect, but we're not equipped to test cardiac enzymes here. That will tell the story," the doctor voice advises. "Can I tell him you'll meet him at the hospital?" the in-control male voice asks.

"Can I talk to him?"

"They're putting him in the ambulance now, but I'll tell him you'll see him at the hospital."

I leave a brief note for Roxy, explaining what I know of the situation, saying that I probably will be home very late and will try to call later. On my way to the hospital, an ambulance passes me with siren blaring and lights flashing. I assume it is Frank and say a prayer.

It's amazing what a crisis can do. For me, it puts everything into perspective.

Emergency rooms–always the same, always different. So many changes over the years, technologically, but some things never change. Flashing ambulance lights. Paramedics exchanging shouted information with ER staff juggling victims from a three-car pileup on the expressway. Worried, anxious faces of people in the waiting room. The ubiquitous TV in the corner broadcasting the evening news; the stock market is up, the economy is booming, but no one is paying attention. A gray-haired woman fingers a rosary.

"I'm here for Frank Zowicki." Breathless from anxiety and running from the parking lot.

The admitting clerk hits a few computer keys. "He's being admitted. I'll let his nurse know. You're a relative?"

Dr. Marino from Urgent Care called me...said you would be doing his cardiac enzymes and told me to meet Frank here."

"And you are?"

Omigod, who did Frank say I am? His wife? Girlfriend? Wives get in and girlfriends...maybe not.

"His wife." *Sister Mary Vincent, forgive me; as God is my witness, what can I do?*

"His insurance information?"

"Frank has it."

She types rapidly without looking up. "I'll let you know when you can go back and see him."

A half hour. An hour. A ballgame's on. An hour and a half. Finally, after two hours, I hear, "Is anyone here for Mr. Frank Zowicki?" *At last.*

The curtained cubicle at the end is his, #14, I'm told by the ER secretary, and I can go back.

He is gray, not even pale, but ashen. *His color couldn't have been this bad, or I would have seen it...or would I, with everything in my crazy life and...*

He opens his eyes and sees me. I shift his arm so it's not on the IV tubing.

"The elephant sitting on my chest feels a lot smaller." The oxygen tube in his nostrils helps him breathe. The monitor above his bed records his vital signs, which seem to be stable, but what do I know? I'm a school nurse, not a cardiac nurse.

"Frank...What happened?"

"I wasn't feeling right all day, and I thought it was indigestion, so I took some Tums, but they didn't help. When I started sweating and couldn't breathe, I figured I should stop off at the doctor's."

"Thank God you did. Dr. Marino thinks it's your heart."

He nods weakly. "Yeah, they're doing more tests–an angiogram to look for a blockage."

*After that...possibly bypass surgery.* "How do you feel now?"

"Better, but like I've run a marathon...exhausted."

I smile–Frank running to the corner, let alone a marathon, is almost beyond comprehension. "This could be a wakeup call to watch your diet, start some kind of an exercise routine..."

❖

I am at Frank's side before and after his angiogram and the angioplasty to reopen the clogged artery. I'm there when the flowers and get well card arrive from his work buddies. That seems to cheer him up. One of them even visits after work, which leaves him happy, but exhausted.

Helping him get better becomes my number one priority; everything else fades from my consciousness. Colin is at day care while Stephanie works part-time at Starbucks. I haven't been with Jeff for days, not since Frank's heart attack, and I only talk to Christa on the phone. Roxy is at school during the day; she and Steph fend for themselves in the evening. God knows they're capable.

Christa phones me at Frank's hospital room on Friday afternoon. "How's it going? How's Frank?"

"He's good, taking a nap right now. We were out walking the halls earlier. I guess it wore him out, but he's supposed to be walking a couple times a day."

"You sound exhausted. Listen, we're going out to dinner tonight, just the two of us. What time should I pick you up?" Christa asks, apparently not taking "no" for an answer.

Having someone else take charge is enticing. "I'll go home, shower, and be ready by 7:30," I offer. The past few days have been a blur of hospital visits, then collapsing at home. Besides, Frank is clearly out of danger and will soon be discharged.

"Good, I'll make the reservations and see you then. It'll be a surprise."

"Who was that, honey?" says Frank, opening his eyes.

After his heart attack, Frank started calling me 'honey' and 'sweetheart.' He seems so thankful that I am at his side.

"Christa. We're going out to dinner tonight. Roxy's at Katelyn's, so that'll work out fine."

"Good, you need to go out and have a good time. See a movie or something."

"I'd probably fall asleep at a movie, but it'll be good to go to dinner. I'm going to take off now so I can get ready and relax a little before dinner. Is there anything you want me to bring tomorrow?"

As I bend over to kiss him, he whispers into my ear, "Elaine, I know this has to be a real drain on you, but I just want you to know I really appreciate it." He doesn't release my hand.

I am suddenly suffocating with panic. Heart pounding, reverberating in my ears, I want to get out of that hospital room as fast as I can. My face fires up as the walls close in around me.

"See you tomorrow." I squeeze his hand and pull away.

"Love you, sweetheart." His eyes are moist...he looks so vulnerable lying there.

I practically run down the hall to the elevator, nearly colliding with a young, attractive nurse who is caring for Frank. "You're leaving early today, Mrs. Zowicki." I don't have the heart to tell her I'm neither Mrs. Zowicki nor the dedicated wife I appear to be.

"Yes, I'm going to dinner with a friend. A–a girlfriend. We used to work together. A long time ago. I'll have my cell phone with me–the number's in the chart." So busy am I doing 'totally responsible, loving wife and devoted friend,' that I nervously offer more information than necessary. *"I can always tell a liar a mile off," Sister Mary Vincent used to warn us. "They talk too much."*

"Have a nice evening," she says as she hurries down the hall. The elevator door opens. I feel like I have just escaped from a prison sentence. I'm free, at least temporarily.

At home the comfort of a soothing bath, candlelight, and a glass of Chardonnay help soften the edges of the day.

I can only tolerate soft clothing next to my body; my favorite pair of jeans and a pink cashmere sweater. I put a little bit of perfume in the hollow of my neck, and melt into Frank's oversized recliner in the living room, waiting for Christa. With Nurse Jane Fuzzy Wuzzy a bit fuzzy from the wine, it's a good thing I don't have to drive or make any decisions. I'm in a twilight sleep. *Scalpel...forceps...gauze...a little more gauze ...retractor ...sponge ...THERE! Suction ...Yes, we'll remove this irritating mass of tangled nerves and before you know it, Nurse Jane, you'll be free...*

The doorbell rings, and I struggle to get up from the depths of the recliner. Christa is upbeat and fresh, her long hair shining and framing her open, smiling face.

"Elaine, you look great, a little tired, but great." We exchange perfunctory hugs.

She scans me carefully with a trained eye. "You need some pampering...that new French bistro, Omar's." French bistro registers expensive. Christa must read my mind. "It's my treat."

Christa drives us back to her apartment after a wonderful dinner of *coq au vin*, crusty baguettes, and pinot grigio topped off with raspberry sorbet. It's the best meal–the only real meal–I've had in days of power bars and yogurt and hospital cafeteria food.

She puts on a CD of soft music, and sits down on the sofa, motioning for me to come join her. With her arm around my shoulder she whispers, "Don't worry, it's going to be all right." I do something I haven't been able to do for a long time; I cry. Short, jerky sobs at first, and the release feels so good, I don't stop. The whole time Christa rocks and cradles me, whispering, "It's all going to be OK." I believe her. My physical and mental exhaustion finds an outlet as well. I sleep deeply and wake up, still on the sofa, refreshed and mentally clear; feeling better than I have in a very long time.

Christa makes us scrambled eggs, toast and coffee. "Thanks for being there for me last night," I say over my steaming mug of coffee.

"You had quite a cry."

"I feel lighter, like I have some energy for a change. Does that make sense?" I ask.

"It does if you consider the weight of whatever it was you let go of last night."

"Thank you, Counselor Christa," I smile. "But seriously, it felt like the floodgates opened and there was no stopping the deluge."

"What do you think that was, last night?" she asks.

"I don't know. I think it's years of pent-up frustration and anger at my ex-husband, and anger at Frank for having a heart attack. My father died of a massive heart attack, did you know? One minute he was sitting on the bed putting his socks on and the next minute…gone. My mother was with him."

"So what does that *mean*?" she persists.

"It *means* that I shouldn't keep things bottled up inside. Is that the answer you're looking for?"

"Hmmm," she muses.

"Being stoic hasn't helped me all these years. It's time for a new approach." I grimace at my professional-ese in response to her professional "hmmmmm," and sip my coffee.

"What about Frank?" she asks, looking at me with electric blue eyes. "Can you honestly say that you still love him? Have you ever loved him?"

"I'm not ready to abandon Frank. He needs me, especially during his recovery."

She sighs deeply, as though from her core. "Don't you realize that I need you, too?"

I can't imagine...what I could have that she needs...

"A lot."

"Christa..." She leans forward on her elbows. "I don't...It's complicated. I have a life with Frank, then there's Roxy and Stephanie, and Colin." *And Jeff.*

"I'm not giving up easily, Elaine. I want to be a part of your life. A big part."

I put my empty coffee mug down on the table. "Everything's up in the air until Frank's recovered... "

She looks away, sighs again as silence settles between us. When she rises to pour coffee, I see an attractive young woman who's been in disappointing relationships though she could probably have anyone she wants. *Why wouldn't she want...what she wants? What DOES she want?*

"What do you want, Christa?"

She swallows once, clearing her throat. "Alone it's just..."

*Peaceful...serene...no one pecking at me for attention...*

"...I don't know, except that I'm tired of it."

*It's exhausting...*

"Seeing couples...doing things together...shopping..."

*Fighting about the food bill...*

"Someone who's there for me."

*Don't we all. But then...they're...there.*

"Having dinner together at a restaurant..."

*Screaming at each other when they get home – or in the car, or in the bedroom, of course.*

Looking out the window, she continues, "Sharing a crummy day."

*Like anyone cares to ask or listen.*

"Good sex."

*How long has it been since Jeff... how about since ANY sex?*

"You want a lot."

She turns away from the window and faces me. "I am a lot."

❖

Christa pulls into my driveway. Before I get out of the car she hugs me to her and whispers, "Let me be there for you."

The quiet, empty house seems strange this morning–a nice strange. With Stephanie and Col living here, there's never a dull moment. Colin's first year passed so quickly, and soon Frank will be coming home, and I'll be his nurse, his own private duty nurse, until he's ready to go back to work.

Thankfully, school will be over in a matter of days, but it is usually one of the busiest times in the year. There's a lot of juggling every year–packing the office and ordering supplies and sending health files to the middle school–in addition to the regular, day-to-day routine, which never lets up. Then Roxy…I'm losing track of her, and she's in danger of becoming "the forgotten child" in all of this, and now, with Frank recovering, more than ever. If she can find a summer job with her black nails and lipstick and spiky unnatural black hair, I'll be surprised, unless it's at some tattoo parlor, God forbid. But any job would help her use her vacation time; still, even with that, it's like I don't know who her friends are anymore, and I don't even know who *she* is anymore. Then, too, we need to start thinking about college, maybe visiting some–if that's what she even wants to do. Who knows anymore? And if she does, there's the issue of grades, test scores, and finances. Tom'll have to help, he'll just have to. With Stephanie's college, it was one long battle with him over every little thing, even down to toothpaste and whose turn it was to drive her back and forth for holidays. Talk about a pain in the ass! Finally, it was just easier to do it myself, which is what he probably wanted in the first place. The divorce decree provided for the girls' college depending on his ability to pay, and he kept insisting his "ability" was limited. Probably that won't change, but with child support ending in a year, he could use that money…but that's money I won't have to help her. Damn it, and with Colin and Stephanie living here…

Forget Frank, who begrudged Roxy the showers she took even before Colin and her sister came to stay. Not to mention how he raised hell when "his" bills for gas and light skyrocketed after that.

That stingy bastard. He sat down and pro-rated the utility bills, even the water bill, probably down to the baby's bath water.

Mental note to self: no more cheap-ass men. Is Jeff cheap? All we've ever done is gone for coffee a couple of times, and have wine at his place, so who knows?

Frank will be home soon, begging for beer and nachos. And getting Mr. Couch Potato up and to his cardiac rehab exercises will be a real treat. He's not good about taking meds, either, so it will mean keeping a close eye on him to be sure he takes them on time, but without seeming to hover. Good God, it's as much acting skills as it is nursing.

And this for the man who refused to meet my grandson at the hospital…that man who never wanted Stephanie and Colin to begin with, the man who's kept mental balance sheets of who did what, who used what, and who paid for how much. How much–with him, it always comes down to that–how much.

And what of Christa? Yes, she is a lot. How will she figure into all of this?

❖

I pull up a chair as Frank reads a brochure on cardiac rehabilitation. That apple on his abandoned dinner tray reminds me that I haven't eaten anything since breakfast at Christa's. The same young nurse that I nearly ran into yesterday comes in to take Frank's vitals: temperature, blood pressure, and pulse. "I hear you may be going home tomorrow, Mr. Zowicki."

"If everything checks out in the morning," he confirms.

"Your temperature and blood pressure are fine. Have you been walking today?"

"I walked half-way down the hallway and back this morning."

"You need to walk once more this evening…the whole circle. It helps keep your lungs clear." Deftly, she checks the pressure dressing on his thigh, where they inserted the catheter for the angiogram. Her "perky nurse" routine is annoying me, but Frank is beaming, eating it up.

I am doing 'exhausted working housemaid about to become an exhausted working housemaid plus live-in nurse supervising a recovering cardiac patient,' and trying to cover all the bases while downplaying my anxieties.

"You OK with going home?" I ask, acting nonchalant while glancing at the next day's menu and waiting for Perky Pants to leave.

"Yeah, but a little nervous, too," he admits, taking one last look at the nurse as she leaves.

"Hmmmm?" *This is a common reaction for cardiac patients who are being discharged.* "No doctors and nurses checking on you constantly, giving you medicine, changing your dressing. It's a little scary."

"You'll be fine, Frank. You'll have your own private nurse."
*Free of charge, of course.*

"I know. If I go into cardiac arrest, though, I'd like to die in the arms of that little nurse."
*I'll bet you would.*

"You'll probably just let me die." His eyes crinkle at his own attempt at humor.
*Don't tempt me.*

# *Elaine*

J eff and I lie on his bed, bathed in afternoon sunshine that tells me the July heat outside continues unabated. Dust particles filter through the rays, gilding our naked bodies. I close my eyes and imagine us on the bed from different angles: from above, from the window. Feeling almost transcendent after ending these weeks of celibacy, I paint the scene in my mind's eye: light, shadow, texture, color, and the composition of the two figures, side by side. "What are you smiling about?" Jeff asks as he slowly runs his hand down my neck, between my breasts, over my slightly rounded belly, to the mound of coarse, dark hair interspersed with gray.

Without opening my eyes I reply dreamily, "I was just picturing the two of us...here...in this bed. I'm going to paint it."

I feel moist lips over mine and continue my fantasy, as our bodies do the work of passion. This is what sustains me.

When we awake from that most restful sleep, the sun has slipped perilously close to the horizon, waiting to be engulfed in neon-pink clouds.

"You know how I haven't produced any new paintings in a while?" I ask. "Well, I have an idea that I've been thinking about. Want to be my sounding board?"

"Do I have a choice?" he smiles.

"Not really," I laugh. "My idea is to paint you– nude maybe. You really are kind of handsome, you know."

"I always think I'm too different looking...like some kind of Mediterranean fisherman instead of a blond-haired golden boy."

"Believe me, Jeff, you are fine," I say, making that last word five syllables long for effect.

His smile is shy, embarrassed, but clearly delighted. "Sure, it'll be fun. We could use the space here. Our own private studio."

❖

On the way home I stop at the grocery store for chicken breasts and green beans for dinner. At least we were all eating healthier, but Roxy complained that if she ate one more boneless, skinless chicken breast, she would begin clucking. It seems impossible to find a recipe that everyone likes. A nugget of resentment, like a tumor, has been growing within me, fertilized by a lack of time for painting, reading, or even relaxing by myself.

The blaring sound of a TV commercial plus the whirring of the exercise bike as I walk in the back door tell me Frank is putting in his miles. Thank God for garage sales! Frank would never have bought a new one.

"Chicken breast for supper," I call out in greeting.

"Jesus Christ almighty–not again." His groan says it all.

"Hello to you, too, dear." *I am doing my best June Cleaver, but I swear, if I weren't holding grocery bags, I'd throttle him with my strand of pearls.*

"Did you get me my salt-free pretzels?"

"Of course, dear." *May you choke on one.*

"Well, bring 'em to me, would you? I don't want to miss any of Judge Judy."

"Is Roxy around?"

"That Judy is a ball breaker, I'm telling you. In this one case…"

"For God's sake, Frank, powerful, confident women are not ball breakers. Get over it." I put the pretzels in a plastic bag to loop over the handlebars.

He tears himself away from Judy's latest scolding to look at me. *Dammit, the one time he decides to pay any attention to me, and I have to be wearing what I wore to Jeff's…a new skirt – a skirt, no less! And Jesus, can he smell Jeff on me? I think I can..and I do not want to go upstairs and shower it off.*

"These are the sticks. You know I like the others better."

"These were the only ones they had." *Must be a run on salt-free pretzel twists for recovering cardio-curmudgeons.*

"Huh." He chews reflectively. "You sure are dressed up."

*Okay. I can do 'This old thing' or maybe 'It makes me feel sexy and desirable, you old fart.'*

"Yeah, right. There's a hot young stud in the produce department. Let me tell you, how I love to look at the lettuce these days…"

He snorts dismissively, staring at the tacky redhead defendant with the tight T-shirt. She is ranting and crying at the same time, snot running down as she waves her arms in the air. Is he staring at her face or her boobs? Frank hasn't initiated sex, a common situation with post-cardiac patients, so I feel less guilty about seeing Jeff. At least Frank doesn't challenge my occasional time away. After all, what's he going to do–throw out his nurse, cook, and housekeeper?

❖

Roxy is the first to notice the smoke coming from the sauté pan with the chicken breasts. "Yo, Mom, what are you trying to do, set the place on fire?"

"Sorry. Guess I got distracted," I say as my mind snaps back, and I turn on the fan before the smoke alarm goes off. Sometimes I fantasize about running away: perhaps a little place in Santa Fe. I close my eyes and feel the intensity of the dessert sun as it drops toward the western horizon.

Frank comes up behind me and lays a meaty hand on my aching shoulders. "What's wrong...got a headache?" He asks, unusually upbeat. Clearly, Judge Judy's latest ruling must have pleased him.

"Yeah, I'll be fine." *If I can get 1000 miles bewteen us.* I step away from him. *How can he not smell Jeff all over me? Thank God for the smoke.* "How about I put a little more onion and garlic in with the chicken? "

❖

July melts into August and with school scheduled to start in a couple of weeks, I have some preliminary work to do before the term starts, so I've been spending time at my office. Frank's been back to work for a month, but decided out of the blue to take some vacation time with his fishing buddies. He was probably eating fried foods and pork rinds and drinking Jack Daniels, but I was happy he was out of the house for a while. Gave me more free time...for Jeff. Whole days at the office usually wound up being half-days at most, and the rest spent with Jeff. Sometimes we even worked on the painting of him, though we usually ended up in bed.

Colin was demanding a lot of attention with Frank gone, probably because the little guy's gotten used to the time that Frank's been spending with him; when I get home they're at the park or building with Duplos or watching a cartoon video. Clifford the Big Red Dog is Col's favorite, but Cookie Monster is Frank's. Since his heart attack, he's a different man with that little boy. Anyway, Frank enjoys this time, and Stephanie seems pleased. I figure the male influence is a good thing for Colin, who wouldn't let Frank alone when he came back, smelly fish clothes and all.

Stephanie seems more attentive to Frank; doing errands for him. "Hey Frank, I'm going to the store. Do you want anything," she asks.

"Yeah, get me some lottery tickets; here's a twenty." Frank holds onto the bill as Stephanie reaches for it, and playfully tugs it toward him. They exchange a look.

## *Stephanie*

After I had Colin and came to live with my mother, I saw how she was with Frank. I just didn't see them together, you know? He was like always at the TV and she was either at work or class or tearing around with laundry and cooking and bitching about the house being trashed all the time. Bitch, bitch, bitch. God, I hope I'm never like her.

He treats Mom like some kind of servant since he's back from the hospital, and the two of them are up in each other's faces half the time, with him ordering her to get him this and get him that, and her telling him he's no invalid and to get off the damn couch and get it himself–not pretty. And she's become like some kind of a Food Nazi, with those gross tofu burgers, and throw-up soy tacos. Why do we all have to suffer with this bogus food? I'm not the one with the heart attack.

Roxy's got it easier because she can get away to her friends', but when she's home, Frank's at her about turning off lights and picking her clothes up off the bathroom floor, and when it comes to her showers, you'd think he was standing by the door with a stopwatch. No wonder she's gone all the time. And it's not like I can just bail. Much as I love Colin to death, there's no way I'd be here if I had a choice. Working at Starbucks barely covers his daycare and diapers, even with tips. And you know, it's like, I've learned to unbutton a few blouse buttons and lean over when I pour that morning coffee for the suits who tip well. It's definitely time to start toilet training my boy, and get him out of those expensive diapers, and forget those Pull-Ups–they're worse yet. At least Mom gets a kick out of getting clothes for Colin, and the things I find him at garage sales are in good shape–outgrown, not worn out. Now that it's November, though, the garage sale season is over.

I shouldn't rag about the food here because it's free, and what would we be doing without it? It may be gross, but at least it's healthy. Colin, poor kid, doesn't know any better.

What's funny, you know, is that Frank's actually nicer to me and the baby lately, even though he's such a jerk to my mom and Roxy. It's "up yours" to both of them, but to us he's almost human.

Must be Colin–gives him a grandson, after all; he'd never have that otherwise. Not that I mind the time he spends with the baby. Gives me a chance to chill while the two of them hang like best buds in front of the tube or when Frank gets off his butt and takes him to the park down the block. Naturally, Col comes back covered with sand from the sandbox, but it's all good and it helps tire him out so I can get him into bed. It's one way to burn off all that energy that he seems to have so much of. Is that the way it always is, because he's a boy?

Anyway, we're stuck here for a while, so it's better to kick back and smell the roses, like Mom used to say–before she went all ballistic with soybeans and low-salt and that crap chicken.

Just as well she's all into the health thing because if she ever took her head out of the freakin' wok, she'd see that Roxy– little Roxy, that poor kid–is really going Goth, big time, with all that gross black leather and chains. Better than going druggie, and I don't think she's into that, at least not yet. Not like I was pure, you know. But that's the point–I do know. And Mom doesn't…totally clueless.

The last thing I remember about her and my dad was that they fought all the time, and when they weren't fighting, it was because one of them wasn't around, usually him. I was 14 when they got divorced, and Roxy was in second grade. No age is good…but for a teen when your parents finally give it up, well, that really sucks. So there I was, with this sucky life and stuck with Roxy half the time when all I wanted to do was go out and hang and maybe par-tay. Sometimes, I dragged her along with me, and if Mom ever knew, she'd kill me, big time. So much for my "adolescent development years" and all. I survived the jerky guys and the booze and the pot and pills and all, but the idea of Roxy doing that shit freaks me out.

At least she's going out, and me–not! Bet Liam's out there, for sure. I wish we could have made it, though. I thought he'd make a good father. He seemed to like kids; I didn't think it would be that big of a deal when I got preggers.

Maybe I should have stayed in Ireland. Then Liam would have felt close to his son and they would have bonded, like a family, you know. He e-mailed and called for awhile after Colin was born, but then the novelty wore off. Six months ago he sent Colin that birthday present–a soccer ball, wouldn't you know it– but not a dime of child support. He emailed the other day, wanting to know what to send for Christmas. Duh, Liam, how about some cash!?

I haven't been with anyone since Liam. It's not the sex I miss; it's having someone next to me on the sofa and to cuddle with at night. That is so totally missing. Like I say, I have this sucky life.

Pathetic–that's me. I keep hoping they'll hire a guy at work– a hottie would be great, but any dude would do. But for now it's just women bitching at work and even if some guy would be hired, we'd either be fighting over him or we'd scare him away or he'd be some kind of perv. Besides, once these dudes find out I have a little kid, they bail.

Even Frank's starting to look better. How pathetic is that? For sure, the weight he took off is a help, and it doesn't hurt that he's been working out. That's me–pathetic, right? Am I a perv, or what?

Once at dinner, Frank said the house would be paid off in a few months so I figure he's got some bucks. I see the way he looks at me–no, make that my boobs-when I come downstairs in my nightgown.

Mom's so busy nagging me, and telling me Colin's always running around and getting into things like it's my fault, you know? Duh, Mom, he's a boy–get it? When he throws his food around at dinner, it's like my mother's gonna jump over the table or something. She says it's no way to raise a child and preaches at me, "Discipline, Stephanie. Don't think they let him get away with that at daycare. You have to discipline him." If only she'd get some kind of life and get off my case. Like, I'm tired, too, and who needs her all up in my face? My sister's lucky she can get away.

So back to Roxy, she's still a good kid, but she could go either way, you know? I told her to lose that black lipstick and nail polish, but does she listen? Not. With her, it's just her friends, you know, and they're goth freaks, even Katelyn and we've known her since she used to play Barbies back at the old house. She's got this shoe polish black hair instead of her natural blonde–who wouldn't kill for that–so go figure.

When Roxy came home with blue streaks on half of her hair and green on the other, well, duh, Mom, why the drama? Why the big surprise? Like your little girl hadn't been all up on the black dog collar look and leather bracelets and shit? What did you expect? Yeah, Mom, it's a heartbreak all right; you got this slacker daughter with a hyper kid heading into his terrible two's and a punked-out kid of your own you barely see, and when you do, she's into Smashing Pumpkins with the head phones and all, drowning out you and everything else, but you're so busy whipping up another tofu-bean sprout stir-fry that you don't even see that you don't even see her. So how lame is that?

## *Elaine*

Migraines suck. If you've never had one, be glad. First, it's that pressure behind the eyes, and then it's like a veil comes over your head and distorts everything. Sounds are garbled and muffled, and your vision blurs. Anything needing higher mental facilities–forget it. You couldn't add a column of figures or make a decision to save your life. You really shouldn't drive a car when you have a migraine, but sometimes I've just had to rely on my higher power and radar to get home and into bed as soon as possible. When you have a mild one, you can still function with the help of some Advil, and work can even be a welcome distraction. Moderate migraines impair sensory perception and judgment. You can still try to work, but it's best to leave important decisions for another time.

A full-blown migraine is everything I've described–the distorted vision and hearing–plus extreme sensitivity to loud noises and light with the added bonus of nausea thrown in. For some who actually throw up, it seems to help, but not me. And while we're ruling things out, add Imitrex to the list. When this latest wonder drug came on the scene, people who once shuddered at the sight of needles gladly injected it at the first sign of an impending migraine. And for many, it really was a wonder drug. But for me, my fingers and arms tingled, then became numb, and the left side of my face actually sagged like I'd had a stroke, complete with dropping eyelid. So no Imitrex for me. Too high-risk.

Driving with a migraine is flat out dangerous. Driving with a migraine into the afternoon sunlight would be impossible without very dark sunglasses. This is a really big, bad one; one that's sent me home right after the school lunch mayhem, and it's a miracle I made it through that. All I want to do is get home without killing anyone, then climb under the covers in a quiet, darkened room. Dear God, just let me sleep through the day, through the week, make that two weeks. Sometimes sleeping works, and when I wake up, it's so much better; even if I'm a little slow and groggy, at least I can still function.

Oh, shit, shit, shit! Stephanie's old beater is in the driveway. It's Tuesday, her day off, and Colin...oh, please God, let Colin be napping, or at least at the park with Frank. Grab the lunch sack and water bottle. Leave the tote bag in the car. Just the purse and now I'm out of the car, unsteady as hell, which only makes me more sick to my stomach. Hang onto the railing and steady yourself, girl. Take one step at a time, slow and easy. Bed'll still be there. One. Another. The last. There—piece of cake, right? Oh, Fuzzy Wuzzy, stop with being perky, already, and just get yourself inside.

Before you know it, I'll be asleep upstairs, and thank God it's quiet. In fact, even though the migraine's giving me a buzzing sound in my head, it's absolutely quiet in the house—dead stillness—where are they? I set my purse down on a kitchen chair gently, silently, as though making a sound would be some kind of sacrilege. If Colin's sleeping, so much the better, and why risk waking him up? Maybe Stephanie's napping, too, and Frank's probably at rehab.

There are a few lunch things in the sink, including Colin's favorite bowl and cup, but there's no way I can wash them now. They'll keep until dinnertime—and there's no way I'm going to be cooking, either. I'll leave that to Stephanie, wherever she is.

Upstairs, and bed—that's the goal, with a couple of Extra-Strength Advil from the medicine cabinet on the way. Only garden variety Advil in the kitchen.

The stairs seem steeper and they have somehow multiplied so I'm hanging on to the railing, hauling myself up like I'm climbing mountains. At the landing I lean against the wall for a moment—then slowly, carefully, up four more and I'll be in my room...sanctuary...the bedroom door. Which opens.

What I see is my 24-year-old daughter Stephanie coming out of my room, stark naked.

She screams.

I scream, almost falling backward when I look into the room— my room—and see Frank sitting on his side of the bed—our bed— also without a stitch on. We lock eyes for one long, horrible moment before my gaze shifts to Stephanie.

If I had a gun, I'd kill them both.

"Mom…"

Only holding on to the banister keeps me upright.

"Take it easy, Mom."

I open my mouth to speak, but some kind of primitive screech comes out instead.

Stephanie's face is drained of any color as she reaches toward me and I lash out, catching her on the throat and knocking her sideways with strength I never knew I had. She gasps for air, smashing into the wall, and I'm gasping, too, heart pounding in my chest, everything like a dream…my head is spinning…

## *Stephanie*

Can't breathe… my neck…hurts, Jesus, I didn't see it coming. Ohmygod ohmygod, I am so busted…just lay here 'til it's over. Frank…thank God he's got her…can't attack me again. Is that Colin…waking up…with all this noise? What if she tries to take him…away from me…I've got to get to Colin…if I can just get up…to my feet…steady…to the room and get him out of here…never seen her like this before… "Colin, Mommy's coming." Does he hear me…can barely talk…hurts. Coughing, "Mommy's here." Has she totally lost it? Is it safe for us here anymore?

## *Elaine*

Frank's voice booms through the cloud of buzzing noises in my ears. "For God's sake, Elaine, are you crazy?" He leans toward me and my hands are like windmills pummeling him as he pulls me up to his chest, containing me in his powerful arms.

Choking, crying, screaming, I fall against him, barely able to stand.

"Die! I hope you both die. I hate…"

Colin's cries cut through the chaos, echoing from his room through the hallway.

Stephanie groans from the floor, where she lies, and reaches for the wall for support. She coughs, hand at her throat. "Mommy's coming…" she says hoarsely, struggling to her feet.

I try to push Frank away. "Don't touch me, you bastard."

"Control yourself. Do you want Col to see this?"

"You should've thought of that…" I land a punch with my fist, hard, into his side.

"You need to lie down."

"In there? Are you nuts? After you screwed my daughter on that bed?"

"Shh, Elaine. Colin–think of Colin."

"Damn you, Frank! " I wrench free and aim myself to the bathroom, locking myself in and flinging open the medicine chest. The bottle of Extra-Strength Advil is almost full.

The pounding on the door echoes the pounding in my head. "Open the door, for God's sake. Don't make me break it down."

"Go ahead, you son of a bitch."

"Get your ass out here, or I'm coming in."

"Go to Hell."

The baby's cries seem closer now, sharper. Stephanie must have taken him into the hallway.

"Mom, let me in." Her voice, a harsh whisper, can barely be heard over Colin's wails.

"You could have killed her, Elaine, for Chrissakes. I should take her to the hospital."

"Never mind, Frank. I'll be OK." I hear Stephanie say through the door, and she does sound bad. My stomach clenches, cramping and almost doubling me up as I lean over the toilet, emptying myself of acid-tasting bile again and again, ridding myself of my wretched life.

## *Stephanie*

How was I supposed to know she was going to come home early? And the way she freaked out. She scared the shit out of me…busting my chops…thought I was a goner. If Frank hadn't grabbed her, she probably would have stomped on me when I was on the floor, barely breathing.

It's not like she's got exclusive rights to him. Frank came to me all acting like a free agent, saying he didn't even "do it" with Elaine anymore…and God knows, I was hornier than hell. So it worked for both of us for a while.

For sure, I've got to bail…she might try to poison my food. And what about Colin? Do I want him around Psycho Grandma–not!

# Elaine

Betrayal is such an ugly word: uglier yet when it's done by two of the most important people in my life: Stephanie and Frank. I'm angrier with Stephanie, though. I know how her mind works. She took advantage of Frank's insecurity after his heart attack and gave him the reassurance he needed, at least temporarily. She played her part to the hilt. She ought to get an Academy Award.

Every time I think about taking her in with the baby, I get furious all over again. Anything of hers I find lying around the house, I throw in the trash, especially her underwear. It's not easy to let go of my anger. If there's something positive that came out of this whole incident, it's that it speeded up the inevitable: Stephanie and Colin's moving out. I probably would never have forced the issue if this hadn't happened. As it turned out, they were packed and gone within the week. Not a homeless shelter; no way are my grandson and his mother going to live in a shelter, but some place Frank found for them.

Frank–I was so busy nursing him back to health–a lot healthier than I realized. I saw him as a patient; then there was Stephanie, who saw him as a man.

And looking back on Thanksgiving just a few days ago, with all of us around the table, heads bowed, giving thanks–Frank sure had a lot to be thankful for–what a sham!  What a lie–one big, happy family.

But was it a lie to work so happily together in the kitchen with my mother and my girls, full of turkey, dressing and pie, washing, drying, stacking and of course, talking, talking talking– and just plain being together? That was real, or it seemed real.

Had nothing to do with where we live or Frank or anything. Just me and my girls. Could we ever have a moment of closeness like that again? My gut tightens with the loss and grief…the emptiness.

Emptiness. Despite all the business in my life, I feel it overshadowing everything else. What was there inside me before? Fantasy? Illusion? Did I ever have anything real with Frank, or some kind of picture I painted to cover over the ugly spots? Do I even know what's real any more?

It adds a layer of work to everything, just to get through the day, and especially, it adds a layer of work…to work.

Mrs. Rothrock asked me the other day if I was okay, and if she sees a change, then I have some serious acting to do at school every day. I just don't know if I'm up to it. The time off for the holidays gives me a break, but away from school is just as bad, only different.

Frank and I can never go back to where we were before. There are women who can overlook infidelity, but I'm not one of them. I cheated with Jeff, but honestly, that was different because I tried not to hurt anyone and I kept it separate from my life with Frank. I never rubbed Frank's nose in it, and dammit, if I'd known how quickly Frank was bouncing back, I'd have done a lot less nursing and a lot more bouncing around in bed with Jeff.

Life goes on. Stephanie is out of the house, but not out of the picture and I still see Colin occasionally when I pick him up from daycare after school. We go to McDonalds and he plays in the ball pit. His mother picks him up there after her shift and takes him home to their tiny apartment. I wonder how she's making ends meet. Is her father giving her money?

I've got to get on with my life, and moving west to Santa Fe is looking like the way I'll go. My best watercolors were painted there. The light, the atmosphere…they'll calm and heal me. Still, I'll miss the people I love.

## *Frank*

I really messed up. I blame myself for what happened. Sure, Stephanie came on to me, but I could have stopped it. Let's face it, though, when a young, attractive woman comes on to a middle-aged man after he's had a heart attack, you're not going to turn down an opportunity like that. I'm only human. Stephanie made me feel like a man again. There will always be a place in my heart for her and Colin, and even though I'm glad about that, I'm not proud of what I did.

Looking back, the only way it could have ended was badly, but I wasn't thinking about the future at the time. Now, Elaine and I are barely talking to each other. I know I'm not a great talker, but we were close before all this happened. Now that's gone.

# Roxy

My family is a bunch of freaks, for real. I still can't believe Stephanie and Frank were doin' it, gettin' jiggy, you know, in Mom's room when she walks in. Dude, it makes me want to toss my cookies…how gross is that? What was Steph thinking? Is my sister *that* desperate for a man?

When I graduate next year, I'm getting the hell out of here as soon as I can…to New York or something and do music, you know… that's what keeps me sane…Blink 182, Radiohead, Weezer, Red Hot Chili Peppers. Yeah, I'm really into alternative…the ones who play because they love it, not because they're fishing for a big record deal. They won't sell out no matter what.

Katelyn and I have been buds forever, since we were little kids. We used to play Barbies and those Strawberry Shortcake dolls, you know, the ones that smelled like strawberries and blueberries and all. Once I found a box of my old dolls in the back of my closet. How old school to think I used to play with them…it made me a little sad, too. I swear, my mom still thinks of me as that little girl, still playing with dolls back in the day. Sometimes she is so out there. No wonder, between her and ol' Frank and everyone else around here, I'm not home any more than I have to be!

Anyway, Katelyn's always gonna to be my bud and all, but she's been getting all preppy on me lately. Gap jeans and even A & F tops, sometimes. Seems like she's totally selling out, talking about going away to school. Not me. Dude, that's totally bogus. When I'm done with school, I'm done. I don't care what my mom says about getting an education and a profession. I could care less about that. I want to go to New York and join a band. I can sing…I was in chorus sophomore year. Besides, it doesn't matter how well you sing. Look at Bob Dylan. He grew up in some God-forsaken place in Minnesota and went to New York. The rest, as they say, is history.

The homeys I hang with now, some of them have garage bands and let me sing. We had an awesome night at some dude's party for his lame-ass birthday a week ago and I totally rocked.

Yeah, it's like forever before it's road trip time, but once I'm out of here, I'll never be like my sister. How lame is that—in her twenties and living at home with a kid—no way. I don't want kids, they're a drag. I love Colin, for sure, even though he can be one real pain, but no way will I do the mom thing. I'm gonna get a part-time job so I can get me some dead presidents in my wallet and bail right after graduation. Sorry, Mom. I love ya, but get over it.

## *Elaine*

It's been almost 10 years since I attended an Al-Anon meeting. It's like AA, only for relatives and friends of alcoholics. It feels comfortable being back down in the church basement and seeing some old friends. Of course, the faces are different, but the stories are the same. My husband drank...my father...my mother abandoned us when I was 12...

"Hi, I'm Elaine. I haven't been to a meeting in a long time. I've been divorced from my alcoholic for about 10 years, but things have gotten crazy in my life lately, and this seemed like a safe place to come." Safety and refuge from Tom's drunken tirades and beatings–the memories flood back.

"Hi, Elaine," the group speaks as one voice.

Just like that. It's like I have never been away. The warmth and acceptance wrap around me like a favorite down quilt. After the speaker and a discussion of the first step–the one where we admit we are powerless over alcohol and that our lives have become unmanageable–some stay for 'fellowship,' to talk to old friends, sponsors, or to make new connections. The usual pot of coffee sits on a Formica countertop in a corner of the room.

I am talking to a newcomer who is fascinated by my years in the program. She comments on how "together" I seem. I reassure her that outward appearances can be deceiving and that despite my calm outward appearance, my world is falling apart at the seams. From the group of women gathered at the coffee pot, I distinctly hear an Irish brogue. I turn and see an attractive, sixtyish woman who is uncovering a plate of homemade macaroon cookies. "Nora? How are you? It's been years!" I say.

"Elaine, I recognized you as soon as you came in. I'm so happy to see you. Can I give you a hug?"

"Of course. How is your family?"

"Oh, that's another story altogether! Do you have about an hour and a half?" she teases with sparkling blue eyes. Nora is just as I remember her. Her short-cropped gray hair emphasizes those eyes and her wide, generous mouth. And, as usual, she's fluttering around the coffee pot like a mother hen, attending to everyone's needs.

"Jack died three years ago from liver cancer. Even though he was sober for years, you might say it was the drink that got him in the end. It was a sad day," Nora says, offering the plate of cookies my way. I take one, along with a cup of coffee.

"What about your daughter and granddaughter?" I ask, biting into the soft moistness.

"God have mercy, they drift in and out of my life. They're out of my life when Peggy has a boyfriend and a job, and back in my life when there's no boyfriend, no money and she's back on drugs. I pray to get custody of Angelica and raise her properly." She speaks without bitterness in her voice; only acceptance of the situation and a deep, longstanding weariness. Nora seems to have stayed upbeat no matter what life throws her way.

"But ,Elaine, dear, tell me about yourself. I never hear from you anymore and I'm your sponsor."

"I know. I'm sorry. Things started getting better for me, and I guess I felt I didn't need meetings anymore. I read the literature every day for years, though."

"Sure, that's an easy trap to fall into. You're here now, though," she says in her comforting Irish brogue.

"Yes, but my life's changed, and it doesn't have anything to do with alcohol or drugs."

Nora's open face encourages me to speak further. I'm sure she's remembering my days with Tom, when I never missed a weekly meeting, lived for them, in fact, until I summoned the courage to leave him, that handsome, charming Irishman I'd met at a high school dance. St. Mary Queen of Martyrs had invited the fellows from Trinity for a sock hop in the gym, and when a tall fellow with devilish blue eyes asked me to dance a slow dance to a golden oldie–"Summer Place"–I was a goner. So were my parents, until I was spending too much time with him and not enough with my school assignments, and then they proclaimed him to be uneducated low class, and therefore, unsuitable.

Not so his immigrant, old-country parents. They saw me as a healthy prospective bride for their strapping son; an excellent breeder, his father once said of me, and I was so young, I'd found myself beaming at his "compliment."

One riotous wedding later–plus the births of our two daughters–and I was no longer beaming. Tom's charm was wearing thin. He was a good hard worker, a skilled carpenter who wanted to become a contractor one day, but he partied hard as well. He spent more and more time drinking at the local pub with the boys, and less and less time at home. When he was home, he was either passed out drunk or nursing a hangover. At least Frank's not a drinker, a plus that I think attracted me to him.

Nora," I say, returning to our conversation. "I've been living with a man, but..."

❖

We are the last ones in the church basement after cleaning up together. We walk to our cars, and Nora gives me a hug. "Don't be a stranger, dear."

"I won't, I promise"

While driving home, I feel a peacefulness I haven't experienced in a long time. All the usual tension in my shoulders is gone. The amazing thing is that Nora isn't shocked to hear the things I've done. Even if she is, she wouldn't judge me.

All week I look forward to the next meeting. Afterward we talk over coffee and freshly baked scones (Nora, of course).

"Do you want to know the real reason why I stopped coming to meetings?" I ask.

"I'm here to listen."

"As I got deeper into the program and saw the power it had over me, I started to get scared. I began to think it was really some sort of cult. Looking back I guess it was the feelings: the unconditional love and acceptance that frightened me. It was uncomfortable for me to have feelings like that," I say, staring off into some indeterminate distance."I know this sounds strange, but it wasn't because I didn't like the meetings; it was almost that I liked them too much. I felt like I was becoming addicted to them. I caught on to the steps very quickly, and I was afraid that I was using the program as a crutch, yet I had never felt better, more focused in my life. Does that make sense?" I ask, shifting my gaze to look at her.

Nora returns my look with a calm, almost angelic expression, a quality I love about her, though I know she's no one's idea of an angel. "For someone who has never experienced unconditional love and acceptance, it can be a very scary feeling. Good, but scary. Sometimes we retreat back to what we know," Nora says, in no way judgmental.

"God, Nora, I feel like a fool. It's like I never learned a thing. At least I'm no longer married to an abusive alcoholic, but my life is spinning out of control, again."

Being married to Tom was a roller coaster ride, to say the least. That was part of the attraction, living life from one crisis to another. The dysfunction dance is intricate and tenuous, but not difficult to learn. Repeat the pattern a few times, and you've got it down pat for a lifetime. The real difficulty comes when you get tired of it and want to learn a new dance. Unlearning the seductive rhythm can take a lifetime.

## *Nora*

Once a sponsor, always a sponsor; like a priest, it's forever. God knows, there's been many over the years. They come and go, but I'm still here, a permanent fixture, you might say, in the church basement. Coffee and macaroons feed the body, and the Program feeds the spirit. Some believe in God, some don't, but we all believe in a Power greater than ourselves.

When Elaine first started coming to meetings she was no different from any other first-timer…unhappy and confused, desperate for answers. She wasn't broken, though, like so many are. Her spirit was strong. You could see it in her eyes…a spark. I was drawn to her energy, and pleased when she asked me to be her sponsor. Silently I prayed to Blessed Mary and all the Saints for guidance as I always do with someone new.

Elaine quickly blossomed, working the steps and relying on the fellowship of the group. It's been a long time, about ten years, but I remember her speaking at a couple of meetings about a step or tradition. She made an impression on those listening; I could see it in their eyes, and on their faces. And just as quickly as she came to us, she was gone. Stopped coming to meetings, stopped calling me and stopped returning my calls.

But they almost always come back, if not to this group, then to another one. Life becomes unmanageable, again, and the memory of a more peaceful time brings them back

# Elaine

I t's lonely at home without Stephanie and Colin. I miss his activity and laughter. Frank and I barely speak. We have never discussed "the situation"–what was happening between the two of them. I don't want to know the sordid details. I am miserable, and I guess that Frank feels the same, judging from the way he mopes around.

The high point of my week is going to my Al-Anon meeting on Sunday night. I look forward to the speakers, and talking to Nora and the others afterwards. I've been baking cookies to take along. The meetings are a constant in my life, a refuge. I always leave there feeling good. The challenge is to figure out a way to carry those good feelings over to the rest of the week.

It was on my second time back that Nora asked me to be the speaker at the next meeting, to tell my story, as so many members before me have done. The idea is that we can always learn from each other.

"I don't think I can do this," I told her, panic causing my heart to race.

"I wouldn't have asked you if I didn't think you could do it. It's not like you're a newcomer. I'm confident that you could help people by sharing your experiences and how you've grown," Nora said.

Flattered, but nervous, I agreed and thought about it all week.

Grown? How come I feel like a hamster running around in a wheel and getting where–nowhere? Maybe Nora sees something I can't right now.

When the time comes, I decide to speak from my heart and hope that the words flow naturally:

Hi. My name is Elaine, and I first started coming to Al-Anon meetings about ten years ago. At that time my life was out of control. I remember lying on the bed crying and sobbing. I called the counselor at the rehab hospital where my husband was in detox. He told me that crying was a natural process and I should let the tears flow. I was afraid they would never stop. He assured me they would. The last thing he said before he hung up was I should go to a meeting. The rest is history. That man saved my life. I came to meetings here for about two years. I didn't have any trouble with the first step, believing in a power greater than myself. I got as far as the fifth step, but I never made amends to the people I needed to. Bottom line is, I stopped coming to meetings and here I am back again to finish what I started. I'm really happy to be here. The great thing about the program is you can always come home again.

I stop for a sip of coffee and see others doing the same. Where would we be without it?

As for my ex-husband, Tom, we met at a high school dance when I was a senior. My dad dropped me off with my friend Mary Jo, saying we were both crazy since Mary Jo and I had insisted on riding with the windows rolled up so we wouldn't mess up our bouffant hairdos. It was over 90 degrees out, and Dad was furious. We both had on sleeveless linen dresses, like the kind Jackie Kennedy wore. The dance was crowded and it was stifling inside the hall. I had my eye on a tall fellow with sandy red hair. He kept walking by both of us and grinning. Later I learned he was checking us out for himself and his brother.

Some say that men unconsciously seek out women who are like their mothers. I, on the other hand, was looking for someone as unlike my father as humanly possible. My father was uncommunicative; he barely spoke. I rarely remember him smiling except for one time, when he was watching TV and Marilyn Monroe was singing "Happy Birthday, Mr. President." He smiled then and his eyes lit up.

Tom, on the other hand, was animated, cocky, and reckless; the charming 'bad boy.' My parents were disappointed, but we married the August after high school graduation—a typical Irish wedding, if you know what I mean.

Glimmers of recognition register in many people's eyes; I can see it. Is my story really everyone's story, after all? Affirmed by their apparent understanding, I continue:

It came as a shock the first time: "Get me a beer," he demanded. Not "Please," or "Would you?" Learned behavior, I assumed. Anyhow, I was dumbfounded.

"I'm not your maid," I responded indignantly.

"Just get me a beer! "

Just like that. Instead of bailing out of the relationship, I was too embarrassed to leave. I vowed to myself that I was going to make it work, no matter how young we were. What a fool I was! The only one I was hurting was myself, and later, my two daughters.

After seven years of constant fighting, I felt trapped and thought of ways to escape the marriage. I imagined affairs with other men, but never acted on my fantasies. All the time I was sinking deeper into depression. After Roxy, my second child, was born, my depression became severe. Tom was barely home. He would go out drinking with his friends after work and come home at two in the morning. This went on for months. I wasn't sleeping, partly due to the depression, partly wondering where he was, what he was doing, who he was with. After not sleeping for several nights, I took a handful of antihistamines, hoping they would make me drowsy so I could sleep. I see now this was a subconscious attempt at suicide, that I had been pushed to the edge and was not in my right mind.

A few people nod their heads. This is familiar territory.

I must have had a guardian angel sitting on my shoulder because, after I finished puking my guts out, I realized I had nowhere to go but up and vowed I would get my act together and get out of the relationship for my sake and my children's.

As my self-esteem improved, I refused to take Tom's abuse. I stood up to him, a little at a time. Although we continued to sleep in the same bed, we no longer had sex.

I suspected that he was sleeping with other women and couldn't stand the thought of him near me. After one particularly nasty fight, I retreated upstairs to our bedroom. Tom had been drinking, of course, and decided he would demand his 'marital rights.'

At this, I see a couple of women shake their heads, their mouths set, hard…bitter? Am I bitter?

I had been crying on the bed when Tom stormed in and locked the door behind him. He had a wild look in his eyes as he approached. Animal instinct took over as I tried to get away from him. He threw me back on the bed and forced his knee between my legs, allowing him to enter me. It was rape, pure and simple, but I knew that resisting further would only result in injury. All the time he called me a selfish bitch. Survival meant disassociating myself from my body. I never felt so worthless and alone.

My anger and resentment turned to hatred. If I'd had a gun at that time, I would have shot him. The intensity of my anger frightened me, and that is something very important that this program has helped me deal with—my feelings.

Shortly after that, I developed a plan, daring to hope that I could become a nurse. I began taking one or two evening classes at the local junior college and, occasionally, a Saturday class, too. If Tom didn't come home, I left the girls with my parents. He didn't see the need for me to go back to school, but in general he was happy about the possibility of a second paycheck. A favorite taunt of his during arguments was that I "never contributed" to the family. I would prove him wrong.

After two and a half years of classes, I was ready for the clinical rotation they only offered during the day. I made daycare arrangements for the girls with a grandmotherly woman who lived close to the hospital, and watched other students' children. During this time Tom and I ran hot and cold. We would go for weeks without an argument, and then, just like the pressure building up in a volcano, the need for a crisis, just as powerful as a drug, would fuel the cycle of bickering, arguments, and an explosion. Like clockwork, the cycle would repeat itself.

Nora's gaze is a mix of encouragement and maybe a hint of sadness. Is she re-living her own story with Jack?

During our marriage, Tom had moved back in with his parents several times, each time returning home after we had both cooled down, usually just a matter of days. The last time he moved out, I told him I didn't want him back. It was over. By then I was an RN and only mildly surprised that he already had an attorney, plus a serious relationship with another woman.

So, that's my story and it's far from over. That's just the first act, and I'm determined to get it right.

After a moment of silence, they applaud.

## *Nora*

That's my girl! God forgive me, I'm not taking credit, but she has a gift, a definite gift for reaching the group. She's no first-timer, that's for sure. So much more insight, she's got, than that scared mother with two little girls who first crossed this threshold. A blessing, she is. Elaine's a blessing.

# Elaine

**M**y eyes open slowly, and I'm not sure where I am or how I got here. Judging by my surroundings it's a hospital intensive care unit. I stay perfectly still assessing the situation. There doesn't seem to be any pain. White curtains are on either side of me. Straight ahead are automatic double doors, and beyond those a long corridor. Next to my bed is an empty chair. I want to get my bearings before calling the nurse.

The last thing I remember is taking Colin on an outing to storytime at the library. Oh, my God! Colin. Is he all right? A nurse appears at my bedside. My heart is racing and it registers on the monitor.

"It's OK; you're in the hospital. You were in car accident. You've been unconscious for almost a day. Welcome back," the nurse says.

"Colin…Is he OK?" I ask, my voice scratchy, my throat dry.

"He's fine. From what I understand, you were rear ended. That's what the paramedics reported. Your grandson was safe in his car seat," she replies.

"Thank God."

Hesitantly, I move my right arm, then my left. OK–that works. Now the toes, then the feet, one by one, then both legs. So far, so good.

"I want to go home."

"Probably not for another day at least. You have a concussion. I'm going to call your doctor and let him know you're awake."

"Does my family know?"

"Your daughters and husband have been keeping vigil. The night nurse finally told them to go home and get some rest; I'll call them now."

I try to prop myself up on my elbows and fall back down onto the bed. The muscles of my arms and chest are sore. I decide there's no rush to get out of the hospital. An excuse to postpone any big decisions. Like I haven't been postponing. Three weeks since finding them together, and I'm still in limbo, almost a state of suspended animation. What am I waiting for? A Sign from God?

I flip the mirror up from the bedside table to look. Omigod — my eyes are sunken into sockets that are purple, rimmed by a sickly yellowish-green and my forehead's black and blue. I touch the bruised parts tentatively with my fingers.

The first person I think to call isn't family or friends, but Nora. She isn't home, but I leave a message on her answering machine. Not too frightening, just a few words… that I was in a car accident and am OK. Then Christa's machine. Then Jeff's. Exhausted from that huge effort, I curl up in a fetal position and immediately fall into a deep sleep.

My eyes open more readily this time, floating in that twilight state between sleep and consciousness. Dusk is fading to darkness. I sense a presence on the room and moan softly as I turn to see who's there. Nora's at my side, fussing and cooing over me like a mother to her injured young. "Girl, I came as soon as I got your message. It's going to be all right, you know," she says, stroking my battered head. "Is anything broken?"

"No, thank God, but I've got a concussion. What are you going to tell the group about me?"

"I'll tell them our dear Elaine was in a car accident, and she's recovering. I'll also ask for their prayers to God or a power greater than themselves," she said with a twinkle in her eyes. "Do you know when you'll be able to go home?"

"No. At first I was in a rush to get out of here, but now…I'm not sure."

"Give yourself time to heal. Roxy and Frank can manage on their own for a while," Nora says.

"Yeah. I can't do anything now."

"Ah, someone's been working the steps. Good for you. What better time, no distractions." Nora kissed me gently on the top of my head, preparing to leave.

"What now?"

"For now, try to rest and not think too much."

"Thanks…for coming," I say softly.

She squeezes my hand. "I'll be checking in on you. Call me if you need anything"

Which is when the calls start. First Roxy, so scared I wasn't ever going to wake up, crying even as I reassure her; then Frank, dutifully mouthing concern which I blow off when the red light blinks, signaling another call—this one from Christa, who wants to rush over.

"Christa, that's lovely, but I'm exhausted…even talking is a lot…"

And the light blinks again. Can I not get a moment's rest here? "Christa, there's another call waiting. We'll talk tomorrow."

Sweet Jesus, am I up to another call, another explanation, another reassurance? No.

What I need is peace and quiet, which I still don't get when they transfer me to another floor with a roommate who's disoriented and moans throughout the night calling for Winston Churchill. "Mr. Prime Minister...Mr. Churchill..."

❖

Frank takes me home the next morning. The quiet only emphasizes the huge barrier between us. I brew a cup of green tea and make my way to the kitchen table, briefly using the chair back for support as I place the teacup on the table. I feel old and tired and sore, so sore. The empty chairs are pushed close to the table, whose top has been sponged clean. The counters are clean, too, and the only things in the sink are a couple of cereal bowls, coffee mugs and a couple of spoons. Someone's even swept the linoleum. But there's a heaviness in the air, and the morning sun fills the kitchen like smoke. Frank sits down across from me, glancing at my tea. "I could have done that for you."

*Since when, I wonder. Has he ever made me tea? And this clean kitchen—is this what it took to get them to pitch in? Would they be washing down the walls if I were still lying unconscious? Or laying a new floor if I'd actually died?*

The slight edge in his voice tells me there's something on his mind.

"It's done." We sit silently as I sip my tea and he gets up to putter with the coffeemaker.

"There's half a pot left."

"I'll make us a fresh pot," he says, dumping it out, then managing to throw away the grounds and even rinse the things in the sink and–be still my heart—get out the dish soap! Frank washing out the cups? When Stephanie was here, was he doing Stephanie's dishes...along with doing Stephanie?

"You'll want to see Colin soon." It's more of a question.

"No. Not for a while. Not like this."

"He'll still love you with black eyes."

"I don't want my face to scare him."

He turns, scrutinizing me. "Well, he's still little, yeah...."

"You don't have to make yourself look at me. Really." He doesn't shift his gaze. "Stop staring at me, Frank! "

"It's just...I feel bad."

"You should."

"Well...I do." For a moment he cannot meet my look, staring down at the worn Formica tabletop.

"Sleeping with my daughter in our bed..." Hard to hear myself saying these words so directly, so nakedly. Maybe it took a head trauma to make it happen.

"What can I say?"

"Whatever's on your mind. What's left to lose at this point?"

"Don't get me wrong, Elaine, it was a big mistake, I know, a...a huge mistake, and I don't know how it..."

"How it happened, Frank? You don't know how you happened to wind up in bed with her, naked, screwing her? You were hearing voices? You had a vision she was Joan of Arc, and the next thing you knew—with Col asleep in the next room, for Christ's sake—" At this, I have to stop for breath. "You were all over her, inside her..."

"That's enough."

"Is it? Is it enough, Frank? I mean, how could you?"

He gets up, shaking his head, reaching for the coffee.

"And I nursed you after your heart attack. Is that the thanks I get? Is it, Frank? I want to know—tell me! And don't walk away from me!"

He moves toward me, his face twisted in anger. "All right, Elaine, all right! What do you want? I can't undo what's done." He's gripping the carafe so tightly, his knuckles are pale.

"Are you still seeing her?"

"Oh, shit..." Another head shake, like he can't possibly believe this.

"Well, are you?"

"After I grabbed you from falling down the stairs and kept you from killing your own kid—after all that, what do you think, Elaine? Jesus God Almighty!" He slams the carafe down, sloshing the hot coffee all over the table top.

Some super strength from who-knows-where catapults me to my feet and I'm standing toe-to-toe against him, a couple of fighters in the ring.

"Tell me. I want to hear it from your lips. Are you still seeing her, yes or no?"

"No, dammit. I'm not. Are you happy now?" He looks down to me, a full head taller, and I step back.

"Happy? Is that what you want? That I'm happy? Like I could somehow be happy?" My voice gets super-shrill. "That's a joke! …With this mess?"

"Can't we just go back to the way things were?"

Is he some kind of alien being? "That's impossible," I say, and I feel the truth of it, the plain and simple truth of it bouncing off the four walls. "I won't be here."

❖

I'm beginning to understand why people drink too much or take drugs. Sometimes our outer shell has been worn away by life and we need something to dull the pain. I think I'd be quite good at it, alcoholism, that is, for a short stint, anyway, but I'd quickly tire of being out-of-control. I went to an AA meeting once at the urging of Tom, who tried to convince me that I was an alcoholic. I loved it, the meeting, that is. I cried from my soul, and felt total acceptance from the alcoholics, all men except for myself. I think Tom felt that if we were both alcoholics, it would give us a special bond we lacked even though we had two children together. I'm not and it didn't. It gave me some insight, however, into the lengths he would go to keep our sick relationship going.

It was peaceful every time he'd retreat to his mother's for a few days, and a welcome relief from wondering when he'd be home after work or if he'd be home at all. How she put up with it, I'll never know, but to hear him tell it, his mother was a saint on Earth, his refuge from a cold, demanding wife.

His returns, at first, felt like new beginnings, like we could make a new start, but after the first few times, I wasn't so happy to see him at the door. I knew the pattern by then: he'd be ready to see the girls, take them to the movies, give me flowers and kisses, and even go to AA meetings sometimes. He'd stop drinking for a while. He would be happy at home for a time. In his own way, he loved me, loved the girls, but sooner or later he'd slip away, back to his cronies at the pub, and back to his other life away from us.

Then he'd roll in at two or three in the morning, drunk, and the next thing I knew, I'd be calling his job, saying he'd caught a virus. Over time, the situation would disintegrate to bickering, then more than the occasional late night, and then shouting matches followed by binges when he'd be gone for days. When he'd show up, bleary-eyed and stinking and sick, he'd greet me with a contrite apology, swearing he'd never touch another drink.

"I mean it, never again a drop, as God is my witness," he'd say, sinking down into his old leather chair with a sigh of relief, and everything in me wanted to believe him, wanted to believe he was home for good.

The last time, though, I wouldn't even let him in the door.

*Not again. I can't let myself live like this anymore, let alone the girls. Better he's gone than this.*

Dirty, disheveled, and with a stubbly growth of beard, he stood there as he had so many times before, hesitantly, as though needing permission to enter his own house. He'd lost so many keys, I'd long ago changed the locks for fear of who might have found them, and had come to recognize his particular, tentative knock on the door that signaled another remorseful homecoming.

*No more. Go away. Go to your mother's or back to the bar…not here.*

"But, Elaine…"

"No buts. Just go. I want a divorce."

❖

Leaving…the first time's the hardest. Saying good-bye to the house we'd had—not a mansion, but nice, with a family room and two bathrooms and a garbage disposal.

Leaving a life. Packing up Roxy's stuffed animals and dolls, Stephanie's posters and paperbacks and roller blades. My wedding ring…

Just Roxy's things this time, and my own…no ring…was that part of the problem, or just as well, I wonder.

Does it matter, after all? Frank and I sit silently for a while. He asks me in a low voice, "You won't be…"

"No. I won't be here. I'm leaving."

"No way…where would you go?"

"Away. Out of here." I think about Roxy. Will she go with me, this close to graduation? Stay with a friend? Her dad's new family? I doubt they'd welcome her, but Tom certainly couldn't turn her away. She's only 17. She's like me; she's curious and likes to try new things. I envision her coming with me, the two of us in a hacienda in the southwestern desert, reminiscent of Georgia O'Keeffe at Ghost Ranch. My reverie is interrupted by Frank's forceful response.

"So that's it? You're going to up and leave and to hell with everyone else! What about Stephanie and Colin? You couldn't wait to have them come and live here, and now that it's all screwed up–"

"Yeah, Frank, 'screwed' is right–"

"You shut your mouth, Elaine, you just shut up. You hear me?"

I close my eyes, as well as my mouth, trying to block him out, trying to ignore the queasiness that could mean the start of a migraine. Or am I just hungry? When was the last time I ate real food?

"Well, to hell with you! I only wish you had told me earlier. At least then I might have had a chance to start a new life, too. But you go ahead and worry about Elaine. You're good at that." I sit quietly and listen to his ranting, but it won't change anything, not the way I feel. He finishes his tirade and goes to the family room, to his recliner, and turns up the TV volume.

Do I have what it takes to create a new life for myself? I've never been away from my family for an extended period of time. I want to be strong, but being 50-ish not a woman's most self-confident period. I've read about women who come out on the other side of menopause more self-assured than ever, veritable dynamos of strength and creativity. I'm not there yet, still struggling to accept the changes my body is going through.

Menopause is like adolescence: you wonder who you are and where your place is in the world. You question everything you thought you knew about yourself. Some days you drive to work literally chomping at the bit, eager to tear into the new day. Other days you doubt every decision you've ever made, and over-analyze your choices. The good days are usually about feeling well physically, no headache or other aches or pains. The bad days are about hormones gone awry. Your body has taken on a life of its own, foreign from the intimate relationship you shared in the past. In the midst of all this turmoil, it still remembers to have a period occasionally. The nerve!

Jeff finally catches up with me after a couple of days of phone-tag. He sounds genuinely upset as I tell him about the accident and wants to see me, but I won't until I look less frightening. Not until all the bruising's gone. We agree to meet on New Year's Eve. I see Christa once at her place when we order in Chinese food and watch a couple of old movies. It's a comfort, watching Bogie and Bacall, munching popcorn together on the sofa, the best post-accident therapy I could ask for. Except maybe for Jeff, but I'm still bruised.

At home, the house is quiet with an edgy silence broken only by terse questions: "What? You forgot to buy coffee? I'm outta underwear. You're not doing wash anymore?"

*"Whatever." Do your own, dip-shit. It's taken you how long—three weeks, maybe, to realize I'm not doing that anymore?*

Still healing from the car accident, the colors around my eyes start to fade somewhat from purple to blue-green. While going to work, grocery shopping, the bank, the cleaners, I notice people looking at me, stares of pity or disgust. What...do they think I was abused? God, I hate that, more than the bruises. By wearing dark glasses, I realize what it must be like hiding signs of abuse. I don't like the feelings; even though my bruises are from the accident, I feel isolated, not to mention ashamed, trying to cover them up. I feel like I need to carry a sign saying, I AM NOT A VICTIM OF DOMESTIC VIOLENCE. This really sucks.

All around me on this last day of work before Winter Break are Santas and Rudolphs and Frosties, along with neon blinking candles and lawn ornaments of the Nativity. Throughout the school I've been bombarded for weeks with bulletin boards full of snowmen and good wishes for the upcoming "Winter Holiday Season," and announcements of the kids' choral program and flyers for food drives and locations of the drop boxes for donated clothing (separate from food, please). No surface is free of cardboard snowflakes and holly leaves and ornaments; besides the ones on the walls and classroom doors, they hang from the ceiling—have these teachers nothing else to do?—and assault you, holly leaves almost poking your eye out as you come down the hall. Holidays are definitely health hazards. All this cheer makes me sick. Deck the halls – I'll deck the next person who asks me what I'm doing for the holidays. Ending a life and trying to start a new one.

And still getting some Christmas things for Colin and Roxy. After all, they're my family and it's not their fault. And certainly, something nice for Jeff...and Christa.

As for Stephanie and Christmas spirit–ho, ho, ho. That skank, that slut, and how I got her I'll never know because she certainly doesn't take after my side of the family. She is keeping a low profile, calling occasionally to let me know how Colin is doing. Other than that, we don't speak. Just like I don't speak to Frank.

Holidays are hard enough as it is, what with family dinners and who gets Roxy for Christmas Eve vs. Christmas Day. And will Tom pick her up or do I take her to his place? And will I even see Colin this Christmas? Will Stephanie take him to Tom's on Christmas Eve and stay over there for the whole holiday? He always favored her, and now with Col, his grandson...

It certainly won't be the same at my sister's holiday table this year, and the inevitable questions: Where is Frank? Where's Stephanie and the baby?

Hell...maybe I'll just spend the day in bed with the covers over my head.

## *Roxy*

Katelyn says I'm welcome at her crib for Christmas, and with the wacko scene at home, I'd like to be, like, "Katelyn, girl, Yo! That rocks and I'm over there, like now"–but my mostly absentee dad insists on having "his girls" over for the holiday–just one, big, happy family. Like, who needs to eyeball his new rug rat, and all, with Pop-sie all lovey-dovey with Family Number Two, you know? What's suckier–watching him drool over cutesy wife or swig down the Jim Beam? Jeez, he's my dad, but no wonder Mom split.

Least Stephanie has the baby, Big Grandpa's Number One Boy. Colin keeps her busy–duh, yes!–in the middle of a family we are no part of, no way, not now, now ever, throw up!

Which is what I want to do when he gets all up in my face, telling me to lose the make-up and the black clothes–and the chrome studs and all–like lose myself, dude! Like, go pour yourself another drink, Big Guy, and make sure your insurance is paid up.

## *Elaine*

The stores are no pleasure with all the other last-minute shoppers vying for parking spaces and the shortest check-out line as Bing Crosby croons about a white Christmas and someone's grandma gets run over by a reindeer. Still, I manage to find *The Lion King* movie for Colin, a few Hot Wheels, some khaki pants and a dress shirt, and a cardigan sweater that matches his green eyes. A great holiday outfit for my handsome grandson when Stephanie and Roxy take him to his granddad's on Christmas. For Roxy, gift certificates for Old Navy and Tower Records. Stephanie—forget it. Ditto for Frank. For Jeff, a super-soft cashmere scarf in burgundy, with fine threads of navy and charcoal and an occasional bright orange that keeps it from being too staid. He can think of me every time he wraps it around his neck against the Chicago winter.

For Christa, I splurge on an Italian cashmere hoodie, irresistible in pale blue with gray undertones. Exactly the kind I wish someone would buy for me. Christa—thank God for Christa!

"You can't possibly have Christmas Eve at Frank's place. You know it'll never work," she says, offering to put up a tree and even bake cookies to make it homier for Colin. "You'll all come here. Roxy, Colin...his mom..."

I'm so grateful I want to cry.

"You might as well stay over on Christmas Eve. We'll be cooking in the morning."

Yes. At the last minute, I accept her invitation to spend the holiday together. Christa's cooking turkey breast on Christmas Day, and I'll bring over some wine, cheese and crackers for a nice, low-key day, the only kind I feel up to less than a week after my accident.

❖

Christmas Eve is anything but low-key as Colin tears around, exhilarated at the new environment, the tree, the pretty packages under it that include a large one Christa bought him. In fact, Christa's made certain there is a small gift for everyone beneath the Scotch pine in the corner of her living room. She's an attentive hostess serving eggnog, cookies and cocoa in this neutral space that lets us be together, at least physically, as a family.

Stephanie's got Colin in cords and a red and green striped long-sleeved knit shirt, and she looks neat, still in her Starbucks shirt and black pants, but Roxy seems to have gone over the top in black Doc Martens, black tights with multiple holes, a red micro-mini skirt, topped off with a man's green cardigan golf sweater that appears to be one of her thrift store finds. The whole outfit looks like a thrift shop ensemble, actually, down to the fringed black shawl over the sweater. With the white face powder, black eye liner and black lipstick, it's so, so festive. I wave Christa away when she comes into the room with a camera. No family pictures tonight, please.

Christa's flowing black velvet skirt is topped with a soft red silk top, clearly designer-level expensive, bearing an exquisitely embroidered partridge in a pear tree on the left breast pocket. With a simple gold chain around her neck, she's the soul of elegance, and in my navy velour running suit, I feel like a nursing home resident who's been wheeled into the day room for a party. I'm a train wreck is what I am, a mass of bruises and aches.

'Tis the season to be anxious, fa-la-la-la-la…oh well, relax and enjoy it.

But there's no relaxation in store. Col senses it's a special evening and won't be still, not even for cookies. Christa follows him around, nervously placing breakables on high shelves, and warning him away from her ceramic Christmas Village buildings she's arranged on the coffee table with cotton batting to look like a deep, fluffy snowfall. This year's addition to the old-fashioned post office, general store, train station, diner, church, apothecary shop and school house is the gas station, one that she bought specially since her dad, dead now for less than year, was a mechanic who owned a gas station in Ohio years ago.

Colin's not listening, and just wants to pick up everything; he opens the cabinet of the entertainment center and spills Christa's CDs all over the floor as his mother, my ineffectual, no-good daughter, tells him "no," without any attempt to actually do anything.

So I do.

The least I can do is re-stack the CDs and try to redirect his attention to the plate of cookies. "Look, Colin; chocolate chip cookies. You like chocolate chip cookies. And cocoa." *They'll probably keep you up all night, but that will be your mother's problem.*

When I offer him a small cup of cocoa (plastic, thank God, and barely half-full), he grabs it out of my hand and races over to Christa's old-fashioned village on the coffee table.

"Colin," Roxy says, "don't," a shout echoed by her big sister on the couch.

"Don't run with that," says Christa, two steps behind him. He grabs the little Mobil gas pump as she bends down for it.

"No," I cry out, and again there is an echo in the room as both my girls yell at him in unison.

He laughs out loud as if it's a game, whirls around and collides with Christa, the cup of cocoa in one hand, and the ceramic gas pump in the other.

What happens next is like a slow-motion movie where you know what will go down; everyone does, but no one can stop it. The cup flies from his hand, a wave of cocoa suspended in mid-air for a moment, a very long moment, until it splashes all over Christa's silk blouse.

"Oh, no," the adults moan, focusing on the brown stain spreading all over the embroidered partridge, the pear tree, and down the front, then turning our attention to the gas pump, which is by now tumbling end-over-end in an arc through the air, again and again, headed toward the brick fireplace. It shatters into pieces with a sickening crash.

Christa's mouth drops open, horrified, a look mirrored on Roxy's face as I jump up from my chair, corralling Colin and depositing him on the couch between his aunt and his mother, who's speechless, looking stunned.

"Do NOT let him off this couch," I hiss, following Christa into the kitchen.

What do I say? I'm mortified, embarrassed for Stephanie, who seems to lack the good sense to be embarrassed at her son's behavior.

"Christa, I am so, so sorry. Please let me replace it for you... the gas station. I...I'll go and do that the day after Christmas, and...oh, Christa." I go and hug her, so sad and sorry for my clueless family.

She pulls away, smiling ruefully. "Elaine, Laney, it's not your fault. I'll put on something else, and we'll go back and salvage the evening. We'll open the presents; that'll be good."

Well, if she can do 'hostess soldiering on,' then the least I can do is match it with my best 'gracious, grateful guest,' and that's what we do, going back into the living room, Col firmly in place on his mother's lap despite his wiggling attempts to break free. Roxy's sponging off the champagne beige carpet with a bathroom towel–thankfully, not a fancy holiday towel. "I think I got it all. It was only a few spots." *Of course–all the rest wound up on Christa, ruining her beautiful blouse, and...*

"This is for you." Christa hands me a wrapped gift sporting a matching bow and tag.

She turns to Roxy. "That's fine, the carpet's fine, you sit down, and here—this is for you and your sister." She hands two small packages, also beautifully wrapped, to my younger daughter, who retrieves a box of Fannie May hostess mints from under the tree and gives it to Christa.

"From me and my sister. Merry Christmas. And thank you."

"Yes. Thank you for having us over for Christmas Eve," Stephanie says. "I'm sorry about my son." His head's thrown back against her chest, head-butting her. "He can be a real handful sometimes."

*You think?* I fetch my present for Christa. It's not nearly as fancy in appearance, tissue papered in a Rudolph the Red Nosed Reindeer Christmas bag. Tiny bags from me hold Roxy's gift cards, and yes, the ones I bought for Stephanie, too, at the very last minute. I wrapped Colin's presents in Disney paper, knowing he'll probably not even notice as he rips it off.

Things move quickly then as tissue and wrapping paper litter the floor, and Colin happily plays with Hot Wheels on the couch, ignoring Christa's gift of a Field's Christmas bear.

I exchange glances with Christa, who says, "You first." We're the last to open presents. I fumble with the red foil wrap and try to keep it intact. The box is lightweight, which should be a hint, but when I part the tissue paper and see my gift, I'm bowled over. It's a cashmere hoodie—the hoodie I bought for Christa, but in lavendar. I hold it to my cheek,  feeling its softness. I rise and go to her chair, where she's removing the top layer of tissue from the gift bag and sees her blue sweater, just like mine. We meet in the middle of the room, hugging, both of us in tears, both of us beaming.

❖

After a night spent on Christa's couch, I'm lured into the kitchen by the smell of coffee. Before I reach the coffeemaker on the counter, the sound of Christa's sobs grabs my attention.

She's seated by the table, which has a half-full cup of coffee, a tube of Super Glue and the fragments of the miniature gas pump, which she is trying to mend. Impossible! There must be over a dozen tiny pieces. She makes no attempt to disguise her tears when she turns to me, staring at the chunk of ceramic she holds before her.

"Dad used to take me to his gas station on Sundays. He'd clean the place up while I'd sweep the garage floor…and then when we were done, we'd drink bottles of Coke and share a package of Twinkies. We never told my mom about the treat. It was our special…" Her voice cracks. "Our special time together." She breaks down, her arms on the table cradling her head. When

I place a hand on her arm, her sobs deepen, shaking her shoulders, and it's as though I feel her loss reverberating through me as well.

Of all the pieces Colin had to break, it had to be that one. Tomorrow, if I have to go to five stores, I'll find her a new one.

"Christa, oh honey, I'm so, so sorry."

"There's so many good memories of me and my dad. Nothing special. Just little things we did together. Made up for my mom..."

*I'm beginning to see why she's rarely mentioned her before...some issues there...*

And the way he died..."

How Christa made every effort to see him as much as possible throughout the chemo and radiation, and all. And I always sensed it was some kind of effort for her to be around her mom.

"I tried..."

"I know you did..."

She lifts her head, turning to me. "I wanted to be there..."

"And you were. He waited for you. He waited to see you one last time."

"He seemed all right, stable, you know?" She's hiccupping, so maybe the worst is over. "He did, and even my mother thought so, too. We both thought it was OK for me to go home."

"How could you have known? How could anyone? He hung on and saw you, and sweetie..." I hold her face in my hands, gazing at her, "Seeing you and speaking with you—is what gave him that last bit of strength."

"Maybe..."

"No maybe—yes."

She shifts her head to look at the ruined gas pump. "The gas station. It was just my way of having him here for Christmas."

"Oh God, and Colin..." Now I'm crying, too. "I hoped for the best, that Steph would control him and he'd behave, but honest to God...now, after last night, I have to wonder if he's OK." I choke at this, maybe from crying, maybe from more. "The way he totally ignored us, and then laughing like it was some kind of joke...and then the way he was butting his mother with his head..."

She's wiping her face with her hands, and I'm doing the same. "I know. Stephanie seems so hands-off with him. You were the one who stepped in. He needs limits when he starts acting that way."

"You see it, too. When I see him, now that it's not every day, it's more obvious to me."

Taking a deep breath, Christa rises and heads to the coffeepot. "It's not an issue that's easily resolved, but if you want me to talk to Stephanie, I will. "

I sigh, grateful at her generous spirit, but unsure. "Thank you. Let me think about it." She pours me a cup of the fragrant hazelnut brew, then tops off her own. After a couple of sips, I marvel at how much better I feel. "It's Christmas Day. Let me get dressed and I'll help you get that turkey breast started and in the oven."

"And we'll put on some Christmas carols."

*And hopefully dry our tears for the day.*

And so we do.

## *Christa*

Christmas Day with Elaine—soothing, healing even, once I got past that thing with the gas pump and my dad. But I'm glad it happened. He's dead–what?–six months, and I never really cried 'til now. In a crazy way, I'm grateful to Colin for breaking it since it helped me make a breakthrough of my own.

Oh, that boy—Stephanie could really benefit from a parenting class; she could see she's not alone and there are ways to cope with kids like Colin, ways to manage that frenetic energy of his. This is Laney's grandson, after all, and I've dealt with kids like him before, though not as young. I'd like to get Stephanie's take on Colin and find out what's going on at home. It might not be a bad idea to observe him at daycare to see how he interacts with other kids. If Elaine's OK with that. And Stephanie. Is she in denial about her son, or just generally shell-shocked by life, I wonder. To wind up in bed with her mother's boyfriend, and in *their* bed–that says so much about anger, and resentment, not to mention the boy's deadbeat dad in Ireland, and having to move back in with her mom. No wonder Colin's acting out. And no wonder Elaine wants out with Frank.

But today was a day of healing for both of us. We cooked, listened to Christmas music, ate, ate some more, sat around and watched *It's a Wonderful Life,* had some wine and snacks and listened to more Christmas music. Just the two of us in our cashmere hoodies—blue and lavender—and neither of us discussing anything in particular after that early morning intensity, but with easy, random talk flowing, throughout the day, along with some wonderful wines that Elaine brought. Then at dusk, we're sitting around with coffee and pie on the couch, talking about nothing, and out of the blue she tells me she's leaving; not just Frank–and the sooner the better, as far as I'm concerned– but leaving. As in moving away. Away, away. To the Southwest. And not in a year or two, but soon.

I can't believe it. She's leaving, and she's my closest…what? Friend? Yes, of course, my dear soulmate, but I still would like it to be more, even though I've had to set that aside for the sake of the friendship. And she is leaving. Leaving me.

Then she tells me she can't even see me on New Year's Eve.

## *Elaine*

Thank God for Revlon Concealer. Without it, I could never let Jeff see my face since the bruises are still apparent, at least to me. To celebrate New Year's Eve, plus seeing each other for the first time since the accident, we'll go out, in the city of course, not my suburban neighborhood where I might run into someone who knows me. How would I explain this younger man with me–on New Year's Eve?

*"Oh, please meet Jeff. He's my nephew, in from Pennsylvania for the holidays. I'm trying to fix him up. Know anyone hot?"*

Or: *"Have you met my yoga instructor? I've become so supple since studying with him."*

Or: *"This is Jeff, my Zen Master. He was an electrician, but decided to become a Zen Master because it was a great way to meet women."*

Or better yet: *"Oh hi, please meet Jeff, my stud-muffin. Say hello, Jeff."*

Our first real dressed-up date, and how adolescent does that sound? Does my hair look OK? How's my makeup? Do I look fat in this? He told me to wear something nice, but not too dressy, whatever that means — men! Who can I ask? Not Frank-duh! Christa's already upset I'm not spending the evening with her, so that's out of the question. My darling, philandering daughter, Stephanie–not. Well, that leaves Roxy.

When she opens the door, the full blast of her music almost knocks me over. In my black suede ballet slippers, tailored charcoal slacks, ivory blouse with sheer organza sleeves and ruffled, deep V-neck, and pearl stud earrings, I stand before her, smelling of Calvin Klein Obsession and, probably, anticipation.

"How do I look?" I resist the temptation to twirl around.

She looks shocked, her eyebrows shooting up into her long, shoe polish-black bangs, part of which are held off her face with a heavy silver comb sporting a death's head. "Wow! You look hot! Where are you going?" She grins, hopefully in approval.

"Just meeting some friends in the city. What are you doing tonight?"

*Liar, liar, pants on fire—oh, Sister Clotilde, you used to look at me and see right through me. And here I am, how many dozens of years—and hundreds of sins—later, lying to my own daughter, my own flesh and blood. Oh well, what she doesn't know won't hurt her.*

"Just goin' to stay over at Katelyn's. But Mom—turn around. I want to see."

"If you like." *Oh, good, I get to twirl.*

"I can't believe it's you. This is awesome. Totally bitchin' with your hair curly like that."

"I had it done; and a manicure, too. Look—I never had one before."

She stands back, appraisingly, perhaps seeing me for the first time. "You need some serious bling."

"Bling?" *Am I so out of it?*

"You know—rings and things." She flashes her fingers with at least eight rings on them. "Chill for a minute."

She makes a path through a pile of clothes on the floor (please, let it be dirty laundry she was sorting, but I doubt it) and manages to open an overstuffed dresser drawer. More clothes land on the floor. "Ooh, I was looking for this a couple of weeks ago." More rummaging around, then, "Here—this will be bangin', for sure."

*Bangin'—yes, I most likely will be…*

She flourishes a necklace that's a heavy silver chain with a center of three long strands of rhinestones hanging on both sides of a silver skull that's at least two inches wide.

"Oh, honey, do you really think it's me?"

*I hope not.*

"Trust me Mom, this is one wicked look. Bet no one else there has one like it."

*No doubt, dear.*

"Thanks, Rox. I'll take good care of it."

I turn for her to fasten it round my neck and feel the heavy skull land between my boobs. And then there's the faux rubies in the eye sockets. Now *that's* a look.

## *Jeff*

Is this Elaine I see at the restaurant? I thought it was when I helped her off with her coat, but then I saw this Goth thing—this *thing* hanging down that must have weighed a dozen pounds, and it's a freakin' skull with ruby red eyes, like some kids in my classes wear. What is she thinking? That it'll make her seem younger to me, is that it?

Then she says her kid gave it to her to wear, and I can't help it, I've just got to laugh out loud. With the tailored ensemble and pearl earrings, and all, then this, this…Is she a closet Dead-Head? And I didn't know it after all this time? What kind of overage hippie do I have on my hands?

"You're…different. Is this a new look for you?"

"Do you like it?" She sticks her boobs out halfway to my face.

"What other surprises do you have for me?" I say, lifting the silver skull and hefting its considerable weight in my hand. And forget the ruby eyes—those dangling rhinestones!

She turns around and fumbles with the clasp. "Help me take it off."

"No way. Leave it on. It's hot. And right then and there, I nuzzle her neck, which smells really good.

❖

So does the calamari and pasta, when it arrives, along with some chianti. But the food, good as its reputation, doesn't keep me from noticing that a lot of men—and women—are staring at Elaine. She looks really fine, but are they gawking at her or the skull that's the size of an egg? That silver skull—I can't wait to get her back to my place, with her wearing it in bed. What other surprises does she have for me? Hope she doesn't want dessert.

"Does Madame wish a dessert menu?" This waiter has obviously been enjoying the place's cuisine, and must weigh close to 250. He has good manners, though, and hasn't once stared at the skull. And yes! She says no. Also declines my offer of a movie—great. Fortunately, this Italian place is not too far from home.

# *Elaine*

I thought Jeff's eyes would bug out of his head when he saw the necklace. When he laughed, I had to laugh, too. Definitely a good start to the evening. He's taken me to a really nice place, with linen tablecloths and waiters in black slacks, white shirts and aprons around their waists, bowing every time they approach the table. Jeff looks more dressed up than I've ever seen him, with that "European Fashion Model Look" definitely going on with a sexy five o'clock shadow, charcoal turtleneck under a black wool jacket, and tight black leather slacks. Oh, baby! Is it warm in here, or is it a hot flash?

But the way he keeps staring at me all evening. I can't think it's my boobs since he's certainly seen them plenty of times, so it has to be Roxy's skull necklace. Where does she find these things? And people are looking at us. So what if they are. Let them think whatever they want to. Jeff likes my look, and that's what matters. I have the scarf I bought for him, but don't know if I want to give it to him here or not. Has he anything for me? I don't see a package.

If I thought shopping for that scarf before Christmas was hard work, that was nothing compared to the day-after-Christmas crowds. I needed replacements for Christa's holiday blouse and Christmas Village gas station. Should I have worn a Kevlar vest as protection? Probably. And a football helmet. Those bargain hunters at Field's were vicious. It was overcast and windy, but with every Christmas thing in the place at 50% off, it's no wonder those people were jamming the doors, all of them—of us—on a mission.

Really, they showed no mercy, and a whole mob converged on the holiday decorations when the store opened at seven. I grabbed the next-to-last "Christmas Village" gas station while most of the others were vying for the church and school house, almost tearing them out of each other's hands, for God's sake. At least it was quieter in Women's Apparel, but there were no more "Partridge in a Pear Tree" blouses to be had. I had to settle for Three French Hens, but at least that was half off, too. Good thing it was available in size 6, or it would have meant two turtledoves—not the signal I wanted to send to Christa.

But Jeff is certainly signaling me with his bedroom eyes, so forget dessert and coffee, along with his offer of going out for a late movie. I'll make coffee at his place.

As the valet goes for my car, Jeff's all over me, kissing me where the skull ends and my boobs begin. Is it me or the skull or the fact that it's New Year's Eve?

"Whoa. Let's save it for when we get home."

Will the concealer hold up? I'll suggest candles just in case.

❖

"Coffee? Or wine?"

We opt for wine, toasting each other and our first real New Year's Eve date together. Last Christmas holiday, Jeff was visiting his relatives in the East, and I cooked on Christmas Day to avoid my sister's usual overcooked turkey. New Year's Eve I spent with Frank and a plate of nachos in front of the TV—of course. Just the two of us, and Dick Clark, with Colin upstairs asleep.

Now it's a totally different scene. Jeff's lit the candles and turned off the lights, so it's no surprise when he starts groping me on the sofa.

"I have a gift for you." I move to retrieve the gift-wrapped box from my oversized shoulder bag. He jokes that I probably keep a change of clothes in there along with a first-aid kit.

"Well, I have something for you," he says, reaching into his inside jacket pocket. He pulls out a small, square velvet jewelry box, and my heart stops.

Omigod, I bought him a scarf – cashmere, yes, but a scarf!

"You go first." Jeff hands me the dark blue box.

Now my heart's racing—jewelry from Jeff. This sure as hell beats nachos with Dick Clark.

Slowly I open the top and see inside the most exquisite cloisonné pill box, which I gently take from the ivory satin lining.

"Oh, Jeff, this is the most beautiful gift I've ever received. Thank you."

He gives me that killer smile. "For your headaches." He kisses me sweetly on the lips.

After stopping, then racing, my heart melts. Wouldn't it be something if it was *my* turn to be ambulanced to the hospital?

"Open yours."

He does, ripping the paper off that I'd so carefully chosen— silver bells on a blue foil background. That's totally lost on him, but I guess that's just a guy thing. There goes the top onto the floor, then the top layer of pale blue tissue.

"A scarf, and it's really soft." He holds it in one hand and strokes it with the other.

"It's cashmere. Do you like it?" *I hope so. I really took a long time picking it out.* "Whenever you wear it, you can think of me—that we've been together almost two years."

"Come here." He pulls me to him on the sofa. Before kissing me, he whispers, "Thank you," and I wrap it around his neck.

Which is where it remains—that and the notorious skull necklace on my chest, minus everything else—until the wee hours of the New Year.

## *Christa*

What am I doing, sitting home by myself on New Year's Eve? Watching old movies on video? I'd feel better if I had an inkling where Laney was, and with whom. So mysterious, she was, about her "previous commitment," and I certainly wasn't about to ask. Especially when she came here two days ago with the new gas station and Christmas blouse. I mean, what could I say? And who am I, really, to say anything to her about her life or how she chooses to spend her time?

When you get right down to it, who am I to her—or to anyone? Will we ever be more than just friends? Is this what I really want? What do I really want? A commitment, yes, from a man or a woman who's smart and caring and attractive, and who makes me laugh. And it doesn't really matter, male or female.

Anyway, there's always the comfort of watching Katharine Hepburn and Spencer Tracy. *Pat and Mike, Adam's Rib*—classics, and for New Year's Eve, *Woman of the Year*—not me, for sure, but definitely Hepburn, a woman for all years. At her best with Tracy, the man she had an affair with for decades; the man who wouldn't leave his family for her. Yet it was his "Katey" who nursed him when he was dying. She didn't attend his funeral out of respect for his wife and son. How many holidays she must have spent away from him.

Dammit! I am not going to be sitting here alone next New Year's Eve, no matter what.

## *Elaine*

With the New Year here, Stephanie and I seem to be settling into a routine. She brings Colin by the house on Tuesdays after work. Some Thursdays, too.

If it's a day when I've cooked, they stay for dinner. I look forward to seeing my grandson, and love playing with big Legos, Hot Wheels, Elmo, Big Bird and trucks in the living room. When Frank gets home from work, he does, too, once I'm out of the way and in the kitchen.

Still, it can be stressful when they're here, even for a short time. Frank and Stephanie in the same room. Stephanie and me in the same room. Frank and me in the same room. My God, how did we get to this terrible place? To think it's come to this...and I'm still here...

Sometimes, even being in the same room with Colin can be a drain. It's not all his fault. Stephanie lets him eat what he wants, and he still throws food on the floor, and when we're talking and he's being loud, she just talks louder.

I jump in. "Excuse me, Colin, but adults are talking. You need to quiet down." He usually gives me a blank stare before running back into the living room.

Of course, that's nothing compared to his behavior at Christa's on Christmas Eve. I've seen many hyperactive kids as young as three years old. Is it Stephanie's poor parenting or does he have a medical problem?

Does he even understand what I'm saying to him? I'll bring my audiometer home from school and test him to be sure his hearing's not impaired–if he'll cooperate. Otherwise I'll have to take him to a specialist. I don't think Stephanie ever applied for health insurance at Starbucks, and if she did, I can't imagine how she would pay for it.

She seems to be trying to set some limits, but with mixed results. Sometimes a stern "No" does the job, but all too often he just ignores her. He seems to listen to me most of the time, so what's the difference? Does he understand that I mean business? When I tell him to stop throwing things or I'll turn off the TV, I really do it, but Stephanie's inconsistent, and sometimes just threatens without following through. With her, it's often a matter of empty words, and small as he is, Colin knows this, just as he knows he has to behave at daycare, that they mean what they say there or it's a "time out" for him, and that's that.

He's had more than his share of time outs, that's for sure, or that's what Stephanie says his teacher's told her.

Stephanie tells me about her concerns for him, maybe because I'm her mother; maybe because I'm a nurse. Colin; his boundless energy and his inability to sit still unless it's in front of a television set. I've seen it, too.

On one particular afternoon Stephanie is noticeably quiet and thoughtful while I putter around making chicken chili. After awhile she says, "Liam and I have been talking lately, e-mailing, actually. It all started when I sent him an e-birthday card. He e-mailed me back, asking how Colin and I were doing. He said he'd been thinking about us, but figured I probably hated him."

"Do you?" She's fidgeting in the chair, shifting forward, back. That plus a certain shiftiness in her expression and her unwillingness to meet my gaze make me sense a revelation about to come, recalling her as a nine-year-old looking left and right, never at me and finally confessing she had a note for me from her teacher; I knew that meant nothing good.

"No, I never hated him. I was angry because he didn't try harder to be a part of our life; I was looking for an opportunity to draw him in. I thought Colin's birth would bring us back together..." She pauses, but I can't tell if that's out of disappointment or an attempt for drama. Drama; I think she's doing 'plucky single mom faces the cold, harsh world.'

"But..." A rueful shake of her red ponytail. Yes; she's definitely doing 'sadder but wiser'...and she wants something.

She continues more briskly. "Anyway, when it didn't happen, I figured the best thing to do is move on with my life"

"Does Colin ask about his father?"

"The kids at daycare talk about their dads, and he asks me about his. I tell him his daddy lives across the ocean in a country called Ireland. He asks why his dad can't get on a plane and come over here. I can only tell him it's more complicated than that. Then he asks why can't we go over there."

She shifts again in the chair. "It got me to thinking"

"You're going to go see him?" How, I wonder, with only a part-time job and expenses...

"Maybe, but here's the thing. I need to see if there's a future for us."

It's dawning on me. Yep, she wants something. She's setting me up to ask if I'll watch Colin while she goes off to Ireland, again. And probably pay for her plane ticket. My muscles begin tensing, first in my neck, then my shoulders. "You're hoping that you two will get back together? Then what? Are you going to live there...and what about your son?"

"Honestly, Mom, I know you've put up with a lot from me." She at least has the grace to look contrite for a moment. "But I'm just asking for this one last favor. Can Colin stay with you? If it doesn't work out between us…" Her voice trails off theatrically, "I'll let it go and forget about Liam. I feel like I have to give it this last try to see if there's still something between us. I feel like…I owe it to Colin."

She is totally doing 'finding a family for my little boy'…and a meal ticket. My gut instantly tells me this is a bad idea, and everything in my 12-step program, too. I would be allowing her to use me all over again. I could see her staying in Ireland, leaving me to raise her son, never seeing her own child for months or years at a time. Colin with a 52-year-old "Mom."

"Why don't you bring him? Doesn't Liam want to see his son?"

"Colin would be better off here with you, Mom."

"…And who's going to pay for Colin's daycare and diapers and clothes and shoes and doctor bills?" My voice climbs several octaves at least.

"Frank will. He is already."

She is so matter of fact, I am stunned speechless. That's what I am. Of course he was still seeing her, and it was one thing to think he might have been helping her get a place for a while, but supporting her child?…after all the cheap-ass grief he's given me about Roxy? So Stephanie's got it figured out, and she needs a granny-nanny so she can high-tail it back to Liam—minus Colin. How cozy.

"With you and Colin and Roxy and Frank—it could bring all of you together again," she says in her most earnest voice, a smarmy smile on her face.

What is this, a recipe for Home Serenity from Dr. Stephanie, TV Therapist of the Slash-and-Burn School of Relationships?

I can't help it. Laughter that simply cannot be contained explodes uncontrollably, huge spasms that rock me as I howl at this latest proposal.

*Is this an appropriate response, Elaine?* I can just imagine Counselor Christa peering at me over her horn rimmed glasses with professional detachment as tears run down my face and I snort and hoot like a maniac.

"Mom…"

There's no way to tone it down, even with my hand over my mouth. Tremendous waves of laughter escape, bouncing and echoing off the plaster walls.

"Mom! What's wrong with you?"

She looks so irritated, which only makes it worse. Beyond speech, beyond reason, beyond thought, I hold my stomach, unable to stop the laughter that's become an ache.

"Grandma?" Little Colin sticks his head around the corner.

"You're not going to do this for me, are you?" Stephanie hisses, her tone suddenly gone ugly. "Not a big surprise. It looks like Colin and I are going to Ireland, no thanks to you. I don't know if we'll be back…ever."

A brief pause, then another outburst explodes. Unable to speak, I'm doubled over, waving my arms around, gasping.

Stephanie pulls Colin to her. "Grandma's not well. We have to leave."

So much for daughterly concern.

"Let's get your jacket on, Col. Here."

Though laughter feels like it is literally pulling me into pieces, I feel strangely calm inside. My twelve-stepping has paid off and no amount of Stephanie doing 'big-time Guilt Trip' will change my mind.

"I'm not cooking tonight," I manage to say, barely able to rise from my chair, and feeling the latest wave of hysteria as Stephanie whisks Colin past me, but not before I land a kiss on his head.

## *Jeff*

We were celebrating New Year's Eve when Elaine said we'd been "together" for well over a year–going on two, in fact. Whatever. God knows this is the strangest, what should I call it, *relationship?* I've ever been in. Somehow it seems to have worked for both of us, but I've had to face the fact that my work is suffering. I haven't painted in too many months.

The last painting I did that I really liked, the one of the *Rubenesque Woman*, as Elaine calls her, was before I even met Elaine, so I guess I can't blame it on her, or can I? The stuff I've done since being with Elaine is derivative, third-rate, but whenever I work up some sketches, it's always the same old thing.

I know blocked, I've been there before and it's bogus. I find any excuse…arranging the next show at the gallery, critiquing students' paintings, working at the frame shop, doing anything but my own art, and when I do have some free time, it's spent with Elaine.

I like spending time with her and all, and not just in bed…we go to the galleries…Museum of Contemporary Art, the Terra, and, of course, AIC. And she gets it…what it's like to paint, and not have time to do what you want to do, what you *need* to do. *Stagnant*, that's the word for this place I'm in, so there's no way to keep doing what I'm doing, which is nothing. Which means I break out and try something new. How do I break new ground? At least new for me? This sucks, and I'm going to have to make some big-time changes. Time to clean house, damn straight.

For starters, there's no real reason to stay on at the frame shop now that the gallery's doing better, so I should get out of there, for sure. One less distraction, one less remnant as I morph into a better place.

A place where I feel I can breathe. How can anyone create if they're strangling—Jesus, Mary and Joseph, as Elaine would say. So for sure, wouldn't you know it: she goes and gives me a scarf which I swear I could feel tightening around my neck—doesn't that say it all? I mean, she's a good woman, but there's a time to move on…

## *Elaine*

Two weeks later I drive Stephanie and Colin to the airport, to say good-bye to my little guy, mostly. His backpack is stuffed with snacks, books, paper, crayons, his favorite stuffed animal, and his raggedy blanket. He's thrilled about the trip on an airplane as much as seeing his father for the first time. I wonder if Liam's the one paying for the plane tickets. Oh well, there are credit cards and it's not really my business. Colin picked out a special gift for his dad: a small teddy bear wearing a sweater with an American flag across the front, and holding a flag in its paw. He reminds me again and again that *he* picked it out for his daddy.

Hugs for Colin, over and over. My only grandchild will be across the Atlantic. I'll miss him so much. Our trips to the library, park and McDonalds ball pit–I'll miss those, too. Who knows what will happen, but at least Colin gets to meet his father, and maybe they will become a family, the three of them. It hurts so much to see him leave, though. How I wish Christa could have been with me for this, but wouldn't you know it, with her busy schedule...So I drive home missing that little boy, but if they can start a new life... if that's where this trip is taking them...

## *Christa*

Hated to lie to Laney, but the thought of going to the airport and seeing her say good-bye to her grandson—all that drama. I'm just not up for it right now. Good thing Stephanie's leaving, but in a way, it's too bad. In time, Elaine might have gotten comfortable with the idea of my talking to Steph about Colin, maybe even having him tested and evaluated, but there's nothing I can do to help with the situation if they're living in Ireland.

Maybe it's all for the best. Who knows? Did I really want to get more involved with Elaine and her family, especially after that episode, no, that revelation—about Stephanie and Frank? And with Elaine so...unavailable to me in so many ways...not just sexually but in every sense. I have to make an appointment, for God's sake, just to see her for coffee and a sandwich, and aren't we—weren't we—best friends? Probably a good thing that I've distanced myself from the whole scenario—Elaine running around in five directions all the time; Frank screwing her own daughter right under her nose; that little grandson who's obviously in trouble and needs some kind of professional intervention, and his mother who's totally in need of some parenting skills...not to mention Roxy, the aspiring goth queen...

Sometimes I think it was meant to be. Taking a long, hard look at my life has helped me pull back from Elaine, especially since running into Mercedes at a movie after the holidays. Ironically, in a way I have Elaine to thank for all of it. If it hadn't been for her gallery show, I wouldn't have met Mercedes to begin with. Then bumping into her in the theater lobby just after she's back from a year's sabbatical of painting in Spain? And going out for a drink with her and her friends? Tell me that's not karma? That we connected after so long–over a year? Are women the direction for me now? And why? Not to run away from men, but a running toward…And with Mercedes and her friends, all successful, accomplished women, I feel like it's a homecoming for me.

Coming home at last– to everything I never thought I could have, only dreamed about: a sweet, soft, tenderness, animated conversation, a passion for the arts, the slow sureness of a lover who knows a woman's body. No wonder it's been so easy to wind up being…with her? I guess I am 'with her'; of course I'm 'with her,' though it's all so new to me. These last few weeks have been way beyond a whirlwind–more like a culture shock that surpasses the sex. Which is fantastic. Is it the newness, the feeling of freshness that comes with hope and new beginnings?

K. D. Lang, Tret Furie, all the other musicians…the films and books and plays and lesbian history–or herstory, is what it's called–I never knew were there. The underground newsletters during the McCarthy '50s, the bar raids, and now the new openness, with music festivals and lesbian book discussion groups…Sometimes it's overwhelming; trying to take it all in. Every lifestyle has its culture, and Mercedes is doing her best to immerse me in it.

There's so much catching up to do.

## *Elaine*

I t's President's Day, a school holiday, and I decide to treat myself to an adventure; a much needed distraction since I haven't seen Jeff since New Year's Eve. What that's about, I just don't know. I had a great time, and he did too, or so it seemed. But was that real or some kind of New Year's Eve illusion? It was OK to let a week go by after that without hearing from him, but when it turned into two weeks, I got concerned and left a message. He didn't return my call. Or the one a few days later.

No middle-aged stalker chick am I, but still…why hasn't he called? How adolescent is that? Am I still a teenager waiting for the phone to ring? Not a thing about getting together, not even on Valentine's Day—especially on Valentine's Day. It's one lousy feeling, and takes me back to the days before I met Tom when a guy wouldn't exactly break up, he'd just vanish. Please don't vanish, Jeff. Was I fantasizing that we'd run away together, two painters living in a thatched hut in Tahiti? How Gaugin is *that*—

dream on, girl, you know how *he* turned out. But I miss Jeff, miss our talk and his energy as much as I miss lying next to him. It's hard as hell living in Stephanie's old room, and under Frank's roof, even though I have no one but myself and my own procrastination to blame. Haven't even told Roxy about moving—she should get high school behind her before I uproot us. After that, I don't know. She refuses to consider college, and doesn't seem too serious about finding a part-time job, which God bless her, wouldn't be a bad thing. Especially since she'll have to find something after graduation.

But today's a good day to clear my head and drive into the city. Too bad Christa couldn't come along. When I invited her this morning, she reminded me that President's Day isn't a holiday for her clients; they need her as much today as on any other day. So I'm doing Chicago alone. To get away—from what? The reality of finishing up the school term before I can relocate? Missing the life I thought I had?

My first stop is North Michigan Avenue, the Magnificent Mile, a street that defines urban chic. If you want to know the latest fashion trend, take a stroll along the Mag Mile. It's exhilarating to be among the trendsetters, and only one block west of the Museum of Contemporary Art, its modern façade punctuated by white marble steps spanning the length of the building. The last time Jeff and I were at MCA, the exhibit was photography of major cities, not the typical skyscrapers and landmarks, but back alleys and side streets that the tourists don't see: the heart and soul of a city. Being there with him was like having a private tutor—a really handsome private tutor—discoursing on the art of catching light and freezing the perfect moment.

I decide to eat lunch at the museum's restaurant, its balcony opening to a courtyard and a view of the lake. Seated nearby is a young mother with her child, which makes me think about Stephanie and her childhood. My perception of her formative years is very different from hers; she sees herself deprived of the love of two parents, growing up in a dysfunctional and chaotic household. I, on the other hand, saw it as survival; she never wanted for anything; she was warm and fed, had books and clothes and music and knew I was there. From her point of view, it just wasn't enough.

Lost in introspection, I don't notice a tall, handsome man approach my table.

"Mind if I join you?" It's Jeff, but he's not smiling. He leans down and kisses my cheek; a chaste kiss that says we were once lovers and now are...what?

"You look great, Elaine. Are you still keeping the universe from spinning out of control by sheer will power?" He is not wearing the scarf I gave him, and his eyes are as cold and green as the lake.

Did I miss something? Six weeks ago we were passionate lovers and now I get a kiss on the cheek?

So what's up? Why is he doing 'sarcastic stud' when he was once so sweet? And not that long ago. But maybe to his generation, anything lasting over a year is a lifetime.

"You do, too–just great. I was concerned about not hearing from you. Is everything OK?" I'm doing 'self-possessed, middle-aged woman.' "Please—sit."

He does as I take a deep breath.

"I've been up to my ears...new students in a whole new graduate class, with some very promising painters there..." he looks away. "So I've been tutoring some of them privately." *Hmm.*

"Really, it's so refreshing to see young artists developing, it's awesome; almost...empowering, even. Makes me feel energized."

"Oh?" *I'll bet.*

He goes on. "I mean, you wouldn't believe some of the new artists we're taking on at the gallery. Such talent—so edgy and urban. I'm in charge of putting together a show for this fall with a focus on the next generation of painters." He looks at me, his eyes lighting up at this.

"How exciting for you."

This goes right over his head, he's so self-absorbed. "It's all good, for sure. And there's a project of my own I've started, too." He's not making consistent eye contact as he begins gesturing in the air. "It's in partnership with some of these younger artists, and it's like a series of canvasses on the same figure, the same woman, you know, but different parts of her body, and different views and in different light, and by three different painters, plus me. And it's coming together effortlessly, seamlessly. What makes this all come alive, so totally, totally alive is more than the passion of the idea, more than the contrasting techniques and lighting, and even more than the energy, it's the model, I mean she..."

I tune him out, unable to hear any more for a moment. How do I fit in with this NEW! IMPROVED! Jeff, if at all?

"…Is so exotic, just embodying the mystery and allure of the Orient…Did I tell you she's Japanese?" He rattles on, "And her proportions…"

*You have her bra size?*

"She's just a joy to paint…"

*No doubt.*

"Her spirit—she's so carefree and spontaneous—just animates her poses like you wouldn't believe."

"Oh, I would, believe me." And before he can take a breath for his next exaltation, I add, "Well, it's all good, is definitely what it sounds like." *Yes, and you've been so busy…I mean, SO busy…and couldn't pick up a phone. To call me. I see. And you are SO interested in my life, you don't even ask what I've been up to.*

"And it's been a busy time for me, too, Jeff." He looks momentarily startled to have his monologue interrupted.

"I drove Stephanie and Colin to the airport not that long ago. They're in Ireland with Liam, maybe trying to patch together a life, maybe not. If nothing else, Colin will finally get to meet his father. Who knows where it will lead. They might stay in Ireland, with or without Liam. It's really up in the air."

It's hard for him to change gears, so caught up is he in his own enthusiasm. Clearly my news pales in comparison. "Sounds like it's up in the air, for sure." He considers me, perhaps seeing me for the first time today. "Ya know, some people attract chaos, and I think you're one of those. I don't mean that in a bad way… train wrecks just seem to happen around you…you have this tendency to attract negative energy."

*Your energy was pretty damn positive around me, buster.* "Hold on while I get my crystals and incense out." My mouth is too tight to even attempt a smile.

"I know that sounds goofy, but in your case it's true. You should get one of those pictures that show the colors of your aura. I bet yours would be brilliant oranges, reds, and purples," he says.

He leans back in the chair, stretching his long legs and torso, locking his hands behind his neck. It reminds me of that night in his gallery so long ago when he was evaluating me then, just as he's re-evaluating me now.

"Santa Fe. I'm moving there. To paint." And then I know I will, that I will really make it happen. "Thanks to you, Jeff. You've been a great teacher."

In more ways than one.

He sits forward, surprised. "When?"

"As soon as school's out."

"You've got ten times the energy and guts of women half your age. I'll miss you."

For the first time today he seems sincere. I glance at my watch, "Need to be somewhere." *Anywhere but here.*

We leave the museum together, and as we walk down the marble steps, he stops and hugs me. I just stand stiffly, not letting myself respond.

"Good-bye, Elaine." His dark wavy hair is the last thing I see disappear into the crowd.

Then it hits me, all the losses I have endured: betrayal— Frank with Stephanie; her flight to Ireland with Colin; and now Jeff's good-bye. Lightheadedness overwhelms me, and my knees buckle. I sit on the cold steps, tears silently streaming down my face. *What a sight I must be, a middle-aged woman crying on the steps of the Museum of Contemporary Art after being dumped by her younger lover. Talk about doing 'Portrait of a mid-life crisis at the MCA.'*

A guard approaches. "Ma'am. Ma'am, are you all right? Can I get you a cab?"

"I'm fine. Yes, fine. I just dropped my...dropped a..." *A little piece of my heart.* "A pen. It dropped from my...from my purse."

Which I clutch to my side as I stand, aiming myself down to the sidewalk.

❖

Alone in the safety of my car—at last, cut off from the world. No one even knows about Jeff, so who could I reach out to, even if I wanted to? Who can I share this pain with? No way with Christa. That would be stretching the limits of our friendship beyond the breaking point, especially when she wants more from me—or thinks she does. Or thought she did, I'm not sure any more. And she is my only real friend, God knows, and I can't risk losing that.

Here I am in the same parking garage Jeff walked me to how long ago—how many lifetimes ago? Get over yourself, Elaine. God, this is so Drama Queen— he left you and that's that. What did you expect? It was a miracle it went on as long as it did, so be glad and grateful – grateful? –yes, dammit, grateful that you had what you had together, whatever that was, for as long as it was. But it hurts, just the same. I thought after New Year's...could it have been the skull? He didn't return my calls after that, even after he gave me that lovely pillbox, which I will treasure…

Dammit to hell, Jesus, Mary and Joseph! What a fool I've been. He was probably screwing every little chick that came along, God knows he had ample opportunity. When did we see each other, after all – once, twice a week, at most? Plenty of time for him to be banging those sweet young things with their taut stomachs and smooth skin; their long legs and firm tits and NO stretch marks—Oh sweet Jesus, what was I thinking? I deserve to suffer. Oh, Mary of Perpetual Guilt and all the Saints, deliver me.

Where is my rosary? The one I got on First Holy Communion. That is all I need for this scene, for heaven's sake— get a grip, girl—it's over, and no amount of second-guessing will bring him back. Go get some hot coffee—the 24-ounce size. It'll brace you 'til you get home for a good stiff drink.

Which can't be soon enough for me. It's about time I sat down and took stock of everything.

❖

First things first. Roxy's here and not on her way out, for once. She's sitting down to a can of Coke and a bowl of God-knows-what from a can, nuked in the microwave. All I know is it's orange and has pasta in it—and what does that say about me? Sure, she's old enough to find her way around a kitchen, but I'm her mom, and still…

A huge sigh escapes me, followed by an equally large breath. This is hard. Maybe not hard as telling her about divorcing her dad, but hard. She barely glances up at me when I sit across from her, so engrossed is she with her snack.

"Rox. How was school today?" She looks at me like I'm a space alien.

"Same old, same old." Her black nail polish and the orange sauce make a contrast best called interesting.

I stare at her for a long moment. *My little Roxy—my baby.* " I have to talk to you. This is difficult."

Her eyes, outlined in heavy kohl, widen in apprehension. "Yo, Mom, don't tell me you're gonna have a baby!"

*Sweet Jesus, no, thank God it's not that – can you imagine? – and it would be Jeff's. That two-timing dog. As God is my witness…*

"Mom? Hel-lo?"

"Oh no, honey, it's not that, but…" Jeez, how can I go on? My heart is breaking for all of us, Jeff too, that lousy bastard. "We're moving. Away from here."

"How far away?"

"Far."

"I'm not going." She shovels a spoonful into her mouth.

Here's where I have to do the 'understanding parent in charge of things': "I know this is a shock."

"No duh. I've got over three months 'til graduation. Then, Mom—I am SO outta here."

"I didn't mean this minute. We both have school years to finish. I was talking about June or July."

"When I'll be gone," Roxy says in a tone that tells me she's serious.

"Where will you go? Wouldn't you consider going to school?"

"*Not*. Mom, I told you I'm not interested in college." She takes another bite of her pasta. "I'm bookin' to New York. To be in a band."

"A band? What band? You're not even *in* a band."

She sends me a withering, 'you are so clueless' look as she does 'long-suffering teen forced to deal with dimwit Mom.' "Duh, parental unit. Earth to Mom…I've been singin' with some garage bands in the 'hood. Nothing big, just hangin' and all…but it rocks."

I feel my mouth drop open—literally. "I had no idea." *Oh, Holy and Divine Saints! She's right—I don't have a clue…not with her; not with Stephanie and Frank; not with Jeff.*

"No shit." She brings forth a large belch.

"*Excuse you!* You were not raised that way, Missy."

"Yada, yada, yada."

So it's come to this—both my daughters take after their father's side of the family. Praise Jesus, my father isn't alive to see this. May he rest in peace; he must be spinning in his grave.

"We need to talk more about this another time. I need to think about it."

Roxy takes another bite and chews slowly, considering. "Yeah, whatever. But I'm going."

"So am I. That's what I wanted to talk to you about. I…can't stay here any more."

"Ya think? It's been bogus here for months, like, lots more than the usual bogus, you know?"

"You could move with me."

"Like, where? New York?" She momentarily brightens.

"No. Like Santa Fe."

*Not.*" She finishes her can of Coke, conversation over.

"We could call your dad. You might stay with him for a while."

"Throw up!" *Yes, seeing you eating that glop does make me want to. And whose fault is it, that you're eating such…where's the glass of milk, where are the homemade chocolate chip cookies I should have baked for you?*

"You can't stay here without me after graduation."

"Damn straight. Not with Perv-O Frank." She chews reflectively. " Katelyn. I'll stay with her until I can leave."

"I'll talk to her parents." Another sigh overtakes me. "I'm so sorry about this, but there's no way…"

"I know old Frank won't miss me. I sure won't miss him."

## *Christa*

So she's really going to do it. It's about time. I wouldn't spend another minute under Frank's roof. It will be tough for Elaine to wait it out with him until the school year ends. As recently as a few months ago, I might have wanted to offer her a place to stay, but even then…no…and certainly not now. But it's good she's leaving. I'm glad for her. I'm glad for me, too.

In the past, I might have felt abandoned by her move, but now I see it as the best thing all around: I'm involved with a wonderful woman, new friends and an exciting new life; Elaine needs a new beginning as well. And Santa Fe's far enough away so that she won't be reminded of old haunts every time she gets in the car to run errands or go to a museum…and I won't be tempted. Tempted to fall back into wanting her again? Unlikely with all the excitement in my life right now, but you never know.

# Part II

# *Elaine*

The summer sky in Santa Fe is brilliant blue, with the blazing sun casting deep shadows. It reminds me of a happy time in my childhood when possibilities were endless during summer vacations from school. I want to save this moment for a time of self-doubt. I still have to find a job, but putting my fate in the loving arms of the universe seems easier than I could have imagined as I explore my adopted city.

For the first time in my life I live alone. No parents or sister; no husband; no children; no boyfriend. Alone. Just me and the four walls, and and when I come in, it's quiet, orderly, and I don't have to walk on anyone's emotional eggshells but my own.

The noisy air conditioners in the windows barely keep the afternoon heat at bay in this casita I'm renting, a two-bedroom house on East Palace Street within walking distance of the Plaza. An adobe wall surrounds the postage stamp-sized property with a courtyard in back and a garden in front that's enclosed by a black wrought iron gate. Beyond the gate is the narrow sidewalk and street. The little compound of casitas has a feeling of safety and security. Inside my house are warm wooden floors and plaster walls that I judge to be from the 1950's. The dining room contains a black wrought iron light fixture hanging over a heavy pine table with matching chairs and a hutch, and an arch connects that space to the living room. There, a beehive shaped fireplace fits snugly into the corner. On the long wall (painted a dingy gray, like all the rest of the walls) hangs an Indian blanket in hues of red, gray and black. A well-worn sleeper sofa faces the fireplace. A comfortable reading chair, accompanied by a quaint, Art Deco floor lamp, angles toward the fireplace. The narrow kitchen's wrought iron light fixture reveals outdated, but functional, appliances (at least a step up from Frank's) and wood cabinets painted mustard yellow (throw up!) and a matching door. It opens onto the back courtyard, littered with dried brown leaves blown into the corners.

The back garden could once have been lovely, judging from its remnants of tangled brown vines and a tall piñon tree that needs pruning, but still commands attention. Though the courtyard's fallen into ruin, I see possibilities for a cactus garden along with mesquite, sage, rocks, and grasses and even a feeder for hummingbirds. The metal bistro table and chairs are at least serviceable, though in need of fresh paint.

The bathroom is reminiscent of the 50's as well; the bottom half of the wall behind the bathtub is covered with shiny, pink ceramic tiles accented with a single row of black, and the tub itself is chipped in spots, albeit a vintage claw-footed treasure I will repair. The former occupant apparently tried to tile over the original floor, which shows through in the areas where the upper layer's cracked and missing. The larger bedroom is sunny, with windows looking onto the back courtyard, and the six-foot tall adobe wall. The bed frame made of rough-hewn logs is probably the newest piece of furniture in the room. An antique dresser with mismatched knobs and a corner table with a battered TV sprouting bunny ears complete the decor. The smaller bedroom's empty. It will be my studio. Despite its shortcomings, I fall in love with the place immediately and begin unpacking my meager possessions, full of plans for redecorating the inside and replanting the little gardens outside. My books, computer and painting supplies can wait.

The casita is only a few blocks from the Plaza, the center of town and a hub of activity. I dine there on my first night at a café that serves spicy tortilla soup and enchiladas. While reading the local newspaper's employment section, it seems the Southwest is in dire need of healthcare workers, especially nurses, and although there are many positions for hospital nurses, I want to work at an alternative medicine clinic. My money will last six or eight weeks, I estimate, and I don't want to take early retirement, which would decrease my monthly benefit. Therefore, I need to find a job fairly quickly, but I don't want to "settle' for the first position to come along. After all, I'm starting fresh, on *my* terms.

My first week in Santa Fe is about getting my bearings: finding the grocery and drug store, cheap places to eat, and most important, the home improvement center. It's a time of thorough cleaning, repainting, repairing and replacing. Glad I budgeted for this, though I didn't foresee needing—or wanting—so much.

First things first: a pair of heavy duty rubber gloves and a can of cleanser do wonders for the sinks and tub, and a bucket with Soilax for the walls brightens the rooms and freshens the air. Wouldn't you know it, I moved here in the hottest month of the year. The sweat has long ago soaked my T-shirt and cut-offs despite the best efforts of the air conditioners, but it's good sweat, the kind that comes from hard work.

Scrambled eggs and toast revive me long enough for a soak in my newly scrubbed tub. It's so relaxing after my hard day's work, I'm nodding off and happy to collapse into bed and fall immediately into a deep, uninterrupted sleep. The next morning finds me a little stiff and sore, but filled with an enthusiasm that I haven't felt in years. My new, clean walls. My new bedroom. My studio. My new little house. My big new life.

The pedestal sink sparkles, and even the tub looks so much better. It will be better still once I use appliance touch-up for the chips. And maybe some bronze accent paint for its feet. As for the floor, unless I undertake a major renovation, camouflage might be best for now.

Speaking of floors: Flax Soap with a bucket of warm water and a mop gives new life to the hardwood floors throughout, even the one in the kitchen. The wear marks give them character. I wonder who else has lived here and walked on them. Next time I run errands, I'll get that touch-up paint for the tub. For the kitchen there's the necessity of a fresh coat of paint on the cabinets and door. The right color could rejuvenate the room; something to contrast with a whole new color scheme throughout, now that the walls are clean. And something for those awful pink bathroom tiles.

❖

I'm so excited I can hardly wait to unpack my bronze spray paint to accent my tub's claw feet. The man in the paint section was a doll, helping me with everything I need to paint the tiles a pale color, then showing me all the Santa Fe decorator colors. Navaho white for the walls overall. Brick red cabinets and door will transform the kitchen. He helped me find matching brick red spray enamel for the outdoor table and chairs. I couldn't resist the large pillar candles, a woven multi-color runner for the dining room table and Indian-patterned area rugs (all on sale!) for the dining room, living room and bedroom. I may go back and get matching ones for the kitchen and bathroom.

❖

A week later I stand in my new home, surrounded by freshly painted walls, all in Navaho white, which makes the place lighter and appear twice as large. The kitchen door and cabinets are so much easier on the eye (and on the stomach) in brick red than that hideous mustard, and the rug there picks up the red color and echoes the white kitchen appliances and black wrought iron light fixtures.

In fact I've matched the rugs throughout, in the bedroom, dining and living rooms, as well as in the kitchen, and in the bathroom, one covers the broken floor tiles. The formerly pink tiles there now match the walls throughout in a nice, neutral Navaho white, making the rug a focal point.

I'm especially proud of the dining room, so much more inviting now. The centerpiece of pillar candles on the table runner makes it a pleasure to eat there. I plan to use the hutch to display a set of dishes I haven't found yet, but right now, photos of Colin and the girls take up most of the space.

Amazingly, the Woolworth's had everything from tacky tourist souvenirs to some really nice things, and I found a black and white throw that covers most of the couch. Its Indian-inspired pattern (of course) matches my new bedspread, which replaces the chartreuse chenille beauty that had been there.

Maybe the most affirming part of this makeover is the fact that my paintings hang throughout—in the bedroom, living and dining rooms, and even in the kitchen. They remind me I have a small body of work to my credit, and that it's one I need to build on. Especially since I also have a gallery exhibit under my belt, thanks to Jeff. Jeff—I wonder how his artist's eye would view what I've made of this place, with my art throughout? I wonder if he'd see it as the place of warmth and refuge it's become for me.

Best not to think about him after all this time; best to keep moving, especially now that I have my studio set up and ready to go.

Next on my list are the gardens, and one night's devoted to drawing up plans. I'm at the garden center bright and early the next morning, waiting for someone to arrive and open the place that should have been opened 20 minutes ago. How Midwestern of me. I'll have to adapt.

One nice thing about being the first customer is getting undivided attention from someone who seems to know native horticulture. She helps me select a variety of cacti in various shapes and sizes, a mesquite bush, a couple of Russian sage plants, and garden tools–a start. I can always come back for more and do my wash at the same time in the nearby laundromat. Which will probably be tomorrow or I'll be out of underwear. Maybe tomorrow I'll buy some instead and use the trip as an opportunity to explore a new street.Now that the place is spruced up inside, and I'll have spent today planting and pruning front and back, an outing would be terrific, even if just a few blocks away. Returning to my freshly planted gardens and inviting interior will be a treat.

❖

The morning sun greets me as I check on my lovely new courtyard garden. As though the cactus were going to sprout feet and run away in the night? Actually, I have my first visitor: a small, skinny, calico cat dashing behind the mesquite. Is she here to use my garden as a litter box, or is she scrounging for food? She looks like she needs a meal. OK, Elaine, we're at the crux of our first big decision here—to feed or not to feed, that is the question. Sweet Jesus, she's peering out and meowing like a poor abandoned thing, which she may be since I see no collar on her. So what are we going to do, Elaine? And where does this royal 'we' come from? She's begging for food and water, and in this heat...

After consuming some cool water and a can of tuna she gulped down, she's now lying down (settling in, are we?) in the shade at the edge of the garden, washing up and pausing every now and then to gaze at me with yellow eyes that seem to size me up—as a soft touch? As a possible new home? She's on her feet and approaching my chair, bit by cautious bit. And of course she's cautious. Who knows what she's been through? Nurse Fuzzy Wuzzy to the rescue again.

"Hello," I hear myself saying. *What, after a week alone, I'm talking to stray cats? I'm now doing 'lonely middle-aged woman who takes in cats.'*

"Looks like you enjoyed your breakfast."

"Meow." Sounds like thanks to me.

❖

Several days later, a visit to the laudromat's a necessity. I'm almost out of new underwear, bought from Underpinnings on Washington Street. My stock of canned tuna's just about depleted, too, thanks to my morning visitor who's become my buddy at breakfast. And lunch. And dinner. And face it, Elaine, the cat has no one but you, so she's not going anywhere, and the two of you are a team. Time to get her to a vet (exam, shots, flea collar— omigod) and yourself back to the supermarket for cat food, litter, and a grooming brush. A job would be nice, too, if I'm going to keep paying for these things. It would also keep loneliness at bay.

A man lives in the casita on the west, but so far, it's just been a few nods and waves of acknowledgement as we pass each other. The same is true of the young woman who lives east of me, and seems to be alone except for her gray tabby.

I miss Colin and Stephanie more than I did in Chicago and have no way to contact them except by old-fashioned snail mail which seems archaic in this age of high-speed Internet and satellite phones. My mail is being forwarded from Chicago. Stephanie recently sent a postcard of the impossibly green Irish countryside declaring that things are good with Liam and that Colin enjoys riding ponies and playing on Liam's family farm. With no phone yet and no e-mail, I must settle for what little information I can get. I mount the postcard on the refrigerator with a red chili pepper magnet.

A trip to the vet's made possible via a pet carrier borrowed from my accommodating neighbor, Trish, who's a silversmith by night and a sales clerk by day. The exam reveals that my new friend, Callie, my calico, is young, basically sound, and in need of shots and spaying. Not to mention treatment for worms, fleas and ear mites. Oh, I need a job.

When the phone line's activated, the first person I call is Roxy, who's sharing Katelyn's room back home—her home, no longer mine, I remind myself.

"How's it going, Mom? Have you gone to any coffee houses? Have you, like, gotten high yet?" She asks, laughing.

"Come on, Roxy, I'm not even here two weeks; besides, you know I'm not that kind of girl," I joke.

"Oh yeah, I remember: no sex, no drugs, no alcohol," Roxy shoots back, mimicking my mantra to her. "Just remember, that goes for you, too, young lady," she says, in her best imitation of me. I miss her energy and unique perspective on things. If she were here she would quickly find her way into the alternative culture and probably help me find a job. I can't blame her, though–she's looking for her own adventure, not mine. Only after I've hung up do I remember I haven't mentioned my cat. Maybe next time we talk.

Standing at the kitchen sink with my coffee cup, I realize that living alone requires big adjustments. A package of frozen chicken breasts defrosts in the refrigerator, even though I only need one piece for tomorrow's dinner. Cooking chicken breasts makes me think of Frank and all the healthy meals I tried to make for us.

I'll feel better when my kitty's home tomorrow evening after her surgery. She'll need a soft bed—a great use for that old chenille spread–near a litter box so she doesn't have to go far while she's recuperating. Maybe have a celebratory chicken dinner and invite Trish next door as a gesture of gratitude and friendliness.

## *Frank*

There's nothing better than a cold beer, nachos, and my favorite chair. Add to that a game on big screen TV, and it's primo. No more Roxy playing loud music and emptying the hot water tank in the shower. Yeah, and no more chicken breast and tofu stir fry and God only knows what other crap Elaine had me eating for dinner. I never get tired of pizza, burgers, and Hungry Man TV dinners. Or fried Walleye right out of the lake. That's my job when we're up there. The guys love what I do with fish and pan-fried potatoes, maybe even more than my bacon and eggs. Those guys–buddies for years, and family to me.

Soon it'll be time for another long weekend up at the lake, but for now, here I am right back where I started before Elaine and her kids and grandkid moved in. Yeah, it's nice and quiet now, that's for sure. Who needed that kind of aggravation?

Just as well those McElroy women are scattered to the four winds; Elaine in Santa Fe, Roxy staying with her friend, and Stephanie and Colin in Ireland. That little guy's the one I miss. I used to like seeing him after work and we'd do stuff together. Boy stuff. Poor kid—surrounded by all those wacko chicks, except for maybe Stephanie, and the best thing about her was her hot bod.

That all seems so long ago. I might never see Col again, unless Stephanie comes back to the States, and even if she does… Who knows, she might get married and have more kids. She might be married now for all I know, and it's not like Elaine's going to call and tell me the latest news about the kid she damn near could have killed. I wonder if she even knows herself. Or cares.

This damned heartburn is really bothering me. I should cut back on the nachos. If Elaine was here she'd kill me. I wonder if there's any Tums in the medicine cabinet?

# Elaine

Job-hunting can no longer be postponed. According to the want ads there are many positions available at the hospital outside of town, but a clinic that focuses on nutrition, herbal remedies, and alternative treatments such as acupuncture, will be more to my liking.

With my computer's Internet set up, Stephanie and I begin e-mailing regularly. Her messages sound upbeat. She and Colin and Liam have bonded. During the week they stay in the city where Liam works at a bank. The weekends are often spent at his family farm. According to Stephanie, Liam's parents adore Colin, their only grandchild. They dote on him and I get the impression that they would like to see Stephanie and Liam marry as soon as possible.

Until Stephanie gets around to finding a job, she's receiving a government "dole"; a stipend for Colin, who has dual citizenship and therefore qualifies for assistance. Having a daughter on the equivalent of welfare is a first in the family, and nothing I'd want known.

Will they remain in Ireland if they marry? I envy Liam's parents who get to see Colin all the time and watch him grow. Stephanie mentions that they are planning a holiday sometime in the coming springtime, a tour of the Irish countryside in Liam's tiny car. Making plans so far in advance...hmm. With mixed feelings of loneliness and jealousy, I am happy that things are finally coming together for her.

❖

Despite a couple of weeks of answering ads, sending out resumes and posting "Position Wanted" notices on message boards around town and on the Internet, I haven't had as much as an interview. A hospital job could be mine tomorrow, but that would be a last resort.

Callie, who's perky and loves her catnip mouse, is putting on weight. Having a cat for company is a pleasure, and, as Rox reminds me, "Cats rock, Mom. Yo." She is currently sharing Katelyn's aloof Siamese, Queen Jojo. Roxy sent me a picture of her recent appearance onstage—well, not a stage, exactly—more like a coffeehouse, but still...She seems to have a couple of facial piercings, but I'm not saying a word because I'm happy she's got a part-time job there and is talking about taking a couple of community college classes. Since Katelyn's ending up there, school's starting to look a lot better. As long as Tom and I share the cost, it's fine with me.

I'm homesick for Chicago, especially as I think of the coming autumn with the leaves changing, though I'm told the mountain aspens in New Mexico are lovely. Still, my casita feels more and more like home with my little purring friend who surveys her courtyard with territorial fierceness each day, prowling for the foolhardy interloper who may have inadvertently blundered in. You go, Callie-girl!

Ever since she lent me the cat carrier and recommended her vet, Trish has helped orient me to my new neighborhood; from the best places for fresh produce to the location of the post office and the cleaners. She really liked the lemon chicken-with-rice I fixed for us, and has had me over for her veggie lasagna with pine nuts. Through her, I've also gotten to know Tristan my neighbor on the other side, who is an architect. What he's done with his casita! I guess he actually owns his; I hadn't known that was an option. The track lights and the new slate floors he's put in it are incredible. Warm desert tones throughout, and the new appliances—Frank should see them! When I get a job, I might go a similar route. One step at a time, Elaine. One day at a time. Which reminds me: Need to contact Nora and let her know I'm still alive.

❖

All of a sudden, it falls into place: I find a job with an alternative healing center. I start in a few days. Clients are seeking relief from headache, back pain, and anxiety and are usually in search of generally healthier lifestyles. Compared to Chicago pay scales, it's less, but I wear street clothes with a lab coat, which eliminates the cost of having to buy uniforms.

The Serenity Spa and Holistic Healing Center specializes in a variety of treatments for body and soul: hot rock massages, mud and seaweed wraps, yoga and aerobic classes, and alternative medicine utilizing acupuncture and herbs. The philosophy of the Healing Center is that the mind and body are inseparable and must be treated holistically. The wooden double doors keep out the scorching summer heat; calm and coolness prevail inside. A scent of eucalyptus permeates the air. Small upper windows provide soft light, giving the impression of being cut off from the hectic world outside while still being connected to the elements of sun and sky. Staff speak in their "spa voices" a few decibels up from a whisper, and move purposefully, not hurriedly.

At the reception desk, women clients are directed to the left and men to the right, down wide, gently descending steps, to the separate spas. A staff member shows clients to the changing area where they select a locker and inside is a white cotton robe and shower clogs. After changing they are given a tour of the luxurious facilities: a sauna which emits the eucalyptus vapors that greeted me; treatment rooms where massages are performed; and the "quiet room" with cushioned lounge chairs and bowls of fresh fruit and pitchers of water infused with cucumber in the morning and citrus in the afternoon. The "quiet room" opens onto an outdoor courtyard with an in-ground whirlpool, and a cold "plunge pool" to stimulate circulation after the hot whirlpool. Also in the courtyard are individual showers, partitioned but open to the elements and complete with all showering necessities: shampoo and eucalyptus-scented foaming gel. From the "quiet room" a doorway leads into a large outdoor area surrounded by a high wall, down wide steps leading to a swimming pool-sized meditation pool surrounded by comfortable lounge chairs and lush tropical plants. Clients are free to relax, meditate or read at their leisure.

My role in this tropical paradise in the desert is to prep the clients before they see Sondra Sandoval, M.D., the medical director and a renowned holistic healer. Weight, pulse and blood pressure are routine for any doctor visit, but what sets this visit apart is the detailed health history that includes diet, exercise, sleep pattern, occupation, family history, stress level, chronic illness, even sexual satisfaction. Finally, I calculate body fat percentage by using calipers on the abdomen, thigh and upper arm. Dr. Sandoval reviews the information before she sees the client and evaluates treatment options; it could be acupuncture for chronic headaches or herbal treatments for illnesses that Western medicine typically treats with medication or surgery.

It's all a big change from Chicago, which I occasionally miss, but where in Chicago would I have desert sunsets, my own casita with courtyard gardens and terrific Southwestern cuisine at any number of local cafés? Not to mention the fact that almost everyone in Santa Fe, from local real estate agents to store clerks (especially store clerks!) seems to be in the creative arts. The man who sells me stamps by day writes his novel at night, just as the plumber doubles as an actor and lighting tech in the community theater. My new job is a crucial step in the transition to life here.

❖

Christa's call comes the day before I am scheduled to start. I've kept her updated on my move and she's excited for me. Would I mind if she comes to visit sometime around the end of August? Perfect—the annual Indian Market is the third weekend in the month and attracts top Native American painters, potters, weavers, basket makers, and silversmiths. I've heard the Plaza will be jammed with people and that wealthy collectors and owners of prestigious galleries congregate by the exhibitors' stalls in the early morning hours so they're among the first in line. Some, I'm told, even sleep in bedrolls in front of the more famous artists' booths. It's not to be missed, and a wonderful opportunity to see work from some of the Southwest's most creative talents. Jeff would love it. Odd–I haven't thought about him in at least a week.

## *Nora*

Thanks be to God she called, and didn't just disappear again. A sign she's growing and learning to trust. She's in Santa Fe, my Elaine. A beautiful place, I'm told, even a spiritual one. She knows I'll always be here for her, no matter what or where, and that she's always in my prayers.

I wonder, though. Santa Fe is so far away. Is it a geographic cure she's seeking? And what of her grandchild back in the old country? I know how it feels not to see Angelica for weeks, not knowing if she's safe, wondering where she and her mother are. Praying night and day, until the only thing I can do is let go and let God. At least Elaine knows where Colin is and that he's being cared for, but that's little consolation for not seeing him, especially at Christmas or his birthday.

Elaine remains in my heart, along with everyone I've ever sponsored. She holds a special place, though. No matter if she were to walk through that door tomorrow, or if I don't see her for another ten years, she's always with me.

# Christa

Nothing could have prepared me for the quality of light; the light that has drawn artists since the '20s, and seeing it makes me know why. No wonder Elaine loves it here. And what she's done with her casita goes way beyond charming…with the added touch of that little cat sitting in her lap every night, the two of them surrounded by her water colors in such a picturesque setting—it's almost a painting in itself. If I had any talent, I'd try to paint a picture of her here.

But how could I think I have any talent after seeing the paintings and pottery and all at the Indian Market? Loved the energy and variety of the whole thing, though not the heat and the long lines at the porta-potties. Found an exquisite silver ring with a turquoise stone and matching earrings. Those, plus a couple of hand-woven baskets and a Santa Clara pot will be wonderful reminders of this trip. Good thing I'm staying with Elaine because the hotels are jammed, as are the cafés and restaurants. Once the weekend's over I'll be able to take Elaine out for some nice dinners and explore a quieter Santa Fe while she's at work…visit the Palace of the Governors, the Museum of Fine Arts, the Canyon Road galleries, and of course, the new Georgia O'Keeffe Museum. Maybe I'll buy a couple of O'Keeffe posters for my office.

After such busy days on my own, it will be a pleasure to sit and relax with Elaine and her cat and watch the colors of the sunset. I can't imagine her ever sitting still long enough for something like that when she was in Chicago. Some new balance seems present in her life, and it's all to the good. This place seems to have calmed her, brought out a stability in her I haven't seen for years, if ever. Maybe she can find her way to peace here.

Peaceful or not, finding the right time to tell Elaine about Mercedes could be tricky. And is that what I want? More to the point, am I ready to? Especially since I'm not sure I can even talk about it yet without crying. It's still so new and raw…

Getting away for a little while was a good idea. I hope it will give me a new perspective.

Which I desperately need. Can't believe Mercedes dumped me for another woman—a younger woman. That bitch. How can I compete with a 20-something photographer who's gorgeous? Like that's how Cooper's wife must have felt about me, the 'other woman.' Either way, both ways, I'm screwed.

Another breakup, another heartache, but with a woman. What is the difference, I wonder? Is there a difference in how it feels, when you come right down to it?

But her skin was so soft, and her tenderness...and I had never felt such a capacity for tenderness in myself, such an easy openness...I miss feeling that way...I let her in, let her know who I am, and now that person who knows me...has left me.

Must try to see the whole thing for what it was...which was everything for me, but what, I have to wonder, for her? She was honest about it, I'll say that for her, and she tried to let me down gently, not in a public place like a man would have done. No, just the two of us together...At least I had that. I couldn't help breaking down, and she held me. Which made it worse.

Was it my inexperience? How I hated that, like being some kind of virgin all over again, when what I wanted was to instantly be confident, suave...but at the same time, have all the highs that come with a brand new kind of love. Did I want too much from her too soon after all these years of feeling starved inside? Would it have turned out this way no matter what?

Breathe...Smell the mesquite in the courtyard. Be here now.

Here. Now. Tonight's my last night here. Is it the proverbial 'now or never,' or just one of any number of opportunities to let Elaine know about the big change–make that changes—in my life during the last six months? I never said a word about Mercedes or my new friends or the new me, even before Laney moved. Maybe I was just plain scared I'd lose her friendship, lose her...Then why say anything now?

## *Elaine*

At first I thought Christa was enjoying the change of scenery, but after a few days it's clear that something's on her mind. Occasionally I sense she's about to open up, but then she changes the subject, switches gears, and gets busy doing 'I'm fine...everything's fine...aren't we all fine?' If only she'd tell me what's up, but all in good time I suppose.

When I get home from work she is waiting for me with a warm hug and smiling face. It feels good to be held by another person. How long has it been since Jeff?

Well, the rest is good. Work—work is fascinating, and doesn't even feel like work. The clients at these beautiful surroundings range from wealthy individuals who want optimal health to desperate souls seeking non-traditional treatments when they've exhausted the options of Western medicine. One socialite flew in for a day's worth of massage, body wraps, facial, the works, and left "rejuvenated," while another client, still a young man, was brought to my office barely able to sit upright in a wheelchair. His mother, who brought him here as a last resort, had to speak for him. Each day brings me gratitude for my time here and all the beauty that surrounds me.

And beauty abounds: not just the sunrises, but the subtler shades of red and purple on the mountainsides after the sun's set and before darkness falls; and Callie's transformation from a skin-and-bones, flea-bitten creature to a well-fed, shiny-coated companion who allows me to share space with her. Christa loves her, and Callie's warming to this houseguest who was kind enough to bring her a box of designer cat treats.

Christa's treats extend to me: some evenings she takes me out to sample the wide array of Santa Fe cuisine, everything from pizza and tamales, to upscale Italian.

Other nights we have a drink in the courtyard and stay home to cook up great veggie meals with the fresh squash, broccoli, and zucchini from the food co-op Trish told me about. In fact, one night we invited her over for pasta primavera we'd pretty much created on the spot, and Christa took us out to Pink Adobe afterwards for an impromptu dessert of their specialty: apple pie drenched in rum sauce. Yet another treat! She said she'd read about it in a Santa Fe guidebook. Gotta start reading those tourist guides!

Before I know it, another weekend's upon us, giving us the chance to explore the outlying area together. Abiquiu and, of course, Ghost Ranch, and the Ranchos Church just outside of Taos. She insists on buying me a large Acoma pot as a house gift—perfect to put by the fireplace. We take in the rugged terrain that's so unlike the Midwest, curse our inability to follow a map, but somehow we manage to get to where we're going, never mentioning the fact that Christa will soon return to her life in Chicago.

## Christa

Saying good-bye to Elaine made me wonder if I'll ever be able to tell her about Mercedes. Each day that passes makes it less likely. In my head I know that's partly a defensive thing: telling would make it real, something tangible I could never take back; not telling lets me delegate it to some shadow-land in myself, which denies its importance, and that's not right. It was real, and it was important.

I'm sure Laney sensed something was on my mind. She knows me—but she doesn't. And that's a wall I've built.

Maybe when I return over Christmas.

## *Elaine*

That visit helped me see how far I've come, and not just the distance in miles. My space is mine. I can eat what I want, when I want—or not.

My time away from my job is mine, and for the first time in my life, I have no one to praise but myself for things accomplished and no one to blame but myself for not painting or not journaling or not being creative.

With so many artists around here, it almost feels like I'm pressured to create, and maybe that's all to the good. I set myself the goal of daily journaling and the far loftier one of developing a series of watercolor studies of the Santa Fe hills at different times and under different atmospheric conditions—how very Monet, but without the haystacks.

When I'm outdoors sketching and painting, I sometimes find I'm talking to myself, and not about the landscape. I imagine conversations with Stephanie, Roxy, Jeff—even Frank—and catch myself speaking out loud. So who cares if someone comes by and hears a crazy lady in a floppy straw hat talking to no visible person? I've gone from doing 'Lonely middle-aged lady who takes in cats' to 'Eccentric old loon in the desert'—now there's a progression!

The days grow cooler, the tourists are plentiful and the spa's appointment book is filled. Between work and painting and taking care of Callie and the casita and occasionally socializing with Trish, Tristan, and a few others I met through them, I barely have time to jot a couple of paragraphs in my journal each night before falling into bed.

My calls to Roxy, and occasionally, Katelyn's mother, Pat, lead me to believe the girls have settled into a routine of classes at the local college, part-time jobs, and—this from Pat, not Roxy, dating a pair of "really cute, really nice" identical twins named

Brian and Michael. Apparently, they're into the "grunge" look, but come from a good family Pat knows from church, where they served as altar boys. This means a lot, and I'm less inclined to worry. It sounds like Pat's got a handle on everything, and though she's too proper to have ever asked, I send her monthly checks for Roxy's keep.

I've known Katelyn since the girls were small and played together, and I never worried when Rox was over at her house. It's a good place for my little girl, and maybe the most stable environment she's ever had. Jesus, Mary, and Joseph, what does that say about me as a mother?

Stephanie's having a hard time mothering Colin, who's well into the "terrible two's," and loves running around the farm on the weekends, but drives her crazy in their tiny city apartment during the week. She's just had her 27th birthday, and I have to wonder how long she thinks she can continue living like this. What about school or a career for herself? And in the short term, God help her in the winter weather when it'll be harder to get that boy outdoors. She's at least thinking about a job for herself and daycare for him. A good daycare setting might be the best thing for both of them. She'd have the opportunity to develop her resume and he'd have contact with other kids on a regular basis, and maybe make some friends there. How will he react, though, to classroom rules?

❖

Thanksgiving makes me glad and grateful to be here despite memories of last year's turkey feast at Frank's, with the girls, Mom, and Col. The thought of him makes me heartsick—will I ever see that little boy again, and if I do, will he even know me?

The sweet part of Thanksgiving is knowing that Christa will be flying in with Roxy for Christmas, less than a month away. Tomorrow I'll start shopping. Sending authentic Indian moccasins to Steph and Colin in Ireland could take some time. As for Christa and Rox, I can't think what they'd like—but something will catch my eye. Just no more cashmere scarves.

For today, I content myself by serving free turkey dinners and dishing up apple pie to the needy and homeless. Then it's home to bake an apple pie, my contribution to Trish's Thanksgiving gathering, an event I'm grateful for. There will be a few people there I've met, so it won't be like the only person I know is Trish.

❖

The day before my guests arrive from Chicago, I arrange gifts around a small artificial tree in the living room. The terra cotta crèche I found at the flea market goes on the dining room hutch by Colin's most recent photo as I offer a brief, silent prayer for his safekeeping on this, our first Christmas apart.

The flight's on time, and Roxy dashes over and throws her arms around me. Is this the Roxy I knew six months ago? She still has the black lipstick and nails and God-knows-how-many rings and bangles and piercings, but I sense a definite change as she hugs me and says, "YO! Mommy! It's your long-lost daughter." A single look tells me she's well, thriving, even, in contrast to Christa, whose dark circles under her eyes combined with a tightness around her mouth suggest fatigue and tension.

When I hug her, she feels rail-thin beneath her long coat though the smile she gives me is genuine.

Over the weekend, we do museums together and admire the many handcrafted gifts on display, especially Christa, who makes a big drama out of her "secret shopping" for me in a couple of the stores. Roxy reminds me of her "B" in Sociology and "C" in English Composition, maybe hoping to leverage that into an additional Christmas gift.

"Mom, I got a 'B' — as in 'boy,' Mom-sa. Listen up, not a 'D' for 'dog.' A big 'B.' And a 'C' for 'Callie the cat.'"

"You've told me at least five times. Yes, Rox. That's great." *Really, it is. And she looks healthy. Not exactly 'Sally Field in Gidget,' with all the Roxy-esque goth adornments, but healthy.*

Unlike Christa, who's lost so much weight, though she certainly didn't need to. Whenever possible, I offer Christa nourishing food without seeming like a hovering Fuzzy Wuzzy, but she just picks, moving the food around but eating little, which worries me. When I am at work she takes Roxy to explore some of the outlying areas: a couple of pueblos, with lunch in Taos. They return, triumphant, with a handmade Taosaño drum–which Roxy enthusiastically demonstrates–that Christa's going to use in a drumming circle she's joining. This is news to me—I don't see her in a drumming group, but who's to say she can't change? After all, I have.

Roxy and Callie are a duo, with the cat rubbing at her ankles all the time until Rox picks her up or finds a piece of yarn and ties a bit of cellophane to its end. Callie loves chasing that thing around, and Roxy giggles like she's a little girl again. Christa and I just have to laugh. The cat even snuggles up to Roxy's side of the sleeper sofa at night, abandoning (sob!) me. Christa, who has the bed, claims she feels left out of this "feline love fest," but I doubt that.

On Christmas Eve, we—and many others—bundle up and walk into town at dusk. Santa Fe's narrow streets are alight with farolitos, paper bags filled with sand and candles on rooftops and sidewalks. Along the way, some houses have small bonfires called luminarias in the courtyards where people gather for holiday cheer and call out to us as we walk by.

"Hard to believe it's cold enough to snow," says Christa. "It doesn't feel like the Chicago winter, even though I can see my breath."

Roxy blows on her hands. Her gloves are of the fingerless variety, perhaps to display her many rings.

"Warm enough, Rox?" No matter how old she gets, I guess I'll never stop thinking of her as my little one. She's done up in a black fleece hoodie beneath a down vest, and I have to wonder if she's properly dressed for the temperature.

"It's fine." She turns to me, grinning. "And this place is, like, bangin', yo! You go, Moms."

Just as I smile back, I catch sight of Trish across the street, and she's so bundled up in scarf and cap I can barely see her petite features. We wave to each other, calling out, "Merry Christmas." She'll be stopping by later on for a glass of wine.

We've become a crowd as we approach the Plaza and its surrounding area, all decorated with lights. Groups of musicians perform here and there in front of galleries and warmly dressed hosts offer hot cocoa and cider by restaurant doorways.

"Mom, take this," says Roxy, handling me a steaming cup. "Christa, yo. You, too."

We huddle together, gripping our hot drinks in the cold and giggling, partly from the giddy good feelings swirling around us as much as from some kind of silliness at the three of us here in the cold desert city of Santa Fe—on Christmas Eve. Who'd have thought it?

Roxy looks up and shouts, leaving me deaf on one side for several days at least. "Mom! Snow!"

Yes, it falls gently in tiny flakes from the star-studded, navy sky, dusting us, this community of celebrants in my newfound home.

"Chicago has nothing like this. Families take their kids to see the window displays at Fields," says Christa, "but it's like half the town is out here tonight, taking in the lights and music."

"And it's like everyone's homeys at this par-tay. With lots of hot dudes. *They've* got it goin' on," she says, spotting a trio of young men, all with cloth guitar cases slung over their backs.

They may be on their way to a gig in front of someone's shop, I'm thinking as I hear, "Hey, you," and I see my neighbor, Tristan, coming over to us.

He's with a young woman almost as tall as he is, and an equally lanky, bearded young man. He introduces them as his daughter, Susan, and his son-in-law, Greg, and I'm seized with a moment of happiness for all of us here this evening with our families. They move on while we linger with our cocoa a bit longer.

Arm in arm, we three walk around the Plaza, then up one street and down another, occasionally calling out greetings in general, high on the Christmas spirit. Eventually the cold drives us in the direction of home, past the Cathedral of St. Francis, glowing with candlelight inside and out..

"Come in with me. Just for a minute." Christa and Roxy find seats in the back of the church while others fill the pews for Midnight Mass.

A large Nativity Scene is set up close to the altar with donkeys, sheep, horses, cows, shepherds, and an angel surrounding Mary, Infant Jesus, and Joseph. All appear to be made of ceramic, and the people have Hispanic features with dark hair and skin.

Many pots of white and bright red poinsettias decorate the base of the high altar and are in front of the statues of Mary and St. Francis. The smell of burning wax from the votive candles mixes with a slightly musty scent in the cathedral that's well over 100 years old, and more and more people arrive for Mass. Some gather in small groups at the back of the church for quiet conversations, and I see Roxy and Christa speaking together in a rear pew where they're the only occupants so far, but probably not for long.

The stained glass windows feature St. Francis, depicted with rabbits, squirrels, and deer as a bird perches on the shoulder of his brown robe; an image mirrored in the statue of him by the votive candles.

This saint brought me Callie; of this I'm sure, just as I'm certain he's watching over Roxy-girl and my dearest friend. My daughter catches my attention and smiles at me, and so does Christa.

I drop a few coins into the small metal box and light a candle to this saint, thankful for the three of us together on this beautiful, holy night.

## Roxy

Mom-sa likes the oldies CD I burned for her, and she gives me a bitchin' sweater. It's long so I can wear it with leggings, and it has a big collar to pull up in the cold. Stylin' colors, a mix of gray and black, my fave, and it wraps around, tied with a matching belt. Even her taste has improved since she's been in this rockin' place—all these like Indian dudes and painters and freaks and rockers. Lots of bands around, I can tell from the posters, and if I had known…wish Katelyn, Brian and Michael could be here. What a par-tay.

Well, Callie looks stylin' in the goth kitty collar I gave her, complete with tiny chrome studs. The little kachina doll I gave Christa might give her luck, and she can wear it around her neck on a chain. Gotta say, she is one sneaky chick, getting me that bracelet I liked in Taos, like, right under my nose, duh, and me, like, clueless. Girlfriend Christa's keeping my secret, too—that Po Po dude, all flashing his lights and pulling me over like I was some kind of gangsta. Putting his freakin' badge all up in my face for a few triflin' miles over the limit through some Hicksville burg. OK, 20 miles over. Whatever! Like, with books to buy for spring term and all, I did NOT need that ticket, but no way can I ask either of my parental units since they pay for school. So there goes more than a week's worth of coin, and all over a speeding ticket. At this rate, how will I ever get to see Smashing Pumpkins?

Gotta call Katelyn and Michael to wish them a big M.C. Soon as Mom's done talking with Steph. Wonder what made my big sis pop for a trans-Atlantic call. For sure, she wants something. The rug rat's not talking—how can that be?—but Mom's hanging in there trying to get him to say something. Anyway, Steph-ola's going to be there awhile, or so she says, with this Liam dude who never gave her jack after he knocked her up. Sucks, but it's not *my* life. Which will mean some rocking good par-tays when I get back—just in time for New Year's Eve.

Mom's jumping up and down like a kid—what's with her? All of a sudden this is morphing into major news. Now what?

The minute she's off the phone she's hugging me, crying, and yelling those things she says like "Saints be praised," and "Thank the Lord!"

"Yo! What's shakin' with Steph?"

Then it's the bomb: "We're going to Ireland! Your sister's getting married!"

## *Christa*

What is it about being there that makes me feel better? I've gotten out of town before, taken a break from my clients, but nothing's ever felt so laid back. That sense of all those people coming together on Chistmas Eve…no way do we have that here. There's a connection there: to Nature and to each other. Even the guy who gave Roxy a ticket was a sweetheart compared to Chicago cops, but she was all stressed about never having money to go to some concert. She should be glad he was so nice.

Really, even through a tourist's eyes, everyone seemed very nice—friendly and more open than I'm used to. Myself included. Wish I could have magically whisked "Santa Fe Christa" back to Chicago (in denim skirt and silver-buttoned blouse with tooled leather cowboy boots and matching back pack; Stetson and squash blossom silver-and-turquoise necklace included). But without Laney…it wouldn't be nearly as good.

Nothing seems to be much good since Mercedes. And nothing much seems to be left of it, either. The people I met were *her* friends, and didn't really become mine. The places we went—well, it's not as though I couldn't go to the coffeehouse or to a girls' bar alone, but to walk into a place knowing no one is hard, and the alternative might be seeing some of the people I met—only to risk being snubbed by them. Maybe the only thing that would be worse would be to run into Mercedes and what's-her-name.

What seemed like a good idea in Santa Fe—my beautiful drum—doesn't make much sense now. A lot seems to work for me there, but not here. I can't really compare vacation time to everyday life, but I have to wonder if it's the place or Elaine or both that make the difference.

The picture of her sitting with her cat—I can't get it out of my head. How much more at home with herself she seems.

Home—another New Year's Eve alone at home! Last year I swore…never again…and here I am: "Loser Christa" in fuzzy pink slippers, a pair of Cooper's black socks, ratty old robe, stained sweat pants, a David Bowie "Ziggy Stardust" T-shirt, TV remote and no prospects whatsoever included.

Elaine never mentioned having plans; is it too pathetic of me to call her on New Year's Eve? What if she's not there? What if she is…but not alone? Could she have met someone? Maybe she's out with that cute neighbor of hers, Trish? But we didn't see much of her over the holiday. Still…

Christa, girl, get a grip. Forget it. Make a bowl of popcorn. Watch Dick Clark in Times Square. Watch the ball drop at midnight. Go to bed. Get a cat—and a really nice bed for it, just like the one I gave Callie for Christmas. I'm sure she's used to it by now.

## *Elaine*

New Year's Eve. A year ago I was wearing a three-pound skull around my neck and Jeff had on that beautiful scarf I gave him. This year, it means Callie purring on my lap and Dick Clark hosting the New Year's Eve Countdown on TV. Even though it won't be too long until Christa's back here over Easter, this place feels lonely and empty to me now. It's just me and Callie, and thank you, St. Francis, for sending her to me. These last few days since they've left have been too quiet, which baffles me—after all, didn't I spend years yearning for peace and quiet?

And Stephanie's going to be a June bride and is inviting her father, too—that's still sinking in. Roxy and I will fly there for sure, no matter how hard that is on the budget. Maybe I could pick up some shifts at the hospital. I'm so excited, and June will be here in a heartbeat. A dress—a mother-of-the-bride dress. Something nice. And Roxy will be her Maid of Honor—another dress, plus accessories. Looks like I'll be keeping a close eye on my budget.

Speaking of finances, Christa really went all-out with holiday gifts: that Indian silver bracelet for Roxy and the suede vest she gave me—so soft it's to die for. The L.L. Bean khaki color Pet Place Mat for two cat bowls—the first portion of the "pet ensemble" Christa had brought with her from Chicago—was a hit with Callie right from the start. As for the matching, color-coordinated L.L. Bean cat bed…well, it was a big hit with the humans; unfortunately, I couldn't get the cat to go near it, let alone on it, even after I rubbed it with catnip behind Christa's back. I assured Christa it was just a matter of Callie adjusting to it, which she would most likely do in a few days. We were still waiting for that "adjustment" when Roxy and Christa flew back to Chicago. It got to the point where I contemplated rubbing a little oil-packed tuna on it—not. Finally—it took me back to the days of Stephanie and her "blankie"—I tucked a piece of the crummy old chenille bed spread over the L.L. Bean fleece-covered cushion with "Callie" in tasteful script lettering. The cat loves it now. Note to self: keep reducing the size of the old spread until it's history before Christa comes in April.

Weekends at the hospital are killing me. They're always short-staffed, and it's always the graveyard shift, which means going from St. Vincent's to the spa on Mondays. But I'm making extra money for Stephanie's wedding, and have found the most perfect mother-of-the-bride dress in a yummy shade called 'champagne ice,' with coordinating shoes and bag. More than I wanted to spend, but this is special.

Stephanie must have chosen her colors by now; it's February after all, and Roxy'll need to start looking for her outfit. In fact, it's Valentine's weekend, and before you know it...

## *Stephanie*

Mom freaked. I mean major, total meltdown. Guess she was all ready for the June mother-of-the-bride scene, so my news, well...

"What do you mean, you got married? I've been working my ass off to make money for airfare and outfits, and now you say there's not going to be a wedding? Your sister's going to be crushed, Stephanie, crushed. I mean devastated, do you hear me?"

*Yeah, Mom, without a phone.* "I'm two months pregnant, Mom, and we had to get ourselves to the priest ASAP, make everyone here happy, and go on from there."

"What, again?" Her screech almost knocked me over. "What were you thinking? Didn't you and Liam learn the first time? Nobody here will be happy, I'm telling you."

"I thought you'd be thrilled to have another grandchild."

"To add to the other one I never see. Don't bullshit me, Stephanie, of course I'd love another grandchild, but that's not the point. We were looking forward to a wedding, even your father. I bought the most beautiful dress, which God knows if I can return."

"Is this about a dress, Mom?"

"No, it's about you being irresponsible, Stephanie—again. This is a major disappointment to us. We wanted to be part of your wedding—your father and your sister, not just me. Plus, none of us has seen Colin for a year. Who knows if he even remembers me, his own grandmother."

No doubt she's red in the face, rubbing her forehead like she does. Really, I feel bad for her and all, but shouldn't she be congratulating me? "You could maybe come here for a fall visit, after the baby's born—if you'd like."

"No way are we even continuing this conversation now, Stephanie. I'm just too upset. Good-bye." So that's how it went.

Guess that means Mom won't be sending me a wedding gift.

## Roxy

My sister—she could screw up a one-car funeral, you know what I'm sayin'? All it would've taken was some condoms until June, but NO! Hate to say it about my own big sis, but was she, like, switched at birth? Steph is acting like some kind of hoochie mama, knocked up twice—how ghetto is that? And Mom and I and Dad, too, were all buzzed about flying the silver bird across the big pond, Euro-virgins, all of us.

Damn you, Stephanie! Even pregnant, you could have pulled a wedding together in a couple of weeks, and invited us early. And we'd have been there, pronto. Telling us now—Bogus! What, you didn't want us there to begin with? Maid of Honor for me, Momsie-of-the Bride and the Big Guy walking you down the aisle, Steph—none of that now. When I talked to Mom, she was crying so hard...and me, too. We wanted this so much. And Dad—Jim Beam's his best bud now for a while, you know?

For once in your life, Stephanie, could you ever think of someone besides yourself? You better have it goin' on good over there with your new family and all, because no one here's looking to see you anytime soon.

When—if—I get married, I choose the people I know won't let me down. My girl, Katelyn, number one, 'cuz she's keepin' it real, ya know? And I'm for real when I say not only do I not want you as my Matron of Honor, ex-sister, I do not want you in my wedding party, and don't even want you there at all—period.

# Elaine

A routine of working, painting, and writing gets me through the winter despite my despondency. When will I see Colin again? Will I ever get to hold the new baby? It didn't sound like much of an invitation.

Roxy still sounds so down. Nothing to look forward to, she tells me, even though she's seeing a lot of Michael, but when I say I'll fly her here for spring break, she refuses. She's juggling part-time school and work, so at least that doesn't give her much time to brood...or does it?

Work. Work is good. I concentrate on the new landscapes I started and a still life with my Acoma pot and some candles. Standing at my easel in my studio brings back memories of Jeff and those classes—and our times together. I wonder if our public display in the studio became the stuff of urban legend. At least I have him to thank for my one and only gallery show, and that's a start. Trish thinks I should persevere.

In March, I get up enough nerve to bring my new work to a local gift shop to sell on consignment. The owner, a lively septuagenarian named Sophia, accepts my paintings and invites me to a painters' group she's started, a loosely knit collection of local artists who meet monthly to share their latest efforts, but mostly just to socialize and support each other.

The meeting's at the shop, which sells everything from hand woven vests to incense, jewelry, pottery, CDs and hand-printed stationery. I'm eager, but nervous about attending it and deciding what to wear; a flowing floral skirt seems too 60's, jeans with wear holes might be OK, but a paint-spattered T-shirt screams *trying too hard*. I want to be artsy, but not too stylish; I want to fit in. Funny, in my fifties to be worried about dressing to please others.

❖

There is no one, single style; Ingrid has coarse gray hair pulled back in a bun, wears a multi-colored caftan, and speaks with a pronounced Boston accent. Chuck, a Ph.D. in physics who teaches at St. John's College, has swarthy skin and beautiful silver hair gathered in a ponytail tied with a leather strip. Cowboy boots, jeans, and a plaid shirt complete the look. David and his partner Steve are attorneys from New York who now work for the State of New Mexico. With their khaki slacks, oxford shirts and soft loafers, they look dressed for casual Friday at an office. Yvonne has a cigarette permanently attached to her lips, chipped red nail polish and deep creases around her eyes and brow. Like me, she's a transplant, but from Nebraska—is anyone in Santa Fe actually from Santa Fe?—who's trying to make time for her painting as she works as part of a road crew by day. Mental note: purchase moisturizer with sun block.

Sophia introduces me as a painter from the Midwest who's an R.N. working in alternative medicine. How differently I would describe myself: a nurse and single mother and part-time painter who's in Santa Fe to find myself. But isn't everyone here trying to do that?

We're squeezed into the shop's back room; a jumble of boxes piled against the wall, a dented metal desk cluttered with papers and lit by an overhead fluorescent fixture, and a few folding chairs. We sit on Indian rugs, sip wine, and talk. Sophia, who laments that her floor-sitting days are over, sits in a chair, and addresses her conversation to Steve, who seems excited to show some sketches from a class he's taking. From what I gather, that's where he met Yvonne, and how she's ended up here. Chuck's telling David about some movie he's seen by a director I've never heard of.

Sophia, with her miniature water colors of desert plant life and her big, welcoming smile, is the brightest star in this loosely knit constellation of artists she's attracted. I'm looking forward to her next gathering when I overhear Ingrid in a deep discussion with Yvonne about whether or not they'll go to 'a sweat' over the weekend. A sweat? I have so much to learn.

Like learning to find a balance between work, home, art and reaching out in an effort to meet people and become part of the community—something new to me now that I'm no longer reacting to everyone's demands. I've gone from years of being "on call" to a completely different lifestyle. For one thing, I leave work at work, something that was impossible with my old job. Money's tight, but there's room in the budget for the occasional treat and the big dividend is time and energy to call my own.

A new wardrobe's out of the question, but there's not much I need. Besides, shopping's an adventure at the local thrift shops, some of them with designer clothes. Feeding Callie costs very little and cooking for myself doesn't cost that much since nachos, snack foods, beer, pizza and bloody steaks are no longer on my shopping list. Now it's fresh fruits and veggies, chicken breasts, whole grain bread, red beans and rice, pasta, cat food—and of course, coffee. Where would any of us be, I wonder, without coffee?

# *Christa*

**W**hy Elaine thought it would be *"fun—great fun"* to break *our necks hiking up a sheer slope I will never know. She's all perky and energetic, like her buddies from the painter's group, and that one woman, that Ingrid—has her enormous English Sheep Dog with her, the size of a pony, only it pants and drools…and drools…and pants. Oh God, this is no way to spend an Easter vacation. For a city chick who never hikes, this is cruel and unusual punishment for all those missed aerobics classes at the gym. Yvonne, that butch-y little number who does some kind of road work, says the view will be worth it, but the trail's washed out every five minutes, and even when it isn't, it gets steeper and rockier. This is one "Rocky Horror," but if I so much as suggest a rest they'll think I'm some kind of a limp dishrag. Which I wish I had for my forehead right now—soaked with cool water.*

"Excuse me? Trail mix?"

*No, I don't care for any soy-granola-crap trail mix with organic figs, probably, thank you very much.*

"Maybe later, Ingrid. Thanks."

Along with a little pure oxygen and a Margarita. Too bad the sheep dog's not a St. Bernard—then at least he'd have a cask of brandy on him.

"Energizing…revitalizing….yes, Ingrid. Yes, it certainly is rejuvenating up here."

My God, are these people all high on drugs? If only I could sit down and pull off these damn boots. I should have known when Elaine told me to pack "comfortable" clothes and hiking boots for "a little walk" up Aspen Vista Trail. Two hundred and fifty dollars for boots? Like Eddie Bauer will ever take them back after this?

Now Ingrid's giving The Beast some water. To make more drool, no doubt.

It's amazing how he laps up the water—quarts and quarts that she has carried up here in a mega-water bottle on a shoulder strap. If he drinks this much, what must he eat? A side of beef at a time? Now he's drooling again—all over my boots. Did Eddie Bauer make them doggy drool-resistant? Probably would have run me another $50. If only I'd known.

"What? Oh, yes, Laney, I'm sure the scenery will be fantastic once we get up there." *Scenery? What about the landscapes at the Art Institute, if she wants scenery? And will we ever get to this place supposedly renowned for its view overlooking all of Santa Fe?*

"We're what? A half-hour away from the mid—"

The mid-point, we're not even halfway there yet? Another 30 minutes of Gargantua the Great drooling on me, and that's just to reach the halfway point? Omigod. And now this Hound of the Baskervilles has taken it into his 80-pound head that I'm his buddy and is sniffing me up and down, tongue out, drooling— again. And that ridiculous little nub of a tail, wagging so hard his whole bottom half—his whole BIG bottom half—is shaking back and forth. Must be my magnetic personality—now he's sniffing my crotch, and with great enthusiasm, I must say. Oh, please— my dates usually buy me dinner first. Men–they're all the same.

"No, really, I'm fine—everything's fine. Yes, he does seem to like me, doesn't he?" *Lucky me.* "Nice doggy. Nice Thatcher." I pat his giant head.

Oh, no. He thinks I'm encouraging him. Now he's standing— STANDING—on my foot, crushing it.

"Get OFF! NOW!"

I'll never make it. I can't go on. Somebody put me out of my misery.

"No, really, Ingrid, it's fine. Yes, he's very…friendly. Just get him off me—please get him off my foot."

And get me off this damn mountain! Somebody please give me a goddamn gun so I can shoot Elaine in the head because she clearly hasn't used hers in quite some time—and then myself. They'll tie our bodies onto the back of The Giant Woolly Mammoth, and he'll carry us down, panting and drooling, drooling and panting. My corpse—covered with dog drool—will be presented to the local undertaker—who's probably also the saloon keeper as well as the town's mayor and postmaster. It'll dry all over me, all over my face, and when my body's shipped back to Chicago, the embalmer will think I died of some dread skin disease and call the Center for Disease Control. Where they'll dissect me and send packages of what-used-to-be-Christa all over the world for research. At least my death will be for the advancement of science.

Jeez, high-altitude delirium must be setting in; this is sounding more and more like a plan…Why's everyone stopping? What's everybody looking at up ahead? And exclaiming over? Laney's pointing at something in the distance and even the dog is running up ahead, barking.

"What? The overlook? I'm coming. I'm coming, Elaine,

yes…in a minute…" *More like a day…I'm crippled for life—what's left of it.* "I'm fine, really…yes…"

YES! Omigod, it really is, it's breathtaking…spread out all beneath us, around us—the city and outlying desert and the mountains beyond that. It really is incredible—and fine. God, I love this place.

## *Elaine*

Poor Christa! What blisters! Not that she's got a lot of weight on her feet. She's still thin, but has started to gain a little since the holidays. And she doesn't look so tired—or at least she didn't until I had to change all that with a crippling hike she now calls "The Trail of Broken Feet." Really, I feel responsible for her aches and pains and, oh God, her feet! No stilettos on that girl for a while, at least not 'til the swelling subsides.

But Nurse Fuzzy Wuzzy jumps right in with a little Neosporin ointment, some gauze and tape, and more gauze and tape—and topped off with my soft leather moccasins. Yvonne builds a fire in the fireplace to take the chill off the air while I minister to "The Walking Wounded" whose feet are up on the coffee table resting on a bag of frozen broccoli florets. Good thing the broccoli will go with the dinner. Some red wine courtesy of Ingrid helps, and even Callie's washing herself contentedly on her now spreadless (thank you, St. Francis!) bed, seemingly unaware of Thatcher who's quiet in the front courtyard. A hot nourishing supper of chicken enchiladas, Spanish rice, the broccoli, and salad leaves us little room for Yvonne's peanut butter cookies with a fresh pot of coffee, but we manage to make short work of them. It's a mellow scene as Ingrid lights offerings to the gods, sending them aloft in the fireplace as Christa dozes on the couch.

❖

Her feet are in no shape for sightseeing today, which might not matter since it's Good Friday and a good day to spend the morning drinking coffee and coloring eggs while an apple-cinnamon coffeecake bakes. Christa's fine for sitting-up tasks, so she's in charge of stirring the dye tablets in water and vinegar while I run cold water over a dozen hard-boiled eggs. We're dunking them in the dyes when Christa asks me out of nowhere, "Remember your gallery show?"

Memories of Jeff wash over me. "Yes, of course," I reply after a moment, wondering where he is now—and with whom.

"Remember Mercedes—another painter in the show?"

*Omigod, how could I forget—you went on and on about her like she was the Second Coming.* "Yes, I think so."

"I've been trying to find a time…"

Long pause. Callie comes over and rubs my leg, begging for a treat. "Find the time for what?"

"Not find the time; find *a* time…to tell you…" Christa dunks an egg up and down in the purple dye.

"What?" Another pause, longer this time. "Is that a question or a statement?"

"A wish," Christa says. "That I hadn't waited so long to tell you."

I try to make her meet my gaze, but she remains fixed on the egg, by now a deep purple. So I do 'understanding friend who doesn't have a clue.' "You know you can tell me anything."

A long breath, then her words come spilling out: "This is hard. So hard. It wouldn't make any difference if I didn't care what you think about me, but I do, Laney, you know I do, and I just don't want to risk all that's good between us, and saying anything about it now……"

I remain quiet, giving her every opportunity. But why, WHY must I do 'Mother knows best'? When she stays silent, though, I have to ask, "'Saying anything now'…you mean…is it something I've done?"

Christa takes a deep breath and finally looks at me. "It's nothing to do with you. But Mercedes…we were lovers last year for a while…six months, and it was wonderful, but now it's over…I haven't seen her since the end of July." Her voice cracks with heartfelt emotion.

"It's over?" *Mercedes? Of all the women in Chicago…that one? Jeez, does it matter who? Poor Christa. But no wonder she called last August and asked to come out here for "a change of scene." And maybe why she was so thin and tired-looking at Christmas.*

Callie jumps into her lap, and Christa, weeping, cradles her in her arms and strokes her. Though tears wet her fur, little Callie doesn't try to get down. She just snuggles deeper into Christa's arms.

"I'm so sorry. I had no idea. Why did you wait so long to tell me? Or even when it was going on, and you were hap—" *Duh, Elaine. Wrong word, girl, bite your tongue.*

More crying, louder now. "Honey, I'll get you some coffee. Or tea." *And Kleenex.*

"No, I don't want anything."

Her tears subside. *Was I this pathetic when I broke up with Jeff? Not! And best to keep that whole episode to myself, at least for a while longer.* "Some nice, hot tea. Herbal. It'll calm you." *I must be channeling a World War II London Fuzzy Wuzzy soothing Blitz victims: 'Have a nice, hot cuppa tea, dear, and you'll feel better. Buck up, now — we are British, so keep your powder dry.'*

"I don't want to be calm. Shit, Elaine! I have feelings! I am not some goddamn fracture you think you can splint up." Callie jumps down and dashes for her bed.

"I didn't mean anything…" *Jeez, excuu-uuse me. And with her bandaged feet, she's not likely to get up and leave any time soon. I'm stuck with her, tears and drama and all. It's you and me, Callie, and Tropical Storm Christa.*

"I'm sorry if this makes you uncomfortable, Elaine, but it's who I am — a lezzie, a dyke, OK?"

"What do you want from me? I had no idea."

"Well, you damn well do now, so take a good, long look: no more straight best friend you used to meet for dinner — when you had a moment to spare. Here's Dyke-y Christa. What? You didn't notice how short I'd cut my hair? You certainly didn't say anything. And what about my cargo pants? And this flannel shirt from The Gap?" She tugs at the red and blue plaid.

"I thought you were dressed for our hike."

"Dammit, Elaine! What do I have to do, wear a shirt that says, 'I'm dating your sister'? And you, lucky you, you're the first and only one I've come out to, Elaine. You hear that? That's big, that's huge, jeez, it's who I am." Her face is blotched with tears and frustration.

I rise and back toward the kitchen. "I have to check the cake in the oven."

"Yeah, right, Elaine, you're good at that — check up on the cake instead of people."

*My God, is this Frank morphed into Alien Christa?* "You're not yourself, Christa." *Four more steps and I'll be in the kitchen. With the coffee.*

"You wish, Elaine. This is who I am — a woman who loves women, and I was dumped, dammit, dumped by the only woman I was ever with. And I'm alone, and it's worse than being alone after Cooper." She stops long enough to take a breath. "You can't 'fix' this with gauze and hot dinners and coffee and coffeecake." Another breath.

"I meant well." *Is she revving up for more? Will she ever wind down? Three more steps...*

She half rises from her chair then slumps back down, grimacing with pain. "Meant well—why didn't you ask me why I looked like hell over Christmas instead of force-feeding me, huh?"

Two more steps and I can stick my head in the oven. Unfortunately, it's turned on.

"I was concerned, but wasn't sure..." Christa glares at me taking the cake from the oven. Pouring us two fresh mugs of coffee, I spike them with Bailey's Irish Cream from the holidays. I tentatively approach the table—my table—and set a mug in front of her. "Please don't throw this at me."

She grasps the cup of hot coffee in her hands, while I wait for...what? I wish I could be busy licking my fur like Callie. Christa sips, takes another, then a good, long gulp. I sigh, relieved, and chug some down myself. It's sweet and warm. Christa silently stares down at hers. When she looks up, the tears still flow but her face seems less strained.

Her voice is soft now. "Will you still be my friend?"

"Always."

❖

How can I even think about planning dinner with this hanging over my head? I'll just walk the aisles with the cart 'til I get a grip. Am I as dense as Christa thinks I am? Really *clueless*? Dinner...oh yes, that's why I'm shopping, after all—and to be alone where I can quietly gather my thoughts after Christa's Revelation this morning. Really, I didn't have a clue, so I guess she's right. All I can do is try to listen and empathize with her pain. I certainly can't offer advice about something so foreign to me.

Fish. It's Good Friday, after all, and I promised Christa fish done Cajun style. Definitely fish.

"Two tilapia fillets, please; no, better make that three." And what to have with that? Wild rice, yes, and a veggie, of course.

It's not like I haven't had a million things going on in *my* life...Jeff; gorgeous, hunky Jeff giving me the old heave-ho at the MCA, no less, and Stephanie and Colin heading off to Ireland, and Frank, God, don't even think about Frank, that s.o.b. and the car accident, and the move. Sweet Jesus, Christa, cut me some slack.

I'll never look at a woman with short hair and cargo pants in the same way again. Especially if she's wearing a plaid flannel shirt. Holy Mother of God, who knew? I certainly didn't. And how was I supposed to? Read her mind? Now that I know, of course, it's a whole different story. Need to find out all I can about, you know, lesbians. Is there a book, books I can read? I want to do this for Christa, my dearest friend. I'll make up for my faux pas.

"Paper bags, please."

As soon as I get home it'll be a whole different ballgame. I'll be doing 'Enlightened Elaine whose best friend is gay.' No, seriously, I hope this doesn't affect our friendship. It can't. We need each other; Christa to cry on my shoulder after her break-ups, which should be pretty interesting from now on, and me to rely on her for reality checks.

Maybe I haven't been tuned in to her needs. No 'maybe'—not at all. Was it because of New Year's Eve a year and a half ago, the Year of the Ruby-Eyed Skull? God, I hope not. From now on I'm there for her. Whatever she needs. I wish she lived closer, not just flying in for visits a few times a year. We need to talk about that. Would she consider moving out here? Starting a whole new life?

## *Christa*

Is there any good way to come out? I don't mean the actual physical coming out, the act of "doing it" that "first time," which for me, was beyond good. No, I mean the disclosure of it to parents, coworkers, friends; the acknowledgment of it— The Annunciation, some call it. If coming out to Elaine is any gauge, I'll stay in the closet 'til I'm motheaten.

Maybe it's easier for others who have known they're gay since they were kids, or at least teens. Did I ever have a clue back in Ohio? Looking back, there may have been faint glimmerings then, but I thought being gay meant being all butch and playing a lot of sports. But even the thought of it was scary, and the risk...Mercedes told me her parents threw her out when they found her with another girl, also 17. Forget telling my mother. Maybe it's a good thing my dad is dead, God rest his soul, though I never thought I'd live to say that, and especially because of who—what—I am. Which is not the person he thought I was.

Who knows if Dad would have been OK with it?

Elaine seemed shocked. How can I stay here another three days? But I'm barely in shape to hobble from the table to the bathroom and back, so I'm not going anywhere soon. Good thing Elaine's at the store to buy fish for a traditional Good Friday dinner—that's us, nothing if not traditional. Well, she's out of the house, and it couldn't have happened soon enough—talk about needing space! This is a good time to journal and try to figure out where all that rage came from. Poor Elaine—clueless and taking refuge in the kitchen. I actually saw fear in her eyes…did she think I was coming unglued? She just happened to be in the wrong place at the wrong time. All my pent-up anger and frustration and fear of rejection hitting her in the face. For a minute, I thought she was going to climb out the window and run down the street, screaming, "Crazy lady! Christa Alert."

Not crazy. Just crazy-mad and alone, figuratively and literally. So I'll take my journal and a fresh cup of hot coffee, minus the booze, and hobble my way out to the courtyard table. Callie, too. The sun can only do us good. Elaine will be back soon and fix us a late lunch.

How mellow sitting here in her garden, my feet up on one of the red bistro chairs. Even though the air is crisp, the sun's rays penetrate to my core and the sky is impossibly clear and blue. Callie is enjoying it, too, stretched out contentedly near my feet. What an uncomplicated life she now has…eats when she's hungry, sleeps when she's tired. I should write that little gem in my journal.

Friday April 10, 1998…Today I came out to Elaine, who didn't know how to take it. She acted like I was a freak. "You're not yourself, Christa," she said. Damn straight. Bad pun. I can't stay mad at her, though. She really was clueless. It was almost funny to see her hovering around, making coffee, checking that cake in the oven, doing, doing, doing. That's Teflon Elaine; if you keep busy enough, nothing can stick to you. The next time can only be easier. Please, let it be easier.

Was I angry at Elaine or at Mercedes? Or myself, for doing nothing to improve my dismal life?

It gets harder as we get older, and coming out when I did…I feel like I was the world's oldest closet case. No wonder Mercedes left me for someone younger, someone who'd been out and in the life for more than a minute, unlike me. No steep learning curve there. No *having to stop and explain background and history and even the slang. With Mercedes and her friends, it all seemed to flow so easily, so smoothly, with a shared wealth of experience that made me feel like an outsider. I was never her peer, plain and simple, so that even someone a dozen years younger is more on her level than I am. Or maybe I could ever hope to be. Whether I like it or not...*

What's up with Callie? She's on her feet pacing back and forth. I've never seen her so tense before, like she's looking for something, her ears cocked. The fur on her back stands up and she stops in her tracks, facing the back wall. She must see something, but what? A mouse? Or some kind of lizard—one of those Southwestern geckos you see in designs everywhere around here? Harmless, but they have teeth, I'm pretty sure, and I wouldn't want Callie to get bitten or anything. Maybe it's a spider; one of those big spiders with fur coats and all. Jeez, for a little cat, she's twice her size, all her fur standing on end in spikes. She's stopped moving now, and so focused on whatever she sees that she ignores me when I speak to her. Could it be one of those tarantulas? Do they have them out here? I don't like this at all. There are all kinds of creatures in desert country, like poisonous spiders and scorpions...Suddenly a snake slithers into view, a big snake. It's coming from the garden, with instantly recognizable diamond-shaped markings on its thick body. It stops for a moment...a long moment...then its triangular head slithers slowly toward her...us. As it winds back and forth, the eerie warning from its rattlers is chilling, making the hair on the back of my neck stand up, just like Callie's fur. She arches her back and a feral, guttural sound emerges from deep within her throat, a sound that changes to a high-pitched hiss. I'm sitting straight up and holding my breath as she stands her ground as if protecting me, but the snake advances toward the house, and the deadly thing inches closer to us, pausing as its forked tongue flicks in and out—sensing us? Neither Callie nor I move a muscle, paralyzed as we are with fear of this creature, now only a few feet away. Every muscle in Callie's compact little body is tensed, as if ready to pounce at the oncoming snake.

"No!" I shout and fling the only weapon I have at the snake... the mug filled with steaming coffee. It crashes to the ground, a few inches from the threatening reptile's head, shattering, and spraying hot coffee on its sinewy form. It shudders from the burning liquid, a chain reaction of contracting muscle traveling down its long body to its rattles, which whirr and clack furiously. Before my eyes, it transforms itself into a coiled mass with its head extended toward us, jaws gaping wide open. Omigod, I can see its fangs! The scream I hear—it's mine, and in desperation I rise from my chair and hurl my journal, which glances off the side of its head as he strikes so quickly, he's a blur.

Forgetting my sore feet, I scoop Callie up and manage to move faster than I thought I could toward the back door, knocking over one of the chairs and almost tripping and falling less than three feet from the rattlesnake, whose fangs have pierced the cover of my journal. He shifts his head toward our direction and for an instant I'm rooted to the spot and look into his glittering, unblinking eyes, literally staring death in the face. Callie struggles in my arms, sinking her claws into my hand, and I fight to hang onto her, all the while scrambling toward the house. Behind me, the rattles make their deathly sound again, and I cannot keep a scream from bursting out of my mouth, as wide open in terror as the snake's was in attack. Frantically, Callie claws at my face, and I feel the pain of tearing flesh as my one free hand scrabbles jerkily toward the door knob. C'mon, open up, you damn door.

Omigod, it's opening at last, but he's right behind us. Will he follow us in and come after us? Quick now, a leap and we're inside, the slam of the door reverberating throughout the room. Callie jumps down and dashes into Elaine's room when I hear someone pounding on the front door rattling the glass in the pane.

"Elaine, are you all right? It's Trish. Open up! I heard you screaming." She's frantically yelling through the door.

"I'm coming, hold on." Breathlessly I open the door and Trish just about tumbles in to the living room.

"Christa, it's you. I heard a commotion and screams…are you all right? Your face…your hand…you're bleeding."

My wounded hand instinctively goes to the right side of my face, and when it comes away smeared with blood, I realize Callie's done some real damage and barely manage to make it to the couch before collapsing and bursting into tears. "The courtyard…" I motion in the direction of the back door. "…a rattler."

Trish rushes to look out the kitchen window. "Yes. A sidewinder."

"Don't open the door!"

"He's leaving. There's a small hole under the wall by the tree. Don't worry; he's as afraid of you as you are of him and probably just wants to get as far away as possible."

She tosses her thick, dark hair back, away from her face. How can she sound so together? "I threw the coffee mug at him...scalding hot coffee and all."

"I'd say he had good reason to leave." She looks at me, her brow furrowed in concern as she brings a wet cloth from the kitchen. "No, no, no, no, no, no, no—don't touch your face. Here. I'll help."

I didn't even know I was doing that, but I was, and I'm grateful when she sits next to me and dabs at my cheek and jaw. "Callie didn't mean it. She was as scared as I was."

"Try not to cry. It'll only hurt more." I close my eyes for an instant and when I open them, Elaine's standing over me, a look of horror on her face.

"Jesus, Mary and Joseph..."

Trish is mopping my brow with the wet cloth, her brown eyes narrowed with worry. "You passed out for a minute, honey." She turns to Elaine. "I heard an unholy uproar like you wouldn't believe. A sidewinder got into your patio. Christa threw hot coffee on him."

"And my journal, too. He bit it." My voice sounds weak and far away.

"He's gone now," Trish says to Elaine. "Your cat panicked and scratched Christa, but the two of them made it inside safely."

"Holy and Divine Saints!" Laney makes the sign of the cross, kneeling close to me. "You could have been bitten."

Trish nods. "I had a feeling the snake was back. Winston has been acting odd lately, standing at the back door, and hissing."

"Back? My God! You mean the rattlesnake lives here?" Elaine says. "In the neighborhood?"

"Not usually, but snakes and lizards and such turn up once in a while. And not generally poisonous, even then. Remember, they were here long before we were," Trish says, seemingly unperturbed, though I can't imagine how.

"He bit my journal."

"Never mind about that. Put your feet up. You've had a fright," Elaine says.

"Yes." Even speaking simple words is an effort.

"We'll get you something to eat. I don't think we ever really got around to breakfast today. And I'll put some Bacitracin on those scratches and some ice," Elaine says. "Where's Callie?"

"In the bedroom. She was a hero out there, ready to pounce, but I don't think she had a chance against it."

Trish studies my face intensely. "I think the bleeding's stopped." Her small mouth's a straight, serious line.

"I'll probably be scarred for life."

Elaine scrutinizes me. "They're surface wounds. No scars. You need to eat something now. Maybe an egg and some coffeecake."

"Should I put on a pot of coffee?" says Trish.

"Yes, and I'll get a blanket."

Which she tucks around me while I hear comforting kitchen sounds of drawers opening, water running, the clatter of plates and silverware, and then the wonderful noise of coffee brewing. The smell alone is enough to revive me.

❖

Once I've eaten a hard boiled egg, some of my energy returns, so I can fill in the story for them—the sound of the rattles and that awful look in his eyes when he held my journal in his fangs. Elaine seems like she's going to cry any minute, and Trish strokes my hand, comforting me. Callie re-emerges cautiously before making her way to her cat dishes, where she stuffs herself, no doubt having worked up an appetite today. Speaking of which, Elaine's coffeecake is so good, I ask her for seconds. At this, she beams as though she's won the Pillsbury Bake-Off. Nurse Elaine's ministrations have pulled me through for another day of skirmishes with snakes. Just give me a cup of scalding coffee, and I'm ready.

Next thing I know, Elaine's waking me up and the sun's shifted. Trish is reporting "the incident" to the local animal control officer and will re-join us soon for an early dinner, she tells me, and do I maybe want to freshen up? Considering I've worn these clothes through two major crises, one of which involved loss of blood, I'd say that's a good idea. Hot water. Shampoo. Solitude. Heaven.

# *Trish*

After the day's adventure, it's a wonder Elaine can pull together such a lovely meal. A candlelit dinner "will help us unwind," she remarks, and we do over her excellent spicy tilapia and broccoli with wild rice. Even poor Christa enjoys it, with her battle wounds. Of course, Callie, our resident Guardian Feline, gets a taste, too. I wonder what she'd tell Winston about it all, if she could.

With wine, coffee and a lemon cheesecake I picked up, we're happily stuffed, but Christa starts weeping.

"Why today?" she asks between sobs and hiccups, and the only thing I can think of is that there's never a good time to find a sidewinder sharing your space, so why NOT today?

"After all that happened this morning." Huh? This afternoon's Killer Snake Attack wasn't the whole deal? That wasn't enough? Elaine nods. So, when do I get to know?

"Even before the snake, it was a rough day." Again, Elaine's nodding. Maybe someday I'll catch up. Well, I'll refresh my coffee in a minute.

Christa manages, "Never again, a day like this—"

OK, I have to jump in. "Being that close to a rattler must have been terrifying, for sure, and getting your face scratched..."

"There's...more." OK. I figured that.

"You want some hot coffee, Christa?" Anything to make it easier for her.

"Like you wouldn't believe...oh, Trish, you've been so terrific today, I feel I have to let you know what's going on." Finally! Inquiring minds want to know.

She raises her eyes to me, a darker shade of blue now after her tears. "Over a year ago, I realized I was gay, and even became involved with someone for a while. It's taken me forever to tell Elaine, my best friend, and I finally did this morning. What a day!"

"I'd say so."

"Why it took me so long to come out to her, I just don't know."

"I was clueless," Elaine says, "And it didn't help things this morning."

"Oh." *Uh, oh.*

"I didn't know what to expect, really. I mean, I'd never come out to anyone, you know," Christa says, "but I'd heard other people's stories..."

*I'll bet.* "How are you feeling now?"

"Wrung out. Between broken feet, snake fright, head trauma and the biggest thing, coming out…"

"Not about to go dancing at the closest girls' bar, huh?" I smile, hoping she'll smile back.

At last! Her face brightens. "I'll be happy for a good night's sleep."

"When I came out," I begin, "I was 22 and living in Boston at grad school. My parents in Kalamazoo were in complete denial and kept reminding me about 'that nice boy' who'd taken me to Prom—gayer than pink mink, and if only they'd known! *Christa's looking surprised, but relieved, probably because she realizes she's not the only one in the room, but omigod—Elaine looks positively stunned. Well, I'll forge ahead just the same.* "My folks even told me where he'd gone to work—San Francisco, of course—and that I should look him up! Before I knew it, my dad wanted me out of the house—'HIS house'—and to take my stuff with me. My mom was sobbing that I'd only done this to hurt them, and that Dad should pipe down, or the neighbors would hear, God forbid."

"Some friends I have…had…said their folks were a lot like that. As for my parents—my dad's already gone, and I could never tell my mother. It would kill her," Christa says.

"If that's the case, the landscape would be littered with the corpses of dead mothers, so I don't think so," I try to reassure her.

Finally, Christa laughs, a big belly laugh from deep inside—such a good thing to see!—that turns into an equally large yawn. Just then, Callie comes into the dining room carrying a scrap of chenille that's a sickly greenish-yellow and looks like it's definitely seen better days.

Elaine bursts out in a huge guffaw. "Now this," she says to no one in particular before turning her attention to Christa. "The cat bed—that beautiful bed…"

"The one I gave her for Christmas." Christa glances at the fleece-covered cushion in the corner with "Callie" embroidered on it, but looks baffled at this sudden switch in the conversation. As am I.

"Yes. Well…" Elaine looks embarassed. "You may remember she was taking a while to adjust to it."

"And she has—such a good girl." Christa addresses this last comment to the cat. "No more sleeping on that hideous old spread."

"I helped her make that adjustment. For weeks, and with cat nip sprinkled on the bed. But she always wanted that chenille bedspread. When I put it away, she prowled the place, yowling for it. Finally…"

Callie chooses this moment to hop up into Elaine's lap, and she laughs again, though I'm not sure what the joke is. "Well, eventually, I used the approach I tried with Stephanie when she was four and refused to give up her 'blankie.' I took a chunk of the old chenille spread and wrapped it around the cat bed so she'd sleep on it—which she did."

At this, Christa looks horrified. "But that bed…that beautiful L.L. Bean bed…"

"Well, Callie was a hard sell." Elaine presses on. "She's…strong-willed, not just about the bed."

The look on Christa's face is pathetically crestfallen. "I even had her name monogrammed on it."

I remind her of the cat's limited reading skills, and Elaine interrupts, eager to explain her method of weaning Callie from her beloved chartreuse chenille. Really, I thought Callie had better taste than that.

Elaine warms to her topic as though giving a major presentation at a nurses' convention. "Bit by bit, I cut the fabric smaller and smaller until it was just a square on the center of her fleece-covered bed. And she accepted that." Elaine smiles at this. "In fact, she loved it. Loved her bed, loved her little square of chenille that she snuggled when she slept, and for a while I even thought of letting her keep it."

"In the middle of that lovely bed?" Clearly, Christa can't believe what she's hearing.

"But I didn't have to decide. One day it was just…gone. I thought she'd finally tired of it and that I'd never see it again…"

Just then, Callie jumps down to the floor and carries her precious scrap with her to the bed. Wrong, Elaine.

## *Elaine*

Trish will come over tomorrow to help Christa hobble over to meet Winston and see how she's made a workspace for her jewelry designing in her second bedroom. Frankly, it will be good to be here alone with Callie and my thoughts. Not only is Christa gay, but so is Trish! I don't get it—she's never, ever worn cargo pants. And her hair is long and straight. Thank goodness Callie was around to change the subject. I never thought I'd be glad to see that old rag again, but thank you, St. Francis. Any more coming out stories, anyone? Callie? Have you been secretly involved with that cute little Siamese number down the block? Granted, her hair is awfully short…

Christa's looking forward to it, and that's good. As I remove the bandages on her feet, she talks of nothing but Trish's coming out to us, which was a revelation to her, too. A bit of ointment and we'll leave those blistered feet uncovered for the night, then see how they're healing in the morning. She's winding down, relieved her feet feel better, and we talk quietly, bringing to an end a day in which not much happened — eggs dyed, fish bought and eaten, a snake frightened off — oh, and Christa came out, too.

❖

Christa returns from Trish's place with renewed energy and enthusiasm and for the first time in a long time, seems upbeat. I don't see much of those two for the rest of the holiday weekend, except for Easter dinner at Trish's. Sunday evening Christa says Trish will drive her to the airport in the morning so I won't miss any work, and then surprises me for the second time this weekend by announcing she may leave Chicago and move out here.

"So many gay and lesbian people in this area," she explains. "Surely, as a lesbian therapist, I could establish a thriving practice here."

## Stephanie

Spring here is so uncertain, and I can't find Colin's sweater — the one Grandma Maggie gave him for turning three. It's thick and warm, and I don't want to forget packing it. Maybe the Chicago Bears sweatshirt his Auntie Christa sent, too.

At last. The Wanderer returns. Damn Liam for leaving me stuck here, packing for all of us and not lifting a finger.

"Just like you to turn up when I'm almost done." He thinks that devilish smile of his will soften me up. Wrong. Colin's been tearing around the place all afternoon, waiting for his da to come home and wanting me to pack every blessed truck and car of his, as though there weren't any of his toys and things at the farm.

My boy's up in his dad's arms, begging to wrestle with him, but that won't do. "Liam, put him down, will you? I don't want him all revved up, or he won't eat his supper."

Liam grins at me. Clearly he's in a good mood about our honeymoon trip. "Jaysus, woman, he's my own son, isn't he? Can't I play with him? I won't see him for a week."

Good. Let his folks cope with this child 24/7 for once. With Maggie's arthritis so bad, she'll need all of John's help to keep up with him, and for a whole week—but that's their problem. And how I'll manage when the baby comes, I'll never know. I'm so tired. "Just put him down, Liam. Damn it, make yourself useful and carry these suitcases to the door, will you? I'll get supper on the table."

❖

Colin's eyes are half-closed as I put him into his crib for the night, and the sweet smell of him, warm from his bath, fills me with love. His favorite Bob the Builder pajamas are getting small on him. How did he get so huge? I have to keep myself from giving him a great big hug, he's so dear, but then he might waken and he wouldn't be such a dear thing then. A kiss on his forehead, and I'll leave him be.

I close the bedroom door behind me, breathing a prayer of thanks he's at least a sound sleeper. "I look forward to this time of the day when he's in bed. At least there's some quiet." Liam's sprawled out across most of the sofa, so I push his long legs over to make room. He pulls me toward him and his lips and hands are all over me. "Jaysus, ya dope, the honeymoon's not started yet. Can't you see I'm knackered and ready to drop? We've got to start out early in the morning, or it'll be lunchtime before we get to the farm, and that means we'll have to stay for a bite, and then after that, your dad will take you out to the barns to see some new gadget, and by then it'll be tea time, so of course your ma will insist it'll be dusk soon, and we should stay on for a few hands of cards and a wee bit of supper and leave in the morning. And there it'll be—a totally lost day of our holiday. A holiday we want to spend in Galway City." An enormous sigh escapes me, almost filling the room. His own echoes mine.

"Don't get your knickers in a twist, woman. I'll just go out for a pint, then." He's unfazed as usual.

So this is how it will be? Colin and me and soon the baby, all cooped up here with him free as a bird to go to the pub every night? I had it a lot better in Chicago.

"Don't be too long, OK?" It's true I was short with him, but doesn't he see I'm running around keeping up with this boyo all day and five months pregnant with his child? His second child? Let's see how well his parents do with Colin for a week. They'll need a month in a rest home by the end of it.

"Not at all, but you needn't wait up."

Duh, Liam. Like I would have.

## *Elaine*

The open windows of the casita let the spring air sweep through, freshening the place. It's a joy to look out at the yellow flowers of the cholla cactus blooming in the courtyard; a reminder of rebirth and new life. Going out into the garden was scary at first, but the place needed tidying up, and no way would some uninvited rattlesnake keep me from it. So I clanged on an old tin pie pan with a metal spoon before venturing out, and because Trish swears snakes are deaf, I jumped up and down on the stone walkway for good measure. They were sure to feel the vibration that way. It worked so well I now do this every time. Once every wild creature within five miles has been warned, I let Callie out, but keep a close eye on her. She likes to lie down under the bistro table and wash herself while I sketch.

The breeze today means weighting the corners of the page with a couple of small rocks and I'm in the middle of drawing the piñon tree when a gust sends my charcoal sticks rolling off the table and breaking on the flagstone below. Really, it's not a day for outdoor sketching, and as I gather my things to go indoors the wind gathers strength, reminding me of that day over a year ago when Stephanie and Colin left for Ireland. By now he'll be learning his colors and shapes and how to print his first name. Anyway that's what his mother was doing at three, but who knows what she's doing with him? At least he looks happy and healthy in his birthday picture that Stephanie sent, grudgingly it seems, as no card or note accompanied it. Not even an acknowledgment of the savings bond I bought him.

Callie startles at the sound of the phone, something she's never quite gotten used to, and follows me into the kitchen, rubbing against my ankles and purring. It must be the hospital needing me to work a shift tonight.

The woman's voice is unfamiliar. "This is the American Embassy in Dublin calling for Elaine McElroy. Is this she?"

It takes me a moment to respond. "Yes?"

"We have located you through the information on your daughter, Stephanie's, passport. You have a daughter, Stephanie? Married to Liam Casey, an Irish citizen?"

Rooted to the floor, I can't breathe and can barely manage to whisper a faint "Yes." I grab the kitchen counter for support and Callie continues circling my ankle.

"Mrs. McElroy, I'm sorry to say your daughter was a passenger in a one-car accident early in the morning with her husband, and she did not survive. Her husband is critically injured and in hospital, unconscious. We are very sorry for your loss and are here to assist you with making arrangements for local burial or return of her body to the United States."

Lightheaded, I gasp for breath, and double over as though struck with a blow to the gut.

"What? How?"

"We can assist you with whatever arrangements you prefer. Would you like a moment, Mrs. McElroy?"

"My grandson, Colin—was he with them? Is he OK?"

"According to the local officials, there were only Mr. and Mrs. Casey in the car. The minor child was with his grandparents, the Caseys, at the time of the accident, where he remains, unharmed."

Thank God he wasn't in the car. "Thank you," I breathe. "I'll need to contact them."

"Yes, and you'll need my number here as well."

"A pen," I manage, choking back tears and rummaging blindly through my kitchen junk drawer for anything that writes.

After repeating both numbers, she tells me her name and of the seven-hour time difference.

"I can help you through the procedure and necessary forms when you're able, Mrs. McElroy," she says. "Among other things, we'll prepare an official Foreign Service Report of Death once we receive the local death certificate."

"Yes."

She once again offers condolences and ends the call. I'm doubled over, crying, sobbing, moaning from the overwhelming pain. Please, God, it must be a mistake. Surely this woman will call me back say it's someone else's daughter. My legs give way beneath me, and I slump to the kitchen floor. Callie runs from me, and I am alone.

# Roxy

Crying. I can't stop crying, just laying here and hugging my pillow, and I can't believe it. Steph's gone. She was going to get married, and then she just went off and left us out of the whole thing, like she never wanted us there to begin with. For sure, we were all down on her for cutting us out like that. But now she's gone...

I should never have answered the phone. The minute I heard Mom crying, trying to talk...no way it could be anything but brutal. But this—no freakin' way!

Damn you, Stephanie, why'd you have to die? You put us all through so much crap, getting knocked up, and then with Frank and all, and finally running back to that bogus Liam, who never did squat for you and Colin in the first place.

Back in the day, when I was just a rug rat, you never wanted me around, no matter what I did. I just wanted to hang with you, play Barbies and all, but you just punked me. So I learned to punk you back, like maybe all sisters do. Katelyn's an only, so she's clueless on sibs, you know what I'm saying?

Now I can't even wig out at you, and I'm freakin' mad at you, Steph, so what now, huh? I can't even tell you I'm sorry for being so totally down on you, 'cause you're croaked and took that away from me, too. Bet you're looking down on me right now and thinking, "Oh, I wish I had treated her better." Too late.

Now I'm crying again, hating you, loving you, you're my sister, and the only sister I ever had.

Remember when we washed the cat and tried to get her out from under the bed to dry her off before Mom came home? And then you found out I'd pulled the head off your newest Cheerleader Barbie. You were going to rat me out to Mom and blame Fluffy all on me. But you didn't.

Jeez, you're dead, and I miss you so totally, even though you were such a bitch, and like I say, now what, Steph? Mom called Dad, and he'll be coming by to take me to his crib and all, so I won't be alone—so I'll be "with family." This is one time I'll be glad to be with him and Family Number Two, cutesy wife and all.

But remember those times when he wasn't home and Mom was trying not to cry, but still crying sometimes, crying so hard when she didn't know we could hear, when I got all freaky scared?

Like, what if something happened to her, you know? Those times, you were my family, Steph.

## Elaine

C'mon, Christa, be there—answer the phone. I dialed and re-dialed and re-redialed. Surely you're done with your weekend clients by now—or at least between them. Or back from wherever you've been.

At last. "Christa, thank God."

"Elaine...honey, what's wrong? I just got in and was going to return your call."

For a moment, I can't do it—can't make myself say it to her, even though I've already told Tom and Rox. "It's Stephanie..."

"Is it the baby? Elaine? Can you stop crying? Please? Talk to me, Laney. Take a breath, one breath, a deep breath, and talk to me."

"She was in a car crash...she's dead."

Now it's Christa taking a deep breath, a huge gasp. "When?"

"The American Embassy in Ireland called first thing this morning. Liam's alive, but unconscious and in critical condition. Colin wasn't with them..."

"That's a mercy. Oh, Elaine...how awful about Stephanie. What do you need me to do?"

"Tom and I...we want her buried, not cremated. The U.S. Consul in Dublin's helping me make the arrangements, and I'm covering the expenses there. Funny...I started working those hospital shifts to go to a wedding, and now it's for a..." Another round of sobs hits, and I sink into a chair, struggling to contain myself. "Anyway, I'll be coming to Chicago on Wednesday to see Tom and Roxy before I fly out to Ireland from O'Hare on Thursday evening...could you...?"

"You'll stay here with me—that's a given. And do you want me to go to Ireland with you to..."

"Oh, Christa, would you? That would mean the world. By then the 'Foreign Service Report of Death'—whatever *that* is, but it's something they say I need—it should be ready and so will her...remains...'for transport,' they called it. Then I can bring Stephanie home to her sister and dad. Tom's family has an extra plot in Holy Sepulcher."

Memories of bringing the girls home from the hospital as infants, all pink and swaddled, and Tom, the proud dad—it all washes over me; the good times we had when we were together as a family. The tears come again, and I can't help it. Thankfully, Christa just lets it happen. Where would I be without her?

"And Colin. We have to get Colin. I talked to the Caseys and…"

"Well, Liam's in Intensive Care, right?" Christa's voice quavers almost as much as mine.

"His dad's with him and Maggie's staying at the farm with Colin so far, but that could change any time. Taking Colin for a while will make things a lot easier for them…and for Col, too."

"He has to be confused and scared, even though he's with his grandma," Christa says. "Does he know yet?"

*Omigod, I just assumed.* "I'm not sure. Maggie was upset, of course, and with her brogue and all, I was lucky to piece together what I could before she broke down completely. Poor thing."

"I'm packing a black dress and hose, to be ready if they have a service."

"Yes. I was only thinking of the services here, with Tom and all. He reminded me to pack copies of Colin and Stephanie's birth certificates, just in case. I didn't think of that 'cause there's so much…getting an emergency passport ASAP… having passport photos taken, getting an open-ended plane ticket, digging out my birth certificate and getting the whole business to the post office for overnight shipping."

"You did all that? Already?"

"Well, fortunately, the post office here closes at four on Saturday."

"Elaine, that must've cost a lot. Do you need any money?"

"It was hundreds of dollars…not to mention airfare. I've been saving all my paychecks from the hospital, so it's okay for now, but thanks for the offer. All this running around and attending to things—it's a Godsend. Later it'll hit me. Now I have to act; get Colin and Stephanie."

❖

What now? Roxy's with Tom and his new family. Christa's being my rock. I'll be getting the passport in time for my Wednesday flight out of Albuquerque to Chicago. Tomorrow's Sunday. A day's wait before work on Monday and Tuesday, and the job will be a welcome distraction. I've let the fire die down, and there's a chill all through me and but no way can I go to bed. I don't want to sleep. The dreams…I can't risk the dreams.

Callie, bless her—just the sight of her is a comfort, and here she is in my lap. Wouldn't you know it—after all this time, she drags out that chenille rag from wherever she hides it. What is this—she brings it out for crisis situations, when everyone's been bawling? Her purrs are like a little motor, and my eyes are so tired from all that crying. No matter what I do, I can't keep them open.

An unfamiliar kitchen comes into view. Lacy white curtains blow in the breeze from the open window, which lets in rays of blinding light along with the sounds of bird song and cows lowing. Stephanie comes into the room, a vision in a flowing gown, a smiling sweetly at me and holding an infant. "Oh, and you're here now, Mom. So have a look for yourself. I gave her your name, sure. Isn't she grand, this wee colleen of ours? She's Margaret Elaine Rose."

Rosy she is, with little cheeks flushed from napping and a tiny, rose petal mouth that makes small, sucking sounds as she sleeps. Everything in me opens to the sweetness of this baby girl, so perfect in her white gown, booties, and bonnet. I want to reach out to this angel; I want nothing more than to hold her, but I'm glued to the spot, unable to move.

An ember explodes in my fireplace, and my reverie fades from view. For a few moments, the brilliance of the lingering image is stunning; I'm filled with longing for Margaret Elaine. But then grief, like a hard knot in my chest, overpowers me. So this is what a broken heart feels like. Curled up on the sofa, I whisper a silent prayer, "God and all His saints, help me through this."

## Trish

Christa called me right away, of course, and let me know. I'll pitch in and do what I can, however little that might be: tuna-noodle casserole with potato chip topping to whip up something fast for a friend in need. I'm bringing it over right from the oven, and I'll make sure we sit down together and eat. That way she's had some hot food. And tea. I'll brew a pot of herbal tea and then, if Elaine absolutely wants me to, I'll leave, but at least she'll have had a bite to eat. You can't grieve on an empty stomach. And no one should be alone the first night.

"Christa must have called you," she says when she answers the door. Her eyes are red and puffy from crying. Then she bursts into sobs and throws her arms around me, casserole and all.

"Thank you, thank you," she tells me, as though I brought over a turkey dinner, complete with side dishes.

It might as well have been, because it does her a world of good. "I can't remember eating today," she tells me between bites. When she helps herself to seconds, I know it's helped, at least a little. "You're a lifesaver, Trish."

Hardly that, but I can at least drive her to the airport on Wednesday and look after Callie while she's in Ireland. Elaine can stay over with me these next few days if she needs to, and Christa will be with her once she's in Chicago; her family, too.

Including the ex-husband; is that a curse or a blessing?

## *Roxy*

Dad's breath almost scorches my pink hair black when he comes up from the basement to answer the door with me. Mom looks ready to fall over—probably like me. And she does fall, we all do, into each other's arms, bawling and holding on to each other, with Mom saying, "Stephanie, poor Stephanie," over and over again. Dad's making some kind of moaning sound I've never heard, and gripping us so hard, I'm, like, passing out. It's like he's hanging on, and for a minute, it's his pain, not Mom's or mine, that brings us together, almost like a family, you know what I mean?

Until Cutesy Wife starts in slamming cabinet doors in the kitchen and yelling at their cutesy rug rat in her freakin' cutesy high chair—her way of reminding us it's *her* living room we're in; how rude, you hear me? I mean it's like, we just lost my sister, for real, and Cutesy-Ass is put out that we're here together as a family in HER space? Get over it, moron, before I run in there and slap you upside your head.

Maybe it's just as well. Wanting to bitch-slap my Evil Stepmother from Hell keeps me from thinking about Steph and crying non-stop. Dad pulls away from Mom, goes into the kitchen, and we hear, "What the hell, Cheryl, what are you doing, banging around here, making a racket? Can't you come out, say hello, be a person?" The crash that follows for sure says, NOT! Guess she dropped that pot of poisoned apples.

"Tom, don't bother on our account," Mom-ola calls to him. Yo, like bitch-ola's really gonna bother. "Christa's in the car outside, and I just came to pick up Rox for dinner." She eyes me frantically to hurry up, so I grab my bag, the one I made out of an old piece of plaid blanket with my band buttons on it, and a row of safety pins up one side. Dad calls it my grunge sack. So, like, we're opening the door to bail outta Wigout City when he's back, half leaning against the wall. Good thing. He might topple over.

"Cheryl isn't...herself. I need to stay and...help her out," he mumbles, not even looking at us, and we're outtie.

❖

"No way. Maybe I can't boogie with you to Ireland, but no way am I staying at Blondie's Hell House anymore. Just let me get my stuff and take me back to Katelyn's." Mom gives me a look, like, *whatever,* and takes a bite of her burger.

"Your mom needs to eat," Christa tells me, like I don't know that, duh. But bad enough Steph's dead; I don't need Dad's Family Number Two on my case. No wonder he's always sucking on the Jim Beam. We'll see him soon enough at the funeral. With Blondie, Queen of Darkness.

## *Elaine*

Last time I slept here on Christa's couch was the Christmas we had together with the girls and Colin, when he broke Christa's ceramic gas station and ruined her blouse–and I looked like Rocky Raccoon after the accident—still, we were here, together, and it was the last time we were a family, me and my girls.

Christa was my family, too; we had a sweet, quiet time, just the two of us on Christmas Day.

And Tom—he's lost a child, too, poor man. That low-class, demanding bitch he married is clearly no help. She couldn't even come into the living room to say hello to me. You'd think she imagined me stealing Tom from her, the way she resented me there—in her precious house, like I was an invader. Which, of course, to her, I was.

❖

Nothing prepares you for tragedy. An automatic survival mechanism kicks in that keeps you functioning on a very superficial level, just enough to physically get by; eating, sleeping, breathing. I remember answering the telephone on a Sunday afternoon years ago to the voice of my mother telling me that my father had suddenly passed away.

My first word was, "No," not in a hysterical or distraught way, just "no," that wasn't possible.

It was, though. And the survival mechanism kicked in; I got through it, and so did Mom. Tomorrow morning I'll borrow Christa's car and meet Tom at the casket company to choose one for Stephanie—our last joint decision as her parents. Hopefully, we'll focus on our daughter and not ourselves, even if Cheryl's there—which, by God, she better not be. Please, sweet Jesus, whether she's there or not, don't let it be a fight about money, and who is spending how much on what.

Once we've agreed on a casket, I'll swing by Katelyn's to pick up Roxy and we'll drive to the old neighborhood to see my mother. What to say? Just when we thought Stephanie was building a life...no doubt my mom will have ransacked the attic for some of Steph's pictures, and maybe some things she wants Colin to have now. That picture of Tom and me bringing Baby Stephie home from the hospital...

❖

For a split second upon awakening I don't remember that Stephanie is gone, but the grim reality of her death quickly overpowers my thoughts. What a strange phrase, *Stephanie is gone.* Gone where? Gone from this earth, from me and Colin—from the rest of us.

I need to call Nora. And I guess it falls to me to call Frank and leave a message. And of course, the U.S. Embassy in Dublin so we can streamline the paperwork. And Jeff. No matter what it was or wasn't, he and I were together for almost two years and he'd met my family, my Stephanie.

Now she's dead, alone on a slab.

Nor can my elderly mother, bent over from arthritis and the weight of living alone, who keeps crying and saying, "I can't believe it. How can this be? With her dying so far from us...last time I saw her, God love her, when we were all together..."

It was Thanksgiving 1996, the last time I thought anything made sense in what I saw as my world. Before finding Stephanie in bed with Frank. Before she moved out with Colin. Before having a concussion in a car accident. Before going out on New Year's Eve with the boy toy arm candy who dumped me. Before Stephanie announced her departure to Ireland. Before footsore Christa rocked me with her revelation and morphed into Hurricane Christa, at least for a time. Before Stephanie announced her wedding as a prematurely done deal, without us, because of yet another unplanned pregnancy, and no need to include or even see us, thank you very much.

But also before I turned my life around with my move, which has been good—what a joy, especially redecorating the casita. And my new job at the spa. Even weekends at the hospital haven't been bad, and the paychecks are certainly welcome now. More good things–Callie the cat, and the way she found me, which helped me get to know Trish. Meeting my other neighbor, Tristan. Christa and Roxy's visit and our Christmas Eve walk through Santa Fe and stopping by the cathedral before Midnight Mass. And seeing how Roxy's really growing up. The true rock of friendship Christa has been to me. Meeting Sophia and her painters group, and having my work on display in her shop. My garden, yet another bright spot—unless you count the Visiting Neighborhood Rattlesnake.

My mother's weepy voice pulls me back to the present with a topic I knew she'd bring up. "And Tom? He's paying for the casket and burial? And the luncheon? At a nice place, I hope. My friends will be there."

Roxy, who's toned down her ensemble for this visit, glances up from the chicken salad my mother's fixed for us. My Goth Lite Girl shoots my mother a look, like "Grandma, get over it," but stays mercifully silent.

"We chose the casket this morning, Mom. Tom and I."

"He did the right thing? It's decent-looking, isn't it? Not some cheap pine box?"

A sigh escapes me. "It's carved oak, Mom. It's fine."

She sniffs. "My Harry's was bronze, lined with ivory satin, and with a proper concrete vault and headstone. Tom's providing a vault and headstone, I hope?"

"No vault, but it's a very nice grave marker…pink granite. It's done. Tom'll arrange for the limo, the luncheon and the rest while I get…while I'm in Ireland."

"What, one limo—only one? We're all going to squash in with Tom and what's-her-name…Sharon? And no metal casket…"

"It's Cheryl, Mom, and it's a stretch limo."

Bless Roxy for changing the subject—she really has grown up!—when she asks her grandma for more chicken salad.

Before long, it's time to leave, but not before my mom ends our visit with, "I made an extra pineapple upside down cake for you, Roxy—your favorite. You bring it to that family you're with, whoever they are," she says, thrusting it into Roxy's arms before turning to me.

"It's up to you now, Ellie. You're the strong one. Go and bring our little Stephanie home to her family, and Colin, too…My only great-grandchild, poor motherless boy."

Once back in Christa's car, I'm so grateful Roxy's driving us. I can barely see through my tears, let alone focus on the road. Grieving is the most exhausting, bone-numbing work a body can do. Not to mention negotiating burial costs with your ex.

And I'm powerless. There's nothing to do in the face of this loss but 'let go…and let God.' But I have to wonder—what if I'd kept Colin with me when she left, the way she wanted? Would she still be alive today? I cry not only for Stephanie and her unborn child, but also for Colin who has lost his mother, whose life will never be the same. I cry for Roxy whose sister is gone, for my mother who will bury her granddaughter, for Stephanie's father, and for myself.

## *Christa*

The brogue of our flight attendant lulls me into almost forgetting the purpose of this flight. After a night and day of helping Elaine and Roxy, it would be a relief to close my eyes, drift off, and forget all this sadness and domestic anguish, but Laney turns to me, all teary again. "Should I have let Roxy come along? My God, Christa, the way she sobbed when we said good-bye, begging me not to leave, saying the plane might crash…Even though she's with Katelyn and Tom and my Mom are nearby, it broke my heart…"

I cover her hand with mine. "You did the right thing, even if Roxy doesn't understand that now. She's better there than at Tom's, and we have so much to do when we land. The bureaucratic forms and red tape, getting to the Casey's, collecting Colin…"

"We don't even know if he's been told. When I spoke to him two days ago, I said I was coming to get him, but he seemed to think his parents were still away on a trip, and was more interested in telling me about the cows and ponies. So they hadn't said anything about Stephanie at that point."

"They may be leaving it up to you."

"I'd rather he hears it from me." She pauses to blow her nose. "They're going through a lot. John visits with Liam in the hospital, Maggie's looking after Colin and the farm, and they're taking it day by day."

We fly in silence for a few minutes, and then she squeezes my hand. "I can't tell you how much it means to me to have you here with me through this." Her eyes well up again.

"I know you'd do the same for me. Remember when I told you I wanted to be a part of your life? I really meant it."

After the meal's been served, the movie's been shown, the lights dimmed, and blankets and pillows distributed. Elaine's quiet for so long I think she's asleep, so her voice startles me.

"I can't help seeing Stephanie as a little girl, looking so angelic with her curly red hair, but headstrong, even then. She was a handful to keep up with, and a tomboy, too. How many times I chased after her in the playground, brought her home grimy all over, and plopped her in the tub with her boats and things. I'd sing her songs while I bathed her, and she'd..." Elaine falters, caught up in her memories. "She'd sing with me. Then I'd get her in her pajamas, ready for dinnertime, and after we ate, Tom would kiss her good night—when he was home."

More tears, and again, there's nothing I can do; nothing anyone can do, but I put my hand on her arm for—what? Reassurance?

"She was never much of a cuddler, and didn't like being held, even for a minute. She would wriggle out of my arms and run around, so her bedtime routine was something else...I'd have to read two or sometimes three of her favorite stories before she'd settle down. She loved *Goodnight, Moon*, but Dr. Seuss was the best, so I'd usually finish up with *One Fish, Two Fish* or *The Cat in the Hat*. By the end of the last book, I was so pooped, *I* was the one nodding off."

How lovely to have mothered a child—something I'll probably never know. But how horrendous to have lost her.

Elaine continues, "My fiery little redhead. 'A fierce one,' my in-laws called her. It was almost a relief when Roxy came along—soft, cuddly Roxy. What a joy it was to sit and rock her, watching her doze off in my arms, even as a toddler."

And now she wears spiked dog collars and a half-dozen visible body piercings. No wonder Elaine's dwelling on the past, but it can't really help. How to bring her back to the present? Gently...but before I can say anything, Elaine yawns and abruptly shifts gears as she settles deeply into her seat and pulls the blanket up around her. "Maybe I'll just rest my eyes for a while."

"Good idea. Me too."

And the next thing we know, the flight attendant wakes us up for a bite to eat—some tea and biscuits with jam. As the plane approached the Irish coastline, it seemed impossible that the fields could be so mockingly green, heralding new life, when my dear friend's daughter is dead. Yet despite our shared grief, I can sense that an adventure, although a sad one, is about to take place.

❖

Shannon Airport is surrounded by farm fields in more shades of green than I knew existed. Once we collect our luggage and present our passports, we set out to find a driver who will take us to Listowel, a small town near the mouth of the Shannon River on the southwest coast, and Liam's family farm. Best not to try and navigate on the left side of the road by ourselves in a tiny car with a stick shift. Once word gets out that we're looking for a driver, we have a choice of several and accept the services of Kevin, a soft-spoken college student with reddish brown hair and beard. Our decision is based mostly on the appearance of the car rather than the person. Kevin's Fiat is the newest and hopefully the safest of the lot. Also, no liquor on his breath.

How anyone fits in these tiny cars without serious osteopathic consequences is beyond me—and I'm up front. Poor Laney is tilted sideways behind me, half sitting, half sprawling across the back seat with her carry-on resting on her legs. The way we're jostling, good thing the Fannie May candy from home is in a sturdy box in there, and wrapped in a sweater besides. Between our carry-ons, suitcases and purses—and we're only two people!—I know my legs will never again straighten and that Laney, poor thing, will have to walk with a cane after being extricated from the back seat with one of those "Jaws of Life" contraptions. At least neither of us is driving unfamiliar highways on the wrong side of the road, all scrunched up and barely able to draw a full breath. How could I, with my liver jammed up against my collarbone?

How can *he*? He's got to be over six feet tall, crammed into a mini-cockpit, shifting the gears, working the clutch, driving like a man possessed—we should have made him take a breathalyzer test—and talking nonstop about his cousin Sean who's also in Chicago, and do we know him? And did we happen to bring any White Castle hamburgers?

"Actually, we're here to claim my daughter's body," Elaine says, momentarily silencing him.

"Ah, I'm sorry," he says, "and me going' on and on. I'll shut me trap."

He does. Miles go by with no one speaking until Elaine startles us. "Look! A thatched roof cottage." But we soon see it's just an abandoned, caved-in ruin and are quiet again as we move further from the city into the countryside.

## *Elaine*

What can I say to Liam's parents? We have both suffered a loss, but of course, mine is greater because my daughter was taken from me. Their son is alive, and even though his condition is critical, they have the luxury of hope, which I do not.

I long to see Colin, to hold him in my arms and reassure him. He must sense something's wrong, or at least very different, with John, his grandfather, gone all day, day after day.

I have to move ahead: claim Stephanie, collect Colin with as many of his favorite things as we can manage, and return to the United States. Without delay.

Even this two-hour drive to the farm strikes me as precious time lost, though I know we'll be here a few days at least. Still the sooner I'm on the plane with Colin next to me and Christa, and Stephanie…Steph in the cargo hold…with Tom and Roxy meeting us in Chicago…the sooner the better.

Try to stay in the here and now…looking out the window, I'm struck by the color, not just green, but pasturelands of a resonating emerald green with paler pastures further away in the foothills and some dark green evergreens not far from the road. Sheep and lambs graze in grasslands enclosed by stone fences dividing the land, their woolly whiteness a contrast to the lush texture of the rolling hills.

Black-and-white Holsteins catch my eye as we turn onto the country lane lined with jagged, four-foot tall rock walls to keep the dairy stock from wandering into the road. The beauty of this fertile countryside seems idyllic, but it brings me no pleasure; instead, fresh tears well up in my eyes as I'm reminded again of my mission here: claiming the body of my Stephanie. Sheep and cows have new babies every year, so who knows how many these mothers have over a lifetime? I've only had two, and now my firstborn is gone.

We turn from a single lane road onto a narrower lane, wide enough for only one car and badly rutted. Kevin slows to a crawl to avoid jarring our teeth out of our heads. When we reach the top of a hill the entire farm compound is spread out before us: the gray clapboard house in need of a coat of paint, and the new white barn made from corrugated sheet metal. Black and white cows dot the expansive pasture that ends at the horizon.

We're pulling up to the house and Christa and I are fumbling for our purses to pay Kevin when a large, red dog bounds at us, barking. The door opens and a woman in a matronly housedress comes out as she's wiping her hands on the white apron around her ample waist. Her tight gray curls surround a grim, work-worn face as she yells to the dog to "Shut up" and straightens to look more closely at us, her lips compressed to a thin line. She looks nothing like a warm, nurturing woman, let alone the country grandma I'd imagined.

"Mrs. Casey," Christa murmurs, more to herself than to me. "Hmmmm."

We're out of the car before Kevin can come round and open our doors. Maggie does not approach, so I take the lead, doing 'gracious visitor from America bearing gifts.'

"Mrs. Casey?"

No response, so I do 'Plucky Fuzzy Wuzzy forging ahead,' and introduce myself. "I'm Stephanie's mother, Elaine McElroy, and this is Christa Thompson, my good friend from Chicago."

The dog approaches us, tail wagging wildly. The gray-haired woman regards us stolidly, mutely, taking in our leather shoes and bags, our khaki slacks (thank God Christa's not in cargo pants!) and Polo shirts, two little privileged American peas in a pod. No one's talking here, so I extend my hand, saying an awkward "Hello," which Christa echoes.

The woman extends her cold, fleshy hand to me, then Christa.

"You've had a long trip. Come in. I'll make the tea." She turns to the dog before leading us into the house. "Russell, away with ya now. Go back to the barn."

Kevin brings our luggage into the kitchen, whose dominant feature is a black pot-bellied stove with a tarnished teakettle on its flat top.

Christa pays him with the Irish money we purchased at the airport, and he is on his way with assurances that he'll stay the night in town and come back for us early in the morning for our trip to the Embassy in Dublin. Then he offers condolences again.

"Yes, I'm so sorry for your loss, as well," the woman I take to be Mrs. Casey manages.

"This is...for you," I say, fumbling in my carry-on and thrusting the two-pound box of Fannie May Hostess Mints at her. "Thank you for having us."

"Hmmph." She says. "I'm diabetic, as is John."

Christa glances at me, eyebrows raised.

"But Father O'Malley at St. Brigid's got a birthday coming up. He'll be saying a Mass for my poor Liam's departed wife later this month," she says. The windows let in plenty of late spring sunshine, but I feel a chill in this kitchen.

"Pray God he'll be conscious and up and around, able to attend it. It'll be his farewell to her..."

Her words are interrupted by a rap on the kitchen door. She glances out the window before opening it to a tall man in muddy boots. "Pardon, Missus, but it's part of your North pasture fence needs mending...Three posts...they must've been blown down in last night's wind, but I didn't catch it 'til just now." The brown-haired man looks down, clearly discomforted. "It's six head I count gone missing...'Til we gather 'em up secure again, I did a temporary fix of the fence, I did, but it'll need..."

"It'll need someone with half a brain, is what it'll need," Maggie yells. "You couldn't figure out to check it after last's night wind before you went turnin' out the cows, you eejit?" Her face has grown alarmingly red. With her overweight and diabetes... "Six head gone...six outta forty, and all ya can do is stand here like a gack, James, when you ought to be calling the Kennedys and the Burkes and findin' if our six are over there." She takes a threatening step toward him, and her color's gone quickly to purple. But if I go over to try to calm her, she just might take a swing at me. I exchange a quick look with Christa.

As if seeing that with eyes in the back of her head, she turns to us with a venomous glance before whirling again on James. "And look what you're making me do, in front of me guests, all the way from Chicago. Why are ya standin' there, you're crippled? Ya need me ta hold your tremblin' hand when ya dial, fool?"

His hands are indeed trembling, and he's gone as pale as she has purple. Jesus, Mary and Joseph, we've stumbled into the Bedlam Asylum with a crazy woman in charge…and where is Colin in all this? What's she done with him?

"Go on, call them, then, and get Paddy to help once you find our six. Just pray they haven't wound up on the road, and get your no-good, skinny arse outta me kitchen now before I…"

The poor man dashes back out as she collapses into a kitchen chair, excoriating James and the rest of the "eejit" hired men working the farm. "Apes and retards I'm dealin' with, I am, with John gone to hospital day after day and only me here to run things. Me nerves, me nerves."

*Her nerves indeed. What's become of Colin? Where is he?*

"I'll…get the kettle," Christa offers. "You just stay there, Mrs. Casey." *Where we can keep an eye on you.*

"Sometimes I worry they'll be takin' me off to Limerick's Asylum for Lunatics and Idiots, this work…this stress is makin' me so crazy."

Christa has a questioning look written all over her weary face. Is Maggie serious or is this some kind of cultural humor that doesn't translate? I offer a small, nervous laugh and, exhausted, sit down on the nearest kitchen chair, scanning around for closed doors, a hallway leading to the other side of the house, anything to get the lay of the land and where Colin might be. Christa's spied a box of tea on the counter and a chipped teapot with a metal tea ball hooked onto its handle.

"What is it you do in Chicago?" Maggie inquires.

"I'm a therapist in private practice."

"We deal with our own problems, here, or we ask our priest."

So that works out well — hence the need for that Asylum for Lunatics and Idiots. Anyone else might be intimidated, but not Christa, who turns around from her tasks with cups, saucers and spoons and faces her. "I counsel people with a wide range of problems, and all ages. Children, too."

"Are you married?" Maggie asks bluntly.

"No, and I don't have any children of my own. That's possibly why I enjoy working with them so much."

"What about you, Elaine, you're a nurse?"

"A registered nurse, a school nurse for many years. I recently moved to Santa Fe, New Mexico. That's in our Southwest."

"I know where it is." She was a tough nut to crack. "What about Stephanie's father? Where is he?"

"We were divorced many years ago." *God, I am so tired. How much sleep did I get on the plane? A couple of hours?*

"Naturally," this Woman from Hades sniffs, condescension emanating from her in the face of my American heathenism.

Christa busies herself preparing the tea, humming tunelessly, which I've never heard her do. Probably helps her stay focused under stress. Speaking of stress, I'm woozy from lack of food—when was the last time we ate, after all? Sometime early this morning on the plane...some kind of biscuits. My stomach is twisting from hunger, making noises Christa must hear from the other side of the room. She must be half faint from hunger herself. Jeez, there goes my stomach again, louder this time. I'd love to ask for the candy back, but she'd probably hit me with the box. How would I explain a black eye back in Chicago at Stephanie's wake?—"I was attacked with a box of Fannie May by a crazed Irishwoman"?

"Mrs. Casey, it's been hours since we ate on the plane, and I'm wondering if you might have some crackers, please..."

"Jaysus, what am I doin' here? I baked a nice soda bread over there in the breadbox, with fresh butter there on the plate by the teapot. Me nerves must be makin' me stupid."

"You just sit, and I'll take care of it," Christa says, hastening to the breadbox and looking relieved. She places the round loaf on a platter in the center of the old wooden table with knife, cups, plates, spoons and the biggest mound of butter I've ever seen sitting on a saucer. I breathe a silent prayer of thanks to whatever saint is in charge of teatime—the Irish must have one—and lay into the delicious bread and butter, the sweetest thing I've ever tasted. Christa does the same, practically smacking her lips and thanking our hostess between gulps of tea.

Maggie remains unsmiling at our obvious pleasure with her excellent bread. She opens the built-in drawer under the table top in front of her and removes a bottle of whiskey. "Ah, yes. It'll settle me nerves."

Whiskey and soda bread for an overweight diabetic? Whoa!

# *Christa*

This is the best Irish soda bread and butter I have ever had, and a good thing, too. Poor Laney looked like she was going to drop and I would've been right behind her—as much from the Maggie Drama as from hunger. Mrs. Casey is *so* stressed to the breaking point—she'll be in the hospital herself if she doesn't get it together. It's true she's got a lot to face, and not just having her son injured and hours away—she's trying to keep the house and the farm going while John's with Liam. Guess she's not getting much support from her neighbors and friends. And what about this Father O'Malley at St. Brigid's? Doesn't he stop in to see how she's holding up? Who's to say he isn't after all, but it's clear Maggie could use some help, big-time, and in a hurry. Right now that seems to be us.

Add to that taking care of Colin, who's a full-time job in himself, and you've got the Poster Girl of Ireland waiting to stroke out. And where *is* Colin?

"…Was runnin' around so excited at seein' yourselves that he wore himself out and could barely stay awake over lunch. He's havin' a wee nap for a while." Maggie pauses, and I wonder if she has been reading my mind. "A relief to me, God knows," she says.

Guess he hasn't changed much.

"How is Liam doing?" I ask.

"A coma. And his face, his handsome face, all cut up and bruised. Broken arm and a fractured spine. They say he may never have the use of his legs, but we won't know for sure until he wakes. John's with him. They transferred our Liam from Dublin. Same city where your Stephanie girl's in the morgue. Thrown from the car, she was."

Elaine looks stricken.

"It must be horrible for you…" I say. Maggie sighs deeply, recaps the whiskey and replaces the bottle in the kitchen drawer.

"Me only child," she says. "The Good Lord only gave us the one, and no other for insurance." She looks around at the sink free of dishes, at the damp tea towels hanging neatly on the wooden rack by the stove, and through the window to gaze at the vegetable garden outside. "Could use the help, though I try to keep things up. And I pray the rosary every night that Liam will be whole again, and can be a proper father to Colin."

I suck in a shallow breath of air as I turn to face Elaine. The fear in her eyes scares me as much as Maggie's words. *Doesn't she know why we're here?*

"Can I see him—Colin?" Elaine sounds like a kindergartener asking to use the bathroom. She shouldn't have to ask permission to see her own grandchild. He lived under her roof almost two years, after all. Still, we are guests in her house and country.

"You go peek in on the wee lad. He's the image of his da, he is." She motions with her chin to the closed door off the hallway.

"And does he...know?" I'm almost whispering.

She softens her voice, wiping her hands on her apron. "All he knows is...I told him his ma's gone visiting the angels. His da's away sick and'll be back soon."

Elaine's chin quivers as though she'll cry any minute. No time to waste; let's just get going down the hall to his room.

## *Elaine*

My insides are shaking and tears dribble from my eyes. There's no way I'm prepared to lose my grandson as well as my daughter to these people. I want to set things straight right away, and Christa senses my urgency. As we set off down the hall to the bedroom, Christa takes my arm and whispers, "Wait, don't say anything yet."

On a small table outside the bedroom door stands a framed photo of Liam, Stephanie, and Colin, propped against a vase of wildflowers, freshly picked. The three are sun-kissed and smiling at each other. The resemblance between Colin and Liam *is* striking. The set of their eyes and the bridge of their noses brand them as father and son. My beautiful girl, my Stephanie, is in the middle, embracing them both. I want to snatch the picture and hold it to my heart.

Christa slowly opens the bedroom door and motions for me to look in at the sleeping child. I long to gather him in my arms. Instead, I lean over and brush his forehead with my lips, light as a hummingbird. He slowly opens his eyes and stares at me, then blinks. "Grandma?" he screams, sitting up and hugging me tightly. I sit on the edge of the bed and return the hug. The tears flow freely now. He isn't a chubby toddler anymore; he's a little boy with unruly locks of reddish brown hair falling into his sleepy green eyes—his mother's eyes. "Grandma?"

Christa quietly leaves, closing the bedroom door.

"I'm so happy to see you, I missed you so much," I manage.

"Dora...I'll show you my Dora." He pauses, clearly full of news, with more to come as he jumps from his narrow bed.

*Is this a friend of his from another farm?* "Dora?"

"Ya, from Grandpa. She's mine," he exclaims with delight.

*What could this Dora be?* "Tell me."

"She's a bee-u-tee. Grandpa said so."

"I can't wait to see her." *There I go, doing 'city grandmother from America.'*

"But she gotta cut."

"Oooh. A bad one?" *Nurse Fuzzy Wuzzy can have that bound up in no time.*

He nods decisively. "On her leg. Her mother licked it, but Grandpa washed it anyway. Grandma said he had to." His eyes darken with something that looks like concern...confusion, maybe? "But you're Grandma, too."

Yes. But if I say Maggie is "Big Grandma" and I'm "Little Grandma," then that puts me a rung down. Same thing with "Grandma Number One and Two"—there can only be one Number One.

"Do you know *The City Mouse and the Country Mouse*?" His blank stare tells me he doesn't.

"I'm your first grandma..."

"Colin!" Maggie's voice bellows as she blows into the room. Was she listening at the door?

Think fast, Grandma Einstein. "I'm your Grandma... Grandma Ellie. Can you say that?"

"Well, of course he can. He's no eejit, ya know, with him havin' his dad's brains and all."

"Of course you can, Colin." *I'd kill her right here, right now, with my bare hands if it wouldn't be such a trauma for the child.*

"Colin, you remember me. I'm Christa. Let's see Dora, OK?" Her voice sounds from the doorway. "You and me and your Grandma Ellie. You'll show us."

"I'll start the roast," Maggie says, sorely put upon. "And peel the spuds. There's so much to do. Another load of Colin's wash, too." She punctuates her displeasure with a sigh.

I am in no mood to offer assistance. For all I care, she can slaughter, skin and butcher whatever dead animal she'll serve us. After all, I had to beg for a goddamn cracker. Not to mention stand for her insults. His dad's brains, indeed. Wasn't so brainy of him to knock up my daughter and virtually ignore their child for over a year—you want to talk brains, Big Maggie? I do my 'sweet but condescending smile' and hustle Colin out of the room.

"We'll get out of your way, then."

❖

Dora turns out to be his calf, only a couple of weeks old. She trots around her stall, sunlit from the large windows admitting the afternoon sun, while her mother, a huge black and white creature, spends her time chewing grass in the pasture with other equally large bovines.

James accompanies us, a necessity, he reminds us, since calves are strong and can butt their heads against people as much as other cows, and could easily knock Colin over. Through my nurse's eyes it appears that he rigs a sort of IV feeding station that he hangs from a hook on a post. It's a pail with a large nipple at its bottom, and as he sets it up, Dora nuzzles and head-butts him impatiently, even throwing in a couple of bucks for good measure; once it's ready, she sucks eagerly at the nipple–her cow version of Meals on Wheels, apparently. She also gets finely ground meal. A sack of something called "Calf Manna" leans outside the pen, and James adds a couple of handfuls to the oat-corn mix.

"Keeps weight on 'em, Missus," he says, "while they're bein' weaned and all." Dora bawls her appreciation at this feast, and goes at it happily as her proud owner, my little Colin, looks on— in between dashing around the open space in the center of the barn and screaming her name.

I gather from his babblings that he got her from John just a few days ago. Clearly, she's a great distraction for him, and my heart swells with gratitude for this man I haven't even met.

## Christa

John's grim face is deeply-lined and straight out of "American Gothic," complete with a collarless shirt and dark jacket, but minus the bib overalls.

"Grandpa, look," Colin shouts. "My first grandma's here to see Dora." A pained look crosses the man's tired face.

"I'm Christa, Elaine's friend from Chicago." I extend my hand, which he takes in his—huge, bony and calloused from years of work. "Thank you for having us."

"I'm John Casey, and the pleasure's mine." He shakes hands with Elaine. "You're here for your daughter, and I'm so sorry for your loss."

Laney looks down at Colin, apparently satisfied that none of that registered with him. "Yes. Thank you, Mr. Casey," she says, and John manages a thin smile. "It's John. And you've met the missus."

*Have we ever.*

"How's your son doing, John?"

His face sags with worry and fatigue. "The same. About the same."

"Come on, Grandma, I want to show you the ponies, and Nettie the cat. She's the nice one, and she catches mice," Colin says, taking my hand and leading me out of the barn. He clomps ahead wearing his boots—his "Wellies," he calls them. Both ponies are dirty, white, and look as though they'd benefit from the Atkins Diet and some serious time on a treadmill at the pony health club, but what do I know? They barely pause in their grazing, then resume eating grass. Rosie is the mother of Marigold, John tells us, and both are Connemara ponies.

"Let me ride, Grandpa, so I can show...her"—he momentarily loses Elaine's name, so resorts to gesturing in her direction—"Her! Grandma Lee."

"Tomorrow, Colin." He gives me a sidelong glance. Your grandmother and her...friend...they'll be wantin' to wash up and have a bit of a rest before we eat. And I've got to help James with those strays, then see to the fence. You stay out of your grandmother's way—your Grandma Maggie, I mean. She needs to get things done in the kitchen."

And then he turns, taking the path to the house in long, ground-covering strides.

Scrambling after him is no small task on the rutted pathway, and I'm short of breath by the time we kick off our shoes at the back door. Just as well—Elaine's picked up a wad of cow manure. The kitchen is warm and steamy from simmering pots on the stove, and the smell of cabbage cooking reminds me of how little I've eaten all day. Dinner can't come soon enough, but first a shower, clean clothes and maybe a nap.

"John took your things up to your room," Maggie calls out, not turning around as she stirs something in one of the large pots.

Wherever that is. Guess we'll know when we find our bags. Which we do in the small dormer bedroom upstairs. The old-fashioned double bed has a white spread with a couple of spare blankets folded at the foot. Next to it is a washstand and basin with two washcloths and hand towels hanging from a wooden rod. A pitcher with steaming water and a small bar of soap on a saucer complete our bathing facilities—so much for that hot shower I'd wanted. Not to mention hot coffee. Don't dare ask if the old bat has any. She'd probably have a seizure.

"Coffee, Elaine, and a hot shower–can't come soon enough. Now we eat, get Steph and Colin and get the hell outta Dodge."

"What's Maggie thinking? Multiple injuries and a fractured spine—it doesn't sound good, but she's hoping he'll walk again?" Elaine stops to take a deep breath. "Enough. Now we figure out a plan." She speaks softly, but rapidly. Where she gets this energy after a trans-Atlantic flight, I'll never know. Must be pure adrenaline. "Tomorrow we go the morgue—Number One. Two, get our return plane tickets, and Colin's, too." Elaine is in Super-Fast-Track Mode, pacing back and forth in front of the small window overlooking the pastureland, opposite the door. In case Maggie is listening on the other side?

"Then we go to the Embassy, sign off on the paper work for Stephanie's return to the States and get her death report. I have Colin's birth certificate, and a copy of Stephanie's and my own, to show I'm his maternal grandmother—so hopefully there's no problem getting him back to America. They require Colin in person for this, or I'd never drag him with us on a four-hour drive. He entered the country on Stephanie's passport."

"There shouldn't be trouble, right?"

"He's a U.S. citizen and the son of a citizen. But you never know what the Caseys will try…Hate to say it, but with any luck, another section of the fence will blow down and who knows how many cows will get out. That would keep them busy—and before you know it…"

"We're outta here," I finish for her, buoyed up by a new wave of energy.

❖

"Where's Ma and Da?"

Maggie almost drops the plate of food she's handing to John. "Eat your meat, Colin," he says, cutting off this train of inquiry.

"And chew and swallow before talking," she adds.

Which is all we can do, too, waiting for John or Maggie to deal with the subject. And why are we waiting for them to take a lead they clearly don't want to assume? Elaine looks tight and pinched as she eats. The food is delicious, though, and I make a point of complimenting Maggie on her roast beef and potatoes, cabbage and carrots, grown in her garden, a fact pointed out by John.

"Colin's dyin' to help in the vegetable patch, but would likely be more of a hindrance," he says, smiling at his grandson, who's busy pushing the carrots around his plate. "Best he can do is feed Russell."

"He'll soon be big enough to be of some real help, and God knows, we need it," Maggie says.

If ever there was an opening to discuss Colin...now's the time, Laney. Sure enough, she jumps in.

"Tomorrow we'll need to be in Dublin. At the American Embassy to make the...final arrangements...for my daughter's transport. And we have to arrange our return flight. We bought open tickets."

"We were thinkin' of havin' the service in a week," Maggie announces. "Surely you're not taking her back before then?"

"Actually, we are. Her father and sister and her grandmother are...making arrangements...in Chicago." The two women glare at each other. "You can still have a Mass if you wish. Our family is in America."

Maggie clamps her mouth shut and looks like she's going to throttle Elaine, but says nothing.

"We'll be taking Colin with us tomorrow into Dublin. Kevin's driving us. It's all arranged. You've been so kind in helping us, and we wouldn't want to put you out more than we have."

"What do you mean, you're taking the boy?"

"Where, Grandma?"

"Home to America, sweetheart. We'll need to get the papers in order tomorrow in the city. Then we're taking you on an airplane ride in a day or so."

"To see ma and da?"

"That's enough, Colin," John interrupts.

"When are they comin' back?" His voice verges on a whine.

"Eat your carrots, Colin." Maggie warns him, and it's all I can do to keep from jumping across the table and slamming her with the bowl of her own damned carrots.

"You come with Grandma Ellie," Elaine says, rising and taking his hand, throwing a "Please excuse us," over her shoulder to a Maggie so stunned she just sits in silence, her color rising. John half moves from his seat, but to my own surprise, I place a restraining hand on his shoulder. "No," I say. "He has to know. She was his mother and Elaine's daughter."

## Elaine

From inside Colin's room I hear the raised voices of Maggie and John, somewhat muffled when Christa comes in and closes the door behind her. Still, Maggie's explosions of "Jaysus Christ" and "bloody bitches" come through clearly, with John's baritone rumblings forming a chorus in the background.

Christa settles uneasily on the bed and the big old rocker has plenty of room for me with Colin on my lap, so I take a moment to rock back and forth before saying the words that must be said.

"Your mother..."

"Is with the angels, Grandma Maggie said," he interrupts.

"Yes, she's with the angels, Col, up in heaven. She's not...coming back."

He half turns to face me. "Da too?"

I hug him to me harder. "No, your dad's not in heaven. He's hurt. He was in a car accident...a crash."

"Where is he?"

"In the hospital. Grandpa visits him there."

"Why can't I?" He turns to face me fully, and my heart breaks at his clear, innocent eyes.

"Oh, sweetie, they don't allow children there."

Christa interjects. "But you could make a picture for him, and Grandpa could give it to him. Your dad'll know it's from you."

"He's coming back?" His eyes are wide open with concern.

"I hope so, Colin. I hope he gets better and comes back."

"Now! I want Daddy now!" His face reddens as the first wail sounds and he stiffens in my arms.

Oh, God, did I say too much? Suggest too much uncertainty? But Christa says it's best to be honest and direct.

"I know you do, but that can't happen now," Christa says. "He's hurt—really bad."

"No, he's not! I want him *now!*" I'm amazed at this boy's strength as he struggles, butting his head against my chest.

"Listen to me, Col. Christa's right. Your daddy has to get better before you can see him."

He struggles in my lap to get down. "Your da, Colin. He was in a car accident with your mom."

He's made a connection and turns to me. "My Hot Wheels get in crashes." He mimes this, bringing his two fists together, then "Bang!"

Christa says, "Your dad's car was wrecked in a crash. And your dad was hurt, too."

"I'll take care of you," I tell him. "It'll be all right."

He must sense something in my tone because he suddenly turns away from me and stiffens. "Ma?"

"Oh, honey…"

Now he seems to know for sure that something's bad, and he's thrashing around trying to free himself from this terrible woman with even more terrible news.

I grasp him to me. "Your mommy's dead, Colin. I'm so, so sorry."

"Ma! Mommy!"

I hear a scraping of chairs in the nearby kitchen, and brace myself for Maggie and John's appearance. Sure enough, they're in the doorway in a moment, Maggie's face contorted with rage. "For the love of God, leave the child alone." John places a hand on her shoulder as Colin continues wailing. "Grandpa! I want me Ma! And Da."

John and Maggie are silent. Without carrots for Colin to eat, what can they say?

Christa rises, half inclining her head toward the Caseys, but keeping an eye on Colin. "It's better for him to know it now, as fully as he can understand. It's difficult and frightening at first—for all of us—but far more compassionate overall." Her low-voiced steadiness, her conviction, a self-assurance I have never before heard in her, has quieted the room. Even Colin is still. She pauses, letting her words sink in. "We can help—together. Or we can prolong his uncertainty and pain."

I'm amazed at the professional confidence in Christa's tone. It compels me to look up and meet her gaze wordlessly, as do the Caseys. Is this what they teach in counseling school?

She turns to face Colin fully. "Let's get to work on that picture for your daddy. I know he'll like it." Turning toward the dresser by his bed, she asks in a conversational tone, "Where are your crayons and paper?"

Now I let him get down and watch as he struggles to open the bottom drawer and takes out a box of crayons, then a letter-sized pad of drawing paper. Maggie exhales sharply. We are, after all, invaders in her territory.

❖

John's sitting and holding Colin to him, who's now busy with paper and crayons. Maggie's seated next to them at the kitchen table, cleared now except for a bottle of whiskey and glasses. She drains her drink, shaking her head at us and glowering.

We sit across from Maggie.

"Now ye did it," she snarls. "Are ye happy now? Sure he's all confused. Pair of meddlin' bit…"

"Maggie!" John intercedes. "He'd have found out sooner or later. What's done is done." He pours drinks all around and lifts his glass, "May God be merciful."

## *Christa*

**M**e, too, Grandpa," Colin says, and when Elaine shakes her head, the boy appeals to Maggie with a whine. "You know you let me." Does she think that's ministering to Colin in some helpful way?

She must, because she urges, "Aye, John, give 'em a wee sip. It'll settle 'im, and what can it hurt?" Hmm. Must be a long waiting list for that lunatics' and idiots' asylum.

He's reaching for his glass, presumably to give the boy some whiskey when Elaine rises. "No, John, please. It isn't good for a child."

"And what makes you Miss Know-it-All?" Maggie challenges.

John pauses as Colin chimes in, "Yes, Grandpa, yes!"

"No, John." Laney turns to Maggie. "I'm a nurse. I know whiskey's bad for little kids—all children, in fact."

Maggie turns shrill and mocking. "Ooo-oh, Miss High Falutin' here, telling us what to do, is she?"

"I will not stand here and allow you to give alcohol to a three-year-old."

She waves this away and downs her glass in a gulp, as if for emphasis. "Aaa-ah, I gave a nip to me Liam from time to time, and it was Mother's Milk to 'im."

I can't help but reflect on how well *that* turned out—for Liam *and* Stephanie.

All eyes turn to John. Maggie thrusts her empty glass toward him demanding a refill. For a long moment he does not move. Finally, he says, "Colin, I've a wee bit of a chocolate bar for you in me coat pocket," smoothing things over, at least for now. "Let me go get that for ye." He hands Colin over to Elaine as Maggie's face darkens and he refills her glass.

She's sipping her current drink, and Colin's eagerly devouring his candy, all artwork forgotten, and Elaine's gone pale with what—anger? Exhaustion?—when Maggie starts in again. "As God is me witness, don't think you're takin' the wee one to America." The old woman's face is blotched with resentment, and nothing in her posture suggests flexibility.

"Take me where, Grandma? Am I leavin' too?"

"Maggie, you don't understand," Elaine says. "Next to Stephanie, I'm the closest thing to a mother that Colin's had. I practically raised him, for God's sake," she says, and I can see she's trying not to sound defensive and shrill and barely succeeding.

"Surely. *you* don't understand. He is Liam's son and we intend to raise him until Liam is able. He loves it here. What better place to raise a young boy than on a farm," she says adamantly. She sighs deeply, then passes her glass to John for a refill. He looks questioningly at Elaine, then me, but we've barely touched ours, so shake our heads.

He winces as he reaches for the bottle. "It's me back," he explains. "Too many years of farmin'. Can't do it alone. Haven't for years.

"With the stock needin' feedin' and milkin' twice a day, and keepin' the stalls clean and the fences in good repair, it never ends. And in calvin' season, it's even…" He breaks off, pouring her a generous drink and shaking his head as he addresses his next statement to us. "For years Maggie's been wantin' to visit her sister in The States, but as it is, we can't leave, even with the hired help."

"Aye, and they're all of 'em eejits, everyone of them we've brought on."

"Maggie, girl, we need them. Don't be such a bloody…" He exhales sharply, perhaps because he's in the company of two ladies from America. "…And it's harder than ever with me visitin' Liam. We need these fellows to keep everything going, with you seein' to things, girl, having to run the farm alone on top of runnin' the house and doin' the laundry and cleanin'…" He pauses for a breath. "Not to mention all ye do in the kitchen, and add to that, we've the boy…" We all turn our attention to Colin, who by now is dozing on Elaine's lap. "As it is," he continues, turning to us, "we pay one of the men a bit more so he can tend the garden every other day. It's been hard enough for her to do it when she didn't have to look after Colin, with her arthritis you know."

Maggie snorts derisively.

"Now, Mags," he cautions. "You've had ye hands full, you have, seein' to things by yourself, and with Colin and all…the farm's a full-time job in itself, and with the boy here on top of it all…it's too much for a woman of your years. He'll come back, and maybe by that time, so will Liam, God willin'. Less work and worry would do ye good for a while." She rises, turning on more lights in the old kitchen.

Slumping back in her chair, she whispers, "Sure, I'm tired, Johnny…and not seein' Liam…is breakin' me heart."

"With Colin in Elaine's safekeepin' you could come to the hospital with me every other day or so…see him…hearin' his ma's voice talkin' to him could only do our boy good."

This man, with his farm-worn hands and bent body, his lined face and troubled eyes, speaks from his heart, and better for Maggie to hear it from him than anyone else.

Always prepared it seems, I hand a few tissues to the exhausted old woman, who weeps silently.

## *Elaine*

I tuck Colin into his bed without waking him, making sure his favorite stuffed bear is next to him as John and Maggie finish cleaning up the kitchen and go to bed. Christa's waiting for me upstairs. So much has happened this day, much of it heartbreaking.

When people talk about broken hearts, it's true. I can feel mine go into pieces inside me. The pain of my loss aches within, matched by the sharp hurt of helplessness I feel when I gaze outside myself at this sweet child, this green-eyed boy who's the image of my green-eyed girl, his mother. Even without remembering, he'll never forget this day; the day his world went from the sureness of knowing his mom and dad were there for him, would always be there for him…not. Not ever again.

Angels…I wish they'd help me tell him…I wish they'd bring her back to both of us, God help me, God help us all. But they don't. And He doesn't; stone-deaf all of them.

❖

Colin's cries jerk me from sleep. "Mommy! Ma! I want Mommy!" Feet pound down the hallway from Maggie's room beneath us, and I hear her say, "Colin, love. Grandma's coming."

Christa stirs next to me as he calls out again. "Do you want to go to him?" she says groggily. "I can go with you."

"Maggie's with him and…" I hear a heavier tread on the worn floorboards. "John, too."

"He's used to them. Maybe let it be, Laney."

Hard to do with his wails echoing throughout the house and everything in me wanting to go to him and hold him.

"Oh, Sweet Jaysus, boy," I hear Maggie say before she breaks into sobs herself. I can imagine her reaching out to him in pain, as much for her own son as for the loss of her grandson, and my heart goes out to this strong, stoic woman now reduced to tears and moans.

"Here, now, give him here to me, and mind ye back, girl," John says as the old floor creaks.

Colin says, "Grandpa, me ma. I want me ma. Get her for me, Grandpa."

He sobs again, but more softly. I'm halfway out of the bed when Christa's hand stops me. "No," she says. "Let them have this moment."

❖

We are so tired we fall right back to sleep. After rising at daybreak we're on half-speed, it seems, but after our baths, the three of us—Christa, Colin and I—are dressed and ready for the day ahead, Colin firmly gripping his bear.

Maggie has made the customary Irish breakfast, sometimes called 'heart attack on a plate,' consisting of sausages, eggs, freshly baked scones with butter, and tea with fresh cream. If I ate this way on a regular basis, I would soon be the size of one of John's cows. The dark circles beneath Maggie's eyes match his as they both stare straight ahead in silence. My God, these two diabetics eat mounds of potatoes and bread and scones and drink whiskey besides! What are they thinking?

Christa speaks quietly to Colin, who seems to have forgotten the previous night's tragic scene, as he tells her about riding Rosie, and that he's going to show us. She glances at John, who nods, apparently remembering his promise.

"Maybe when we get back from the city, Colin," she says. "You'll like it there. There's lots of cars and buses, and when we're back here, you can change into your play clothes and show us then. I'll bet it's fun to ride her."

He nods vigorously. "James taught me." He finishes his eggs and sausage as Maggie prepares roast beef sandwiches from last night's dinner, and methodically wraps them in wax paper.

She prepares enough food for a small army, and fills a dented Thermos with hot tea. She reaches for something high in the cupboard, then stops, wincing. "Ah, my arthritis is acting up again." She seems ancient to me with her dowdy cotton housedress and gray frizzy hair, although there's probably not more than ten years difference in our ages. Something tells me to take that photo of Liam, Stephanie and Colin to Dublin for photocopying and possible presentation to the Embassy, so I slip into the hallway for the picture and hide it in my tote.

As we are getting ready to leave, Colin brings some crayons and construction paper from his room. "Grandma Ellie, help me make a picture of Rosie for my da."

"I'll see him today," I say in response to Maggie's questioning gaze, printing Colin's name in capital letters and he copies it as best he can. The result is jagged intersecting black and red lines applied with undue pressure by his tightly clenched fist.

Kevin appears at the back door. Has it really been just a day earlier when we said good-bye to him? Surely a week has passed, though it's only been overnight. Before getting up to help clear the table, (busily doing 'Grateteful Guest from America' with Christa) I silently say the Serenity Prayer: *God grant me the serenity to accept the things I cannot change, courage to change the things I can, and wisdom to know the difference.* Our actions today will change everyone's lives.

❖

Maggie stands at the door waving good-bye, an old shawl pulled across her shoulders in the cool early morning mist. As the little car pulls away, I turn to wave, my heart aching for both of us.

Kevin and Christa are in the front. After securing Colin's car seat, I make it clear we won't leave until he is strapped in, which he disputes, of course, but finally I prevail, sit back and we're off, Colin clutching Bear. Given the bumpy road and the grinding gears, we can't really speak to each other, so I contemplate the lush Irish countryside while Colin complains. In my carry-on are supplies I might need: head-phones and portable CD player for long waits should Colin take a nap, a book, and the small spiral notebook that serves as my diary away from my laptop. And the photo. For Colin there's a few Hot Wheels, picture books and crayons with paper. Christa's holds the Lunch for An Army, plus a couple of small trucks.

Irish country roads are not at all like the smooth asphalt conduits we are accustomed to in the United States; the quality varies from county to county, depending on the area's wealth. Eventually I can tell when we are leaving one county and entering another by either the dramatic improvement or disintegration of the roads. It is not a fluid system that flows seamlessly, and I'm glad that I am not the one behind the wheel. We stop several times as sheep are herded across the road, and Kevin exchanges pleasantries with the farmers. The farmers are not in a hurry, but I am, anxious for this four-hour drive to end.

Christa and I take Colin with us to "the loo" in the building that houses the morgue, and then I present ID and deal with numerous forms. A bookish-looking attendant with horn-rimmed glasses and a coffee-stained lab coat leads me into a cold, sterile room smelling of disinfectant and death. Stainless steel lockers line the walls. My imagination plays cruel tricks on me...Is my Stephanie disfigured? Will I have to see the Y-shaped incision made during her autopsy? I fear the worst. Christa's just outside, keeping Colin busy with books and toys as Kevin waits for us, but I wish she were here with me. Still, knowing she is in the building helps as I take the longest walk of my life.

I follow the attendant to a stainless steel locker. After checking numbers and shuffling papers, he lifts the metal handle and opens the heavy door of the refrigerated compartment. As he rolls out the slab and and partially unzips the body bag, a chill seeps into my heart. Sudden light-headedness overtakes me, and I grip the young man's arm for support. *Be strong, Elaine, You have to be. Colin's just outside and you need to be composed for him.* Stephanie's waxen face is surrounded by a halo of unruly auburn hair that accents the whiteness of her skin. I instinctively reach out to brush a stray strand off her forehead, as I have done so often when she was little. My child, my Stephanie, is like a cold, marble statue.

But no—it can't be my little girl. It's someone else, someone who happens to have red hair. After all, it's Ireland...

"Ma'am?"

I don't answer, and he repeats in a questioning tone, "Ma'am, is this Stephanie McElroy Casey, your daughter?"

No, of course not. She couldn't be. It's someone else's Stephanie. My Stephanie is pregnant and has a three-year-old boy. She's needed. She can't be dead.

"Oh God..."

"Ma'am?"

"Oh...yes."

No, you fool!

"Yes, that's my daughter," and with those words I give up any shred of hope that somehow it is not Stephanie on the slab, that it's all a mistake. I gaze at her for a few moments and gently kiss her good-bye, then turn away.

I feel anything but stable as I half stumble from that place of refrigeration and farewells.

Stephanie's dead, Liam is in a coma, possibly paralyzed, and Colin is for all practical purposes an orphan. My breath is shallow, and I sit for a minute as the room begins spinning. After a moment, a deep sigh from an unknown place within me helps me collect myself. What other places within am I supposed to discover, to draw upon, before this is over?

"Some water, Ma'am?"

I'm grateful for the coldness in my mouth and coursing down my throat, reminding me I'm still alive and able to take on the rest of the day's challenges. And there's Colin's pony ride to look forward to when we return—who knew I'd eagerly want to return to Maggie's place?

With Stephanie's personal effects in hand–that include her U.S. Passport, thank God–and her body released to me for transport back to The States, the next step has to be easier.

Anything would be.

Colin's busy crashing his trucks, but Christa looks visibly concerned when she sees me.

"I look that bad?"

"Just pale and tired. Are you OK?"

"Oh, Christa..." I fall into her open arms, grateful for her never-ending support as a wave of tears rises in me.

Colin looks up. "What's wrong, Grandma?"

"I'm sad," I manage to choke out, drawing away from Christa. "Because…"

He rises, truck in hand, questioning me with his eyes.

"Because your mommy," I pause for a deep breath. "Died."

"Oh." He returns to his trucks, complete with engine sounds and explosions. But he grabs his bear from the tote bag, too.

Kevin's knowledge of the city comes in handy as he steers us through the Dublin traffic to a travel agency for the plane tickets, and then to a park not far from the U.S. Embassy on Elgin Road. Before dealing with the Consulate, some lunch under the trees plus a place for Colin to run around is a must.

Even in the midst of this grief and stress, there's humor as we leave Kevin with an oversized sandwich and fruit as he circles the area in the car. Forget parking spaces! As he passes us for the second time, he sticks his arm out and waves, giving the 'thumbs up' sign and grinning, and I thrust another sandwich through the open driver's window while Colin shouts "Hello!" to him and Christa waves enthusiastically, hamming it up by jumping up and down for Colin's pleasure as much as to relieve stress in general, I imagine. What a collection of characters we are! Others seated near us smile at our performance.

I'm not aware how hungry I am until Christa urges me to eat something, and I bite into the fresh yeasty bread and the salty beef as she steers Colin away from the pigeons and to our bench for some lunch. He's happily munching away and enjoying the sweet, creamy tea when it hits me—my little girl is gone forever—and I have to turn away, not quite suppressing a sob. Christa intervenes, bless her, asking him more about Dora and Rosie.

The flock of pigeons gathers round the bench, naturally, so Christa lets Colin throw them an occasional crust to keep them happy—and him occupied. Hopefully he'll be as good at the embassy.

About a hundred feet away from us, another flock forms around a red-haired woman with a dark-haired pre-schooler, both of them having lunch, it seems. She turns our way briefly and smiles. Then Colin tugs my sleeve, demanding, "Where's Ma?"

There's so much more where that is coming from, and this is just the beginning.

# *Christa*

Colin's holding on to his bear for dear life as we approach the consular officer, a tall, solemn-looking official in iron gray suit and tie. "You're Mrs. McElroy, the deceased's mother, I presume," he says, extending his hand to Elaine. "Please accept my condolences."

After introductions, during which Colin stubbornly refuses to shake hands, we're led to a small office where Laney produces her U.S. driver's license and birth certificate plus a 9"x12" manilla envelope from which she pulls our plane tickets, travel agency itinerary, Stephanie's passport plus copies of her U.S. birth certificate and Colin's, too. She shows "our" official, Mr. Clement, the recent photo with Stephanie, Liam and Colin, and he leaves to make copies of everything, When he's out of the room, we realize Colin's grabbing his crotch and dancing around, "Grandma, I gotta pee. I gotta pee."

"Right." Elaine springs to action and quick as cats, they're out of there, hopefully in time. That leaves me to contemplate the sad detritus of Stephanie's birth, life and death. In addition to her certificate of birth spilled from the envelope, I see Elaine's brought her Baptism, Holy Communion and Confirmation Certificates, her diplomas from middle school and high school, and there's even a Red Cross lifesaving certificate among the papers. Probably every report card she ever received is there, too, and I thumb through the early ones noting her strengths in spelling, history, and reading.

A yellowed program shows she played a turkey in her elementary school Thanksgiving play. A certificate for winning the middle school spelling bee in sixth grade is in here, along with a third place ribbon in a 1986 talent contest. Stephanie in a talent show? She'd have been 15.

After that there's the high school graduation tassel and her diploma–no special recognitions, but she did graduate, and given the party girl she'd been, Elaine must have been grateful.

Tears spring to my eyes as I see the scant remains of this girl's life—a young life ended too soon. Was she more or less than this smattering of papers? A trial to her mother, not to mention her teachers, I'm sure. And what was she thinking, screwing Frank in her own mother's bed? She might've been alive today if not for that and the chain of events it set off. How different it might have been if Colin had stayed with Elaine in

America. Stephanie's motives might have been less than altruistic, but as things have turned out, would it have been easier for the boy?

Either way, in the end, she left us Colin.

And what of him? His short life lived back and forth across the Atlantic, across cultures—his "adjustment issues" don't begin to describe it when you add the death of his mother and the sorry state of his father. It's a blessing he's got Laney, but realistically, it will be tough. She's a 53-year-old single grandma raising a preschooler who's had major trauma. Can she handle it? Probably, but what about that new life in the Southwest she was forging?

Thinking of Santa Fe makes me think of Trish, and how funny it is I haven't thought of her in at least a couple of days, given the whirlwind of getting here and dealing with the Caseys. I'll have to call her and let her know what's happening and when we'll be back. God, I miss her. After Mercedes, I thought I'd never meet anyone again...but now Trish...our daily phone calls...

Elaine and Colin re-enter, followed by Mr. Clement, who's holding papers and announces, "Here's a set of copies for you, Mrs. McElroy, plus originals. You'll find four extra copies of the photo for the deceased's relatives. I'm also giving you the embassy's Report of Death of an American Citizen Abroad, which you'll need."

Colin's making a beeline for the large, antique-looking globe on a walnut stand when I move faster than I thought I could and head him off. Oh, it's going to be a long, long flight home.

The glass coffee table's next as Colin, agile as a monkey, scoots up on it and skims across its slick surface on his belly, scattering magazines, brochures, maps, loose pads and pens and a large ceramic ashtray, which shatters as it hits the polished hardwood floor with a crash. Omigod, it's Christmas Eve all over again!

Laney and I are screaming at Colin to get down in between our apologies to our host, who's gone as gray as his suit. Time to collect our things, pick up the fallen items and make ourselves scarce.

It's going on five in the afternoon when we reach the hospital in Limerick. Visitors to intensive care are allowed only once an hour for fifteen minutes. Elaine's in with her son-in-law while I sit downstairs with Col, snacking on Maggie's oatmeal cookies and reading him some Dr. Seuss and Clifford the Big Red Dog, but he's soon off my lap and running around—after everything that's already happened today.

## Elaine

When I see Liam, I focus on my comfort zone, the medical issues, and try to rein in my feelings. I was unprepared for the young, dark-haired man whose face is a swollen mass of bruises and whose right cheek is covered with a large dressing. His right arm is in a cast. He lays as if asleep, surrounded by medical paraphernalia. The tube inserted in his windpipe is attached to a machine that breathes for him. Does he have a g-tube into his stomach providing nutrition? I can't see it beneath the blanket, but I imagine he must. His IV tubing snakes under the hospital gown, likely a central venous line going directly to his heart, but it's been so long since I worked in a hospital's critical care care unit…His urine fills a catheter bag hanging on the side of the bed.

I struggle to find a resemblance between Colin and the bandaged face of his father, my son-in-law.

Comatose patients have awakened remembering people speaking to them, so I whisper in his ear, "Liam, I'm Stephanie's mother. I'm so sorry about what happened. I hope you will try your best to get better for Colin's sake. He's fine and he sends his love. He made this picture for you."

Does he know Stephanie's dead? Probably not. I put Colin's hand-made card on the bedside table where he will see it when or if he regains consciousness. Have the Caseys been approached about organ donation, I wonder?

These few minutes with Liam drain me. Will I ever see him alive again? Will Colin? Dare I ask Maggie for a few photos to keep his memory alive? Would she part with any, especially to put into my hands?

Kevin will be having a bit of a break—at last—but as I step off the elevator, my spirits dive as I see Christa chasing after Colin as he tears around the lobby with a cookie in one hand and a truck in the other, shouting and heading full-tilt toward a small group of people there. She greets me with a silent look of relief as she scoops him up, preventing his collision into an elderly man with a walker. I still have to phone Tom so he can get me up to speed on the funeral arrangements and I can tell him when to meet our plane. We have a long journey ahead.

On the ride home Christa nods off, but Colin's wide awake, clamoring to be let out of the car seat. He pulls in frustration at the straps as though their constraint is unfamiliar to him. Those frequent weekend trips back and forth to the family farm—didn't Liam and Stephanie make him stay in it? Thank God he wasn't in the car with them when...

"No, Colin, it's not a choice. You have to stay in your own seat. You can play trucks or I'll read you a book, but only when you calm down." He responds with another in a series of protests—"Out, out, Grandma"—shrill cries that I marvel Christa can sleep through. How will we ever make that long flight home?

I dig in my tote for a couple of Hot Wheels cars, but as soon as I hand them to him, he flings one at Kevin's head.

"Shite!" Bets are that our intrepid driver never counted on a day spent circling government buildings and parks, eating behind the wheel with scarcely a break, and being attacked by a three-year-old commando. This last will mean an even bigger tip.

"No!" Instinctively I slap his hand and retrieve the remaining car before he can do any more damage and have us careening off the road. "We don't throw things."

He screams as though he's being disemboweled on the spot, waking Christa, who turns and asks, "What's going on?"

"Oh, nothing. Everything's fine."

Christa makes a face as Kevin remarks, "Bloody little bugger assaulted me with this." He waves the Dodge Daytona muscle car.

*Omigod, does this mean a lawsuit against the two women from America?* "Oh, Kevin, are you OK?" There I go doing 'Fuzzy Wuzzy to the rescue.' Just give me a moment while I unpack gauze, surgical tape, disinfectant, gloves, clamps, sutures, retractors...and a portable heart-lung machine, just in case.

He winks. "All in a day's work, Missus." He calls me Missus—like James called Maggie. Has this day aged me so much? Come to think of it, when was the last time I checked a mirror? When I brushed my teeth this morning? Am I a Maggiemorph?

Resolutely, I stare out the window, determined to discipline this child who's apparently a stranger to most limits. "We'll have to ride this out, I'm afraid. I'm sorry."

And a sorry ride it is, all two hours of it back to the farm as Colin's wails and shouts rise and fade.

❖

As we discuss the next day's early morning departure with Kevin, John comes out of the nearby barn and offers to take us to the airport in the morning on his way to the hospital, bless him. The cost of Kevin's accommodations and services today plus an enormous tip for putting up with Colin more than equal one airfare home. No wonder our young driver is beaming as we say our farewells and he leaves.

Dinner's over, but we can see that Maggie's left us plates kept warm on the back of the stove. She's busy with the dough for the morning's batch of bread, and as she kneads the pale yeasty mixture, the extra skin under her upper arms flaps.

"Ah, you're back. John took advantage of your visiting our son and stayed home, thank God, to oversee the men. And with you having the boyo, it was a holiday for me. Your food's still hot." She stops working the dough to look at us. "My Liam. How is he?"

"No change, it seems." Seeing her face fall, I add, "I'm sorry. We're set to leave tomorrow."

She shakes her head and returns to her task.

I return the framed photo to its place before we enjoy our heaping plates of Irish stew with garden vegetables and warm bread. Bread pudding drowned in heavy cream is dessert. Then there's packing for Colin—the pajamas, clothes, underwear, socks, and shoes he brought for his week's stay here plus some of the toys—the rest we'll buy at home as he needs things. Christa and I both packed black dresses for a service we're not attending. That space could have been used for Colin's stuff. Still, I did leave room for some of his things.

Before long it's Colin's bedtime, and I let Maggie enjoy the pleasure of tucking him in one last time; I will have exclusive rights after tomorrow.

After Colin's nestled in his featherbed, Maggie puts the kettle on for tea. As she pours steaming liquid into china cups, she says, without looking up, "Elaine, we've been talking, and even though Colin's an American citizen, he's happy here with us, the family he knows. And when Liam comes home…"

I didn't allow her to finish her fantasy. "Maggie, I know this is hard for you, with Liam in the hospital and all, but this is what Stephanie would have wanted. And Colin has family at home in America, too, besides me—his aunt, grandfather, great-grandmother—and more." I do not mention Tom's Wife from Hell for obvious reasons.

Her response is the bottle of whiskey, placed with a resounding thump on the old wooden table, plus three glasses. Christa shakes her head, but Maggie ignores her, pouring drinks for all.

"Ah, and what'll it mean for Liam's recovery, havin' his own son whisked away? I don't have the heart to tell him."

"Then don't," I say, leaving my drink untouched as Maggie downs hers. It sounds harsher than I intend. "I'm sorry, Maggie. This has been hard on all of us."

Christa rises soundlessly, and I excuse us both to go pack.

❖

We're organizing our totes for the plane ride home when we hear the back door slam, some muffled conversation, then the scrape of a chair across the floor.

John's deep voice rises up the stairs. "It's the only way, Maggie–how long do you think you can keep runnin' yourself into the ground with the farm and now the boy? He's a handful, and we both know it. Our Liam was never that way. Must be his Yank mother."

"But he's ours, John, no matter if that brassy whore birthed him. That Stephanie…her, comin' here with no job, no money, and her ginger-haired bastard, and then throwin' her loose self at our Liam."

I gasp, turning to Christa, who restrains me with her hand on my arm before I can storm out the bedroom door and confront Maggie. "I'm going down there and kick that drunk old cow in her fat old country ass…first giving booze to…"

"Don't do it, Elaine. For the love of God, we're so close to getting out of here…"

"She can't talk about my Stephanie like that!"

"She's probably wasted already. No doubt she's had three more since we left her. Consider the source, and don't even think about going down there."

John's voice resonates. "But think, Maggie. Liam chose her after all, though who knows why he would have taken on such a piece of baggage as herself. Must've bedeviled him, she did."

"Yeah, a gold-digging harlot she was, spinning her evil web, opening wide her sleek, white American legs…"

"Maggie, the boy'll hear you," John interrupts.

Not even Christa can keep me from bounding down the stairs, running to the table where the two are seated. "You are two of the sickest bastards I've ever seen, and I am not spending another night under this roof." Christa's right behind me. "You have Kevin's card," I tell her. "Call him. I'll pay him overtime to come get us out of this..." Momentarily I'm at a loss for words. "This whiskey-soaked hell hole."

"Elaine." Christa's voice is low and professional. "Taking Colin from his bed in the middle of the night—adding trauma on top of trauma—think about it, Laney."

*Trauma—I'll show that Maggie bodily trauma, by God, and if Tom were here, he'd be whaling on that old bitch.*

"Takin' him from his bed like you took that picture you thought I wouldn't notice. What was that about, now that it's back, I wonder? I can see where that daughter of yours got her ways," she starts, but John interrupts.

"Enough."

"Goddamn right!" I dash for the door to get away from this place, these, these... "Christa," I call over my shoulder, "Call Kevin. I've already paid half his college tuition, and I'll pay for a little more." *That money was for Stephanie's wedding. It all washes over me—the missed joy of seeing my grown up girl being married in a church, seeing Colin there with the ring, and Stephanie's big beautiful smile...and seeing her instead in the morgue.* Loss overwhelms me, my head throbs with the start of a killer migraine, and I collapse, sobbing, into Christa's arms, letting her hold and rock me in the moonlight.

Maggie's shrill tones reach us from the kitchen. "As God is me witness, John, I've done nothing but slave for them since they landed on my doorstep, demandin' this, demandin' that. It'll be a cold day in hell before I lift a finger for 'em..."

"Maggie, girl, no matter what you think of them, you've got to let 'em take Colin for a little while. When Liam's better..."

"And there'll be the divil to pay for lettin' 'em take the lad. The divil..." Her harsh tone diminishes to a low wail of grief fueled by 80 proof Irish whiskey.

## *Christa*

Later, huddled under the feather quilt, we speak in hushed tones. "Colin belongs with me," Elaine whispers. "I was there when he was born, and I took them in when they had nowhere else to go."

"Laney, sleep. I'll sit downstairs with a cup of tea and keep an eye on things…just in case. You never know."

In the end, we wind up sitting together huddled under an old quilt we find in the living room, sipping tea and starting at every sound, however slight as we struggle to stay awake. John and Maggie know every inch of this countryside, every abandoned farmhouse, barn and possible hiding place, and I wouldn't put it past those two…

❖

After an hour we're so worn out we've no choice but to return to the lumpy bed upstairs for much-needed rest. We'll need all our energy to manage a trans-Atlantic flight with an impulsive three-year-old, and Advil doesn't even touch my headache.

It feels like I slept for all of 45 minutes.

Maggie stands at the stove, stirring a pot. She offers no breakfast, but says, with her back to us. "You'll be getting some breakfast at the airport, I guess."

John blusters, "Jaysus, woman," you're embarassin' me now."

I help him set the table while Elaine gathers Colin's last-minute things. He's like a rocket about to blast off. There's no holding him back as he circles the table, arms outstretched as he whoops and shouts that he's an airplane. Oh, we are in for a bumpy ride with him!

Maggie places a large pot of oatmeal on the table with a loud thunk, then goes to her room, slamming the door behind her.

"Don't slam doors, Grandma," Colin says, and John simply says, "Eat. Eat your oatmeal, boy."

We're eating buttered scones when Kevin knocks on the door. His broad smile lifts my spirits, and relief washes over me as he collects our bags and starts strapping them to the luggage rack on the roof of the car. No matter how miserable the car ride and plane trip might be, at least we're making our escape.

John opens the bedroom door and tells Maggie, "Colin's leaving now," and Elaine directs him toward the tearful old woman who presses something into the boy's hand and says, "We gave this to your father for his First Holy Communion, God bless him. Keep it with you always."

Then turning to us, she spits out, "He's Catholic, raised Catholic. Remember that. Mind ye take him to Sunday Mass."

She hugs Colin until he begs her to stop. "Grandma, you're squishing me. I can't breathe!" She wipes her tears away with her apron, and Laney takes what turns out to be a gold Celtic cross on a chain from Colin's hand. Once she's fastened it around his neck, we do not linger.

John ignores us both. He picks up Colin, carries him to the waiting car, and after a hug, places him in the car seat. "You'll hear from us, Colin," he says. "You're in our hearts."

❖

Not even the Car Trip from Hell can diminish our relief at leaving. Colin's repeated attempts to free himself from the car seat work on my nerves, already frayed from this rescue mission of too much bureaucracy, too little sleep, and an over-abundance of drama. Now Colin's thrown one of his books at the back of my head—ouch! How will Elaine manage with this child, day after day? Enough. One step at a time. We get him on the plane. Once we're airborne, I can always make an emergency parachute jump.

## *Elaine*

At last! Wheels up and we're in the air and I breathe out an enormous sigh of relief in spite of my headache, which still lingers. In eight hours we'll be at O'Hare, and I can stand anything—even Colin's head-butting against the back of his car seat and kicking the seat in front of him. It falls to me to stop him, though, when the elderly gentleman ahead turns around in obvious irritation and says, "Please! Control that child." My face flushes in embarrassment as I stammer, "I'm so…I'm so sorry. Yes, of course."

I reach over to his little feet encased in hard-soled leather shoes and fix him with my most serious stare. "Stop," I tell him in my firmest tone. "Remember what we said about a plane ride. They do *not* allow kicking on a plane." *God, there were the arguments over the car seat, throwing cars and books, now this…will life with Colin be one long struggle?*

"Here, Colin, I'll show you how to put these on," Christa says, adjusting headphones to cover his ears. "We'll watch a movie."

Thank heavens for *A Bug's Life*, which keeps his attention for a little while as he holds Bear. Where is Barney when I need him? Christa, poor thing, falls asleep, and I have the luxury of my own thoughts.

Has this nightmare really happened? Did Stephanie really die, leaving me to save Colin from those two, especially that

Maggie...how she raged at James and everything else around her. Between the overweight, diabetes, starchy diet and all that whiskey, it's a wonder she's still alive. Her weight alone...There I go, doing my Nurse Fuzzy Wuzzy self, when I should be wishing that evil fat fart croaks tomorrow—without any CPR intervention, thanks very much.

But still, Maggie's only child is comatose and will probably never regain consciousness. Even though I lost one child, at least I have another living, functioning child at home, waiting for me to return. No one can replace Stephanie, for all her faults, but at least I'm not left childless as Maggie is, realistically.

What a life that woman's had—a dairy farmer's daughter then a dairy farmer's wife. It's all she's ever known. No wonder she resented the footloose redhead who captured her son's heart.

Stephanie's remains are being flown to Chicago from Dublin, due to arrive just after we get in from Shannon. I'm counting on Tom to be there.

As usual, in times of crisis, my mind automatically shifts into hyper-efficiency mode. Tom's made all the funeral arrangements, but Colin will need clothes for the funeral and that's my job now.

Colin's new fit of kicking and another complaint from the man in front of us break into my thoughts, and when I try to hang onto Colin's little feet, he kicks and screams, "No," as though I'm torturing him.

Everyone stares like they've never seen a misbehaving three-year-old before. "No kicking or I'll take the headphones away." His response is to wrench free as his face reddens with the effort of arching his back in protest.

I dare not risk taking him out of his seat during a tantrum. I just hope he doesn't have to go to the bathroom any time soon! Christa's roused from whatever sleep she's managed to get, and retreats down the narrow aisle toward the galley. She soon returns triumphantly with a small bag of pretzels and a questioning look for me. I nod, and she hands them to Colin, who tears it open with his teeth and not so much as a "thank you."

"What do you say, Colin?" He stares at me. "We say, 'thank you,' Colin."

"Th...thank you," he, manages, stuffing his mouth with pretzel after pretzel. They seem to have some kind of calming effect for he's soon quiet and watching the movie. Until he suddenly shouts, "I never rode my pony for you! I want to go ride Rosie. I want me Ma!"

People turn and stare. Have we spirited this child away from his mother? At this rate, international agents will be escorting us off this plane at O'Hare with charges of trans-Atlantic kidnapping and abuse facing us. They'll whisk me and Christa to some windowless back room with a bare light bulb and threaten to beat us with rubber hoses...and God have mercy on the case worker assigned to watch Colin.

More shrieks for his ma and da, more disapproving looks from the other passengers, and I'm more than ready for one of those in-flight cocktails. Maybe Maggie was on to something...we've gained time flying west, so it's not even noon for a pre-lunch drink, but who cares? More than six hours to go...I never envisioned any of this when I set out to bring him home.

Small trays of food appear that distract him, at least for now. The male flight attendant stands over Colin. "Can he have a set of wings?"

Christa intercepts the wings, and says, "These could come in handy. Thank you."

And do they ever. One lunch, a movie, a trip to the bathroom and three Dr. Seuss books later, Colin is head-butting again and crying out for Rosie and his grandpa. Are we stuck in a time-warp, doomed to fly endlessly? By now, every passenger passing our seats either sends us an angry look or mutters about "uncontrollable brats." Except for the older, grandmotherly types who sigh sympathetically and offer to say novenas for us. I'm ready to try that myself, even without the rosary beads, or maybe a shot of morphine for my head when Christa whips out the wings and says Colin can be a pilot, but only if he's quiet and sits still. She plays up these pin-on wings like The Holy Grail, spinning tales of action heroes flying planes, saving the day, getting medals just like these wings, and so on. She's so convincing, she's got me paying rapt attention as Spider Man and Batman join forces to evade the enemy jets and land the plane safely. I can almost hear the sighs of relief from those seated around us.

By the time we land in Chicago, it's lunch time—again—in this Neverending Day, and I stagger out of Customs ready for a wheelchair and a little pure oxygen...but Tom, Roxy, and even my mom are waiting for us. Who knew I'd ever be so glad to see my ex and my mom together...though neither looks very happy.

This is not a joyful occasion, after all, but not made any easier by my mother's barrage of questions for me.

"Helen, they've just come off an eight-hour trans-Atlantic flight," Tom says, taking Colin up in his arms. "Don't you have a special toy for him?"

She takes a small gift bag from her oversized purse and hands it up to Colin as she says to me, "All my friends say their grandkids just love these."

Answered prayers, for the gift turns out to be a small electronic toy cell phone that beeps, clicks, rings, plays music and lights up—Colin loves it, and I relax for the first time in a very long time into Mom's arms as Roxy enfolds Christa, then me, in welcoming hugs. Tom and Mom hug her, too, saying she's been like family.

Hallmark moment though it is, it wouldn't be Tom and Mom together if one wasn't sniping at the other.

She's at him, true to form. "A family style luncheon…and a wooden casket." She practically shudders at the words. "I mean, really, Tom, I'll pay for a proper lunch myself, if it's a matter of money. Someplace we can all order off the menu…"

"Helen, please," he says, turning to me and explaining, "She's been in my face about the funeral since I picked her up."

"Well, it's a matter of showing respect—" she persists.

Roxy rolls her eyes, and I turn and focus my steeliest glare at my own mother, God help me, but all the stresses and sorrows of the last three days combine into the icy-est tone I have ever heard come from my mouth when I tell her, "Helen. Give it a rest."

Mercifully, she does, even as we trip over each other getting into Tom's mini-van and secure Colin into yet another car seat, and I sincerely thank her for this Miracle Toy that so occupies him. She's mollified when Tom takes us to lunch where we can all order off the menu.

## Roxy

After a night with Mom and Colin, Grandma was looking pretty frazzled, but she insisted on going shopping with us yesterday. Buying Colin some funeral threads was a scene. Once we figured out his American sizes, Mom bought him Gap Khakis and a dress shirt. But the clip-on necktie—bogus. Grandma wanted him in a two-piece suit, but Mom held out for practicality, even when Grandma moaned and groaned about her friends being there and offering to pay to make the little guy look like—what—a mini-undertaker?

That was nothing compared to my sister's "laying-out" clothes. I thought the two of them would wind up bitch-slapping each other in the maternity section of Carson's. Finally I grabbed a crème-colored satin blouse and a knit top in teal to go over it, practically threw them at Mom, and announced I would find a plain charcoal skirt. It's all good—they went for it.

By then, I was like, so creeped out shopping for my dead sister—my *dead sister*, for real—that I couldn't wait to get back to Katelyn's crib and crash, forget Grandma's offer to take us out for a late lunch, I just had to book, I was so freakin' bummed. I was boo-hooing like a banshee with the covers over my head when Katelyn came in, and she was like, "Dude—are you wiggin' out?"

No way could I stop, so she ran for Pat, who just held me for a while, and then it was better. No need to track down Mom, who was probably dukin' it out with Grandma over the right shade of lipstick for Steph. Like it makes a difference, duh.

## *Helen*

Our Stephanie looks beautiful; so peaceful lying there, like something out of a fairy tale with her long red hair loose around her face. She has my mother's rosary in those slender white hands. Her wedding band's a gold Claddagh ring. I have to admit that Tom's florist did a nice job with the casket spray—miniature roses in pale coral surrounded by calla lilies, resting on her little pregnancy mound, poor, sweet thing. Not one death, but two. Maybe it was a baby sister for Colin and a great-granddaughter for me to fuss over. Oh, dear, I just can't keep from crying, and I thought these two hankies would be enough. My mother embroidered them especially for wakes.

The tissues are over there by that woman…my God, that woman…with her, her…bosoms practically hanging out of that skin-tight top cut down to her…her…if it were any lower, someone would call the police. With the skirt so short, it's practically up to her…whatever they call it today. The nerve of her! I hope the priest isn't here yet! She could have at least covered her shoulders. Someone should say something to her. Who could she be with? She is certainly not from my side of the family.

No! Tom's coming in and standing next to her, holding her arm like she's his...my God that must be what's-her-name, that little tramp he married. I just hope Ellie hasn't seen this...this public display. And now, oh no, oh no—it's Gert and the crowd from the St. Mary's Seniors, and they're taking it all in. It'll be all over the neighborhood by tonight. At least the seniors from the community center aren't here yet.

Thank God I thought to bring a sweater along just in case.

"Tom, you look so handsome in that dark gray suit and tie. You know, I could use some help with the food, so if you'd let me borrow your lovely wi...And Elaine needs you over there, by the receiving line."

The little slut looks at me like I'm from another country. "Come with me, honey." How she can even walk in those four-inch stiletto heels I'll never know.

She hasn't got a clue in that brainless head of hers when I pull her into the coffee room, and try to hand her my sweater. "Here, dear. Put this on. We don't want you to catch a draft."

She just gives me a blank look with those eyes of hers all made up and lined in black like a raccoon.

Doesn't she understand English? Did Tom get himself one of those immigrant wives you hear about? I'll have to drape it over her shoulders myself, I suppose.

"Turn around dear, and you'll be much cozier..."

The sheer gaul of her! Turning heel and ignoring me.

## *Elaine*

A lot of Mom's friends are here, but where is she? Maybe the bathroom. The place is filling up fast, but Tom's next to me now. And here come my sister and Stuart.

"Denise..." We hold each other, sobbing. Have I ever been this relieved to see my big sister?

"What can I do, Elaine?"

Stuart leans over, kissing me on the cheek and holding my arm in his big, square hand. "How're you holding up, Ellie? It's a terrible thing." He turns to Tom, leaning into him as the two men shake hands and thump each other on the back. Tom looks good in that suit. His graying hair has just been trimmed. If only he had been nicer to me and stopped drinking...

Christa enters, and we nod. She's perfectly turned out in a long-sleeved black dress and pearls and black pumps. She kneels in front of the casket then rises and comes toward me.

Roxy's hugging my sister and they're both in tears. It's the first time I've seen my little girl cry since she was in middle school. She's grieving hard for Stephanie, maybe wishing they'd been closer. I know I am.

"Tom's done a fine job," Christa says, holding me. "And the flowers are lovely." She's probably referring to the casket spray saying "Loving Daughter and Devoted Sister" that Tom chose for the three of us, though an arrangement of roses—an enormous bouquet of red American Beauties from Colin saying, "Beloved Mother" stand at the head of the casket. Next to his are yellow roses from my mother and pink ones from Tom's mother, Fiona. At the foot are lilies from Tom's brother and sister-in-law. My sister, Stephanie's godmother, sent white carnations in the shape of a cross, and Christa has sent a multicolored arrangement with bright tulips and daisies.

These flowers and their banners saying daughter, sister, mother, granddaughter, niece, godchild define the roles she played and line the walls by her casket.

Stephanie's casket—what horrible words. What mother ever expects to bury her child? Tears overtake me again—for the umpteenth time—and Tom takes me in his arms for a moment, and I can't help wishing he would hold me, support me, comfort me, as a husband consoles a wife and she in turn eases his pain.

And where is Mom? I need her. Another group of her senior citizen friends is forming in the corner. I can place two or three faces, but that's all...and besides, I need her close to me where I can see her, like a child needs to see her mother is nearby.

"Roxy, please find Grandma."

## *Roxy*

"Cheryl, is my grandma in there?"

"Is that who that was?" She goes to my dad's brother, Uncle Andy, my godfather. I haven't seen him and Aunt Maureen in like, years, and my other grandma, Grandma Fiona, is with them, and she's all boo-hooing even though they've just arrived and she hasn't even seen my sister yet.

Of course Grannie Fi wraps me in a killer clinch and kisses me on the cheek with her double killer old lady breath, but she's my grandma, too, is what Mom would say.

I manage to do both my aunt and uncle in a single hug. "Catch you in a minute. Mom's sent me to find Grandma Helen." *Later, dude. For all I know, she's outside tokin' on some of that prime weed I hear seniors can get. Wouldn't mind some of that myself, Grandma.*

And here she is, stirring her coffee. "Been lookin' for you Grandma. Mom needs you out there with her."

"OK, dear. Do you want something to eat? I brought my lemon squares—your favorite. Your sister…she loved them, too." Her eyes get all misty. Poor Grandma. Poor everyone.

I give her a big hug. "It's OK, Grandma. I miss her, too." For a sec we stand there, hangin' out, hangin' on to each other surrounded by countertops full of nut rolls, muffins, taco salad, chips…the whole Food-for-a-Grieving-Army thing. "So you met my dad's wife—Cheryl."

"What a piece of work. I tried to give her my sweater so she could cover up decently, but she…she just ignored me."

"Sounds like her."

## *Helen*

I'm standing between Ellie and Tom and say to him, "Your wife, wherever she's from…This is a wake," I whisper so no one can hear, "and people don't go a wake parading around with their…bosoms hanging in people's faces. She should show some respect. Cover her up, Tom, in the name of all that's decent." *It's bad enough Roxy is done up like a…an I-don't-know-what in that leather vest and boots and wrist band…and you and Elaine let her…You think I don't see those pierced holes in her eyebrow? At least she dyed her pink hair black for the services, but it's such an unnatural shade. And why she has to wear three earrings in each lobe, well, I just don't know.*

"Tom? Tom?" *Why is everyone ignoring me?*

## *Christa*

Elaine's mother sits next to Tom's on the couch in front of me; the two barely have time for greetings before a crowd of seniors converge on Helen, all commenting on the flowers and how lovely Stephanie looks. I can't help overhearing;

many speak quite loudly, probably due to hearing loss. Some wear hearing aids. When Tom's mother's friends arrive, I can imagine what the decibel level will be then.

"Helen, dear, where is her little boy—that Irish child?"

"Colin's here in America with us now. Today he's with that nice family—whoever they are—that Roxy stays with. I can never remember their name."

If she was about to say anything more, forget it. All their eyes turn to follow Cheryl's languid, hip-swaying progress across the room. She has *got* to be wearing the Uprising Strapless Wonderbra. Her boobs are spilling out of an off-the-shoulder, low-cut knit top trimmed with lace. Her tight black pencil skirt only emphasizes her "come-hither" stroll toward Tom, and with her hair piled up high and black eyeliner with blue eye shadow, she looks like she's in a 1960s time warp. The three old gentlemen with Helen make a beeline to offer condolences to Cheryl; poor Helen reaches for the rosary in her lap.

## *Roxy*

Finally! Michael's here with Brian and Katelyn. "Dude," he says, taking my hand and halfway leaning into me, then pulling back, clueless. "It's like, freakin', you know?"

"Bummer," his brother says, hugging me, and then all three of my buds are hugging me, and things feel a little better.

"We're outta here," I tell Mom and Dad, who look at me like, 'not,' so I explain it's just outside for a little while.

Wouldn't you know it, even surrounded by a bunch of seniors, Grandma Helen spots us and calls over, "Roxy, come here and introduce me to your friends. Is this that girl from the nice family you stay with?"

*Duh, Grandma.* "Yeah, Grandma Helen, this is Katelyn. And this is Brian and Michael." I nod at Grannie Fi who's next to her. "And this is my dad's mom, Grandma Fiona."

"Bless your mother for looking after Colin," Grandma Helen says. "How's he doing?"

"Fine."

"I'll bet your mom's busy just keeping up with him," Grandma says. "Such energy he has!"

"When I left my mom was making a big bowl of that Play Doh stuff with him, and they were going to use food coloring to make it like, red and blue and stuff." She's like, really getting into this, all smiles. "She used to do that with me, too, and I helped roll it out flat and we made Christmas ornaments—angels and Santas with cookie cutters, and sometimes trees and bells, and I'd roll tiny balls in different colors and decorate all my trees and bells, and the gingerbread men, too." Katelyn's getting all back in the day, and before she morphs into a five-year-old, it's "Back soon, Grandma," and we beat feet for the nearest door, but not before I hear her say to Grannie Fi, "Such a nice girl, that Katelyn—too bad Roxy doesn't dress more like her."

## Elaine

I'm not surprised the Caseys made no attempt to find out about the arrangements. No flowers; not a plant. I'll be shocked to get so much as a card from them. Shows how much they cared about Stephanie, the mother of their grandson. And she was cared about, damn it. Not just family, but some old friends from high school stopped by, and a few she worked with at Starbucks from a year and a half ago.

The place is thinning out after being full of Tom's people, but most of them have gone across the street to the corner bar. At least some of them were still here when the priest led us in prayer. Nora was here for that, too, bless her. Roxy had a couple of friends from school besides Katelyn and the fellows, and I almost fell over when I saw Mrs. Rothrock leading a contingency of at least a half-dozen people from school. And speaking of falling over...could it be?

That man signing the visitors' book...tall, thin...carrying a large portfolio-sized package wrapped in brown paper...*Oh, sweet Jesus*...I grab the arm closest to me for support, thankfully my sister's and not Tom's. She turns to me, eyebrows raised, and I shake my head. "No...nothing. Just someone I haven't seen for a while."

## Jeff

Honestly, if I hadn't known it was Elaine, I might not have recognized her. Drawn, pale, exhausted...this is not the woman I knew. And black is not her color. True, she's lost her daughter, but she looks so much older. When I approach and kiss her cheek, it's awkward, not only because it's been so long, but because I have to set this down before taking her in my arms for a moment and whispering my condolences. She starts to tremble, so I step back. Her face starts to, like, crumple: chin quivering, eyes closing and squeezing out tears. She's wailing and sobbing in an eruption of grief. Everyone in the place quiets down and stares at her, and two old ladies on the couch make the Sign of the Cross. The woman next to Elaine—her sister?—holds her, murmuring...

## *Denise*

OK, Ellie, let it out, hon. This is the first I've seen you cry, and it's good, it's all good. You need the tears. That's all a part of it, and for good reason. All part of the healing...Stuart, get us some tissues, will you?" *Thank God for Stuart. He not only has a handful of Kleenex, he takes my sister outside. She can cry as much as she needs to. This fellow who's come by for my sister, and who's standing here with a big package done up in brown paper and tape...who is this guy, anyway?*

"My sister's exhausted. She just got back from Ireland with her grandson and...Stephanie. It's been terrible for her. For all of us. I'm Denise Stratton."

"Jeff Dvorak. Elaine studied painting with me at the Art Institute."

*And this causes such an outburst?* "Yes, you were with... that gallery..."

Tom steps forward. "Tom McElroy. Stephanie's dad. This is my wife, Cheryl."

This Jeff person can't keep from glancing at her cleavage— who could?—then looks away quickly. "I'm so sorry for your loss..."

## *Jeff*

This Cheryl chick—is she in costume? Is it some kind of fashion statement? Or just bad taste? Elaine's ex is all over it, grinning like a jackass...all that attention for his trophy wife...and the bimbo will probably dump him in a heartbeat...

## Elaine

It's only me and my sister standing together by the casket. I wish Andy and Maureen had stayed longer, but they had Fiona. If only I could have left with them...but there's no running away. I'm tired, hungry, thirsty, and my feet are killing me. No sooner am I back in this place when I see Frank, another Man from the Past, kneel briefly at the casket, then turn my way. Oh God! He looks like hell. His color is ashen. Reminds me of his heart attack. He's shrunken from a robust man to a puny guy with a paunch. No—I can't do 'Nurse Fuzzy Wuzzy to the rescue.' There's nothing left of me.

"Elaine, I'm so sorry." His cold hands tremble when he takes mine. Then tears stream down his face as he struggles to say, "She was so young...so beautiful and full of life."

What can I say? Words escape me. Does he think I don't remember? He fumbles for his handkerchief and blows his nose loudly while I exchange a look with my sister.

"Thank you." Finally, he leaves, but not before he encounters Cheryl and stands, momentarily transfixed, like a stunned deer in her 38EE headlights.

## Frank

I'm standing here, taking a piss when it hits me–this guy in the next urinal is Elaine's ex....And wouldn't you know it, her artsy gigilo, Jeff, what's-his-name, comes in — was he screwing Stephanie, too? She looked so good, not really dead; I can't help remembering when we were...Ah, jeez, I feel so bad.

## Christa

Could it have gone on any longer? I could have cheered when the funeral director ended the evening with The Lord's Prayer and the Glory Be...and announced we'd gather here tomorrow morning at eight. Now it's just a matter of retrieving our empty plates from the coffee room and it'll soon be home and a hot tub.

"Helen, your lemon squares were a hit," I say, "and Denise's chips 'n taco salad, too. Not a crumb left."

"I'm starving," Elaine says. "By the time I got in here for a cup of coffee, they were both history. You know your lemon squares are the best, Mom." Cheryl's contribution looks untouched, however... hors d'ouevres made of some kind of cubed meat (somewhat darkened from sitting out) on Ritz crackers with toothpicks holding green olives.

She offers the plateful to Elaine, who waves it away.

"No, really," Cheryl says, "they're so good—Spam on crackers with olives...and pimentos."

They're displayed on a flimsy paper plate bordered with holly leaves and red berries. She sighs, then places her culinary masterpiece on the table. "I worked hard on these," she whines, putting plastic wrap around the whole unappetizing mess. Someone should warn Tom not to eat it.

Speaking of warnings, Helen turns to him with, "Dear, I know you'll make sure your...wife...is properly dressed for the funeral tomorrow."

Tom pauses. "What?"

"You know what I mean. This isn't a bawdy house."

My mouth drops open, and so does Elaine's. The room is hushed with one big drawn breath as we wait.

His face reddens. "Give it a rest, Helen. Enough."

"No, it's not enough. I tried to cover her up, I was so mortified—for all of us, with her done up like a...a tramp!"

"Tom," Cheryl's voice turns shrill. "Are you gonna let her say that about me?"

"This is my wife you're talking about, Helen..."

"She won't listen to me. Even offered her my sweater. I tried."

Cheryl snorts, "Tried to put some old pink thing on me. Smelled of moth balls."

"Liar! That's lavender sachet, you ignorant..." She breaks off and says to Tom, "Honestly, for a while I thought she was one of those immigrant wives you hear about—from one of those Eastern European nations..."

Roxy interrupts, grinning, "Yeah, Trailer Park Nation, Grandma."

"Shut up, all of you! And stop talking about me like I'm not here." Cheryl looks trapped, scanning the room—for an escape hatch?

"Ya know, it's a look," Roxy remarks to no one in particular. "Kinda retro. The stilettos are totally bitchin', and I'm gonna get myself a pair. On sale at Payless."

Helen gives her a horrified look, whether at the notion of four-inch heels, or setting foot in Payless I'm not sure, but Our Little Goth Girl persists. "She's, like, outta some kinda time warp." Roxy starts doing an impromptu version of the Timewarp Dance from the *Rocky Horror Picture Show*.

## *Elaine*

Christa starts laughing out loud, and it's all I can do to keep from cracking up myself. The sight of Roxy dancing while Cheryl's damn near quivering with outrage—how dare we not appreciate her culinary talents and fashion sense?—would be enough to set me off, but I feel one of my God-awful headaches coming on, and then the grief hits again, only this time I'm not only sad, I'm mad, really crazy mad.

Damn you, God! Just when I was finally getting my life together, you took my Stephanie away from me, from her child, from all of us. You make me slog through cow shit and endure hours in a sardine can of a car with my screaming grandson, not to mention an eight-hour trans-Atlantic flight with more screaming, kicking and mayhem to retrieve him from his grandfather and that overbearing, hateful, alcoholic, whiskey-pushing, fat assed, miserable grandmother from Absolute Hell—and my daughter in a body bag. Now this...and a migraine on top of it!

Naturally, my mother's unstoppable, and goes at Cheryl like a pit bull with, "You come sashaying in here with your...your front hanging out like, like...cantaloupes!"

"More like honeydews," Christa murmurs in my ear.

That does it.

## *Christa*

Elaine's high-pitched, hysterical laughter shocks us all; an unearthly sound, almost inhuman. We're frozen in place for a second, speechless as she seems to come unglued. The sound lingers even after she stops abruptly.

"Ellie, dear, are you all right?" Helen asks anxiously.

"No, dammit, I'm not all right," she says, sitting down. "I'm exhausted, I'm hungry, I'm jet-lagged, I've been on my feet in heels all day, my ankles are swollen, I'm getting a headache, and my daughter's out there in a casket."

Cheryl turns, facing Tom squarely. "The casket you spent a fortune on, Tom. You should think of your family, the one you have now."

Like Elaine hasn't spent a penny? At that, Roxy starts winding up, swinging her grunge sack to hit Cheryl, yelling, "Just what ghetto are you from, fool?" as she closes in for the attack.

Elaine manages to grab her wrist. Roxy says, "Just once Mom, c'mon let me have just one swing at the beeotch."

"Tom, Tom!" Cheryl shrieks. "Your daughter's assaulting me. Your family's insane. You're a bunch of whack jobs, all of you. Get me outta here now."

"Cheryl, that's enough," he says. "Go get in the car."

"And take your dog food on a cracker with you." Roxy spits.

I can't keep from laughing at that.

Cheryl tries for something resembling dignity when she sniffs that she's left better places.

"Like the Tobacco Roadhouse and One Hour Nap Motel," Roxy says.

Tom wheels on her. "I said enough. Both of you. You, Roxy. Go sit by the casket. Now."

By now I'm choking, trying to keep from laughing out loud.

"I'm outta here. You're lucky if you see me tomorrow," Roxy says.

"Just be sure you don't wear those dog collar things, dear," Helen says. "And no torn sneakers."

## *Stephanie*

What a cast of characters. Roxy, you go, girl. Wish I'd had the chance to slap The Hairspray Queen upside the head. I'd have gone for it, for sure. Sorry, Dad, but your tarnished trophy wife is a big step down from Mom. As for Cheryl and her overachieving mammary glands, what nerve! This wake was supposed to be about me.

Which it was, for all of ten minutes until Dad and Bombshell Cheryl arrived.

But at least I look good. Thank you, Roxy, for making sure they didn't have me laid out in some old lady dress. And even though I'm pregnant—and dead—I don't look fat.

Speaking of death, I want you to know, Mom, that my untimely demise was the farthest thing from my mind when Liam and I set off on our honeymoon. I can see how hard this has been on you. I'm glad you brought me home to be with my real family. Thanks, Mom, for taking Colin, and yes, it's what I want.

My dear, sweet Colin, I didn't want to leave you, but Grandma Ellie is the best one to raise you. Listen to her; don't be like your naughty ma, causing her heartache and grief.

Dearest Liam, don't be angry that my mother took Colin back to America. It's where he belongs…where I want him to be. I hope you'll get to see him grow into a fine man. It seems you're the forgotten one, hovering somewhere between earth and me. But your time isn't over yet, and no one knows what the ending will be. The gentle touch on your lips is my good-bye.

Please, Mom and Dad, think of this as a second chance to work together for your grandchild. Be consistent and speak with one voice. For sure, this is funny coming from me, but things look a lot different from where I am now. I see both of you talking together in the parking lot, and Dad is taking your arm, like he should, walking you to Christa's car and the two of you hold each other for a second. Like a mom and dad about to bury their daughter.

### *Helen*

No one should go to a funeral on an empty stomach. My Ellie sat up half the night, crying, poor girl. I know—I sat up with her, the two of us. It's going to be the hardest day of her life today, and the least I can do is make sure we all have a good, hot breakfast in us.

"Colin," I say, "I love how you love my pancakes," and I mean it. How he packs it away, even asking for more bacon. I guess that's how they ate on the farm. And the way he drinks his milk—such a blessing to have a good eater. But he does jump up and run around a lot, even in the middle of eating. If Elaine has to put him back in his chair one more time…

She's making an effort with her eggs and coffee, and that's better than nothing, but I wish she'd eat more. She needs to keep up her strength.

We'll be leaving soon, so while I'm dressing Colin in his new clothes, maybe Ellie will take a few more bites without him to worry about.

❖

The final good-bye—I had no idea it would hurt this much—for me, for any of us. Little Roxy is crying so hard, I'm scared for her. It was her big sister she lost, and all I can do is hold her, hang on to her, and cry with her. Fiona's leaning on Tom for support, and tears just stream down his face, poor man. He has one arm around his mother and the other around Ellie, who's beside herself, saying "Stephanie, Stephanie," and it breaks my heart. Just before the funeral director closes the lid, she puts a framed photo of Colin, Stephanie and Liam in the coffin and kisses her girl good-bye.

❖

The incense is so thick around us, and Tom, Stuart, Andy, Denise, Maureen and Roxy take their places as pall bearers by the coffin for the recessional out of the church and into the rain.

By the time we reach the cemetery, it's raining harder, and there are more prayers and farewells in a small sheltered area. Just as the funeral director announces the service is concluded, wouldn't you know it—some old man from Tom's family opens his big mouth and says, "Say good-bye to your mother, Colin," and that starts it! We had some trouble with him during the Mass when Roxy had to take him to the back of the church and quiet him down—twice—but that's nothing compared to the commotion he raises here—kicking, screaming for Stephanie and his father, working himself into a state. Tom and his brother take him and that old bear of his to the car with them, and just as well; it gives the rest of us some peace on the way to the restaurant.

Which isn't bad at all. Thank God Tom and Elaine listened to reason. I mean Short Sammy's House of Gumbo is not the place for a proper funeral luncheon, and I don't care how much Elaine took Tom's part in this. What was his second choice, I wonder…Lame Willy's Chicken Shack?

Especially with all my friends here. How did they think we could eat that spicy food? At least here at The Blue Rooster we have a choice.

And everyone's reasonably presentable. Tom must have talked to that wife of his because she's in a black suit; form-fitting, but at least it's buttoned. Roxy's very toned down for the day; I have to hand it to her. She looks almost normal in a long black skirt and top, and none of that spiky jewelry. It's a shame she had to go and spoil it all with those men's Army boots, but the skirt almost covers them completely. Poor Ellie looks pale as bread dough. How she'll manage with Colin, I have no idea.

# Elaine

If anyone tries to give that child one more extra dessert, one more piece of candy or one more glass of pop on top of all the Italian beef, mostaccioli and ice cream he put away, he's going to get sick right here, all over everyone, and it'll serve them right. Shifting him from lap to lap with Fiona's brother, Malachi, making gloomy pronouncements (between gulps of whiskey) — "Ah, 'tis a sad day, with the lad's mother in the ground…" — enough!

Fiona picks up her part of the dirge, repeating Colin's a "poor, wee motherless lad…with his dad as good as dead or worse" while Tom gives him more ice cream — more than enough! But when I tell them to stop, they stare at me like I'm some kind of wicked witch denying this child comfort, yet what they're doing is satisfying their own morbid fascination. Col's not able to understand that we buried his mother today, and loves this table full of adult attention. They delight in his Irish expressions like "Da" for his dad and "jumper" for my mother's ever-present sweater but are less charmed when he spills his third glass of pop and bursts out with, "Shite!"

"No, Colin, that's bold!" I can't let him get away with this.

After a couple of nervous laughs, but definitely none from my mother, they resume with offers of treats and everything but a new pony, a bicycle with training wheels, and a trip to Disney World. Some even stuff money into his little hands, saying, "Your Grandma will open a bank account for you when you get home."

How much longer 'til I can escape? They can leave; they've had drinks and food and more food and more drinks and some even had coffee, so what are they waiting around for? I swear if I hear one more person promise to say a novena, I'll strangle her with her own rosary beads. Mom looks like she's ready to drop, and Roxy's so fidgety it's like she'd love to bolt any minute. Colin's been freed to dash around the restaurant and he's running from one table of people to another, laughing and shrieking, leaving cash on the floor. Tom looks drained, and he's also had more than his share to drink. He rises slowly and with effort, retrieving the bills of various denominations for me. I stuff them into my purse, leaving Tom to corral his grandson. This, of course, sets off a frenzy with Colin yowling "Put me down, Grandpa. I want down!"

I want to go home to my casita; away from these relatives I won't see until the next wedding or wake. Away from this chaos. I want to stop doing 'bereaved mother of the deceased.'

Things will be different in Santa Fe, I hope.

Right now I'm hoping Tom doesn't give Cheryl any grief; for once, she's doing the right thing and taking the car keys from him. He's clearly in no shape to drive, but wouldn't you know it, there he goes with, "Honey, I'm fine, really." Please, no more. No more tragedy.

Judging from the look on her face, it's not the first time, so I'm really not surprised when I see them in the parking lot—Tom slumping into the passenger seat and Cheryl standing by the car, sobbing.

## *Roxy*

We're back at Grandma Helen's, and it's like we can't get outta our funeral threads fast enough and into sweats. Even Grandma's in a robe and slippers. Momsie's collapsed on the couch while the rug rat's watching cartoons, and it's freakin' wierd to be here in the middle of the afternoon on a week day.

I'm no sooner in the easy chair when it's, "Roxy, could you come here and help me with this?" and I'm thinking, *Duh, now what,* but I say, "Yeah, Gram."

"I have some things for you," she says, which makes me want to roll on out, but I can't, so she's showing me old picture books of Steph's and a "grandma" card my sister had crayoned when she was about seven, and even an old teddy bear.

Is this what's left of my sister? I sink my face into the bear, hoping to what...smell her, feel her in this thing, like, that's gonna happen, Rox, but I'm crying, and so's my grandma, like we haven't cried enough. Then the doorbell rings.

## *Christa*

Roxy's wiping away tears when she answers the door, and Elaine sits up on the couch, looking worn out.

"Don't get up, Elaine. I brought your package over. You left it in the trunk last night."

*Uh oh,* her eyes say, so I put it down next to her. Helen comes into the room dressed for bed, but still the hostess. "Hello, Christa.

How about some tea? You look so pretty—still dressed up. Sit dear, sit."

I've been in heels for two days and happily kick them off. It's nice in here, with just the few of us, some afternoon sun at last coming through the clouds, and Colin quiet by the TV. Helen heads to the kitchen though I haven't answered her.

"What's in there?" Roxy asks.

"Just an old painting I did." Something's off in Elaine's tone.

"Let's see." Clearly, Roxy's interested.

When Elaine shakes her head dismissively, I add, "Yes, please."

Roxy's ripping off the heavy kraft paper with her black lacquered fingernails, and stops halfway through with, "Yo! Mom! He's got it goin' on!"

Indeed he does. It's Jeff, reclining seductively, stud muffin that he is, with not a stitch on…

Roxy's got the rest of the wrappings off in a flash, and we all stare silently, in appreciation, no doubt. Elaine looks at me mutely for support, and I'm beginning to see why…

Helen's voice reaches us before she does. "Would you like regular or herbal tea? I have…"

She never finishes that thought. Instead, as she sees the painting her eyes widen and she barely manages a faint, "Oh…my." At least she isn't holding the tea tray.

❖

"Nothing could have prepared my mother for that—a naked man on a bed—and in her living room," Laney says, flushing. "And after the day she's had, it's a miracle she's still standing."

Actually, she isn't. After hiding the painting behind the sofa despite Roxy's protests, Helen was the perfect hostess and served tea and cookies. She took to her bed right after tucking Colin in, and we haven't heard a peep from either of them. Roxy's out with Michael, who's probably getting an earful, so it's just me and Elaine at the kitchen table, two glasses and Helen's bottle of "medicinal" brandy between us.

"It's been over for a long time…I should have told you…" She can't look at me.

"Yes, you should have. If not right away, at least when it ended. I thought we were close, Elaine."

She keeps staring down at her glass of brandy. "Steph and Col were with us, and Frank was unbearable, and Jeff was…there. Young, handsome…and interested in my work."

"I told you about Mercedes. Willingly. You never said a word about Jeff. Would you, if it hadn't been for the painting?"

"He made me feel…"

*No doubt.* "Hmmm."

"Oh Christa, I should have told you…" Finally she looks up at me. "I had no reason to keep it from you. I don't know why I did." She traces the rim of her glass with her fingertip. "And you've done so much for me."

*Damn right.* "Didn't you trust me?"

"It's that…looking back on it…" she breaks off, staring at the refrigerator. "It wasn't you…"

"Can you answer me, Elaine?"

She glances my way before returning her attention to the refrigerator. "I'm sorry. What was the question?"

"About trusting me." The sadness in her eyes adds years to her face, already aged by the past week's events. I'm just as sad when I say, "Let me know the answer…sometime." And I'm out of there.

## *Elaine*

Another flight with Colin, this time with the ever-fascinating electronic cell phone toy (extra batteries in my tote, of course); then the shuttle bus. Thankfully he naps on the seat next to me as the arid landscape welcomes me home.

First thing yesterday I cut up every paper grocery bag of my mother's and used them to wrap the nude of a male hottie—then hustled it over to the nearest FedEx, Colin in tow. Our reward was breakfast at McDonalds and an energetic half-hour in the play area.

When we returned, Helen had the table set for our "ladies' luncheon" with Pat and Christa, our gesture of thanks for all they've done.

Christa called Helen with apologies—not that I expected her to show up after that conversation about Jeff—still, it stung me, so how could I think about eating, even Helen's famous pasta salad, turkey sandwiches and sherbet served with the good china and silver, all on top of a lace tablecloth? "Mom, you fussed. I could've helped if you'd waited."

"It was nice to just putter alone in my kitchen, dear. After all, it isn't every day I meet that nice lady our Roxy stays with."

"Pat. Her name is Pat…"

❖

Today I can't wait to get home and putter in my own kitchen. Trish and the smell of fresh coffee greet us at my door. She's holding Callie while Colin's grabbing for her tail, and the poor cat jumps down and races to the bedroom. To retrieve her precious chenille scrap, I'm sure. This does not bode well for Callie; for any of us.

Col's pulled cars and trucks out of my travel tote and on the floor almost before I can sit and catch my breath. "Seems like I've been gone a month, Trish, but it's not even two weeks."

"Callie's made herself at home with Winston; no problem. But you—how are you managing?" She serves me much needed refreshment. Colin's too busy to eat.

Trish's coffee and some kind of wholegrain muffins she's made give me enough energy to wonder—how am I managing? Or are events managing me?

A thud in the living room reminds me the place isn't childproof yet, and I turn to see my coffee table books on the floor. I'll have to get that Acoma pot away from the fireplace hearth and to the safety of the hutch—one of many changes needed with Colin here. Which is what I rise and do immediately after a no-nonsense, "Leave Grandma's books on the table, Colin! Aren't you hungry?"

In answer he takes my hand, pulling me toward the back courtyard. "Out to the cows, Grandma," he says, but when I tell him there aren't any here, this reminds him of his calf, Dora, which he misses, then Rosie, which reminds him he never rode his pony for me, which makes him cry for his Grandpa and Grandma—and his ma.

With all this wailing and tears from Colin, Trish beats a hasty retreat—smart woman—which leaves me here with a toddler having a meltdown and a cat hanging on to her bedspread scrap for dear life. If only I had a scrap…

After calming Colin and getting some canned soup and crackers into him, he snuggles next to me in my bed, and he's asleep within minutes.

That was the last can of soup…we need to shop, ASAP, now that Colin's living here…for soup and crackers, peanut butter, macaroni and cheese, milk and eggs, cheese, juice–lots of juice, bread, jelly, children's vitamins, cold cereal, fruit, oatmeal, microwave popcorn, pretzels, cookies and ice cream.

The kitchen cupboards all need child-proof safety locks, and I'll pick up socket covers, too, so he doesn't electrocute himself. Not that I saw any at Maggie and John's, but that's not the point.

He'll also need at least a half-dozen T-shirts, shorts, maybe a light jacket for starters, and sandals, too. Before we know it, it'll be 90 degrees in the shade.

❖

By the time we return, dusk is falling, and we've gotten his clothes—plus a wooden tool kit with pegs. And a little wooden hammer to pound them.

Finding the socket covers and the cabinet locks was easy enough, just like the humongous cart of groceries at the supermarket—plus the cat food and kitty litter I remembered for Callie and the Ben & Jerry's Chunky Monkey for me. Still, by the time I checked out, Colin started kicking to get out of the cart's child seat and yelling for his ma. "If you're quiet, I'll get you a treat," I say, trying to ignore the looks other shoppers are giving us. How long can I do 'Fine. Everything's fine' when I'm ready to throttle this child I'll be raising alone? More to the point, how can I even begin to pay for these clothes and groceries and…stuff, not just today, but all the time—without a better job?

❖

Colin's pounded his pegs with his wooden hammer, had his bath, a story, a sip of water and a big good night hug and kiss, and is asleep with Bear in my bed—his, now that I'll be using the sofa bed until I get another for him. I forgot to get him pajamas; his are too small, but he looks adorable in them. Tomorrow, another trip to the store…and I have to arrange daycare…then talk to Mrs. Ruiz at the hospital ASAP. I know they need more full-timers there because she's tried to recruit me before.

Bye-bye, spa; bye-bye, painting; bye-bye, life. Good-bye, carefree hikes with friends and quiet dinners.

But he's my grandchild and I helped raise him the first year and a half. We'll bond again, he'll calm down, learn to trust me, and we'll manage.

❖

First things first: safety locks on the cabinets, a good, hot breakfast, then a trip through the Yellow Pages for daycare; I can't do a thing—go back to the spa or the hospital or the human resources department there for a full-time job—without someone to look after Colin. I never thought I'd need daycare again; surely some of the nurses at the hospital know…but to get there and ask, I have to first find someone to care for Col. He's currently terrorizing Callie by trying to grab her and pull her from under the couch; the poor thing's had to venture out for her food dish and litter box at night.

He knows cats and dogs, ponies and cows; probably more than many kids his age. "No, Col. This is Callie, and she's a good like Nettie on the farm, remember?" *Was it a mistake to remind him?* "When she wants to come out, she will, and then we're nice to her, and she's nice to us."

A pouch of cat treats helps lure her to my lap, with Colin under strict orders to sit quietly by me on the floor. He's quick to see how a few treats and a gentle hand soothe her, so when I guide his hand over her soft fur, he's eager to please and touches her light as a kiss, saying, "Nice Callie. Good girl," and she's soon purring and he's smiling.

"That's how we treat animals. We're kind to them and we don't hurt them or scare them. Then they're our friends."

"Not scarey," he says smiling and clearly pleased with this victory. He watches intently as I gently put her down and, happily, he doesn't chase her. "Nice Callie," he says, turning to his trucks. She goes straight to her litter box and within minutes is cleaning herself in a sunny spot by the back door.

"She's washing," he says, apparently satisfied at this, and mimes her actions. He's interrupted by the FedEx man at the door who delivers my painting. The one of Jeff that left my mother speechless, if that's possible. Monday's going to be phone day; calling daycare centers, private babysitters, and the hospital, so while we're out getting pajamas for Colin and picking up my mail, I suppose I should bring that painting over to Sophia today.

She's sweeping the sidewalk and stops, saying, "Elaine, who is that handsome young man with you? I don't believe I've ever seen such green eyes and strawberry blond hair." Colin, spiffy in his new clothes, hides behind my long denim skirt, clutching Bear." I haven't seen you in a while. How are you? You missed our last get-together."

"This is my grandson, Colin. He's living with me now. I'm looking for a daytime sitter so I can go back to work. Do you know of anyone who would be interested?"

"I might know of someone. Let me make a call and I'll let you know."

*Be still my heart! If only...* "Colin, we're nice to the kitty, right?" He's busy now trying to coax Sophia's tabby out of her shop, and chimes in, "Nice. Grandma says be nice. Not scarey." Then, without missing a beat, "My mommy's with the angels, isn't she Grandma?"

Sophia sends me a look which I return with a small nod. She bends down as close to his level as she can manage. "Your grandmother will take good care of you, I'm sure." She rises, motioning us in and asking me, "Is it OK if I give him a cookie? I made them myself."

Chocolate chip cookies, and at the sight of them, Colin rocks back and forth on his feet with excitement saying, "A cookie. I like chocolate chips!" and I realize he hasn't shown such simple, spontaneous joy the whole time we've been together in Ireland, on the plane, at my mother's...he makes short work of the treat, and is talking to the cat who's safely out of his reach on a high book shelf when I begin unwrapping the picture.

"I'm so sorry, Elaine, I had no idea."

"We just got back from Ireland...."

"Is there anything I can..." she says, then stops, her gaze fixed on the painting. "Oh, my, Elaine. That's good, it really is. And in oils, too. You've mostly done water colors. This is your strongest work by far. How recent?

"A year...or so..." *Has it been that long?*

"I know someone who might want to see it, and maybe a few other pieces you've done, but especially this. He's Porter Williams, and last month he opened the Parabola Space Gallery on Romero Street, just southwest of the main drag." She looks at the painting again, then at me. "You said you have some at home, too, right?"

I'm walking on air and filled with hope as we buy Colin some pajamas and a large plastic storage bin for his toys, but I'm back to Earth with a thud at the post office. There, among the many pieces of junk mail, and bills is an Air Mail letter addressed to Colin Michael Casey c/o E. McElroy from the Caseys.

It sits unopened on the kitchen counter beneath the bills.

## Sophia

My daughter's been motherly since she was a tiny little thing, so adding Elaine's Colin to the three she watches didn't seem like a problem. He's the same age as the little girl, Heather, and we thought they'd play together, but the boy isn't getting along with the other kids; just grabs what he wants out of their hands without asking. I've seen it myself; he's learned a little about sharing and he's bright enough, but my Chloe has to remind him constantly. He's certainly having his share of timeouts. Could raising children be so different in Ireland?

To be fair, an uprooted only child who's lost his mother has issues. Chloe tells me Colin's outbursts about his mother are heartbreaking. She's seen some improvement in the week she's had him, but lots of tears, too.

## *Elaine*

Chloe says Colin's doing better, and I'll soon be working four 10-hour day shifts at the hospital, which has its own onsite daycare—thank you, Mrs. Ruiz! She understands my situation; she's a grandmother, after all, and those months of weekend work when I never turned down a shift didn't hurt, either.

And now a gallery show at Parabola Space! How great is that, but how am I ever going to turn out another three to five paintings to "fill out" my part of the exhibit? I mean, I'm grateful to Sophia's networking, not to mention Porter, who owns the gallery, but how will I fit this in? This opportunity to die for? Just my work and one other artist's? What a step up from that group show where I was one of—how many? A lot. I'll just have to, that's all. True, it's not a major show in a big gallery during Indian Market, and it's only for three weeks during the dead of winter, but I'll be seen as a Local Talent and not just another transplant establishing myself here as a painter.

But to turn out more paintings for Porter to see by November! There's my sketchbook of landscapes since I moved here, but it was that picture of Jeff...still, can I do the same quality work here, on my own, without him?

## *Christa*

I'm surprised at Elaine's phone call; not so much that she calls, but at myself—that I'm so happy to hear her voice. She seems upbeat about her new job and Colin.

"What about his daycare?"

"There's one onsite for hospital employees, and the people I've talked to swear by it. During my breaks I can even go down and visit him. And wait 'til you hear this: I'll be in a show; a two-woman show the end of the year. I want to paint you..."

That's how she pitches it: a series of portraits of me...and when can I come out so she can start?

What? Excuse me? "My clients, Elaine. I just returned to them. From Ireland...with you, remember?"

She ignores this, babbling on about needing photos and, believe it or not, maybe using The Trail of Broken Feet as background. She's lost her mind. Next it'll be a picture of me and Sammy the Sidewinder in the courtyard.

"Why me?"

"You don't want to?" Elaine clearly hasn't considered this possibility. "Not even for a long weekend? Too bad we just missed Memorial Day..." I have to laugh out loud. Is she on drugs?

"Stop, Laney. You're running full-tilt with this, and I need time to consider. I'm probably visiting Trish in a week or so, and maybe—"

This silences her, so I hurry to explain. "We became...close ...when I saw you last month, with the snake and all. And we've spoken to each other and e-mailed almost every day since. We're together—"

"A couple? Oh, Christa, listen, in that case, I could do a "Women in Love" series, maybe four or five paintings of you both."

A couple, yes. New, and still discovering each other. I only wish I'd taken an extra day or two and extended our long weekend together. In a few weeks, though, we'll be together again when I come back over the Fourth. Elaine's restrained herself, managing to give me all of nine uninterrupted hours of privacy (only nine?) with Trish before calling to invite us for dinner...and while we're at it, sitting for a few, "just a few, I promise"—photos and sketches. Trish thinks it's hilarious we'll be "immortalized." I love seeing her laugh. She may be The One.

Now that we've been wined and dined and Colin's in bed, Elaine's following our every move with her Polaroid, "for candids, so I can capture the real you," she says, but the shots emphasize the dark circles under my eyes, and Trish's don't look much better. Besides, these pictures make me look fat. My hair's hanging in my face after playing on the floor with Callie and my T-shirt's sticking to me. No way do we want her painting from these, but she persists, promising, "just a few more reference shots so I can get started, and then…" Good thing she's busy working all day tomorrow and Sunday, or I'd leave here with permanent flash photophobia.

And then we get to sit down. Trish brushes a few stray hairs hanging in my eyes as Elaine's hands move rapidly over the sketch pad with sticks of charcoal. In no time she's turned out a half-dozen of us holding hands, hugging, with Trish's head on my shoulder, and me sprawled out with my head in Trish's lap. Finally satisfied, Elaine calls it a night. At least until my next visit. Not a moment too soon, though seeing pictures of me together with Trish makes 'us' more real.

How real, how lasting, is Laney's enthusiasm, I wonder? Underneath the brightness, there's unmistakable fatigue in her eyes. Nervous energy seems to be fueling this excitement of hers more than anything else. She was so busy playing hostess and seeing to Colin that she barely ate. Tonight was no exception, judging from the way her clothes hung on her. With her easel moved into her bedroom, it's like she's never away from work of one kind or another, not even in the room where she sleeps. Mental note: Get Elaine a large, folding screen to divide her art space from her rest space.

## *Elaine*

Tourists clog the streets and stores, even the supermarket. Getting around and getting anything done is a disaster during Indian Market. How those people can take that blazing sun as they stand on line for the Port-A-Potties is beyond me. And to think last August I was one of them.

Now I have to focus on getting in and out of the store without Colin pitching a fit for some candy at the checkout. I'm hungry and tired from working all day, Col's sticky and cranky, but we need to stop at the store for milk and cereal and a few other things. The next hurdle is hauling the stuff out to that oven of a car, and inching home through the traffic and humanity.

Living close to the Plaza has its disadvantages this weekend, like having to park two blocks from the house. Walking in this heat with my purse, tote bag, groceries and Colin in tow makes me sticky and cranky, too.

The living room air conditioner's broken and won't be replaced until Monday, so no oven tonight. It'll be boxed macaroni and cheese with veggies on the side and chilled fruit. "Col, please bring me Callie's water bowl while I start dinner—two hands, Colin."

"So I don't spill, Ma?"

"Yes." It's not the first time he's called me 'Ma,' which still pierces my heart each time he does. When I think of what I've taken on, I wonder, what if something happened to me?

Callie's by my feet, of course, playing 'let's trip Elaine,' and Winston peeks out from my room. He's staying with us while Trish visits Christa; what a great time for her to get out of this tourist onslaught.

"Good job, Col. Now Winston's water."

I open a can of his cat food and some Fancy Feast for Callie, a special treat.

The cats are well into their meals when I turn on the radio and we sit down to our own dinner, tired and sweaty but together, the four of us. "What did you play today?" He doesn't look up from his macaroni. "Did you play outside?"

"Outside…on the monkey bars." He pushes his green beans around on his plate.

"What else did you do?"

"We got to swing on the big swings." He looks up at me, eyes wide. "I went up high, really, really high. To the sky."

I smile the best smile I can muster while chewing, marveling at the wonders of big swings. Before I know it, he's off his chair and heading toward his box of action figures. "I'm done," he yells.

"No, you're not. Come back here and finish your green beans and milk. And share a peach with me." Corralling him's never easy, especially after a 10-hour shift, but I have to do what I have to do.

Once he's eaten, and I've seen to it that he's successfully undressed himself, put his dirty clothes in the hamper and chosen his bath toys, it's into the tub with him, but not for long; early to bed for an early start tomorrow. He protests when I help him brush his teeth with his Batman toothbrush, but he still needs help with that; then it's into his new Batman pj's—way cool. Then we read *Goodnight Moon* and *The Very Hungry Caterpillar*, and after that, a sip of water followed by prayers. Colin's reminded me that his Grandma Maggie always had him pray to God and all the Holy and Divine Saints at bedtime. In the beginning, he would launch into a litany of, "God bless Ma and Da and Grandma and Grandpa and Rosie and Dora…" I've adapted it to "Please God, keep us safe, and remember everyone we love."

Then come hugs, lots of 'I love you's,' and one 'good night,' and he's holding Bear as I close his door. Hopefully he won't appear in my room tonight wanting more water or to climb into bed with me. Or worse, wake up screaming with night terrors that he hasn't the words to explain.

Best to make the most of the opportunity right away. Everything in me wants to collapse on my bed, but I have to paint, at least a little every night. Switching from oils to acrylics makes it easier since they're quick drying and clean up with water, but that doesn't guarantee the energy level I need. Sometimes mixing the colors and feeling the pull of the pigment beneath the brush on the canvas gives me an incredible boost and I continue until my eyes burn. Most often it's an effort, and I wonder how long I can do this. Until you have finished what you need for your big show, girl—duh. Or until I drop to the floor, whichever comes first. At least I go to bed knowing I've done something just for myself.

The annoying buzz of the alarm clock comes as an unwelcome messenger whether I've slept well or tossed around trying to get some rest. What do other menopausal women do? In any case, I'm up at dawn, making sure the cats have fresh water and food, helping Colin dress, giving him his back pack, gulping coffee while I throw a granola bar, a sandwich and an orange in my tote, and getting us out the door by 5:30. It's still a shock to my 53-year-old system. Thank heavens Col's fed breakfast as well as lunch at daycare. Once I take him there, he stows his Teenage Mutant Turtles back pack in his cubby and gets down to the serious business of loading blocks into a dump truck and building roads and houses, but if he's had a troubled night, he might cling to me. In his first days there, he hung onto Bear, bawled, and had to be pried off me by the teacher, Miss Annette, who assured me he'd be fine. Now he's usually OK, though I'm getting some of the same reports on his behavior that I had from Chloe, and especially on the days after those bad dreams.

In any case, once he's at daycare, I'm off to the fifth floor for the morning report when the nurses working nights fill us in on what's gone on, who needs pain meds, who's having surgery this morning, which IVs need changing, and who will be discharged. I hit the ground running, and don't sit down until my lunch break, when I grab a bite and get to put my feet up in the nurse's lounge, the senior citizen of floor nurses surrounded by people literally half my age. The conversation's not deep or meaningful, but still a welcome change before reporting back on duty. It seems as though lunch break's barely over before it's three and time to update my charting, and check my IVs to make sure none will run out during report. Cross fingers, arms and legs and hope that nothing happens to my patients until after four when I'm out the door to pick up Colin. Please, Mr. Jackson, don't die at 3:50; try to hang on 10 more minutes, and then you can go in peace with my blessing.

Collecting Colin means bringing home his latest paintings, drawings and designs made with Cheerios glued onto construction paper. The art exhibit on my refrigerator changes all the time, held in place with magnets of cactus, coyotes, cowboy boots and Stetsons. The day's mail may or may not bring another letter from the Caseys to Colin; do I open them or continue to stack them on the counter? I now have four. If I wait long enough, he'll be able to read them himself, so I'll do Scarlett O'Hara and think about it tomorrow.

Which is a day off for me, and that means sleeping in at least until 6:30 or even 7:00. Eggs and toast with unhurried coffee, followed by errands and, if he's good, an excursion to the park, which he loves. He's fearless on the swings, hanging on the chains and laughing while I push him and he yells, "More, Ma! Higher!" The first time I saw Colin scramble up the steps of the spiral-shaped slide, I held my breath, but he's naturally agile and well-coordinated, usually sliding down five or six times in a row before climbing to the top of the jungle gym–then crossing a little bridge to the tree house, where he crawls through a tube, then comes down through a slide.

Good thing I've been a school nurse, so I can easily deal with all his cuts, scrapes, bumps and bruises. I haven't gone as far as bringing an actual first aid kit to the playground with me, but there's one in the car, just in case.

He usually winds up in the sand box with his little plastic bucket of rakes and shovels, making roads for his cars and trucks, using the dump truck to move the sand. This can hold his attention for as long as 10 or even 15 minutes. When other kids are in the sand box with him, he gets territorial about these public works projects of his and might throw sand or refuse to share until I remind him. Preschool sand box etiquette! So much for him to learn, not to mention the inappropriateness of the Irish blasphemies he's been known to shout at the kids.

"Bloody eejit" and "gobshite" have been known to escape this little angel's lips, much to the dismay of the other adults.

"Please excuse him; he's from another country and just recently moved here," I lamely explain. "Enough, Colin!" I scold. "We do *not* use that language." I imagine the other grandmas and moms and nannies whispering about us the minute our backs are turned.He needs work, to be sure, but the kids continue to play with him, and some even seem to enjoy him. There's one little dark-haired boy who seeks him out every time we see him here, and they race each other to the swings or up the slide. Joshua's mom compares notes with me about our boys' energy, and we're glad they're buddies. Colin's learning how to get along here, just as he is in daycare.

The library story time is another chance for him to be with kids, and he retells the stories to me and likes to sing the songs he learns like "Where is Thumbkin?" and "Itsy Bitsy Spider."

It's hard to balance such a full plate. If it weren't for my art show, I could have more time for chores, sleep, or even the pleasure of reading. But if it weren't for my show, what would get me through this unbroken routine of doing 'single working grandma'?

## Roxy

Mom says the hospital gig is all good, and so's the rug rat, pretty much... She's totally pumped about her show, and she's all about the new pictures she's been painting. Anyway, Momsa wants me there for the opening, or at least to see the show.

She's all like, "Rox, honey, it'll open before Christmas, and remember how much fun we had last year? I can't wait for you to come visit again, sweetie."

*Sweetie. Honey.* Well, maybe I could work it out so I meet up with Christa at O'Hare. She'll be going out there, too, now that she's dating Trish and flies to Santa Fe like, a lot, Momsa says— how awesome is that—you go, Christa! And if this new gallery has anything like those exploding snakes I saw at Mom's other show, it'll be smokin'. I mean, excellent!

Maybe the picture of that studly, bare-ass dude old Mom-ola painted will be there, too.

Speaking of dudes...I tell her The Bomb is that I've met my

258

new boy, TJ, a bouncer at this punk club I've been going to. Michael is so-o-o history.

"Oh," she says, and I can tell she's bummed. "What does he do—this TJ—besides bounce, I mean? Is he in school?"

I'm like, dig it dude, he's in school to be an R.N., plus he's a bouncer at Poison, this new music spot that's slammin'....I want to tell her about my homies, how I chill there, and how fine TJ is.

Instead I tell her how Dad insists I come to dinner every Wednesday and eat Witch Mama's vomit food. This makes Mom happy. Good thing I date a nurse.

Grandma Helen makes me come over for a big Sunday dinner "so we can be together, dear, now that your sister's gone. You're all I have." So, like, with eating here and eating there, and going to school full-time, when do I get to hang with my man TJ, who's hangin' with his books or bouncin'? But Momsa's all good about those Sunday dinners, just telling me to take out my eyebrow ring and nose stud first. There's only so much Gram can take.

One thing we agree on: we both love that she sends me back to Katelyn's with a cake or cookies and bags of snacks "for that nice family you live with, dear." Only when I'm outta Helen's crib do I put my eyebrow ring and nose stud back in. Don't want her strokin' out on me. After all, she's all I have, too.

I wonder if Stephanie can see me at our grandma's table or when I'm at Dad's. Does she know we miss her? Dad doesn't say much, not in front of Cheryl; not to me. But Gram and me, we talk and I try to remember. All that was so long ago and, dude, it's hard, you know, to think of my sister in that casket, and mostly I try not to go there.

## *Trish*

I refuse to take 'no' for an answer. "Elaine," I say, "you and Colin both need to get out into Nature. It's the perfect fall day for a picnic and a walk up Aspen Vista Trail. The whole side of the mountain is breathtaking...golden."

"Oh, please. I could never do it. I went up there with Christa in the spring, and if I was tired then, I'm exhausted now."

"All the more reason to get out into the invigorating mountain air. It'll do us all good." She does not look convinced. More like she's just waiting for me to finish before launching another protest, so I press on. "Besides, it's so close. People come here from...from wherever, to hike the trails and see the aspens. It will be a great change of scene for Colin; something different from the daycare routine."

She seems to waver, then smiles wryly. "Christa called it 'The Trail of Broken Feet' when we hiked it last spring."

"You have that darling wagon you found for Col at the thrift shop. We'll bring it along for him, and put our picnic lunch in it, too."

Before she can find an excuse, I cut off debate. "Great. It's settled then. I'll pick you up in an hour."

❖

Parking's crowded—of course, on such a sunny, crisp day—but we find a spot not too far from the grassy area before the trail starts. Colin insists on pulling the wagon with our lunch, so we dub him the 'Wagon Master,' and let him pick a spot for our picnic.

"Right here," he says, grinning and almost dancing as he holds one corner of the blanket that puffs briefly from a breeze. "We got sandwiches," he announces. "With peanut butter and some jam." We unpack the rest: juice boxes, cheese crackers and grapes.

The yellows, reds and oranges of the fall trees seem to relax Elaine. After lunch we try to take a moment to rest, looking up at the clouds and finding images in their shapes, but it's only a moment because Colin quickly loses interest with the idea of horses and dinosaurs in the bright blue backdrop of the sky.

The hikers and their dogs, especially their dogs, get his attention, though, so he's reasonably happy in the wagon that I'm pulling—for all of five minutes before he's out and pulling it, then back in while Elaine pulls it for a while, and then it's my turn. By the time we reach the overlook, it's full of people with their cameras and dogs, and Colin's fast asleep. Elaine wakes him and lifts him up to see the view, but I doubt it makes an impression since he's out cold again in a minute and stays that way in the wagon ride down to the car.

"So far I've finished two paintings and I'm working on the others," Elaine tells me, taking the opportunity for uninterrupted adult conversation. "How do you manage it, working all day and doing your jewelry at night?" She glances back at Colin. "By the time I get him fed, bathed and settled into bed, I'm ready to collapse, even on days I'm not at the hospital."

"I'm not chasing after a three-year-old, and it's hard. I can't imagine how you do it."

"I have to. It's October, and Porter needs to see my work for this show soon—in a month. The series of you and Christa will be the focus, I'm sure, with whatever landscapes he chooses."

Being the focus, even at a tiny new gallery, could be a mixed blessing, assuming the series is chosen. Paintings of me with Christa as "Women in Love" are nothing less than an open declaration of the two of us as a couple, and Christa doesn't seem too ready for something so public...especially in a commuter relationship, as she reminds me. Like I could forget. We're both such private people. She hasn't been out that long, either, and only with that one woman before me. Could this make or break us? I thought the idea of portraits was so far-fetched, it was funny at first. Now that Elaine's produced actual work and the show's weeks away, Christa's not so sure about this.

Elaine's been going on and on about the various portraits and landscapes she's completed when she breaks into my thoughts, asking, "But what if they're not good enough; if I'm not good enough?"

What if anything we do, or any of us, isn't good enough? There's no real answer. We come here to live and create art and some of us decide it's best to return to our old lives in Minneapolis or Pittsburgh or Boise, but some of us stay. The lucky ones here land a government job with benefits, becoming the civil servants they swore they'd never be. The less fortunate wait tables for tourists. So few of us establish ourselves creatively ...here...anywhere. But at least there's a large community of like-minded souls here who keep on trying.

"They'll be fine," I tell her. "Just fine."

## *Elaine*

Porter was right; they're like bookends holding the space together: the portrait of Jeff lying on the bed hung next to the horizontal picture of Christa with her head on Trish's lap. They'll command the attention of everyone entering the gallery.

Maybe it's the powerful combination of the two paintings, or perhaps that Colin was up half the night with bad dreams and night demons, but looking at this work, my work, makes me almost light-headed. *Breathe, Elaine. That's good; you remember how to breathe.*

It's not exhaustion that makes me dizzy and my heart pound, though God knows, I'm ready to fall over; it's sheer adrenaline and exhilaration at seeing this, my desert scenes along one side of the room and the four others of Christa and Trish on the other.

My favorite in the series is the one of Callie and Christa playing on the floor. She's in a sweaty old T-shirt with her hair hanging in her face, but what we see of her eyes radiates energy and playfulness.

Hard to imagine anyone sweating in this December chill; some say we'll be seeing snow before the week's out. But try explaining the need for warm clothes to Colin, who's so attached to his short-sleeved "Bug's Life" T-shirt that he doesn't want to wear anything else. We reached a deal today: he'll wear his precious ant shirt over a long-sleeved cotton turtleneck. Is this the New Age, preschool version of win-win? I don't remember doing this with Stephanie or Roxy when they were little; I just got out their clothes and helped them get dressed and that was that. Now the kids seem to have the Right of First Refusal, and when did all that happen?

Christa's flying in tomorrow for another long weekend with Trish so the two of them can come to the opening together. Who else will show up? Hopefully everyone in Sophia's group of artists, and maybe a few from the spa and the hospital. Come to think of it, I've sensed something from Christa. Not that I've spoken to her at great length, but when we do touch base about the show's progress it's almost like she's having second thoughts about these paintings. How could she, when she hasn't seen them? The "Women..." pictures will be a total surprise to Trish, too. The only work in the series that anyone's seen is the one Porter chose for my half of the postcard announcing the show: a portrait of Trish brushing a strand of hair from Christa's forehead; an unforced, intimate moment.

The other artist—Zoe, who's been here for years—has a semi-abstract winter landscape of the mesas and hills on her half of the card. Between us both we'll be lucky to get a handful to actually show up at this off-season opening. If we had to depend on me, it would be closer to four or five. Roxy will fly out to visit in a week or so when her fall term's over, but I wish she could be here when the show opens. We need all the warm bodies we can get.

Omigod...what if no one comes? What if no one likes my work?

It's too late. What's done is hung, and I need to pick up Colin. Mustn't dwell.

C hrista's stiffness immediately tells me something's wrong. Is it that she doesn't want people staring at us? It's not like I'm planting a great big, wet one on her in the middle of Albuquerque International Airport for all to see. I'd never do that. We're two women greeting each other with a hug, for God's sake. Like women air-kiss all the time when they do lunch.

Yes, she says, the flight was all right...this silence, though: NOT.

As I drive us home, she looks straight ahead with a fixed stare. "What's wrong? Is everything OK?" She's been concerned about those paintings for some time now, and more so these last few days as the opening draws nearer. It's all we talk about, it seems. No answer. "You seem a little...You're so quiet."

"I almost didn't get on the plane," she says with tight lips. I reach for her hand to hold, but she pulls away. "No. You're driving."

"You're scared. But you did get on the plane, and I'm glad." Truly I am, and the sight of her makes me happy.

❖

Christa's brought an oversized suitcase plus a garment bag, and tried on three different outfits: first, urban sophisticate, then designer pants suit for a suburban soiree, and finally country girl in denim skirt with tan Tony Lama cowboy boots. She claimed they all made her look fat. She looked so gorgeous in all three, I wanted the show to be over right then and there. Finally, she decided none of them were right, and after two different hair styles and a change of make-up (at that point, forget gorgeous— I wanted to throttle her), she settled on the boots, a pair of Calvin Klein jeans with my silver concho belt, and an ivory silk blouse under a butter-soft, toffee-colored, leather jacket. I helped her finish the look with my favorite turquoise earrings and necklace, three silver rings, and a Valium, washed down with white wine.

"C'mon, Mona Lisa, time to go," I insist, and I practically have to throw her in the car.

All the way over, she's been obsessing about how terrible she looked the night Elaine did the sketches and photos, and worse than that, what if she painted us naked, and if she did, does her cellulite show...and will the gallery be picketed by anti-gay protestors.

I suppress a laugh and try to calm her. "Relax, honey. Since Ellen came out, it's chic to be gay. All those little straight girls out there are trying to be like us."

She isn't hearing me, and says over and over, "I don't know if I can do this," (after all those costume changes?) and is literally wringing her hands when we arrive. When, oh when, will that Valium kick in?

The first thing that hits us as we open the door is the center display panel with a large painting of Christa sprawled out on the couch with her head resting on my lap. We're fully dressed, which is more than I can say for the dark-haired dude, also lying down, in the picture next to it.

"Oh, my God…that's…us." She clutches my arm.

"Christa, relax. They're beautiful paintings…and we have clothes on. Let's get a closer look." On the left side of this front portion of the gallery are Elaine's desert scenes, and on the right, four other portraits of Christa and me. These show a closeness, an easy intimacy (probably from the wine at Elaine's that night) without overt sexuality. "See? There was nothing to worry about."

Her grip loosens. "We look…like real people…"

"As opposed to faux people?" I take her hand; it's cold and clammy from nerves. "Sweetie, trust me…you're real. I'm real." I want to hug her, but she might bolt and run.

From the rear of the gallery comes Michael, a local "character" who's lived in a shack up in the mountains for years and comes into town to beg outdated meat and limp produce from the supermarket. Occasionally, this former math professor reads poetry at the coffeehouses, and of course, shows up at every gallery opening in town for the refreshments. Tonight he goes to the counter displaying white wine and plastic cups, hoping for solid food to appear. His off-the-shoulder gold lamé dress shows an alluring swatch of black chest hair that matches his military boots. He's pulled his long, salt-and-pepper waves into a loose ponytail for the occasion, and trimmed his beard as well.

Christa's eyes widen at the sight, and she moves closer to me. "Don't worry," I say. "He's harmless; the town's eccentric mountain man."

"A mountain man…in gold lamé?"

I have to grin. "He tells people he's honoring his feminine energy."

"He should shave."

Just then, Elaine bursts from behind the half-wall displaying her work, and looking like Dude Ranch Barbie in fringed boots and long denim skirt with tooled leather belt. Is the Stetson and lariat in the back? "Thank God. For a while I thought the only person here would be…" She inclines her head toward Michael. "All those late nights, all my hard work, and now…this." She rolls her eyes. Christa enfolds her in a hug. Elaine steps back. "Both of you look…gorgeous." Christa, definitely, but I doubt my black jeans outfit qualifies. Elaine's probably just relieved to see two people here who are interested in her work…and not in drag.

"The portraits of us…"

"Are lovely." Christa finishes my sentence.

Apparently tired of waiting for the food (will there be any at all?) Michael picks up his worn canvas back pack and approaches our little group. I know him by sight and reputation only, so don't introduce him, though I doubt a formal introduction applies here.

Gazing at the paintings of Jeff and the two of us side by side, our resident cross dresser says, "The negative space formed by the juxtaposition of the opposing elements is so compelling…a commentary on the masculine and feminine, adjacent, but discreet."

"Yes," I say, recalling my 2-D Design classes.

He extends a hair-covered hand. "I'm Michael. Don't you find the symmetry of the two pieces pleasing?"

"I'm Trish. I've seen you at some poetry events in town. This is Christa and this is Elaine, the artist. Do you paint, too?"

"No, I'm a poet-mathematician, and I occasionally read…around. Have you seen Zoe's landscapes in back?"

They are, quite simply, no match for Elaine's. But any octogenarian who's lived alone in an ancient Airstream trailer in the middle of sand and tumbleweeds, painting year after year, deserves some recognition. The sun has turned this living legend into a dark brown, reptilian creature with bright, darting eyes. Even though she drives into town in an old Jeep and gets supplies and mail, people have started going out to check on her, just in case. As far as anyone knows, this recluse has been here forever and has no relatives. Porter, resplendent in a grey suit and silver bolo tie, has her ready to receive well-wishers in a battered wooden chair probably as old as she is—but no one's on hand to be received…except us.

It's an awkward moment. She sits enveloped in a woolen serape over a long, worsted skirt, and can't seem to recall Porter;

she interrupts our greetings by asking him, "You…what's your name again? You have anything to drink here?"

"Or eat?" asks Michael.

"I was just about to serve," Porter sniffs pretentiously, producing a can of dry roasted peanuts that he empties into an earthenware bowl. He proudly takes it to the counter, where he pours a glass of wine. Peanuts; not even cashews…

Christa's hand, now warm and dry, squeezes mine. "I changed three times–for this?" she stage whispers into my ear. Michael grabs a large handful of nuts.

"I'll get us some wine," I say. Wrong move. It seems to hit her hard, and only now do I remember she downed a Valium with wine a short while ago. Before long she's started slurring her words and it's definitely time to retreat to the other side of the gallery, where—hallelujah!—another living person has arrived.

He's deep in conversation with our mountain man in gold lamé, who's pointing to the picture of the male nude. A reporter and a photographer from the paper arrive next, doing a feature on Zoe's lengthy presence in the arts community. A woman from the historical society is with them.

Christa spots two more warm bodies coming in the door. "Ingrid!" she cries. "Remember me, the tenderfoot on the trail? Did you bring your giant dog? The one that drools?" Time to get Christa some coffee.

Elaine's here like a shot, greeting these women, Ingrid and Sophia, who, it turns out are from her painting group as is Chuck, the fellow talking with Michael.

When Tristan comes through the door, paying neighborly respects, I throw my arms around him, I'm so glad to see him at Elaine's show. He's with an attractive woman he introduces as a client. He's designing her new home, and he's mentioned Elaine's paintings to her.

People. A potential buyer. It's practically a party.

## *Christa*

We're barely into our first cup of coffee this morning when the phone rings and Elaine invites us next door for fresh coffeecake just out of the oven–and a rehash of her introduction as a bona fide member of the arts community with a real show under her tooled leather belt.

Colin's engrossed in Saturday morning cartoons when I arrive, Trish-less, since she has to work, but he remembers his "Auntie Christa," as Elaine tells him to call me. I rate a hug, especially as I come bearing gifts: a battery-operated miniature R2 D2 robot that beeps and lights up and moves slowly across the floor and a Luke Skywalker T-shirt he insists on wearing over his pajamas—immediately. I leave him to his Star Wars adventures while ads for sugar-coated cereals run in the background.

"There's fruit and coffeecake," Elaine says. She hasn't bothered to dress and is still in a long-sleeved, fleece robe and fuzzy grizzly bear slippers; clearly out of hyper mode now that last night's event's past and people actually showed up. "Thanks again for flying here for the opening. Before you two came, there was only that hairy man…"

"In gold lamé?"

"Stunning," she says and we both laugh.

"Zoe's a character, too, but at her age, she can get away with it. Besides," I add, "she didn't try to carry off the lamé look." It's feeling good to sit here with Elaine, the best it's felt since we buried Stephanie. "Trish and I love how you painted us. We were hardly at our best when you sketched us, but we look good—together." *Funny how worried I'd been—like she'd done paintings of me in bed with Trish, or something, and it turns out they're nothing like that; there's a gentle, tender quality in them, and I hope other people can see it, too. Maybe some will even sell.* "It was a good evening, don't you think? Trish and I had a great time, and talk about your local eccentrics…"

"I'll never forget it. Just as well I don't work today," she says, yawning. "It's catching up with me. Getting those portraits done in time, and working 10-hour shifts and taking care of Colin, not to mention dealing with night sweats…" She trails off, apparently too tired to continue. Without make-up, her drawn features and the dark circles beneath her eyes are easily visible.

"He seems calmer now, like he's adjusting to his new life."

"I had that picture of him with his mom and dad on the wall of his room, but it was too much of a reminder for him. He sleeps better now that I've put it away…"

"For a while," I finish for her, and we share a moment that comes only when you've been through so much together: the Caseys and the morgue and the flight home—not to mention Stephanie's wake and funeral. "You'll have more energy for him now."

Out of the blue, she says, "They write him letters, you know; the Caseys. Look over there, on the hutch."

There must be a half a dozen, all unopened and wedged between framed photos of Stephanie and Roxie as little girls.

Just as I rise, Colin grabs my arm, urging me to come with him into the living room. "Auntie Christa, come play Star Wars with me. I'm Luke Skywalker."

"Honey," I tell him, disengaging myself, "I'm busy talking with your grandma now."

"No! I want you to play now." His body stiffens, arms held rigidly away from his sides, his small hands clenched into fists.

My Professional Voice clicks into gear: "Colin, I said I'm talking with your grandma now. We can play when I'm done."

His face is pinched and red. "Now!" He pitches his R2 D2 to the floor, where it bounces. The rug prevents it from breaking.

"I'll take this for now," I tell him, picking up the robot. The top of the refrigerator should be a safe place.

"You're in time out, Mister! You know better! Go sit in time out by the fireplace," Elaine orders.

He huffs into the living room, I retrieve the letters, and Elaine massages her temples.

"Should I open these?" I say. She nods, and I put them in chronological order by postmark, opening them carefully.

Just as I start reading, Colin announces from the other room, "I'm here!" How could we forget?

"I know, Colin," Elaine answers with a practiced calm. "You've got two more minutes."

Maggie Casey's letters to her grandson bring back to me all those memories of Ireland with its beautiful scenery, but also of whiskey and fights and the Casey's vilification of Stephanie.

My reading is interrupted by Colin who stands under the arch. "You're not done," Elaine reminds him. "Go sit down for another minute…now, or I'll add minutes."

"I hate you, Grandma," he says on his way back to time out.

"I don't hate you, Col. I love you, and I want you to be a good boy."

Head down, he crosses his arms defiantly across his Skywalker chest, but he does sit. "Good job," I whisper to her. "I know how he can be."

After time out we play Star Wars, and I'm Darth Vader, Colin informs me, then a Death Star stormtrooper and finally, Jabba the Hut. Because I look fat? Dueling with light sabers and walking stiff-legged like a stormtrooper wears me out (at least playing a sedentary blob isn't much of a strain), and I happily return his R2 D2 so I can sit down and see what John and Maggie have written.

Elaine's brow is furrowed. "The letters…what do they say?"

Maggie's painted this melancholy scene of the farm without Colin: how much she and John miss him; how his calf, Dora, misses him, and how sad that he's not there to see her growing into a fine young heifer; and how he's not there with them to see his loving father. *We pray the Good Lord will awaken him soon*, she writes. *You must pray, too, and I only hope That One, your other grandmother, takes you to Mass like the proper Catholic you've been raised.*

The other letters repeat these refrains, with the last two announcing their plans for his homecoming: *We want you back with us, your family, so you can see your father. Then we'll all be together, with your da up and around again and being a father to you once more, lad. For this I say the Rosary every evening, knowing you can feel the power of my prayers across the ocean and will return to us.*

"Well, Maggie wants you taking him to Mass. She calls you 'That One,' so I'm guessing she wrote it with a whiskey bottle next to her. She says the calf misses Colin and it's sad that he's not there to see her grow up." Elaine nods, apparently not surprised. "And Elaine, they want him back."

## *Elaine*

Will we be walking into town again?" Roxy asks on Christmas Eve. "Last year was a par-tay with the lights and music and all the people, and we don't want the rug rat to miss all that."

So into his wagon goes Colin, bundled up against the wind and I make sure his mittens are securely clipped to the sleeves of his ski jacket. With a blanket around him, he'll be fine. As for me, I'd rather stay home where it's warm, alongside my cat. Winston's here, too, while Trish is in Chicago, and he has become cat-friends with little Callie. But this walk to the Plaza could become a tradition we'll cherish, and far be it from me to poop on the par-tay. Roxy's disappointed most of the farolitos have blown out in the wind, which whips the flames of the luminarias that we pass on our way to the town center. "The fire," Colin shouts, and jumps out of the wagon, entangled in the blanket. He's up and running toward the bonfire and is halfway to it before Rox catches up to him and carries him back, kicking and screaming. O, Holy Night.

He eventually falls silent as we draw closer to the festivities in the cernter of town. With his aunt steadying the cup, he sips hot cocoa offered in front of a Mexican restaurant while we enjoy a song from a mariachi band. We walk down a single block of the Plaza turning around as the cold drives us into the Cathedral, aglow with light and welcoming warmth. When we walk Colin up the main aisle to see the Nativity, he calls out, "Cows! Look, Ma!"

I do my Catholic best to redirect his attention, saying, "Yes, and that's the Baby Jesus in the Manger."

"I know Jaysus," he announces, turning and running toward the door. Roxy, my agile Roxy, sweeps him up before he's gone too far.

"I'll just be a minute," I tell her. "I'd like to light a candle for your sister."

❖

Once we're home, I start a fire in the fireplace, and we sit by it in our jammies, thawing out and eating Christmas cookies. When Stephanie and Roxy were little, I put a few gifts under the tree on Christmas Eve: one for each of us to open before going to bed; only when they were fast asleep could Santa deliver the rest.

Roxy's glad I've done this again now that Colin's with me, and she makes a big drama out of going to my little artificial tree and helping her nephew choose one of the two things there with his name on them. Of course, he picks the larger one, the one I got him from his Aunt Roxy: a Fisher-Price Playhouse with family figures, furniture, cat, dog and cars. Once we've helped him open it, he's on the floor arranging the little family and their belongings, talking for them and giving them lives together.

The drawstring velvet bag "from Colin to Aunt Roxy" holds essentials for the college student: disposable razors, AA batteries, hand and body lotion, lip gloss, shampoo and conditioner, a pair of black tights, a spare pair of woolen gloves, postage stamps, deodorant, toothpaste, and scented body wash.

"Mom-ola," she cries, "This rocks. "Thanks, Col." She scoots over on the floor and hugs him. I'm delighted to see the two of them together by the tree, and capture the moment with my camera.

My gift from Roxy is a large bag of "holiday blend" gourmet coffee, which we'll enjoy in the morning. Along with it is an oversized Christmas mug in red with a leaping reindeer.

"Look, Col. There's one more thing for you. From Ireland." He couldn't care less, busy with his playhouse family.

It's a beautifully bound book in a slipcase with "The Lives of the Saints" embossed in gold lettering on the cover. According to the title page, the illuminated letters beginning each saint's life are replicas from *The Book of Kells*. I open it randomly to a full-color illustration of St. Sebastian, eyes gazing heavenward, his chest sprouting arrows and his blood flowing freely. Lovely gift for a grieving child going on four, though it's exquisitely crafted, and I'll put it away for him and send them a thank-you. Tucked inside is a note: "Christmas, 1998. Dearest Colin, I can't wait to read this to you when you return to us. With love from Grandma, Grandpa and Da."

Colin gets up and puts the play figure of the mother by the archangel that hovers over the creche sitting on the bookshelf.

"What did you do?" I say.

"The ma's with the angels," he announces, returning to his playhouse. "That's what Grandma Maggie said."

I say nothing for a moment, trying to take this in. "Yes," I tell him.

## *Roxy*

Once we got Col into bed and read him *The Polar Express*, he said his prayers, and we kissed him goodnight and told him he had to go right to sleep or Santa wouldn't come. He's wiped out from tonight, so he does.

We're sipping the tea I made for us—Mom's favorite, peppermint—and wishing the furballs would come out and cuddle with us.

"Don't know how you keep up with him; I'm worn out from one day."

"It's easier when I'm at work and he's at daycare. Your sister was 25 years younger than me, and I can't imagine how she handled it all day, day after day, and in a small apartment."

"I'm never having kids."

"Stephanie said that, too, but I know how she loved Colin. I love him, too, but I'm just one person, and at 53, I don't have the energy I had when I was raising you girls." She pulls an afghan around her and sips her tea for a while. It's like I'm invisible, and I want to go, "Yo! Momsa! I'm still here," when she says, "I wonder how long I can do this."

## *Christa*

It's not surprising," I say when Elaine tells me about her latest Christmas Eve. "Given the traumatic losses he's had." I'm doing 'professional therapist' on the phone. "It's normal, considering his loss, Laney, but you might want to take him to a counselor who's trained to help him express his emotions."

"He is expressing them," she says. "Here and at daycare, too...his teacher, Miss Annette, says he's aggressive sometimes...and he's run away from the group and out the door...twice..."

"In non-violent and healing ways, Elaine."

"Oh. Yes."

## *Elaine*

There's a let-down after those months of preparing for the gallery show and without that deadline for motivation, I rarely paint more than a couple of evenings a week. It's not like I can use a day off to go into the desert like O'Keeffe, find some old bleached bones, and set them up as the foreground of a landscape—not with Colin in tow, complete with cars and trucks and light sabers. Though he'd like the bones. Becoming a single working grandma-mama means struggling to make a few minutes for your creative self, and when you do manage it, you're likely to nod off.

I need a break; everyone needs a break, but what a luxury. Who could take Col for the summer? It's not as though he could stay with Tom and Cheryl. I don't see them as trustworthy. Better Denise and Stuart, but they've no experience raising kids. My mother, if she were 20 years younger, but she's not; with Roxy, there's no way...

And with Colin in therapy once a week...I'm grateful that he's covered under my insurance as part of the family plan. The cost of it is killing, but imagine what it would be like without this blessing of insurance through the hospital?

I asked for referrals at work, and Dr. Park made space in his schedule for Colin. He's warmed up to this small Korean man with a big smile and soft voice, and now accepts these weekly visits as routine. I'm sorry the coverage is limited to eight sessions. His office atmosphere is very non-threatening, with playhouses, play figures and art materials; all part of the expressive therapies he uses.

The changes in Col are subtle but meaningful. Miss Annette at daycare tells me he's less hostile and seems to be improving at taking turns, sharing and getting along with the other kids. When she reports "fewer outbursts," that means a big step in the right direction, but he still walks out of the classroom without permission—every teacher's nightmare.

At home each evening we work on shapes, colors and the letters for printing his name, occasionally for as long as 15 minutes, but it's exhausting to keep his attention on our lessons. "No, stay in your seat, Col. Look over here at these shapes and hand me the circles," So it goes, over and over. Sometimes he sweeps the plastic shapes to the floor and screams, "No!" (so much for those "fewer outbursts"). Lately, though, he's more likely to sort by colors or shapes when I direct him to, and when he does well, he gets rewarded with a new sticker on his card which now features smiley faces, Matchbox cars, Batman and gold stars.

What's troubling, though, is that all too often from one day to the next he forgets what he's already learned. I've worked in settings with kids Colin's age who have disabilities, and short-term memory loss is common. Combined with his tantrums, outbursts at daycare, refusal to listen to adults and his overall busy, busy, busyness—all the time—I think I have reason for concern. I need to speak with Dr. Park.

Jumping to conclusions can be as bad as turning a blind eye, but Christa wanted to observe him even before Stephanie took him to Ireland, and he wasn't even two then. Who could forget that disastrous Christmas Eve at Christa's apartment…the spilled cocoa and broken gas pump from the Christmas Village?

She tells me his losses could be the cause for these problems, or there could be a deeper issue. Time will tell.

❖

Dr. Park starts preparing Colin for the "end of our time together"; his last session will be two weeks from today, and with his background of loss and abandonment issues, this has to be handled delicately. Dr. Park's pleased with Col's progress, and emphasizes his need for routine and stability so he can feel safe…and know I am always here for him. This means continuing to do "Nurse 'Rock of Gibraltar' Fuzzy Wuzzy," 24/7, and putting out my shingle: *Round-the-Clock Healing. No Appointment Needed.*

Christa says I must do some things, even small things, for myself, or I'll burn out. "You're a nurse, Elaine. You know this." I know she's right. Getting my hair cut regularly, shopping by myself and, luxury of luxuries, meeting with my painters group that I've met with all of three times in the last year—any of these things would help. But how would Colin react to a babysitter? And where would I find one?

## *Trish*

Clearly, she's desperate. "Trish, so help me God, I will wash your windows, scrub your floors, anything…if I don't get out of the house and talk to other adults about something other than pain meds and post-op dressing changes I will go live in the mountains and wear gold lamé. Please, please…I'll have Colin bathed and in pajamas and ready to be tucked in. All you have to do is read him a story, and you could bring Winston, too, for a play date with Callie."

A play date for cats? She's not desperate; she's deranged. How can I wriggle out of this? "Elaine, I enjoy Colin, you know that, but babysitting…I was the youngest in my family, and have no experience with kids…"

She cuts me off. "You don't need experience to read him a story book and put him to bed. He'll go right to sleep."

*You lie, Elaine.* "What if I have to, to…take him to the bathroom? There were only girls in my family, and…"

"He does that on his own. No problem."

"Wiping?"

"Oh, he's aces at wiping, believe me. Neither of my girls were such good wipers at that age." She smiles with pride at his achievement.

"Isn't there anyone else? The one time I babysat I was 15 and it was a disaster with those two little girls. My next oldest sister, Greta, had to come rescue me."

"Colin's just one little boy, and I'll be down the street at my painter's group in town. If something happens, you could call me, and I'd fly right back."

Fly right back…right. So here I am with Winston, who seems in no mood for a kitty play date and would rather go off in a corner and sulk. He's missing the Nature Channel special on "Birds of South America." Elaine doesn't have cable.

Colin's watching a kids' movie on TV and barely looks up at me. "Hi, Trish. Hi, Winston," he says. Callie's nowhere to be seen right now. Not play date material.

Elaine tells me Colin goes straight to bed after the movie, and gives me a first aid kit and a 3" x 5" card with Sophia's number, the Police and Fire non-emergency numbers, the number for Poison Control and his pediatrician. Also his therapist. Overkill...ya think? Wait 'til I tell Christa. "You go now, Elaine. We'll be fine. Really."

## *Elaine*

How wonderful it was to relax for a few hours with adults—artists—and talk shop, see people's new paintings, have a little wine...I can't wait 'til next month's meeting...assuming it went well with Col and Trish tonight...

The first thing I see is Trish, mouth open and snoring as she's sprawled out on the sofa, covered with a throw. The floor is littered with every Matchbox car, truck, action figure, building block and stuffed animal in the place, with Colin sitting in the middle of this mess, busy with his Playhouse.

"Colin, you're not in bed?"

"Aunt Trish put me in bed this many times..." He holds up the fingers of both hands. "She got tired and needed her nap, so I tucked her in."

Tucked she is. Until she hears us and jerks awake. "Elaine, I'm so sorry. I tried, but every time I took him back to bed..."

Colin interrupts. "I took real good care of her, Ma."

*No doubt.* "I see that you did. Well, it's definitely bedtime. Let's put your action figures in their box."

"No! I want to play!"

"Now. It's way past your bedtime. Where's the box?"

Trish sits up, blinks. "I'll get Winston and be on my way..."

"Thanks, really. I needed a night out. This," I smile and indicate the toys on the floor, "is nothing."

❖

Thanks to that meeting four weeks ago and the motivation it gave me, I finished a painting of my garden—minus the snake— just in time for this month's get-together. Most everyone said they thought this new focus on a space that's more defined and intimate than my previous landscapes could mean a different direction for me, and Chuck and Sophia were especially encouraging. They urged me to do a series of everyday gardens in Santa Fe homes; a great idea that could lead who-knows-where.

More than anything I want to continue with this group. The constructive feedback gives me the push I need, and I enjoy the socializing, too. It's a welcome change from my daily routine, and an occasional break in Colin's routine is good, too; things are much smoother when babysitting means playtime, not bedtime.

As a matter of fact, when I return I see the two of them have used every Duplo block in the toy box to construct a castle, and they've populated it with action figures, Matchbox cars and Playhouse characters (minus the mother figure, who remains in the box, but is at least in the general vicinity—a good sign?).

"Look what we made," grins Trish, delighted with the creative applications of this new artists' tool. "A Medieval castle!"

"It's a fort," Colin corrects.

"Of course," she says, her joy undiminished. "We've been defending it against Darth Vader and the Stormtroopers. It was awesome!"

"Awesome, Grandma," he parrots. "Luke Skywalker and R2-D2 are the good guys, but the bad guys have Princess Leia and we have to get her back."

They've done an outstanding job and even built a wall around their fort. I'm delighted and surprised at this huge change from their last play date. "What a great fort," I say. "Can I play, too?"

"You be Chewbacca." My hair looks that bad?

"You keep those bad guys out," he directs, and I do my best with guttural moans that apparently suffice, for he's busy having Luke battle Darth Vader while Trish takes a back seat to this action.

After a while, we're all yawning. "Time to call it a day," I announce, and he's so tired, his only request is that we keep the fort and its characters up for tomorrow.

When he asks Trish to come back and play with him some more, she hugs him, saying, "I will…another day," then tells me, "I really had fun." How can I ever repay her?

❖

Colin's started to think of her as a pal and asks her to come over whenever we see her outside. He's becoming quite the host.

He's also losing some of that baby pudge and looks more like a little boy—a big little boy—who needs clothes for his fourth birthday. Hopefully, Tom and my mother will come through again with generous checks, like the ones they sent at Christmas...

And they do, so he has new things from the skin out, as well as the red tricycle from me and the *Mulan* video from Christa. She's out here to see Trish—and me, when time permits—every month or so, so sees Col and knows he'll enjoy it.

The Caseys, on the other hand, send Colin every four-year-old's dream: a Mass card indicating that a Mass will be said for him on his birthday in "his" village church for his safe return to his homeland.

The rest of their gift is a short-sleeved "football" jersey in green and yellow, the colors of a local team, the card says. It's so big, he can use it as a nightshirt. I enclose a photo of him wearing it in the thank you note I write them. He looks adorable with his hair all tousled and his sturdy legs sticking out from under the oversized shirt; I have to wonder if it will only strengthen their resolve to claim him. What if they turn up at my front door one day?

Speaking of my door, I'm in the middle of making dinner one night when it slams...and the house is suspiciously quiet. "Colin? Col?" Nowhere. I'm out the door and on the front step in a flash and see Colin's beloved tricycle is gone. So is he, and the wrought iron gate is wide open. I scream his name, feeling dread engulf me. My heart pounds and stomach twists. How far could he have gotten, and where? I dash down the sidewalk toward the Plaza and catch sight of him pedaling furiously toward the end of the block, fast approaching the street.

"Colin! Stop!" My shout to him is the loudest I can manage, but can he hear? I'll never make it before he gets to the intersection, and he's not slowing down. Omigod, he's getting closer, and people are driving home from work, and..."Col-linn!" Gulping air, no matter how much, doesn't help. I can't run faster. Oh, God, oh God. "Coll-innnn!"

A tall, thin man in lime green Spandex jogs around the corner just in front of Colin, and I scream, "Grab him! Please!"

Time seems to slow as the fellow sees me, then closes in on Colin, grabbing the handlebars with both hands. The back wheels fishtail around, bashing the jogger in the shins, and Colin's flung from the seat, hurling the man to the ground in a jumble of red metal, chrome, tires and green Spandex.

My boy's sprawled on the sidewalk, bawling, the guy's slowly sitting up and looking dazed as he rubs his shins, the trike's over on its side, and I'm screaming, "Are you OK?" Col's scraped his knee and elbow, which ooze red, and he yells, "I'm bleeding, I'm bleeding!"

"Dammit," the man says, and I see it's Tristan from next door. "Elaine. Colin," he says, and though he's breathing hard, he doesn't seem to be in shock.

"Col, your head—did you hit it?" I feel around his head for bumps or cuts. His helmet's at home, of course. The scrapes will need a thorough washing when we get back there, but right now I need to know, "Can you bend your leg? Your arm?" So far, so good.

Tristan's starting to his feet. "Wait," I tell him, doing 'Fuzzy Wuzzy, First Responder,' from my days as school nurse, "Did you hit *your* head?"

"I don't think so." He pats it gingerly. "No."

"Are you dizzy?" He looks flushed.

"No. Maybe a little stunned." He takes a long drink from his water bottle. "I'll be fine."

"Are you hurting anywhere?"

"The bike caught me in the legs, but I think I'm OK." He gets to his feet and I scramble to pick Colin up from the concrete.

"My bike—is it broken?" He's sobbing.

"Let's see, Buddy," Tristan says, righting it on its three wheels. He makes a big show of examining it, probably to distract Col from his wounds, and declares, "Well, she's got her first battle scars, Bud, but mostly just some scratched paint. She'll be good as new with some rest and touch-up." He laughs and takes another long swig from his bottle. "I did a number on mine when I was five, I tell you. Crashed a tree full force, and it wasn't even our own tree." He pauses for dramatic effect, and Col's quit crying by now, all ears. "It was the neighbor's, and he was a mean, mean, dude, I tell you. I was more afraid to tell my mom about his tree than about wrecking my bike."

"What did you do?" Colin asks.

"It wasn't what I did—it's what that dude did, hauling me off to Ma with my busted up bike, and saying I'd have to pay for his tree I broke—it was just a sapling, and it snapped—" Here he mimes breaking a slender tree with his hands—"In two."

"It did?" This boy's enthralled with tales of testosterone derring-do.

The three of us make our wounded way down the street, Colin holding my hand and limping a bit as Tristan hoists the bike on his shoulder and entertains us with stories of his apparently stern mother, "who made sure I stayed safe and in one piece, no matter what. So no more rides without headgear, Buddy."

Colin loves this. "Headgear. Yeah."

"It means your helmet, Colin," I say. "That's if I ever let you on that bike again. And don't you ever go out of the house alone."

Tristan sees us to our home, carefully placing the wounded trike next to our front door, which is as wide open as I left it. "I can't thank you enough," I tell him. "What would have happened if you hadn't been coming around the corner?" Mental note to Fuzzy Wuzzy: call tomorrow and make sure he's really OK...and invite him to dinner sometime soon.

❖

Fear's turned to anger now that I've washed, disinfected and bandaged Colin using plain, flesh-toned Band-Aids; no bright colors or cartoon characters to reward him. "You don't ever leave the house like that, not ever again. Or Miss Annette's room...you hear me?" It's hard not to raise my voice.

"Yeah," he mumbles.

"What were you thinking?"

"I dunno."

"You were so close to crossing the street, Col. A car could have hit you."

"I would have looked first," he whines.

Squealing brakes, Colin lying crumpled on the street, people shouting—the thought is almost overwhelming, and I don't know whether to hold him or spank his butt. "You're grounded, Mister! That means you don't ride the bike for five days. That's five"—I hold up a handful of fingers—"bedtimes, and we're going to mark them off on the kitchen calendar. Together. Starting tomorrow." He stares at me.

He keeps staring at me throughout dinner, throughout bath time—forget working with shapes and colors tonight since neither of us can concentrate—and throughout my single reading of whichever book I grab first. He's never seen his grandma this way.

Once he's in bed I pour myself a hot cup of decaf coffee, and hold it in two hands. Callie's meowing at me, winding her small self around my ankles, and I realize I didn't refill her food and water dishes. "Poor kitty; we forgot you in all this excitement! What were we thinking?"

What was *I* thinking–that I could raise this boy alone in new surroundings with new people? I feed Callie and stand back as she purrs and eats. Would it have been better off for everyone if I'd come home to my place in the Southwest and kept cats? But the thought of the Caseys raising him...my Stephanie's boy, my grandson...no way.

## *Helen*

Such a big boy my Colin's become. And so handsome, with that sandy red hair and green eyes; the picture of his mother, and so much so that every time I look at him, I can barely keep from crying. And I really want to bawl when I see my little girl, so thin and tired-looking from working those long hours and raising that boy. She's aged so much since I last saw her, I barely recognized her at the airport last night. God help that little boy if something should happen to her. She's the only constant in his life.

"Elaine, Ellie, don't...don't ever let another year and half go by like this. Last time we were all together, we buried Stephanie, God rest her soul, but today is different, and we have so much to be grateful for...such a wonderful Thanksgiving."

Did I ever think I'd live to see my whole family here again, around the table? How can we make the most of this day with both my girls here, and Stuart, of course, and Roxy...and dear, precious Colin? Just look at him shoveling in his great-grandma's homemade mashed potatoes "made with lots of real butter, dear," I tell him. Before we sit down to eat, Stuart and Colin play on the floor with that train they got him — genuine Lionel engine, caboose, flat bed, coal car...the whole thing, with train tracks going across the room. And sure enough, the two of them are barely done with dinner before they're back on the floor, playing together...how wonderful to see them. Let them play. The women will clean up, and maybe I can catch Ellie alone in the kitchen while Roxy and Denise set the table for dessert; tell her to buy some vitamins and make-up; maybe give her some money to get her hair colored and styled and some new clothes.

"Elaine, dear, no one could blame you, not a bit with your busy life, but here...get your hair done, put on a little lipstick. You've let yourself go, sweetie, and you'll never find a man looking the way you do…Why are you looking at me that way? What's so funny?"

"In what lifetime will I possibly do that, Mom? In between hospital shifts and grocery shopping, housework and cooking and taking Colin to the park and the library? I barely have time to go to the bathroom, and even then, he's banging on the door for me to come out and play or fix him a snack or take him outside for a bike ride." She has to catch her breath from laughing, but I don't see the humor. "So when am I supposed to meet this guy, Mom? The one fellow I've had over for dinner was my neighbor, Tristan, who helped me with Colin's bike, and that was months ago."

*This could be promising, no matter what she says.* "Honey, I'm sure you fixed him a lovely meal. I just hope you wore some make-up…and a nice outfit. I wish you were here longer. I'd take you shopping."

She's laughing again. "It was no big deal. Just one neighbor thanking another for a nice favor he did for Colin."

"Oh…Colin gets along with him?"

"Like you wouldn't believe. The two of them…"

"What?" I say as she stops speaking in mid-sentence.

"I can see where you're going with this, Mom, and no. Stop it right now."

"I'm sure I don't know what you're talking about, Ellie. I hate to see you running yourself ragged and so tired is all I'm saying. Maybe when Tom takes Colin tomorrow, you can rest."

## *Tom*

Can't believe this little guy's gotten so tall and heavy. He must be almost 50 pounds. And solid. He doesn't wake up when I carry him inside to Elaine and Helen and put him down on the bed. After the day he's had with dinosaurs, Egyptian mummies, and the big gorilla, it's no wonder. We covered a lot of ground at the museum, and what a kick it was to see it all through a little boy's eyes.

"No, thanks, Helen, we had lunch there, and much as I remember loving your pumpkin pie, I don't know where I'd put it. Besides, Cheryl and Tonia are asleep in the car, and I have to get them home."

"It's good you're spending time with Colin," Elaine tells me.

I can't keep from grinning. "Ellie, I loved it. He tore around the place, taking it all in. You know, boys are so different from girls. Once he got used to being with me, he told me about the dinosaurs; knew their names and which ones ate plants and which ones ate meat…Can't wait for another outing with him, and sooner than later. They grow so fast. Maybe next time we'll go to the aquarium; see the whales and dolphins. He'd like that, wouldn't he? Or Brookfield Zoo?"

"Next time he's in town," Helen says, surprising me.

What's up with her? Does she actually approve of my interest in the boy? "Oh, here, I almost forgot." I hand Elaine the wooden T-Rex assemble-it-yourself kit. "We got this for him as a souvenir. Honest to God, I can't tell you what today meant; having my grandson with me, showing him the totem poles I saw as a kid, lifting him up so he could see everything, climbing up the same stairs I climbed…maybe we could drive out to Santa Fe in a few months; do some Indian stuff…take him on some day trips, if you think that's OK."

She gives me the most beautiful, heartfelt smile. "Great, Tom," she says. "That would be great."

## *Elaine*

No one yelled, no one was fighting; with all of us so well behaved, it was a memorable Thanksgiving. It's tempting to think about moving back, but could I endure the Chicago winter with the wind that tears into me and that steel gray sky for weeks on end? Leave my painters group and the friends I've made here? And uproot Colin yet again when Dr. Park said stability was so important for him?

Still, Chicago would give him—give us—the support of family. We'd see my mom a lot and not wish we'd done that when it's too late and she's gone. Be with Roxy before she's starting a life of her own and going who-knows-where. I could get to know my sister again. Col could spend time with Tom and maybe even Stuart…do guy stuff.

Like Santa Fe has no men? My mom would be the first to sniff them out if she were here. Who needs it? My job's hard, but that's true of any city hospital, and the pay here is very good…not to mention the on-site daycare, where Col's used to it and even has some buddies. Between birthday parties and occasional play dates, he's the one with the social life in this family. He's still hyper and has trouble retaining lessons we work on, but I haven't had any complaints from Miss Annette in a while. He has good days and bad, but maybe a few more good. Would it serve any real purpose to move back?

Good thing there's no pressing need to decide right now, but no matter which state we're in, he'll start kindergarten in August, and that means getting his paperwork in order and getting him registered.

❖

*Dear John and Maggie; I thank you for the lovely Christmas gift you sent Colin, and he thanks you, too. I have put the exquisite hand-carved ebony rosary away for safekeeping until he is a little older and can take proper care of it. For now, he is using an extra one of mine that is made of plain plastic, as I'm teaching him to pray the rosary with me. He's getting big, as you can see from this photo, and has learned to print his name, which he's done on this card for you. We work together on his letters and numbers; the usual skills to prepare him for kindergarten. The school district is sending a Power of Attorney form to be completed by you, and returned at your earliest convenience, please, since Colin needs it for his school files. You'll see I'm sending you one of the pictures he's drawn, so you can put it up and enjoy it. He made it just for you.*

*Best regards,*
*Elaine*

C° li n

❖

OK, OK so I'm stretching the truth a little. We don't exactly pray the rosary together on a regular basis…or ever, when you get right down to it, but we could…if he knew what a rosary was…and the prayers to say. As for the picture he made for them, well, he did draw it, after all…for Winston, but who's to know? He has no idea about kindergarten, but he will. Soon.

If, pray God, and I mean this God, we can get that form giving me power of attorney for Colin's welfare. Without it, can I even register him for school? Why, oh why, did I try to play by the rules on this? I should have just said I had no idea of the father's condition or whereabouts since technically, I don't. But, no-o-o-o. 'Fuzzy Wuzzy the Upright Citizen,' had to get the authorities involved, had to Do the Right Thing. The district's mailing may have already reached the Caseys.

# *Christa*

"Calm down, Laney." She's talking so fast, she's almost babbling. Next thing I know, she'll be hyperventilating. She's practically in tears. This is *not* an auspicious beginning to a new year.

"I'm just so worried. What if the Caseys don't get that legal form to the school district? Without it, the court won't grant me legal guardianship of Colin, and without guardianship, I can't register him for school, which is the reason I need to go through all this guardianship stuff, not that I wouldn't have to eventually, but..."

"Breathe, Elaine. Please breathe. What's the worst that could happen? Worst case scenario, they protest and try to get him returned to Ireland and secure Power of Attorney for themselves. Which they can't. He's an American citizen living here for the last two years and about to begin pubic school. Even if they found a court to hear their petition, that could take years, and no court would keep the child out of school until the situation's decided."

"Excuse me? What's the best? I need to hear good things, Christa."

"The Caseys put Colin's welfare first, sign the form and attach documentation of the father's incapacity, and Colin goes to school."

"If they cooperate, everything will be so much simpler."

"Assuming they do cooperate. And assuming Liam's still comatose." I am trying to be my best professional self here, looking at different scenarios. Elaine may not be ready to listen, but she has no choice now that she's approaching guardianship and all it entails.

"Well, they never said...oh, sweet Jesus, I never thought of that. Wouldn't they have told Colin if he's better? I read their letters, and all they talk about is their prayers for him, but nothing about Liam himself. Dammit, Christa, Liam...I never thought he could possibly wake up."

"With all that praying...just don't underestimate the power of prayer. Who knows? I'm not saying he's better; only that we can't assume." I hear her taking deep breaths. "But don't worry because it won't change anything except you'll make yourself sick. Laney. And you can't be sick. Colin needs you."

"True, but so much could go wrong. I hate this helplessness; having to depend on those damned Caseys who trashed Stephanie when she couldn't defend herself. I hate needing them for anything, let alone paperwork for something as important as school."

When I remind her how strong she's been and what she's accomplished so far, I add that I'll soon be living there in Santa Fe. "It's true. I've just decided, and I was going to call you today, in fact. I'm planning a springtime move to Santa Fe, and this commuter relationship with Trish will be just a memory. We'll be able to see each other all the time."

"That's wonderful. I'm so glad for the two of you. And Christa, you'll be here, really here, not just occasional weekend visits!"

"I'll be looking for a place, and I'm not sure if I'll rent or buy to begin with. You know I've loved Santa Fe since my first time there, and now, with Trish and me…"

"We'll have dinners together, and go visit the galleries, and even hike the trail again…I can hardly wait."

*I can wait for a return to the Trail of Broken Feet, believe me. Once was enough.* "I'll never forget it."

"Oooh," she says happily, oblivious to my meaning.

"I'll be at Trish's in a couple of weeks…house hunting."

## *Elaine*

Christa's going to be here. It'll be heaven. My rock; she's seen me through so much: that unspeakable incident with Stephanie and Frank, and then going to Ireland with me…how could I have survived without her?

She was my first visitor here, and now she'll be living in Santa Fe, spending lots of time with Trish, who's another lady I owe, big-time. Trish is one of Colin's favorite play dates for sure, and who knew they'd take to each other the way they have…must be the Duplo blocks.

Whoa…wait, girl. Trish and Christa are a couple, and couples want to spend time…alone. So where does that leave me? Struggling to paint a couple of times a week, raising a pre-schooler, and barely managing a foray to the painters group once a month. Without anyone special in my life. Maybe my mother was right. I'll never meet someone no matter where I go if I don't fix myself up. I look like a troll who needs more than a dab of lipstick and a new hairstyle, though. I need a complete makeover from head to toe, starting with a skin care program and an exercise regimen, not to mention a make-up consultation and a new wardrobe.

I'm going find the time and money…lots of money…for this how? Oh, God, I'm actually wishing my mom were here to help me, give me ideas. Or at least mind Colin now that Trish will be less available. Except that every time Mom calls now, she makes a point of asking about, "That nice neighbor man, that Tristan." Last time she wanted to know his age and occupation.

*Mom…Helen…even if I was screwing this man every night on the roof, I would never say. How about: "He's in his twenties, Mom and in a punk rock band."*

Maybe there's a singles group around? Yeah, filled with 30-year-olds. I'd stand a better chance hanging out with the vets at the VFW hall; claim I was a Navy nurse. Not. Could sign up for the VFW Auxiliary, though.

So here I sit…alone, and in desperate need of a miracle makeover and something that resembles a social life. Before I wake up and realize I'm 65 and still single—raising a teenaged boy on my own.

It's all too depressing with the Caseys and losing Trish and Christa to each other, and looking like crap; wanting to cover every mirror in the house, even though I'm not Jewish. I am aging visibly as I sit here, and there is no patron saint of good looks that I know of, which leaves me praying to Venus, goddess of love and beauty, for some serious intervention.

## *Christa*

More than a big change, it's a big gamble: leaving an established practice; my place that I've gotten just as I want it; my professional associates in Chicago; and the few social acquaintances who have no idea I'm a lesbian; and making this move as a commitment to another person, a woman.

Yet, it's the right next step for Trish, for me, for us. Two years of a commuter relationship has meant long, lonely periods of separation with only holidays together and occasional long weekends and unbelievable air fare costs, but no day-to-day…we really have no idea of each other's everyday lives. Sure, we talk on the phone and email all the time, but moving is a major life change for me, and it's scary. Having Elaine there will help, and I've met a few people through Trish, so it won't be like living in a strange city, knowing no one.

Still…moving so far from my mother; what if she needs me? Either way, Chicago or Santa Fe, I'm not exactly down the street from her. For over a year I've been considering this move, weighing pros and cons, trying to decide and then changing my mind. But one thing I do know: there's a fresh start for me there, where I'll be known as 'gay Christa' right from the beginning, and if I don't do this now, I never will.

## Trish

What, my place isn't good enough? Christa says it's too small. Well…she might have a point since my studio takes up the whole second bedroom, but even so, if it's a matter of space, why aren't we looking for a place together instead of Christa finding her own? Maybe it's not so much the financial differences between us as it is her unwillingness to live together with me–or with anyone, for that matter. Isn't she ready? Or maybe I'm just a stepping-stone to a better climate where she'll establish herself and move on to someone else? True, she's fairly new to the gay life and her first relationship crashed and burned. And no way do I want to pressure her into a decision so important. So living together…that would come only when she's totally accepting of herself as a gay woman who wants to share her new life with me.

## Christa

Asking Trish to come with me when I look at houses may not have been the best idea. I see that now, but the alternative would have been worse, with her getting upset at not being asked. It's hard when you're hurting someone you love no matter what you do. We've been together for what?…Two years, and this means we should have furniture and a mortgage together? What next? An adopted Chinese baby?

I'm not ready for that, though I want to move toward it. Well, maybe not the baby. Living with someone, anyone, would be the first time I've shared space since grad school, and that was a disaster. Soon I'll be 40, though, and what's holding me back? Not Trish, certainly.

Am I already too old and set in my ways to ever accept living with another person…until I wind up at the nursing home?

For now I still need my separate space, no matter how much I love her. I just hope I can find the right house; a house that could be a home for both of us, eventually. And that Trish will be patient.

❖

A month ago I was hoping to find something reasonably OK; now I've seen so many beautiful homes in all styles it's been hard to narrow the field to two. They're both great, full of Old Santa Fe charm, so there's no bad choice. One's on Callecita, with two bedrooms and bathrooms, kiva fireplace, exposed beam ceilings, not to mention a ground floor pantry room large enough for an office, if need be. It's only blocks from the Plaza. The other's on Lejano, a five-minute drive from the center of town, not far from Trish and Elaine. It's half again as large, with two bedrooms and bathrooms, plus a cozy den, kiva, beamed ceilings and mature landscaping that's a pleasure. Both have those red terra cotta-toned Saltillo tile floors I like that are a "selling point," giving the homes…well…Old Santa Fe charm. I've picked up the jargon; pretty soon I'll sign up to take my realtor's exam.

"OK, which do you think it'll be?" Elaine asks. "From what you've said, they're both good. And how about work?" She tosses the question over her shoulder as she runs back to the kitchen to check on the meatloaf she's made for us. The delicious aroma adds to the homey feeling of her casita and makes me yearn to have that feeling about a place of my own.

"That's the final piece, and I should know soon—very soon—if I'm invited to join that practice: Mosaic Mental Heath." I actually cross my fingers…of both hands. "It's right downtown, low-key, yet very professional. I felt so comfortable…"

"You've really got your heart set on it, don't you?" Trish says, squeezing my hand, and she knows I do.

"It would be a relief, for sure. A position here, then a house." *Concrete things to hang on to.* "It's an exciting time."

"I'm excited, too," Laney says, "For you, of course, but for me, too. My mom must have thought I really looked bad at Thanksgiving because she sent me a big check for Christmas, saying I had to—absolutely *had* to—use it for a beauty makeover at a spa, top to toe. I'm only now scheduling it since she called and reminded me to cash the check and use it right away. She must have been thinking there's no time to lose."

I have to laugh out loud. "Laney…"

"There will be enough left over for an outfit; a nice outfit, maybe even designer stuff." She eyes my Liz ensemble. "Like yours."

"We want to hear all about it," Trish says. "I've never been to a spa." She looks at me intently. "Honey, maybe that's something we could do together sometime, if it sounds good…and if I make a big jewelry sale."

"Take pictures. Elaine," I tell her. "We want to see before and after."

"I'll still be Elaine. Just the New! And Improved! Elaine."

## *Elaine*

And I am! Massaged, manicured, pedicured; I've had a facial, haircut, color and style, skin care consultation and makeup. Who knew beauty could be so exhausting? But get ready, world: it's The New Elaine, and before I use this money to pay the rent, I'm running to the mall for a new outfit.

The lady at Dillard's Better Sportswear Department makes great suggestions right down to the accessories, and now I'm Urbane Elaine in my new natural linen slacks, matching jacket and apricot silk blouse. Crème-and-camel leather purse with matching flats and gold hoop earrings included. It's a Total Look. Why waste it? What better place to show it off than Canyon Road? I'll go to the galleries there and maybe even treat myself to an overpriced cup of tea.

And wouldn't you know it—I run into Ron Anderson, a surgeon from the hospital. I see him all the time at work, but when I say hi to him in the gallery, he's just puzzled, like he doesn't know me. Then it dawns on him, and he looks at me—stares—then blurts out, "Oh. It's you. You're all…dressed…up."

Fuzzy Wuzzy be damned. Her Secret Life's out in the open as I flash him what I hope is a dazzling smile. Oh, if only I had flowing hair to fling back over my shoulder.

"Well, it's nice to see you out of your green scrubs," he says, clearly flustered at this New Me. Damn! I should have done this a long time ago. Mom was right.

"See you soon," I say, attempting a runway model's graceful turn as I aim my gaw-juss self out the door.

Three galleries later, I'm regarding some stick-and-plaster sculpture and in the corner I see a well-dressed couple deep in conversation, walking around the largest piece in the place. I can only see the back of his head, but my view of her tells me she's an expensive blonde, exquisitely dressed in a mauve silk outfit. The Hope Diamond's on her left hand.

They both turn to leave, and it registers with me that it's Tristan from next door, just as he recognizes me.

"Elaine? What a surprise. You're looking…so radiant."

You bet, buster. He introduces me to Victoria, a well-manicured little number from head to foot whose gaze rakes over me top to toe.

"Tristan's been an angel, helping me pick out a few things for the home he designed for me and Maury." She takes his arm and leans into him in an intimate way flashing a smile that's a testimony to cosmetic dentistry.

*Look out, girlfriend, this is Urbane Elaine you're talking to.* "How lovely," I say, doing my best to purr. "The work here lends itself to so many possibilities, don't you think? I'm considering one myself." *Liar, liar, pants on fire.*

"Re-al-ly?" Victoria drawls.

How can I mention—casually—my own gallery show? Well, forget casual. Just forge ahead. "Are you familiar with Parabola? I had a show there in December. You remember, don't you, Tristan?" I turn to him, putting lots of sugar in my smile.

"We're ready for a drink after an afternoon of gallery-hopping. Won't you join us, Elaine?"

*I'm dressed for it. Coiffed for it. Would love to do it…if Victoria weren't here.* So I channel Emily Post. "I'd love that, but I have to run…" *Think, Elaine, what ritzy place could you possibly be running to?* "To the spa. I left my watch there. Maybe next time." *Will there be a next time?*

❖

Cinderellaine that I am, I remove my princess clothes and hang then carefully on wooden hangers, throw on jeans, an old shirt and then cook dinner for me and Colin, who wolfs down the hamburgers, Spanish rice and salad like he hasn't seen food in days. I, on the other hand, just pick at mine, mulling the day's developments…flattering hair that makes me look years younger and I can do myself…make-up that's becoming, but will only take me a few minutes. Classic clothes that won't go out of style and look good on me. Dr. Anderson almost didn't recognize me, and Tristan said I was radiant.

He phones just as I'm ready to call it a night, and chats about Victoria and Maury's mansion he designed for them...for her, really, then shocks me down to my blonde highlighted roots by asking when would be a good time for us to have that drink.

*Emily Post, Letitia Baldrige, I need you.* "Such a nice idea, but with Colin...he's in daycare when I'm working, so it's important for me to be with him in the evenings. Why not come over and have dinner with us?"

"Only if you promise not to fuss."

"It's no fuss, believe me. Col and I eat every night." I add my best lighthearted laugh, we set a date for later in the week, and I say good night, fighting the urge to call my mother despite the time difference, wake her up and tell her I've had a makeover, a new look, and now a date. But the shock might kill her.

❖

"Ma, what are these long green things? They look like trees."

*Just be quiet and eat them, Colin. Like we have them all the time.* You remember, honey, these are fresh asparagus. You like them. *Oh, God, strike me dead now.*

"Tristan, some Hollandaise sauce?"

"Ma, what is that stuff he's putting on his trees?"

"Sauce for his trees. Would you like some?"

"Ee-eew. Gross. And why do we have flowers on the table?"

Tristan says, "It's what a gentleman brings to a lady when the lady is kind enough to make a special dinner for him."

"Oh," Colin says. "Special dinner." Then after a bite of his grilled salmon, which he chews slowly and with great suspicion, this boy who has no concentration and lacks focus, miraculously decides to continue a train of thought, and it has to be now. "Is that why you made me take my bath before we eat tonight and put on clean clothes...not pajamas? And not say things like fart, poo and penis?" *Who is this? I never saw this child before in my life!*

Then Tristan laughs and so do I, though I try to contain myself when I tell Col, "That's not polite. What do you say?"

"Sor-ry," he says grudgingly, eyeing me in my "Bohemian Casual" look: embroidered peasant blouse, flowing skirt and sandals, as he returns to stacking his three small spears of asparagus like cordwood.

Tristan says, "I loved eating my asparagus trees when I was

growing up, because I knew if I ate enough of them, I would grow tall as a tree myself...and I did."

"Yeah?" He picks up a spear of asparagus and bites off the tip, making a face.

"Your salmon's delicious, Elaine," Tristan says, ever the gentleman. His clothes are nice; casual, but designer quality: Gucci loafers, khakis, pale blue Polo shirt, setting off his eyes. He continues, "And I love wild rice."

Colin rolls his eyes.

After dessert—peppermint ice cream and sugar wafers to please everyone—I let Col run off to see a video on the TV I've moved into his room for tonight. Tristan and I take our coffee into the living room. After some talk about a couple of commercial design proposals he's got going, one not too far from Albuquerque, he says, "There's going to be the annual 'Gathering of Nations' powwow there during the last weekend in April. Indian nations from coast to coast compete in tribal dances, and there are art exhibits, all kinds of food with great fry bread...maybe you and I and Colin could make a day of it. He'd love the Indian stuff..."

*Think Fuzzy Wuzzy: what's the best drug to subdue this man, tie him up and keep him here forever? How can an attractive professional, gentlemanly man still be single? Trish mentioned once he's been divorced a long time...so have I.*

"Sounds like fun. I have to check my work schedule to see if I'm off that weekend. If not, I'll have to find someone to switch shifts with me for a day."

So we leave it that I'll let him know for sure about my work schedule, and when he gets up to leave, we move to the door, and I realize: it's That Awful Moment. Will he kiss me? On the cheek? The lips? If he does, does he bend to me or do I stand on tiptoes to meet him halfway? This is so complicated—how do people date and survive? It's a non-issue when he gives me a hug, thanks me one last time, and is out the door.

What, no kiss? He's not attracted to me? Not that I imagined him shoving his tongue down to my tonsils, but a kiss...a little, polite kiss.

Is it me? Give it time. It's our first...quasi-date. We've been neighbors for a year and a half and it took him this long to ask me out for a drink. And only when he saw me straight from the beauty factory. I must've looked like a rag every other time he'd seen me. Mom was right.

Maybe it's not me. Maybe he's gay. After all, he's an architect, and that's almost like being in the arts, and I had no clue about Trish or Christa, so maybe he is. Hmmm...the man knows how to dress.

Maybe he thinks *I'm* gay?, I mean he saw my 'Women in Love' paintings at the gallery last year. He surely has noticed how often Christa visits Trish, and how the three of us hang out together a lot...and that Trish has been babysitting Colin for over a year. True, I don't wear cargo pants, but I've considered them. I mean, they make sense when you stop and think about it...all those pockets...

Omigod, girl, get a grip. Next thing, I'll be waiting up for him to call. But he didn't kiss me, and that could mean so many things. He's shy; no. He's old fashioned; possibly. Maybe he thinks I'm not attracted to him; what, I should have flung myself at him? Jesus, Mary and Joseph, I haven't dated in a hundred years. Jeff and I never exactly dated beyond a few walks to the coffee shop and one New Year's Eve dinner, after which he dumped me. Was it the skull?

No wonder people throw up their hands at the idea of dating. It's so complicated. Who pays for what? What are appropriate first dates? Who provides the condoms, if it ever gets to that? For people over 50, it's a minefield whose rules have been re-written since our own mating rituals. Do people today just meet and jump into bed, then tell each other their favorite foods and movies?

OK, Callie, here's the leftover salmon. Enjoy it, girl. It may be the last "special dinner" I ever fix for a gentleman caller. Who didn't kiss me. You, girl, you've been spayed, so you're out of the uproar, the chaos, the insanity. Of course, cats don't really date. You gals just yowl, the guys come over, and no one even buys you dinner first. All things considered, you're best out of it.

## *Christa*

A month in my new place and new practice. I've had to get a new look since my old Chicago wardrobe just didn't work here. Still adjusting, big time—I was gazing outside from my "open living space" and admiring my mature piñon trees, when I saw a flash of motion and realized it was a snake. That brought it all back to me: the terrible fright at the sidewinder in Elaine's courtyard garden; I had to grab Callie and run for our lives. But it's also how I got to know Trish, and she's right when she says these animals have been here long before us, and most are completely harmless. So I guess it's safe to assume that the snake—my snake—is OK. Just not to bother it. I'll try to describe it—long, big and brownish—and maybe Trish will know what kind it is. I guess living a little way from the center of town means not only having more space, but also coexisting with the wildlife. Some places I looked at even had "coyote fencing." Can't imagine waking up to a coyote in my yard—munching the neighbor's Pomeranian, no doubt.

Trish's touch on my shoulder interrupts this train of thought, and she hands me a platter of hot dogs and hamburgers. "Elaine's got the kids playing a game and it's up to us to grill these. After lunch Colin will blow out the candles on his cake and open presents." She gives me a big grin, clearly caught up in the excitement of her little buddy's fifth birthday, complete with four of his friends from daycare—all crowded into Elaine's casita. His gift from me is a pair of handmade moccasins, and Trish bought him a matching beaded wristband, which will be great with the little deerskin drum Laney got him last weekend at the tribal powwow. Col's been talking nonstop about the Indian dances ever since, and even pulled me and Trish into his impromptu dance circle last night. Our Irish lad's gone native.

So once the cake things have been cleared away, he's delighted with his presents, not only the authentic drum, moccasins, and wristband, but a wooden tomahawk and beaded headband with a feather from Tristan, who's hanging the paper maché donkey in the courtyard outside.He organizes the piñata game while we fill a 32-gallon trash bag with wrapping paper, napkins, plates, cups, half-eaten lunches and cake, grateful to be cleaning up with the end in sight. How do people with a bunch of kids stay sane?

Col's kicking his regulation soccer ball (his gift from the Caseys) against the adobe wall, then to the kids, who kick it back. Into the yuccas. When it's his turn to whack the piñata, he wants to use his tomahawk instead of the boom stick. Tristan says no, and Birthday Boy raises his arm as if he's about to hurl it at him in frustration when Tristan kneels down close to Col with some serious conversation between the two, though I can't hear them. Col puts the tomahawk behind his back, shakes his head vigorously, but in the end, reluctantly hands the tomahawk over to him, picks up the stick and submits to the blindfold, thrashing away in the air until he finally connects with a solid thwack. Wrapped hard candies and chocolates spill onto the flagstone patio, and the kids, cheering, are all over them.

Before long Tristan's in the house. "We're all done with the piñata. Parents due soon?"

"Any minute. Come here a second, would you?" Elaine asks, and when she offers him a cold drink, I can see *AGENDA* written all over her. "What exactly did you say to Col that had him giving up the tomahawk so easily...willingly?"

Tristan looks at her, blinks, smiles, and says, "Oh. That. Nothing."

"What do you mean, nothing? If I had tried to get it away from him, you'd have seen Tantrum City, so how'd you handle it?"

His smile grows larger. "Just a couple of guys working it out..."

"So it's a guy thing, is that it?"

He just nods, giving her a big, shit-eating grin. Men can be so infuriating.

## *Tristan*

Colin needs a father-figure in his life, that's for sure. Elaine tries, but it's not the same, especially since she's working full-time. Susan was my little princess, but I was clueless about raising her. Mariel–and the string of nannies–took care of that. I was the bread-winner, and with Mariel's money, that was fine.

Until she decided she didn't want to be married anymore...to me. Work became my life, except for the occasional weekends with Susan, and those were unbearably awkward. She wanted to be with her friends at the mall or the show, and she made no effort to hide it. So we went to a lot of movies together. It wasn't until her engagement to Greg that things improved.

But Colin–if anyone ever needed a dad, it's that boy. Still, what if he looks to *me* as a father, and it doesn't go anywhere with Elaine? That's all the kid needs. But what if it does? Taking on another family at my age, after living alone for 10 years...and how would Susan react? Probably not well, based on her attitude toward some of the women I've dated–and their children. For that matter, how would Colin react, not having Elaine to himself anymore? Either way...

# Christa

After that party, I'm amazed that the boy, all done up in his Indian things, still has energy to kick his soccer ball around outside when two women can hardly get up from their chairs. I move slowly to heat water for tea in the microwave, as though I'm paddling through dry sand. Trish has left to work on her jewelry, and I'll be on my way soon, too. Callie, just emerged from the safety of wherever, checks to see if the coast is clear of strange, whooping children, then settles down to her dinner. Elaine stares into space. "Next year's birthday will be at McDonalds," she says. "Assuming he's still here. No signed power of attorney statement from the Caseys…I check with the school district every week. No information, period. John and Maggie haven't sent him a letter in months, probably since receiving the request from the district to sign the damned document. For his birthday, they sent a regulation soccer ball, along with a birthday Mass card. No message."

"Not necessarily bad news, Elaine. It's not like they're officially denying you power of attorney; they just haven't delegated it."

"So I keep doing the day-to-day grunt work but they hold the cards." Her eyes well with tears—of anger more than fear. "It's put me in a position of absolute helplessness while they sit on their hands and I'm knocking myself out to keep us going. They pray so damn much, but never think to send him a check for his birthday instead of some stupid Mass card that won't buy him new shoes or school clothes. Or school supplies. Or his school shots and check-up. Not a dime have they sent, as God is my witness. And never did Liam send Stephanie a damned nickel the whole time she lived under my roof with his baby. *His* baby, dammit." Her face is flushed with rage.

"No…it was *OK*, in fact, it was perfectly *fine* with him and his ignorant parents to pretend Colin's needs had nothing to do with them…or their wallets. Liam wasn't only emotionally distant for a year and a half when Stephanie lived with me; he was a deadbeat dad, plain and simple. And it was my daughter who got herself and their son back to Ireland. Otherwise, he might never have laid eyes on his boy."

She's practically screaming, and stops for a breath, continuing, "Not that he helped them when they got there. Jesus,

Mary and Joseph...Steph and Colin were on the dole! And no wonder—look who he comes from. The Holy Duo who pray, pray, pray, but are such hypocrites, they do nothing, when you come right down to it...nothing for the child they pretend to care about so damned much. No-o-o." She shakes her head violently from side to side. "They'd have to open their pocketbooks for that, and God forbid, they give the child a penny. Really, Christa, it's no wonder he never sent Steph any child support—he's an apple who didn't fall far from the tree."

She shows no sign of calming down anytime soon, and no wonder. It's been a long time coming, and probably a good thing for her to vent like this. Now she's started waving her hands in the air, though, and I'm beginning to get concerned.

"I mean, Christa, do the math: Colin lived with Steph and me for the first year and half of his life without so much as a pair of baby shoes from his father. Then the two of them are dependent on the Irish welfare system. At long last, when he marries her, and only—*only* after he's gotten her pregnant yet again, he *finally* supports his family for what?—all of three months?—and God forgive me, my girl dies, and I'm back to supporting Colin for the last two years. I've yet to see one red cent from his good-for-nothing family. If they'd taken the price of a regulation soccer ball plus the cost of shipping it here," her voice is rising, "not to mention paying for a Mass..." She's getting more and more incensed. "If they'd sent a check for all that, I could have..." She's screeching now. "I could have bought him something he really needs—like...like..." She exhales a huge lungful of air and, deflated, hangs her head, exhausted.

Her voice is barely a whisper now. "I've got to stop. I'm getting a headache."

"I'll make you some herbal tea, Laney. You sit back and close your eyes. While I'm up, I'll check on Colin." *She's right—on all counts—and has every reason to be enraged. She's been doing this all alone. And what would become of him if something happened to her?*

## *Elaine*

Can it be—answered prayers? Ron Anderson asks me to dinner because he's seen me in something other than scrubs? Blond and handsome, well-dressed...and successful. Word on the floor has it that he's quite a catch despite his recent divorce.

When I call my mom and say the magic words, "He's a surgeon," she's transported—make that ecstatic—and says, "How wonderful! I've been praying, dear. I mean it. I said a Novena to St. Jude for difficult or impossible causes." *That's me, Mom a difficult cause at best.* "A doctor, Ellie! A surgeon! Oh, wait 'til I tell my friends from St. Mary's." She bursts out laughing. "That old biddie, Amelia, always bragging about her son-in-law, the lawyer; well, she'll have an absolute fit."

I interrupt her fantasy with, "Hold on, Mom. He asked me out, but we haven't actually gone on a date yet. And besides, I have to get some new clothes. He's already seen me in my one good outfit." *When he didn't recognize me out of my scrubs.*

"Not to worry. I'm putting a check in the mail today. I'm sure he's taking you someplace nice." *Not like Tom.* "After all, he's a doctor. Now promise me, dear, you won't use part of it to pay the gas bill or something. Go for a classy look, Ellie, wear a dress for a change—something feminine." *As opposed to gold lamé like our local eccentric?*

"Floral, maybe," she suggests with a hopefulness in her tone I haven't heard in years. "Or white. After all Memorial Day isn't far away."

"Don't order any invitations yet, Mom. It's just a first date."

"Yes, yes, I know. But call me, and let me know right away how it went—where he took you—and be sure to accessorize, dear."

❖

On his first day of kindergarten, Colin insists on wearing the cowboy boots Tristan bought him when he took us to the Santa Fe Rodeo a couple of months ago. They've become Col's favorite things, and he would sleep with them if I didn't make him take them off for his bath and for bed. No matter how hot it's been, he wears them every day. With shorts and a short-sleeved shirt, it's not my favorite look, but as Trish reminds me, "Still, it's a look, after all. Give him credit for marching to a different drummer."

The fresh haircut helps, I'll say that. As his hair darkens to sun-streaked auburn, I see more and more of his mother in him. Of course, the only time I've seen his father, he was at death's door in the intensive care unit, so who can say? I certainly don't find any resemblance to the Caseys, thank God, and the irony is, after all my worry, thanks so much, John and Maggie, for your disregard of the school district's letters. In your stupidly or stubbornness or whatever, your failure to grant—or deny—power of attorney for Colin actually worked out, and now he's in school. So much for that.

He's pulling his hand from mine, he's so eager to get in the classroom and show off his boots. This is a whole new chance for him to "do well in school," and a big change from daycare. Now if only he'll adjust. He has a hard time knowing how to act with other kids, and some are more tolerant of him than others. For the last month I've been talking to him about not hitting, not throwing things, not blurting out words I don't even want to suggest to him ("shite" and "bloody hell" come to mind), and most of all, not leaving the classroom on his own. How many times I've told him he can't just get up and walk out—not to get a drink of water, not to go to the bathroom, not to wander away under any circumstances. He tunes me out during  these pep talks, doing 'Colin the Disconnected' when I do my 'Authoritative Fuzzy Wuzzy' voice. "I kno-ow, Ma-aa," he says in a robotic voice, as if he understands.

But does he? And even if he understands, he doesn't always remember. In the heat of the moment, he acts first and thinks afterwards, much more than is usual for his age. Miss Annette says he's behind in deciphering social cues, often blundering his way—uninvited—into a group of kids hard at play. He has no concept of asking, "Can I play, too?"—just barges in. And if they don't accept him into the group, he's as likely to take one of their toys or throw things as he is to storm off, calling them names.

So while other parents wave farewell tearfully, I'm holding my breath, wondering what he might do. It's an effort to keep from shouting, "Remember, Colin, be a good boy…no swearing, spitting, fighting or hair-pulling." What dark looks I'd get from the other adults, all of whom have perfect children, of course. I can imagine the note the teacher might send home: "Dear Ms. McElroy, Colin pushed another child in line today, causing the child to fall down and sustain a head laceration requiring stitches. An attorney for the family will be contacting you shortly. When reprimanded, Colin called me a 'bloody bitch,' which is not appropriate language for kindergarten. Please contact me immediately so you can set up an appointment with me and Principal Stern…within 24 hours, please. Sincerely, Ms. Merry Sunshine."

Snap out of it, Elaine. He's not even through the door yet. I've done everything humanly possible. Helped him study his colors and shapes, counting and alphabet. Maintained consistent rules and boundaries…or tried to. Enforced time out after time out after time out until I ran out of steam…then let him go about his evil ways. Oh, Fuzzy Wuzzy Failure! Now I'm unleashing him on an unsuspecting school district. Shame on you, Fuzzy Wuzzy, but they'll find out soon enough.

Will this change in his routine mean it will be like those early days of daycare…*challenging*? As in hand-wringing challenging? But no matter what happens, this is the start of his school career. And heaven knows, I've seen it all as a school nurse; nothing would shock me anymore.

When Steph and Roxy started kindergarten, my biggest concern was what outfit they'd wear and how I'd fix their hair, and with what color ribbons. Things seemed so much simpler then. True, Tom was drinking and unpredictable, and sometimes money was tight then too, but I was 30 years younger, had a lot more energy, and didn't know all the hazards of raising children.

❖

Or dating.

Like dinner with Dr. Ron Anderson—the surgeon who made my mother's heart beat faster. The floral dress from Dillard's was perfect for the Anasazi Restaurant's soft lighting, and its pattern came close to matching his silk tie. Mom would have loved the picture it all made, as well as his manners. He opened the door of his Jaguar for me and at the restaurant, held my chair out. That was nice, but when he took charge of the menu and ordered for both of us—good thing I was open to buffalo carpaccio with blackberry-whole grain mustard. I'd have preferred the chicken.

He's an accomplished man, but his idea of table talk was a recitation of his accomplishments, professional citations, and fellowships. He monopolized the conversation; maybe he thought I didn't have anything interesting to say.

All my mother could say when I reported this was, "Well, dear, I'm sure he's busy night and day, doing his surgeries and all. Give him a chance."

Actually, I did, and when I finally could get a word in edgewise, I brought up my painting. This brought the semi-interested reaction of, "I see. That's nice," before he launched into the itinerary of his last trip to the Amazon Jungle. "He's well-traveled and adventurous, dear," Mom said when I told her that part. "Wouldn't you like to canoe down the river?"

All I could do was listen to his tales of anacondas and piranhas and ask questions. "Piranhas–they bite, don't they? My grandson would be interested."

"How old is he?"

"Five, and starting kindergarten soon."

Nodding he said, "They grow up so fast. My daughter from my first marriage has a three-year-old who wrecks my house every time they visit. Can't wait to see them leave." He asked me if I golfed or played tennis, and the possibility of playing at his club. *That would mean getting two more new outfits.*

At that point, when I said I did neither, he must have thought I was a mushoom who sat in the dark–Fungus Fuzzy Wuzzy, best sautéed in a little butter, onion and garlic.

OK–I don't do golf, tennis, or adventure vacations, have no medical awards or Jaguar, and for that matter, no connection whatsoever to this man.

"Well, dear, he was just one, and you work in a place with so many–doctors, I mean. And you did get to eat buffalo," my mother remarked.

*Yeah, Mom. Right.*

❖

I'll at least get some more wear out of my 'Urbane Elaine' outfit for parent-teacher conference night. Put my best foot forward. It doesn't hurt to look as good as I can for Ms. Silva. It's only the third time I've worn it; the second was out to dinner and a show with Tristan. This time, he did kiss me—the only thing I didn't share with my mother (thankfully, she didn't ask), who was beside herself with renewed joy (or hope) for me. "See, that spa day and the new clothes did it—and St. Jude–he made all the difference. Now go get a facial, dear, and keep up the good work. My treat." Thanks, Mom. Anyway, does the kiss—a little one—mean he isn't gay? Or doesn't think that I'm gay? Or that he maybe finds me attractive—a little?

In any event, it doesn't hurt to look as good as I can for this meeting with Ms. Silva, but is she going to tell me anything I don't already know? I have to put on my 'receptive grandma' face, though, despite the many notes I've gotten from her about—the usual: hitting, yelling, throwing, disappearing…she looks at me like I can magically fix Colin—as if! As if I haven't been working with him for two and a half years, as I have told her…and told her. We're no strangers to each other—I wish.

"Look, Ms. McElroy, what good work Colin is capable of doing. You see how neatly he printed his name here, and over here, how well he colored this worksheet and completed it. He was so thrilled to get a sticker on this paper." This young woman—is she old enough to be out of school?—is actually glowing, then pauses for The Big Breath. Uh oh.

"However," *Bet I know where this is going.* "These," she says, pushing a tall stack of papers to me, "are what I mostly see from him."

It's obvious some have been crumpled, and one or two show small bootprints as though he'd stomped on them. In contrast to the first two, these worksheets look like he grasped a crayon in his fist and scribbled randomly across the page to finish as fast as possible. His name is barely decipherable. I think of Stephanie at five years old; she was able to legibly print her first name on Valentine hearts she'd made for her father and me. How can there be such a difference?

Everything in me wants to break down in sobs. What good would that do? This is all too familiar, but what can I say to this novice teacher who wants successful students? Have I been too lenient...tying him to his seat until he completes work properly might be the answer. Or maybe I've been too strict and boring, doing the same things with him over and over? But Dr. Park said maintaining routine is essential. Maybe it's time for another visit. After those sessions with the doctor, Colin made some small improvements in Miss Annette's classroom.

Ms. Silva with her long, silver earrings and pencil-slim skirt is staring at me with concerned eyes. What can I do that I haven't tried? Colin's in school less than 90 days, and I've already got a history with her that I never had with either of my girls' teachers during all of their school years.

"Ms. McElroy, I know you have an extensive background as a school nurse, and have seen many students with these same kinds of issues. Difficulties controlling impulses, concentrating, staying on task, completing work...interacting with the other students...he seems to play best alone..."

"He saw a pediatric psychiatrist last year, and there was some improvement...I'm thinking of taking him again."

The sun bursts through the clouds as Ms. Silva's face radiates relief. "Yes, oh yes. That would be a good idea."

She rises, signaling the end to our meeting. And her joy at being off the hook.

Once in my car, I hold my head in my hands, recalling Ms. Silva's words; that I've seen many students "with the same kinds of issues": aggressiveness...impulsivity...concentration and social problems...

Yes, I've had offices full of kids pushing and shoving, in line for their meds. I've seen them, yes. God knows I've seen them. How many meetings have I attended with parents whose kids are just like Colin? How many times have I suggested a trial period of medication to see if there's some improvement? How often have I sat down at a conference table and met with parents who are dead set against meds and made that super-clear? Or the ones who would consider medication, but need more information—a lot more—from their pediatrician? With some of the meds, you see results immediately, with the child at his seat, concentrating, completing work...or not. But you know right away. Sometimes the dosage needs adjustment and the medication turns out to be effective, assuming the parents allow enough time for that.

None of it's a magic bullet, though. The parents have to be right on top of the kid, making sure the assignment's been written down properly, making sure he has what's needed to do the assignment, and then making sure he actually sits down and does the work correctly and completely. Some parents have told me, "OK, it's nine o'clock, he's been working for two hours, but he still hasn't finished a 20-minute assignment; I just tell him go to bed and get some rest. The hell with it. My child needs sleep. He's just a little kid."

I don't disagree; how could I? And this doesn't go on for just one night a week; it's five nights a week for homework and 24/7 for everything else: playing sports or being with friends or sitting down to dinner...it's constant vigilance for the parent. It's exhausting for everyone involved, and often frustrating.

Thank goodness Ms. Silva recognizes I have that information, and tons of experience, but it's a totally different situation when the child in question is my own grandson, my flesh and blood...and it's hard...it hurts so much, more than I ever imagined, to be on the other side of the table.

# Roxy

**N**ow that my man TJ's graduated and gotten his R.N., he's working at County Hospital and gotten his own place in the city—how cool is that? It's just a matter of letting a few people know I'm moving in with him. People like my dad. And Grandma Helen? First is Mom.

"Don't tell your grandmother–either of them. It'll kill them. Does your father know?" Momsa gives me That Look when she doesn't want me to do something, but can't stop me either. She gets up from the couch and walks over to her kiva fireplace, where she's hung two red stockings, one with Colin's name and the other with mine. She pokes and stirs the embers with irritation, but better she's taking it out on the fire than on me. Sparks are flying from the fireplace. Will Mom go postal on me? Will I wind up back in Chicago tonight?

She straightens up and glares at me. "This is *not* the news I wanted to hear. You may be going on 21, but you're still my little girl, and I don't like the idea of you living with this man. Or any man."

*Duh, Mom, like I didn't get that. But it was OK for you to move in with Frank, dragging me along.* "TJ's an R.N. with a solid job and a good future. In a year and a half, I get my B.S. in Biology, and I might go to grad school or get some rocking job at the Field Museum. How sweet is that?"

"Right now you're a UIC undergrad whose parents are helping with tuition and living expenses, and if you think for one minute," (*Yo, Mom, quit waving that poker around before you hurt someone*) "…that I'm going to support you when you're living with TJ, a guy I've never even met—please. Has your father? Your grandmother? Met him?"

"Her face gets this *Uh Oh!* look like she doesn't know if she's going to yell or cry. "Roxy. Please. Don't. Tell. Me. You're. Pregnant."

She leans on the iron poker for support and takes this, like, huge breath and plants her hand over her heart. Seriously.

"Not again. Oh, Sweet Jesus, not again. I'm too old, and I can't take any more. As much as I've been through, I mean I can't, I just can't…"

"No way," I tell her, "I'm not going to do a Stephanie." Then I remember my sister and get all sad about that, and so does my mom, because I see her start to tear up.

"Thank God for that. And leave your sister out of this. Look..." She comes back to the couch, the better to see me, no doubt. "I only want what any mother wants for her child...I just want what's best for you."

*Oh, throw up. If I ever have kids—and I won't—I'll never say that to them no matter what.* "That's what I want, too, and TJ would never hurt me, for real, Mom-ola. I can't wait for you to meet him. He would have come with me for the holidays, but he's still new at his job and doesn't get vacation time yet. Next Christmas..."

"Roxy, who knows about next year? I'm not happy with your news, but you're here with me now for the holidays, you're not pregnant, you're doing well in school—that's all good. And I can't talk about this anymore."

❖

Mom's driving to pick up Colin and busy telling me about his troubles—fighting with the kids at school, tearing up his worksheets and even walking out of the classroom and wandering down the hall—jeez, if Steph and I had ever done anything like that, she'd have been all over us. Stephanie wasn't really wild until high school, partying hardy and never looking back. If Mom only knew half the stuff she did, and Steph dragged me with her for some of it. Now it's Colin who's the problem child, and he's only in kindergarten! What's going to happen in first grade, and will my mom survive it? She's still alive after hearing about TJ and all, but that's nothing. She should be glad; I'm The Good Kid after all, so what's her problem? I'm the least of her worries—as usual. The last time I was here for Christmas, Colin was out of control, running toward a bonfire and all over the church, and I was the one chasing after him. And calming Mom down afterward with peppermint tea.

What if I were pregnant? Is that what it would take to get Mom's attention?

When I was little, it was all about Dad—was he drinking again? How much? Would he come home? Would he be OK? Next thing I know, Mom and Dad split and Stephanie's doing Wild Thing, with me tagging along. Fast forward to Steph doing 'here I am from Ireland...with child,' and she winds up moving in and screwing Old Frank. Eeeew. She's not back to Ireland for a month before Mom decides it's Time To Reinvent Herself—in New Mexico, so it's off to Katelyn's for me. Then Steph gets married—without us—and croaks right after that, so Mom's over to Ireland at light-speed, bringing back Hyper Kid who's been the center of her attention ever since—especially now that he's got "issues."

She's surprised—no, shocked—that I'm moving in with my man? Get real; with TJ, for the first time in my life, I'm Number One.

❖

"Hey, Sport," I call out when I see this kid that's so much bigger than the Colin I remember. And more grown up. I mean he's just had this play date (play dates already?) going on with his bud from school, and he's no sooner out the door than he dashes for the car, leaving Mom a dozen steps behind.

"Hi, Aunt Roxy. Tyler has PlayStation, and we played Crash Bash all day. I beat him, and it was way cool."

Way cool? What happened to the little rug rat who was drooling on Mom's wall-to-wall?

## *Christa*

Tonight's party is so much easier to manage than last month's catered affair. And smaller, since it's just a few personal friends and not all the businesspeople and therapists I've met since moving here—talk about a mob scene in my house, which is not that large. The florist sent over vari-colored poinsettias big as potted shrubs, and those took up a lot of floor space, too, but made for a wonderful ambiance…perfect for a holiday bash meant to impress. Ever since early November it's been a round of dinners and drinks and parties. Who knew relocating would mean so much networking?

After we walk into town this evening, the gang will come over here for hot chili and cold beer. Plus a few snacks and sweets, but nothing fancy. They've been here before, of course, but Roxy's never seen my place with its "Santa Fe charm" and all. Come to think of it, I haven't seen her since Stephanie's wake and funeral when Rox almost got into a brawl with her dad's trophy wife, what's-her-name, Meryl? With the boobs? And the fifties hair?

❖

No black lipstick and nail polish? No studded dog collars? No pink spiked hair? Who is this vision in fashion jeans and sweater? Do I detect the fragrance of Calvin Klein's Obsession instead of Gag Me Gothic Musk? Hmmm. Is it possible Roxy's shed her leather and chrome for a new look? Laney said she works part-time at Urban Outfitters...she must be making good use of her employee discount, and to good effect, right down to her Navy peacoat and red tam—a big change from the last time I walked into the Plaza with her on Christmas Eve three years ago. She was sporting a ragged hoodie and a down vest, then, and fingerless gloves so you couldn't miss all her silver rings. So this is the New! Improved! Roxy who's given up her grunge sack in favor of a neat-looking navy and gray backpack.

Trish is stylin', too, doing 'Santa Fe Cowgirl' in a tan shearling coat and to-die-for cowboy boots, thanks to a big jewelry sale she made to a New York shop.

❖

We're all in high spirits tonight as we head into town, our breath forming little white puffs in the cold, with Roxy and Col behind us, and Elaine bringing up the rear. Keeping watch on us all. Waiting for someone—anyone— to trip and fall or choke on the free cocoa and cookies so she can swoop in and administer life-saving CPR. Ever-vigilant Elaine.

If it weren't for her making that break to come out here, I'd have never hiked The Trail of Broken Feet, or faced down a venomous viper—which led to Trish. Which led to my moving here.

Trish turns to Colin, who's hot on our heels, having broken away from Roxy—yet again. Trish asks what he wants from Santa, and he shouts out, "PlayStation," so she yells right back to him, "Cool, dude! We could play video games together at our next play date when your mom goes out." Does Trish even realize what she just said—Mom?—it's one thing for the boy to call Elaine 'Ma," when she is, after all, raising him and mothering him and he has no memory of Stephanie. Or his dad. But when another adult slips and refers to Laney as Colin's 'mom,' that's big, huge really; it's validation that Colin and Elaine have truly bonded. I'm all goose bumps, and it's not just the temperature out here.

"Can Christa come to our next play date?" Trish asks him, and he stops running in circles as if weighing this.

He eyes me dubiously. "Can she build forts?" Omigod, I'm being evaluated as Possible Play Date Material by a five-year-old. The way he's eyeing me, my other job interviews were heaven compared to this tough scrutiny.

"Oh, I've seen Christa build some wicked-good forts," she says. Is she insane? He'll see right through that one.

He sizes me up one last time, dismissing me with a shake of his head and turning to Trish. "No, just you and me. Not her!"

Ouch! No play dates for me, I guess, and Elaine's busy looking all embarrassed, so Roxy saves the situation, shouting out, "Let's roll, dudes…and dudettes. I want some hot cocoa and cool tunes."

## *Trish*

So our little group moves forward, approaching the Plaza, and I take Christa's hand. She gives me a questioning smile. I smile back, half-cocky. *Sorry, lover, you didn't make the grade; not everyone can be Prime Play Date Talent.* Maybe just as well. I get to play with boy stuff and watch Colin, just him and me while Elaine goes out, and it's good, it's all good. Sometimes makes me wonder if I want one of my own…someday.

Rox is careful to walk on the outside of the sidewalk as she's trying to rein Colin in and hold his hand, but he's having none of it. The lights of the Plaza and some high energy mariachi music draw us into the center of town, and the closer we get, the more he's pulling out of Roxy's grasp, then running down the sidewalk with her in pursuit.

"Colin, wait! Don't run off," Elaine yells after him.

He runs off into the crowd ahead, all of us chasing him and calling his name, but he vanishes into the moving mass of people. Just for a moment until I catch sight of his red stocking cap and move faster than I have in years. I want to grab him in a headlock, he's scared me so much. When he turns and sees me, he gets this goofy grin on his face like we're playing a game, and dashes off again toward the door of a restaurant, but I corral him just in time. "No, Col. You need to stay with us. Seriously."

Elaine catches up, breathless and angry. "No more of that, Mister, or I'm taking you right back home this minute." She puts her face right up to his. "Do you understand?"

He's looking all around at the lights on the trees in the Plaza, at the crowds of people milling around, some with their dogs— on leashes, thank heavens—so he's paying attention to everything but Elaine. She has to take his chin in her hand and make him meet her gaze. "Listen to me, Colin. Do you understand?"

Finally, he gets it. "Yeah, Ma."

"You're not going to run away again, are you?"

"No, Ma."

She gives him a brief, hard hug, then pulls away. "We don't want anything bad to happen to you."

The hot cider and cocoa, the cookies, and the live music help ease the tension. I'm grateful Col's not off and running again. For the time being, at least, Colin's become the model child, placidly holding his Aunt Roxy's hand except when he's sipping cocoa and eating a cookie. Elaine, poor Elaine, seems to be enjoying herself for once. We're all so thankful nothing terrible happened. The phrase "giddy with relief" comes to mind, and Christa, who's usually so prim and buttoned-up, gives me a cookie—and a big hug and kiss—out of nowhere. God bless us, everyone.

## *Elaine*

Col's been good since I made him listen, really hear me—but I don't want to press my luck. I've limited his cookie and cocoa intake so he won't be up all night, and he's got to be in bed at a decent hour since he'll be up at dawn, no doubt, to open presents. Tomorrow when he sees his new two-wheel bike (assembled by Tristan, complete with training wheels, and hidden in his house these last three days), he'll want to ride through the neighborhood—even if it snows.

As it happens, Col tires of the lights and music. Besides, he soon realizes he's cold and announces, "I'm freezing, Ma."

The wind's picked up, giving a sharp edge to the night air, so we're all ready to go back to my place, get in our cars, and head over to Christa's…at least for a little while.

"Yo, Mom. Sounds like a plan," my girl says, probably relieved that our outing with Colin is nearly over. She needs a rest from him. Would that I had such a luxury; he can be wearing.

The Cathedral offers us shelter from the chill desert wind, so we stop in to light a candle for Stephanie. It's still pretty early so the church is nearly empty; only a few old women in the pews. The place is dim: sconces give only faint illumination, and votive candles cast flickering shadows at the back of the church. Incense lingers in the air.

"Light a candle and say a prayer for your sister," I tell Roxy, giving her some coins for the donation box.

Colin watches, then chimes in, "Me too. By myself."

He takes a long, wooden wick, which I guide to the flame of a votive. When it catches fire, he says, "Ooo-ooh." Together, we light a small white candle, I make the Sign of the Cross, and Colin clumsily mimics my motions.

Trish and Christa both light candles, too, maybe for Christa's dad, and perhaps for their own future together.

A sudden draft makes the tiny flames shudder, and the face of the St. Francis statue seems threatening, almost sinister. When I look toward the door, I see a man off to the side leaning on metal forearm crutches. His cap is worn low on his brow and a scarf covers his neck and hangs down over a long woolen coat. When I hear Christa's gasp, I instinctively put my hand on Colin's shoulder and pull him closer to me.

"What, Ma?" He's busy dropping quarters as noisily as possible into the small metal box.

The stranger's face, what I can see of it in the wavering candlelight, is gaunt, but strikingly handsome and somehow familiar. He stares intently, not at me or Trish, Christa or Roxy, but only at Colin, studying his face and clothes as though commiting them to memory.

Christa and I exchange a look of fear and disbelief. When I glance back, the man on crutches is limping away from us, toward the massive wooden doors, and I see that the right side of his face is horribly disfigured with deep, jagged scars. Again, I look to Christa, and when I return my attention to the vestibule, the man is half-hidden in the shadows. The door opens, and he is gone...

I whisper to Christa, "You saw him."

"It was such a shock. If we hadn't both seen him, I'd doubt my own eyes."

"Is it *him*...? Lazarus, raised from the dead."

Christa moves closer to Colin, protecting him...but from what exactly I'm not sure...an apparition?

Roxy and Trish send me questioning looks, and Rox asks, "Mom...What's up?"

"Later," I tell her, in a tone she knows not to challenge.

Outside, the cold wind at our back hurries us home.

## *Roxy*

Props to the decorator—this place is stylin', Christa." Is it ever. Can't wait for the day TJ and I have someplace this sweet. Two bedrooms plus a den, a nice, open kitchen going into the living room, and the wolves howling outside. Do the critters come with the house as part of the "Santa Fe Charm" she keeps talking about? Her chili rocks, too, and Mom doesn't say anything when I have a beer—like I've never had one before, duh. The little dude's all busy with the wooden train set Trish gave him as an early present from one play pal to the other— guess she's trying to keep her 'Preferred Play Date' status. It's stellar how much hanging with Col means to her, and hanging with him isn't always the easiest gig, believe me. Yesterday the two of them holed up in Trish's kitchen and baked chocolate chip cookies together—from scratch—for tonight's little par-tay. For real, the dude's a four-star chef! I'm grabbing another of these killer cookies when Mom comes over to the counter for chili. She's looking all serious, like she has since the church. And not a word from her all the way over here.

"So what was the drama at the church, Mom? Can you tell me now?"

Christa stops pouring salsa in a bowl and gives my mom this *Uh, Oh!* look, and I'm saying, "This is bogus. I'm not a little kid." *What, Mom, you're ignoring me? I crank it up.* "*What* went down back there?"

Trish glances up from the train on the living room floor but goes back to Colin. Wise move—this could be raw.

"There was a man...at the church..." Christa says.

"And your point is...?"

Mom's going all pasty in the face and looks over at Col who's all about the train and Trish. "It looked like...maybe...he could have been..." She's like some kind of zombie.

*Somebody, please—where is my mother?* "Freakin' what—some kind of space alien?"

Christa says, "It was so dark, and it happened so fast, but this man on crutches came in and we saw him staring at..." She breaks off, motioning with her head toward the living room.

"Col?" I whisper, getting caught up in this mystery, big time. She nods.

"I'm going to call the Police," Mom announces.

"What, is that dude a local child molester?"

"Laney, he hasn't done anything...yet. We don't even know for certain that it's *him*."

"Who, *HIM*? John Wayne Gacy?"

"Sh-sh." Mom tilts her head toward the little dude, who could care less about whatever we have to say.

I can barely make out Christa saying. "Liam…it could have been Liam."

*Whh-a-a-a-t? No wonder Mom and Christa are freakin' out. Wasn't he like, supposed to be some kind of vegetable?* "But if it *was* him, wouldn't he come up and say something to his son?" I whisper back.

"And scare the living crap out of him, like he scared us?" Mom says. "Maybe he's checking out the situation…seeing Colin for himself before he…." She stops, slapping a hand over her mouth. "Sweet Jesus, what can I do?"

## *Elaine*

Colin's tucked in bed for the night, finally asleep after all his talk of Play Stations and Legos and bicycles around the tree in the morning, but I can't keep from tiptoeing into his room and checking him…again…just to be sure.

"Mom, you've checked on him three times—he's OK. Now give me a hand with this tape and stuff. Gotta have Christmas ready to go in the morning." She's in the middle of the living room floor with scissors, gift tags, wrapping paper, bows and gift bags all over the place.

"Go for the gift bags, Rox. They're fastest."

"Just come over here and help. You're pacing back and forth like you can't wait to get in his room and check him again…like you haven't done that a minute ago."

*She's right, but if anything ever happened…* "Children have been snatched out of their beds."

"So, Christmas is cancelled because of some dude you saw in the dark who may or may not be anybody?" She gets up, leaving the green and red chaos on the floor. "I'm going to bed."

"Oh, Rox. Don't. I'm sorry to be so nervous; it's just the shock of seeing—"

She cuts me off with a sharp tone I have never heard from her. "I don't want to hear it, for real. Now help me wrap this stuff or I'm done."

OK. We wrap. And tape and tie and stuff things into gift bags (thank God for those!). We've piled gifts around the tree and I'm trying to hurry and fill Roxy's stocking while she's in the kitchen. Three sharp knocks on the door startle me, and I drop the vanilla-scented candle I'm holding. The glass jar hits the hardwood floor, shattering into jagged pieces. A vision of that man in the church fills my head, and all I can think of are the scars on his face and those crutches...and the way he was staring at Colin. Could it have been...was it the dim light...or some shadowy phantom?

"I'll get it," Roxy calls from the kitchen. "What broke?"

The thought of her opening the door to who-knows-what makes me shudder.

"No, I've got it," I'm trying to sound light and breezy like it's no big deal to answer a knock at midnight...but it could be a very big deal. The walk to my door stretches before me as a chasm, one that could swallow us all. *One foot in front of the other...left foot, right foot...we're there now...*

Three more knocks, louder this time, and I'm opening it—to someone...or something...

The shape of a man bends to the side, in the shadows cast by the porch light, which reflects on something metal.

"Omigod!"

"What?" Roxy shouts. "What is it?"

The dark figure turns and faces me. "What's wrong? For god's sake, you're pale as a ghost. What's going on?

For a moment, I really *don't* know what's happening...my nerves are so overwrought I can't make sense of what's in front of me...

❖

Have I lost my mind as well as my memory? How could I have forgotten? It's not like I didn't know. Tristan reassured me—twice—that he'd bring Colin's new bike over on Christmas Eve. Assembled and ready to go.

"Tristan, I am so so sorry, and so embarassed. I completely forgot you were coming over with the bike. It's just that hearing a knock at the door...after midnight...with everything that happened tonight at the church..."

He looks baffled, as well he should. "Wait. Elaine, calm down. What church? What happened?"

"Coffee. I'll make a fresh pot of decaf. Please, Tristan, sit down...this is my daughter, Roxy."

"I've heard about you, Roxy. I'm Tristan, from next door," I hear from the kitchen as I make coffee.

# Roxy

Legs tucked under me, Callie and I cuddle on the couch–after Mom's big, scarey drama, that's about all I can do. That, and explain it to him. "Mom's all bent out of shape about some dude she and Christa saw at the church. Made her scared to open the door. Scared me, too."

Callie's purring now, so she's all cool, especially since I'm scratching her in back of her ears–her fave.

Momsa's recovered enough to bring in coffee and a plate of the Christmas cookies we made together–with Col's help, and he did a good job with us, just like he did with Trish.

"We were at the cathedral this evening," she says. "We stopped to light a candle for Stephanie, and this strange-looking man appeared–out of nowhere. He just stood there, staring at Colin, like, like…I don't know exactly, but it was creepy. And then he…was gone. Christa saw him, too. He walked with crutches, and when he turned to leave, I saw the horrible scars on his face."

"Did this guy say anything?" He sounds concerned. Before he was just confused.

"No…just stared, then limped away. The thing is, he looked so much like…and the age was right…and with his scars, we both thought he could be…"

"Who? What are you saying, Elaine?"

"Liam. We thought it could be Colin's father, Liam…here to take his son…back to Ireland."

If Tristan looked clueless before, he's totally *Duh!* by now. I smile at him. "Don't worry. My mom has that effect on people." Poor guy's trying to make sense of all this.

"But you said he was in a coma and probably wouldn't recover."

Mom nods like, damn straight. "But who was at the church staring at Colin, if not Liam?"

"Did Colin see him, too?"

"Just Christa and me, and she thinks it's Liam, too."

"They're the only two, I guess. I wasn't one of the lucky ones." *Like I'd wanna be–not!*

Mom cuts me a look. "Make fun all you want, but I saw what I saw."

Callie-girl jumps down, probably to dig our her scrap of chenille–it's getting way weirded-out in here. If she could talk, I wonder what she'd say.

# Elaine

You were a doll to put Colin's new bike together. 'Some Assembly Required' scares me," I tell Tristan. *Yes, definitely time to change the subject.* "He gave us a scare in the Plaza tonight–running off into the crowd. Good thing Trish caught up with him right away. We could've used you there."

"Sounds more exciting than my evening with Greg and Susan. My daughter and I haven't much in common, other than her mother, so we talked mostly about their new apartment in New York."

I offer more coffee, but he turns it down. "I have company, it's late, and you two"–he smiles at Roxy and me–"need to sleep while you can. Colin will be up early."

*Definitely. Opening presents, and Mass and Christmas dinner for the three of us, with turkey, potatoes, cranberries–the whole thing– down to apple pie with ice cream.* "You'll stop by tomorrow, won't you, and see Col with his new bike?"

"Wouldn't miss it." He gets up to leave, and I walk with him to the door, where he kisses me good night. Yes, we've progressed in the kissing department from our first chaste kiss that had me wondering all sorts of things. His lips linger on mine, gentle but sensuous, while visions of Tristan and me dance in my head.

"Hey, you two, do I need to come over there?" Roxy says, getting up from the sofa when the phone rings.

The sound startles me, interrupting our kiss. I pull away. What now? After midnight?

"Got it." Three strides and Roxy's in the kitchen.

"See you tomorrow, then," Tristan says. His hand is on the doorknob, and I'm looking toward the kitchen when Roxy comes into the living room, looking serious.

"It's for you, Mom…Maggie Casey…from Ireland."

He turns to leave, but I put my hand on his arm. "Please. Stay."

These few steps to the phone don't give me much time to collect myself. The last words I spoke to Maggie were filled with fury. I was ready to storm out of there and never speak to that hateful woman again.

Pick the phone up, I tell myself. Breathe. Again. "This is Elaine."

Maggie's thick brogue makes it hard to understand her words, but I grasp her message. "It's Liam, isn't it?"

"Me only child–he's gone, he is. The Lord took him away, not six hours ago."

Almost automatically, I say, "I'm so sorry for your loss." And I am. Tears, heartfelt and genuine, surprise me as I cry for this woman who's been nothing but a burden to me...this hateful woman who said unspeakable things about my poor, dead Stephanie, my beautiful, red-haired girl; this woman who treated us with nothing but scorn; this woman...this mother who's lost the only child she's ever had.

Fresh grief for Maggie and John mingles with the grief that never leaves.

Gently, I replace the receiver and close my eyes for a moment, seeing again this stooped old woman wrapped in a shawl and waving to her grandson.

"Mom?" Roxy's voice is tentative.

They're still standing as though frozen in place, waiting, when I go back into the living room.

Slowly, the words leave my mouth. "It's Liam...he died about six hours ago...he never regained consciousness after the accident."

Roxy inhales sharply. "Isn't that when you and Christa–at the church?"

"Maybe...that really *was* Liam–seeing his boy one last time before leaving him."

Tristan and Roxy are beside me, and we're holding on to each other.

I look toward the bedroom where Colin is sleeping. "Our little guy–we're all he's got now."

Photo: Tim Coughlin

Kathleen McElligott is a Registered Nurse and a Certified School Nurse in Illinois where she lives and practices. She has been published in *Arts Alive: A Literary Review; A Harvest of Faith; Real Simple Magazine's* web magazine and three of the "Black-and-White" anthologies: *Things That Go Bump in the Night, Falling in Love Again,* and *Vacations.* She has written feature articles for the *Star Newspapers* and is at work on a sequel to *Mommy Machine.*

# To Order
## Heliotrope Press Publications

effective January 1 2007, all prices include applicable taxes

Please send me _____copies of *Mommy Machine* at $21.75 each.

_____

Add shipping/handling:

　　　　1 copy ............. $4.50
　　　　2 copies ........... $6.50
　　　　For each additional copy ........... $2.00

_____

TOTAL ENCLOSED

_____

Please rush my copies of *Mommy Machine* to:

Name_____

Address_____

Phone/E-Mail _____

Mail this order form with check or money order to:

Heliotrope Press
16911 Cardinal Drive
Orland Park, IL 60467